RECKLESS
Obsession

samantha christy

Books Publishing Group

Copyright © 2020 by Samantha Christy

Cover designed by Letitia Hasser | RBA Designs

Cover photo by **WANDER AGUIAR**

Cover model – David T.

ISBN: 9798638109806

For everyone who has a love of music

RECKLESS
Obsession

Samantha Christy

Chapter One

Bria

Everyone has their own pre-show rituals. Adam and Colin get high. Kurt gets his rocks off with a groupie or even one of the roadies if he's desperate. Louis prays—as if that will somehow exonerate him from his other twenty-three hours of indiscretions. Me—I sit in my dressing room and listen to the opening band.

I look around the small room that's little more than a storage closet. At least I have a dressing room, and since I'm the only backup singer, it's all mine. I'm grateful for that, because even though I've done this thirty-four times before, I still feel nauseous every time.

I lie down on the small couch, careful not to ruin my hair or wrinkle my dress. I breathe in, hold it for a count of five, then breathe out. It's a technique my brother, Brett, taught me for when I'm feeling stressed.

I smile, thinking how I'll see him in a few weeks when the tour ends back home in New York City. Even better, he'll see me, up onstage singing with one of the hottest rock bands around—White Poison.

1

It's been almost three months since the tour started, and I still can't believe I'm doing this. There are only nine shows left and I'm surprisingly okay with that. I suppose I'd be sad if Adam, the lead singer and my boyfriend, hadn't assured me he wants me for their next tour later this year. In Europe!

I stare at the speaker piping music into the room. Wow. These guys are really good. Most of the opening acts are, seeing as they're playing in a venue this large, but this band ... I can't put my finger on it. Their music moves me.

I pull out my phone and find out who they are. Reckless Alibi. The band consists of four guys, all local from Connecticut. It looks like they'll be opening for us for three more shows. Impressive. I wonder what they had to do to get put on the lineup for four shows. Most opening acts get one show—maybe two.

I watch an amateur YouTube video of one of their songs, thinking these guys should be a headline act, not an opening one. But I've never heard of them before, and according to their Facebook page, they've only been a band for three years. That's not a long time in band years.

Their lead singer is Chris Rewey, also known as Crew. He's good. Really good.

There's a knock on my door. "Five minutes!" Aimee yells, and my heart races.

Aimee is one of the roadies Kurt sometimes shags.

Shag. I kind of love that word, especially when the guys say it in their British accents. Though it really just means *fuck*, it doesn't sound so dirty.

The music stops, and I miss it. I vow to download some of their songs.

I get up and check my makeup in the mirror. Sometimes I don't recognize myself, with my fire-engine-red lipstick, glitter eyeshadow and false eyelashes that practically touch my nose when I blink. But it's not my choice how I look onstage. It's theirs. I was told on day one, it's my job to look pretty, sing on-key, take very little credit, and leave quickly. I pull down the skin-tight gold sequined dress to make sure it's covering my ass—another concession I have to make to be the backup singer for one of the most successful bands of our era—then I put on my six-inch heels and head out the door.

Aimee is waiting. She's been assigned to me. She makes sure I'm in hair and makeup when I need to be, and she gets me through the maze of backstage hallways before and after every concert. She's called a production assistant, but really she's a groupie who ended up being hired by White Poison to help them on tour. Funny how they have mostly female "production assistants."

One of the first things I noticed when I came on tour with them was the lack of male roadies. With the exception of the guys who do the heavy lifting and set up the stage, all the help is female. If you ask me, one of their duties is to sleep with the band members anytime said band members want a shag.

It's pathetic. I suppose they all think they'll get to be the next girlfriend of a famous rock star.

I got lucky when Adam turned an eye my way. It wasn't long after the tour started, maybe six or seven shows in, when he asked me out. By then I'd gotten to know the guys well, and I knew Adam Stuart never asked a girl out. He never needed to. Not with all the Aimees around. So when he did, I knew it was going to be different, and it was. We've been dating for two months. *Me*, dating the lead singer of White Poison.

Aimee hands me the song lineup for tonight. It's almost always the same. "When you're out there, watch out for the step down behind you."

"Thanks. I saw it earlier during the sound check."

"Of course you did," she says, her tone laced with condescension.

Aimee, like most of the other roadies, is jealous of my relationship with Adam. In the beginning, I tried to make friends with her and some of the others. It worked until I started dating Adam. Now they barely talk to me unless they're required to. Hell, I'm surprised she even warned me of the potential hazard onstage. You'd think she'd want me to fall and break my leg or something.

We pass the guys' dressing room. Their door is open, and they're huddled together like a team around a quarterback before a play. They shout something in unison and then take a shot of liquor.

Adam sees me and gives me a wink. I blow him a kiss.

I wouldn't even think about going in there before a show. I was explicitly told not to mingle with the band unless asked by one of the members. Almost all the stereotypes I've heard about successful bands are true: the drugs, the frivolous parties, the law-breaking that authorities turn a blind eye to, and the women.

I sigh, thinking I hit the jackpot with Adam. He's not squeaky-clean, but he's not into the bad stuff some of the others are.

Aimee and I step aside when four guys walk down the hall. I recognize them from the YouTube video I watched minutes ago. The smiles on their faces are miles wide. They're patting each other on the back. I can tell they're hyped up.

"Great job," I say as they pass.

"Thanks," they reply.

"Good luck out there," one of them says to me. I think he's the guitar player.

I hear their boisterous banter trail down the hallway. I don't blame them. This was probably the largest venue they've ever played. Based on what I heard, it could lead to their big break.

Aimee leads me to the wings, where roadies are putting the finishing touches on the set. I peek at the crowd. It's another sellout. White Poison has sold out every concert they've played for the past eight years.

I remember listening to them when I was fourteen years old, and now I'm one of them. Well, kind of. It's still surreal.

A hand goes up the back of my short skirt and grabs my ass. I spin around, ready to deck whoever it is.

"Easy, luv," Adam says, stopping my hand mid-slap.

I pull my skirt back down. "I didn't know it was you."

He smirks. "Just how many other chaps are grabbing your arse?"

"You're the only ass grabbing my arse," I say in a hideous attempt at a British accent.

He laughs.

"Hey, did you hear Reckless Alibi?" I ask. "They're really good."

He's only half-listening to me, as he's looking over my shoulder. "You want to do something reckless with me? That can be arranged."

"No. The opening band, Reckless Alibi. They're good. Great, in fact."

"Reckless who?" He drinks something handed to him by a young girl with ten miles of cleavage.

I put a finger on his chin, turning his head away from her boobs and back to me. He shoves my hand away, irritated. And

5

now I'm irritated at him for being irritated with me. Why should he get to ogle the cleavage of another woman?

"I think you should invite them to the after-party," I say.

He glances again at the girl's boobs, and I swear he thinks I'm suggesting he invite her breasts.

"The opening band," I clarify, frustrated.

"Have you gone bonkers? Why the bloody hell should I care about some blokes who don't mean two shits to me?"

I take a step back. "Because you were them, Adam. A long time ago, you were an opening band, too. They're good. You should listen to their stuff."

His eyebrows shoot up. Suddenly he seems interested. Well, not interested but maybe jealous. "They're not coming. Do not invite them, Bria. They won't be welcome. You're lucky *you* were invited."

"I know. You never fail to remind me of that."

"What the fuck has put a bug up your arse?"

"Nothing," I say, seeing Aimee beckoning me. "Have a good show."

He air kisses me so he doesn't smudge my lipstick. "I always do."

His words resonate in my head. Has he always been this cocky, I wonder, or did fame make him this way? I think of the guys from Reckless Alibi. When I told them they were great, they looked genuinely pleased. Grateful even.

I hear the mass hysteria of the crowd when White Poison takes the stage and begins to play. I'm never out there when they go on. I'm not part of the band.

"Come on," Aimee says. "It's time."

I close my eyes and take a few calming breaths. Then I walk confidently over to my microphone twenty feet away from the band. There's a huge smile on my face, not that anyone would notice. They're not looking at me. I look out over the massive crowd and wonder once again if these three months will be my fifteen minutes of fame—or if there might be something more.

Chapter Two

Crew

"Holy shit, that was great," Garrett says, stashing his drumsticks in his back pocket.

"Way better than drugs," Brad adds.

I laugh. "As if you'd know."

"I got high last week, remember? When Liam gave me that pill."

The three of us double over in laughter.

"It was a baby aspirin," Liam says.

Brad is confused by our reaction. "No it wasn't. I got high."

"You felt high because I told you it was drugs and you expected to get high," Liam said. "Shit, it was funny watching you."

"What? No." Brad looks at me. "You knew about this?"

"It wasn't my idea," I say and point at Garrett.

"I should have known. They warned me you're always pulling stupid shit."

"You were getting way too stressed about these gigs," Garrett says. "I had to do something, but I knew you'd never believe it was mine. It was easier to believe it was Liam's."

"Thanks for making me look like an ass," Brad says.

Garrett smirks. "Consider it your initiation."

Brad looks around. "I'll consider *this* my initiation."

Liam pats him on the shoulder. "You're one of us now. We've got your back, you know."

Brad swipes a drumstick from Garrett's pocket and points it at him like a knife. "Don't pull that shit again."

Music pipes through the speakers in the hallway as White Poison plays.

"What are we doing back here when we could be watching them?" Garrett asks.

I shake my head. "We were told to disappear when our set was over."

"Let's go out into the pit. Who'd notice?"

Liam looks at me as if he's on board. Brad shrugs. I step aside. "Fine, lead the way. But if we get busted, it's on you, Garrett."

"Why am I always the fall guy?"

"Because you're the one who gets us to do stupid shit," Liam says.

Garrett walks around us. "Come on. I think I know where the door is."

Five minutes later, after trying eight different doors that lead nowhere, we're fighting our way through the mosh pit to get a decent position near the stage.

"Damn, these guys are good," Liam yells.

"That's going to be us one day," Garrett screams over the music.

Liam high-fives him. "Hell yeah, it will be."

I look at all the screaming fans, then I stare at the band, thinking of what Garrett said: *That's going to be us one day.*

Thirty minutes ago, we were up on that stage. It was great, even if the crowd wasn't here to see us, a nobody band from Stamford, Connecticut. But after being up there, I wonder if all my childhood dreams are about to come true.

I see the girl from the hallway, the one in the gold dress who said we were good. She's not part of the core band. She's their backup singer. Her hips sway and she moves her feet as she sings. When she's not singing, she's dancing in place. I'm mesmerized. Maybe it's the shimmery sequins of her dress. Maybe it's the rhythmic motion of her feet. Or maybe it's the throaty voice that sends chills down my spine when she has a brief solo.

I close my eyes and listen. She doesn't sing long—just a few lines. But that's all it takes for me to understand exactly what it is about her that's affecting me. My stomach rolls.

I turn to walk away. Liam grabs my arm. "You're leaving?"

"I'll meet you back at the hotel."

He looks at me like I'm crazy. "What gives?"

"It's not like we won't have three more opportunities to do this. I'm beat. I'll see you later."

I can feel him stare after me when I walk away, but I don't turn around. I don't want him to see my face. Liam knows me too well. He'd probably follow me. But I don't need him trying to comfort me for the millionth time. I'm sick of his sympathy. He needs to get over it already. *Fuck.* I shake my head at myself. "Pot meet kettle," I say to no one.

I work my way through hundreds of sweaty people, mostly girls. One of them grabs my junk as I go by. "Aren't you the singer of that other band?"

Normally I'd be reeling at getting recognized, but all I want is to get the hell out of here. "You think I'd be out here if I was? Hell, I'd be backstage partying."

She eyes me up and down. "You look like him."

"Thanks," I say, moving away.

When I find the door we came through, I walk up to it but am stopped by a security guard who puts his arm over the door and shakes his head.

"I'm with the band," I say, sounding like an idiot. "I mean, I'm in the opening band. You saw us, right?"

The guy doesn't even look at me. He continues to block the door. He's one big mother. The girth of his arm is bigger than my leg. I reach for my phone, then realize it's backstage with the other shit we left in the small dressing room assigned to us.

"Dude, listen," I yell over the music. "I'm Chris Rewey, the singer for Reckless Alibi. I was up on that stage an hour ago."

He finally looks at me. "I'll give you points for originality, but fuck off."

"I came out to watch their set and didn't think about how I'd get backstage. My bad."

He ignores me.

"Jesus, at least look me up on your phone. If it's not me, I'll fuck off."

He looks irritated, but he gets out his phone. He raises his brows at me. "Well?"

"Look up Reckless Alibi," I tell him. "I'm the lead singer."

He taps on the phone, then holds it next to my head, presumably to compare me to the online picture. He tucks his phone back into his pocket and opens the door. "Don't forget your credentials next time."

"Thanks, and just so you know, my three bandmates are still out there. They'll try to get through this door later."

"Wonderful," he says, heavy on the sarcasm.

"I wouldn't mind in the least if you messed with them."

He laughs. "Name's Hulk."

I try not to react, because this guy could pummel me with two fingers. "People call me Crew." I extend a hand. "Nice to meet you."

He shakes and nods at the hallway. "Get out of here."

Not many people are behind the stage. Everyone is in the wings. I stop in the doorway of White Poison's dressing room. Someone is setting up a bar. He looks up, and I keep walking, knowing I shouldn't be here.

I step on something and lean against the wall to examine the bottom of my shoe. Fucking wad of gum. I pick up a piece of paper off the floor and try to get it off my shoe when I hear voices around the corner.

"God, Aimee, you're so lucky," a woman says.

"I know, right? I've waited so long for this, and it's finally going to happen. He texted me earlier and told me to meet him at midnight. He said I could stay for half an hour and if I told anyone, he'd never shag me again. Oh, my God. I'm going to shag Adam Stuart!"

The other woman squeals. "Exactly what did it say?"

"Here, look."

A second later, they're both squealing.

I roll my eyes. Why do women lose all sense of worth and decency when it comes to rock stars? Hell, even in the small venues we've played, girls came out of the woodwork. They offered to sleep with anyone in the band or even just give us a blow job, and we're nobodies.

I'm not much better than Adam Stuart, however. I've occasionally taken advantage of those situations, welcoming women into my bed. I've never gone so far as to give them a time limit, but they all know it's a one-time thing. It could never be anything but.

I clear my throat before turning the corner. The women look at me from head to toe. Then they look at each other and smile. I wonder which of them is Aimee.

One takes a step forward. "You're the singer for the opening band," she says with fuck-me eyes, leaning forward so I can see her impressive cleavage. "I'm Aimee."

I snort. "Of course you are."

I half expect to hear a 'fuck you' behind me as I dismissively walk away, but I don't. I guess they're used to cocky rock stars. I duck into the dressing room, upset with myself for the nasty comment, and vow never to become a stereotype, no matter how famous we get.

I'm collecting my things when I hear the backup singer's voice again through the speakers in the room. She's singing with Adam, then she sings a short solo. It's so powerful it makes me stop what I'm doing.

What the hell is happening to me?

I turn off the sound, grab my shit, and call for an Uber.

Chapter Three

Bria

Exhausted from the concert, and let's face it, almost three months of being on the road, I lie in bed, listening to Reckless Alibi. They've opened for White Poison twice, and their music touches me in a way I can't explain. It's so personal. It's like their singer, Chris Rewey, is singing to someone every time. Lucky girl.

My phone pings with a text.

> **Adam: How about a little shag before we retire? I won't keep you up late, luv. I promise.**

> **Me: I'm so tired.**

> **Adam: Too tired for me already, are you?**

I sigh and let my head fall back against the pillow. I know all too well the position I'm in. He can have anyone he wants, and he chose me. But I'm not a fool. I know thousands of women are waiting in the wings. It's why I try so hard not to rock the boat. Our relationship is still new. I admonish myself even before I send the text. I let him win too much. On the other hand, I knew going into this he was the one in control.

Me: Give me an hour.

Adam: That's what I like to hear, poppet.

I throw my phone on the bed because that's exactly what I am—his puppet. It's a term of endearment, but it's hardly endearing. He pulls my strings to get me to do what he wants.

A few weeks ago, when we were in Chicago, I wanted him to take me shopping to a few places I'd heard of but had never been to. Instead of accompanying me, he hired a car. In New Orleans, when I wanted to check out a famous nightclub, he got one of the male roadies to take me. He doesn't realize I want to do those things with him. As a couple.

Now that I think about it, what have we really done together? We never go out unless his entourage is with him. The only time we have romantic dinners is when he has them catered in his suite.

As I freshen up, I stare at myself in the mirror. "It's the tour. It's stressful for everyone. Things will change in a few weeks when it's over."

I smile. Convinced I'm one hundred percent right.

I check my watch. I got ready a lot faster than I thought, but I head up anyway.

As I enter the elevator to go up to the private floor the band has booked for themselves, I wonder where Reckless Alibi is staying. I know they aren't here. I've never seen any of the opening acts at the same hotel, and it has me wondering if White Poison wants it that way. Then again, we stay in hotels most people can't afford.

The elevator doors open, and I show the credentials hanging on the lanyard around my neck.

"Is Mr. Stuart expecting you?" one of his goonies asks.

You'd think after almost three months, his security team would get that I'm his girlfriend, but they ask anyway. "He asked me to come up," I say a little too harshly.

Freddie, their manager, sees me and runs down the hall. "Piss off, Cole." He pulls me into the sitting room. "Darling, Bria. Let me pour you a drink."

"But Adam is expecting me."

"He'll only be a moment. He's finishing up with a meeting."

"At this hour?"

He pulls out his phone and taps on it. "Fame and fortune never sleep, my dear."

I take a glass from him and stare into the brown liquor. "Freddie, will it ever change? When we're not on tour, I assume things won't be as difficult or complicated."

He sits down next to me. "Being on tour is the hardest and most rewarding part of doing what we do. It won't be as difficult once this is all over." He gives me a sympathetic look. "Complicated—that's a whole other ballgame."

"What do you mean?"

"Adam is a complicated creature."

Someone races past the doorway. I look at Freddie for an explanation. He rolls his eyes. "Kurt must be at it again."

I laugh, but it's not genuine.

A moment later, Adam appears, stretching against the doorframe. The tag in his shirt is in front. I walk over and finger it. "Are you sure you want me here? Seems like you're burning the candle at both ends. You can't even dress yourself properly. Maybe you need to get some sleep."

"I'll sleep when I'm dead." He pulls me to him and I smell his minty-fresh breath. "Right now all I want is you."

He leads me down the hall, past his room and into Collin's.

"Why are we here?"

"He's out for the night, and my place is a sight. Dirty clothes everywhere. I zonked out and didn't have a chance to tidy up." He starts removing my clothing even before the door is shut.

"Is it true? That all you want is me?"

"What kind of question is that?"

I shrug as he removes my pants. "Sometimes I wonder."

He pulls down my panties and puts his mouth on me. Hard. Then he withdraws for a second. "Maybe this will make you forget."

Forget what? That I wonder about such things, or that I'm not really all he wants?

"Something wrong, luv?"

I smile and shake my head and then pretend to have the most awesome orgasm he's ever given me. I even make sure to squeeze his fingers inside me to make it believable. I know how upset he gets when I don't come. As if I'm broken if he can't get me off.

Ten minutes after I've pleasured him, and he's fucked me just how he likes it, I'm lying beside him. "What's going to happen in two weeks when the tour ends?"

"I'm going to take a bloody holiday, that's what. Lie on some beach where no fans can find me and drink my way to oblivion every night."

"That sounds kind of nice. Am I invited?"

He stiffens. "Uh, it's a tradition after our tours that my mates and I go alone."

I try not to let him see my disappointment. "Maybe we could do something after? Like go out to dinner in a real restaurant?"

He kisses my temple, then gets out of bed and quickly throws his shirt back on—the same way he did before, with the tag in front.

I eye it suspiciously.

"I think that can be arranged. I'll have Freddie clear my calendar the week we get back from Fiji. Sound good?"

I nod.

He hands me my clothes. That's my cue to leave.

I'm still exhausted when I get back to my room, but not so much that I can't listen to Reckless Alibi's full album.

Chapter Four

Crew

I stand in the empty arena, watching the backup singer for White Poison do a sound check. She starts by talking into a mic, then she hums a tune. Then she sings part of one of their songs.

It still pisses me off that we don't get to do a sound check. Do they want us to sound like crap when we get onstage? Our first two nights were great, we killed it. But maybe that was just luck. If the amps aren't calibrated perfectly, Brad's bass can overtake Liam's guitar. My mic could be set to the wrong volume, and Garrett's voice might be the only one the crowd hears.

I get it. White Poison is who everyone comes to see, but you'd think we'd at least get to make sure we're heard properly. Don't even get me started on the other things we're not allowed to do, like *look* at the band. It actually says that in our contract. "As the opening act, you are not to make eye contact with the headliners unless headliners engage in conversation. The opening act will yield to headliners in all ways, allowing them to pass in the hallways without interference and have sole use of elevators and green-room facilities."

I contemplate eating the unappealing sandwich I was given half an hour ago after everyone from the White Poison setup crew had first pick at the buffet.

Suddenly I'm no longer hungry and my eyes become glued to the woman onstage, stunned at what she's singing.

Liam appears beside me. "Holy shit."

We stare at her. Garrett and Brad join us. I'm pretty sure our jaws are touching the floor as she belts out one of *our* songs.

"What the hell was that?" Garrett says when it's over.

Liam grins and lets out a long, low whistle. "*That* was exactly what we've been missing."

"Bullshit," I say.

Liam shakes his head. "You mean to tell me you don't think she nailed it?"

Garrett elbows him and laughs. "Crew doesn't want to lose his job."

"Fuck off," I say.

Liam motions to the woman. "I'm serious, guys. Half our songs have parts that would sound better sung by a woman."

He doesn't look at me when he says it. He knows better. I can't believe he's bringing this shit up again, but he does every so often to test the waters.

"The songs are good as they are," I say, walking away.

"Crew, just think about it," he says. "We need a female singer. You know it, and I know it."

I turn around. "I'm not having this conversation again."

I go backstage and stomp down the hallway, only to bump into the woman who was just onstage.

"*Oof!*" she says when we collide. "Sorry." It looks as if she recognizes me. She holds out a hand. "Chris, uh, Crew … sorry, I'm not sure what to call you. I'm Bria."

We shake, but my bandmates appear before I can respond.

"That was some amazing shit you just sang," Liam says.

Bria turns bright red. "Oh, gosh. You heard that?"

"We did," he says. "And we're damn flattered you know our music."

"I didn't," she says. "Not until the other day when I heard you. I looked you up that night." She looks at us one at a time. "Liam Campbell, lead guitarist. Garrett Young, drums. Brad Templeton, bassist who recently joined the band. And Chris Rewey, lead singer, sometime keyboardist, sometime backup guitarist. You're really good. I'm Bria Cash."

"He goes by Crew," Garrett says, stepping in front of me. "*I* don't need a bullshit nickname. You can call me Garrett."

Garrett never met a girl he wasn't interested in. I feel something unexpected in my gut, watching him chat her up. Nothing big, just a twinge. I don't like the way he's looking at her. Like maybe he's going to make her his next conquest. And for a reason I can't explain—that doesn't sit well with me.

Liam and Brad talk to her too. They're drooling over her—or her voice anyway. I give them a look. They ignore me.

"You want to join us for a bite to eat before the show?" Liam asks.

I kick him. She notices.

"No thanks. I've got plans with my boyfriend."

"We'll catch you later then," I say and pull the guys to the door.

"You didn't have to be so goddamn rude," Garrett says. "We asked her to go to lunch, not have an orgy."

"Let's go. We need to be back in an hour before it starts getting crazy around here."

We leave our gear and go out the back door of the arena to Liam's van, or more precisely, Liam's uncle's van. He owns a car dealership in Stamford. He's also the mayor and the reason we got this gig. He has a lot of political connections. He'll be running for governor in the next election.

No way could we have landed this contract without him. Four shows—that's almost unheard of. We owe him big time, much to Liam's dismay.

Liam pats his jeans pockets. "Damn. Forgot the keys. Be back in a sec."

When he returns, Bria Cash is with him. I raise my brows.

"She got stood up," he says. "She's coming with us."

Bria's eyes meet the ground. "I didn't get stood up. He's just busy, that's all. He has to prepare for tonight."

"You guys won't believe who her boyfriend is," Liam says. "Adam fucking Stuart."

My eyes snap to hers. "*You're* dating Adam Stuart?"

She nods.

"As in he's your boyfriend, and you're his girlfriend?"

Garrett elbows me. "What's your problem, man?"

"Sorry. It's just … nothing."

She eyes me suspiciously. She probably wonders if I think he's too good for her or something, but in the five seconds I've known her, I can tell it's quite the opposite. I contemplate telling her what I heard those groupies saying the other night. Then again, she'd have no reason to believe anything I say.

We pile into the van and drive down the street.

"This place okay?" Liam asks when he sees a diner.

"As long as it's less than ten bucks a plate, I'm in," Brad says. "My bank account is running on fumes."

"How about you, Bria?" Liam says. "You good with this?"

"It looks fine." She glances at Brad. "Not that I'm complaining about the diner, but didn't you guys just get your big break? Don't you have money coming out of your ears?"

Garrett laughs as we get out of the van. "Don't you know how this works?"

"How what works?"

We go inside and find a table.

"How long have you been singing professionally?" I ask.

"This is my first real gig, but I've been singing for a long time. I even cut an album. I spent every penny I had, hiring a band and a recording studio, but I couldn't get my foot in the door. Nobody would listen to it."

"Yeah, we know how that goes."

"Do you? Seems to me you're doing pretty well." She smiles.

I shake my head. "We've been playing bars and county fairs for years. The only reason we're here is because Liam's uncle is a bigwig in Stamford. We barely get paid enough to cover our hotel and travel expenses."

She looks appalled. "How is that even possible?"

"Being able to open for a major band like White Poison— that's our payment," Liam says. "The exposure we're getting is worth more than money at this point. Hell, we'd have played for free. This could finally lead to something for us."

"Still," Bria says, "you should be getting paid what you're worth. From what I've heard, you're worth a lot."

"Thanks," Brad says. "That means a lot."

A waitress puts down glasses of water in front of us and then pulls a pen from behind her ear. "Ready to order?"

One by one, we pick up the menus stuffed behind the napkin dispenser.

"Better give us a minute," I say.

Samantha Christy

"How much do *you* get paid?" Garrett asks Bria as he peruses his menu.

I hiss at him. "That's pretty personal, don't you think?"

She laughs. "Let's just say more than you, but it'll have to last. In two weeks, when the tour is over, I won't get any paychecks for a while."

"Where do you live?" Liam asks.

"New York City."

"Maybe you could sing with us for a few gigs—you know, to tide you over. The money is better than what we're getting here."

I kick him under the table.

"I'm actually going on tour with White Poison again in seven months. They're going to Europe."

"You must have really impressed them," Liam says. "I don't think I've ever seen them with the same backup singer for two tours."

She shrugs. "I like to think I've impressed them, but I'm sure it has to do with my dating Adam."

She doesn't seem like the type of girl who would use someone to get what she wants, and I feel sorry for her. Is she so naïve that she doesn't know he's screwing around behind her back?

A group of girls come in, and two of them look familiar. They were the ones talking about Adam the other night. They hesitate when they see us sitting with Bria but go on by.

"God, I'm so tired of this cold weather," the one I think is Aimee says. "Three weeks from now, I'll be wearing my string bikini on a beach in Fiji. I can't wait."

Bria's eyes widen and get glassy. Her chin quivers.

"What is it?" I ask.

She swallows and dabs at her eyes. "I'm just tired." She tucks her menu behind the napkin holder. "If you'll excuse me, I'm going back to the arena."

"It's half a mile away," Garrett says.

"The walk will do me good, and I've lost my appetite." She peers over to where the girls are sitting. "Pre-show nerves still get to me."

Liam stands to let her out of the booth. "We'll see you later."

She nods. "Have a good show."

"You too." Liam watches her leave and turns back to us. "What just happened?"

I motion to the table of girls. "I'm pretty sure Adam Stuart is screwing around with one or more of them, and I'd venture a guess that maybe Bria knows it."

Brad snorts. "She shouldn't be surprised. He can have anyone he wants."

I narrow my eyes. "True, but he shouldn't string her along. That just makes him a douchebag."

"Do you think he cares what people think of him?" Garrett adds. "He can sit back and count his millions and do whatever the hell he wants."

"That shouldn't include hurting people." I look out the window. Bria shuffles her way down the street. "We should make a pact that we won't end up like that. You know, the stereotypical band guys who are all assholes with lists of riders longer than my dick."

"That'd be a short list," Liam deadpans.

I introduce him to my middle finger. "I get the expensive houses and cars and personal jets, but I think you can have all that and still be a nice person."

"You're assuming we'll make it big one day," Garrett says.

"Oh, we'll make it big," Liam says. "And when we blow White Poison's record sales out of the goddamn water, they'll be begging to open for *us*."

While they're busy dreaming about our future, I pull out my phone and google Bria Cash. I don't see anything about an album, but I find a YouTube video of a high school talent show where she sings a Taylor Swift song. I put in my earbuds and listen to the entire thing.

Chapter Five

Bria

During the van ride to Hartford, I stare at the White Poison tour bus in front of us. I don't get to ride in it. Never have. It's for the band only, so they can sleep, de-stress, or work on new music. Despite being onstage with them, I get to ride in the large passenger van with some of the crew. It's almost impossible to sleep, given its rigid seats and lack of headrests.

Liam's van is behind us. It's even smaller than this one, yet it holds the four of them and all their luggage and equipment. I wonder if there's any extra space. The short time I spent with them at the diner yesterday was better than any time I've experienced on the road with White Poison. They seem genuine and nice, but that's probably because they haven't made it big yet.

I try again to fall asleep, but I can't. I haven't slept more than a few hours since yesterday. Every time I doze off, I hear Aimee bragging about going to Fiji. I turn to the guy sitting next to me; he sets up the band's instruments. "What are you doing after the tour ends?"

"You mean after I sleep for two weeks straight?" He laughs. "I'll do what I always do between gigs—work on my brother's construction crew. He builds houses."

"Are you …" I glance at the tour bus again. "Are you going to Fiji?"

He looks at me like I'm crazy. "Fiji? Where did you get a crazy idea like that?"

"I thought since the band is going, maybe you'd go too."

He snickers. "As if I'd ever be invited."

"So they *do* invite people?"

He gives me a sympathetic look. He knows I'm dating Adam. Everyone does. "I honestly don't know who goes on those trips. For all I know, it's just the four of them."

He's lying. I look out the window, lips tight, and gaze at the snowy hills in the distance, wondering who else has been lying to me.

A few hours later, we pull up at the hotel, the entire caravan still in perfect follow-the-leader formation. That rarely happens. Liam's van pulls in behind us, surprising me. They never stay at the luxury hotels where we bunk.

When I get out, I stretch my legs and catch Crew doing the same. "I thought you couldn't afford places like this."

"We can't, but this is our last show, and Liam's uncle wanted us to go out in style. He booked this for us as a Christmas present. After the gig, we're staying the weekend to unwind and do some male bonding or some shit like that."

"That's nice."

I can't help feeling a little sad that after tonight, I won't get to hear their music in my dressing room before I go onstage, but I remind myself there are only five more shows, and for the first time in months, I feel a sense of relief.

Crew and I are talking when Aimee gets off the tour bus. I feel a quick spurt of anger. "What the …?"

"Everything okay?" he asks.

"No, everything is not okay. I was told nobody else rides with them. It's why I was relegated to one of the roadie vans. I'll catch you later."

I storm over to the bus as Aimee saunters away, her hair all disheveled, like she was sleeping or *something.*

Kurt, Collin, and Louis get off the bus. When they see me, they look guilty.

Adam appears, tucking in his shirt. "Hey, luv. Didn't know you'd be waiting."

"Obviously, otherwise you'd have wiped Aimee's lipstick off your face." His zipper is at half-mast. I point. "Might want to close the goddamn barn door."

"What's got you in a tizzy? I was sleeping. I always sleep on the bus."

I cross my arms. "Yeah, sleeping with Aimee. Not to mention taking her to Fiji."

"Hogwash," he says with no guilt whatsoever. "But even if that were true, you're the one who gets to call herself my girlfriend."

I'm disgusted that he says it like I should be honored even though he's sleeping with anyone wearing a skirt.

"I'm so stupid." Outraged, I look at the sky. "How naïve I was to believe I was the only girl in your life." I give him a hard shove. "And what an asshole you are to make me think I was."

He looks around at our audience, causing me to do the same. Some of the crew are watching, as are all the guys from Reckless Alibi. "This is hardly the place for this conversation, Bria."

"This is exactly the place for it. That way everyone will know what a jerk you are." I glance at Aimee, whose grin is not the least bit apologetic.

He finishes buckling his belt. "You'll find you're the only one who cares, luv."

I stomp my foot. "Stop calling me that."

He tugs on my elbow. "Calm down. Let's go up to my suite."

I jerk away from him. "I'm not going anywhere with you ever again. I'm done with you."

He grabs my arm again, harder this time, and looks down his nose at me. "You're done when I say you are and not a moment sooner."

Crew takes a step forward, but his bandmates hold him back.

I painfully pull my arm free. "Screw you, Adam. I don't care who the hell you are. Nobody treats me this way. I don't care what Aimee and your other sluts do, but I'm finished being your doormat." I turn to the roadies. "Kudos for keeping his man-whoring under wraps for so long. Does he pay you extra for that?"

Most of them look away but Reckless Alibi is ready to come to my rescue if Adam doesn't back down.

"Do you even know what you're doing?" Adam asks with an air of superiority. "Nobody tosses me to the curb. I'm Adam bloody Stuart."

"No, you're an asshole."

I walk away, and he laughs. *Laughs.*

I struggle not to cry, managing to make it around the corner before the tears fall.

I hear footsteps behind me, and whirl around. "Get the hell away from me!" It's Reckless Alibi. "Sorry. I thought it was him." I sit on the curb and wipe my eyes. "How could I have been so stupid? I was a fool to think he was faithful to me."

Liam sits next to me. "You're nice and beautiful and have the voice of an angel. Fuck him, Bria. And fuck White Poison. Come sing with us."

"No offense, but I'm the backup singer for one of the hottest bands in the world. I'm not sure I could be a backup singer for anyone else, plus there's the Europe tour."

He touches my shoulder. "Do you really think you'll be included after what just happened?"

Like a punch to the gut, I realize what I've done. I wasn't thinking of the consequences. I let my emotions get the best of me. Why couldn't I have kept my mouth shut and quietly dumped him? Of course I'm not going to be invited on the Europe tour. I publicly shamed Adam Stuart.

Oh, God, I feel sick. My head falls into my hands. "What have I done? I've ruined everything."

Liam says, "Hold on, Bria. You did the right thing. That prick had it coming. Your career isn't over. It's only getting started."

"You misunderstood," Garrett says. "We're not asking you to be our backup singer. We're asking you to be one of our lead singers."

Surprised, I look at Crew. He's pacing. "I don't know you," I say. "What's even more relevant is that you don't know me. I've never sung with you. How can you make such an offer?"

"Come to a few rehearsals," Liam says. "See if we're a good fit."

I glance at Crew again. He doesn't look happy.

"Don't mind him," Liam says. "He knows we need a female lead. He's fighting it."

I shake my head. "I couldn't. Not if you don't all agree."

Crew kicks a rock into the street. "She's a smart girl," he says before walking away.

Garrett holds his hand out to help me up. "He'll come around. We're serious about this."

"As a heart attack," Brad adds.

Crew turns the corner, looking pissed.

"I don't know."

"Think about it," Liam says, pulling a card out of his wallet and handing it to me. "You've got another week here. Give yourself some time to rest, then come jam with us. It doesn't have to mean anything. It'll be fun, and it will give us a few weeks to work on grumpy."

"Why do you think he's so against it?" I ask. "Other than the spotlight not being solely on him?"

Liam sighs. "He's got his reasons."

Garrett huffs. "Reasons he needs to get over."

"Piss off, Garrett. You don't know what the fuck you're talking about."

Garrett shakes his head. "Still."

"Still nothing," Liam says. "Mind your own goddamn business and let him work out his shit." He turns to me. "Are you okay? Do you need a place to stay?"

"We have separate rooms." I laugh. "Obviously. How else could he shag everyone with a pair of tits?"

"And maybe some without," Brad says.

I turn up my nose at his insinuation. How many people has he been sleeping with? I make a mental note to visit my doctor when I return to the city and have him run every available test.

They go to their van for their luggage, and I enter the hotel, avoiding anyone associated with White Poison.

As I pass the bar, I see Crew sitting by himself, tossing back a shot—two empty glasses already sitting in front of him. And I wonder what his story is.

Chapter Six

Crew

Seven years ago

I can count on one hand the few moments in my life I remember with such clarity, it's as if a high-def Blu-ray is imprinted on my mind. One of those moments was the day my parents told me they were getting a divorce. I was ten. I was wearing pajamas with baseballs on them. I had a granola bar and chocolate milk for breakfast. Then I sat in my room and stared out the window, hoping I wouldn't have to move out of the house where I grew up.

Another such moment was the Christmas when Mom gave me the karaoke machine. The first time I turned it on and sang a song in front of my family, I knew I wanted to be up on a stage.

Today, as Abigail Evans plays her flute for Mr. Hannigan so he can figure out which chair to give her in the school band, I'm certain this memory will become one of those moments.

It's only been five minutes since I met her. Well, technically, I haven't met her yet. She doesn't even know my name. But she's staring at me. She's playing her flute, auditioning for her spot, and she chose me to look at. *Me*. Out of all the kids in this room.

I'm at the height of adolescence, at barely seventeen years old, but one thing's for sure—I've never before gotten a boner in band class. Seventh period has just become my favorite of the day. The rest of my classes will be torture while I wait to see the girl who plays the flute like an angel. Hell, she *looks* like an angel. She's got sun-kissed skin, even though it's cold enough outside to freeze your balls off. Her long hair is brown, with streaks of blonde running through it. I can't see her eyes from here, but I'm certain they must be blue.

Suddenly I'm thanking Mom, who badgered me into taking another year of band. I didn't protest too much, though. It's an easy *A*, but playing the trombone is not exactly my forte. In fact I'm last chair—the worst of all the trombone players at Stamford High. Keyboards are more my thing. It's what I play in my band. But Mr. Hannigan is hardly what I'd call a progressive teacher. He must be eighty years old. I'm not even sure they *had* keyboards when he was growing up.

Abigail finishes playing, and all eyes are on me instead of her—probably because I'm the only one clapping. I look down at my hands as if they don't belong to me. *What the hell?*

Liam rolls his eyes at me, laughing. He's here for the easy *A* too. He rocks the trumpet, but his true passion is the guitar.

"Fantastic, Miss Evans," Mr. Hannigan says. "Why don't you take a seat next to Miss Nevin. Hannah can show you the ropes and bring you up to speed."

A lot of eyebrows are raised. Hannah Nevin is our first-chair flautist. Is he replacing her with Abigail, or did he just make Hannah Abigail's mentor? Judging by the look on Hannah's face, she thinks she's been replaced. She should be. Abigail's *that* good.

I spend the rest of class totally screwing up my part, earning me some biting stares from Hannigan, but I can't help it. How can I concentrate on music when the only thing I can think about is how I'm going to meet this girl? Song lyrics bombard my head, and I wish I had my notebook with me to jot them down.

Forty minutes later, I'm rushing to put away my trombone when Hannigan calls to me. "Mr. Rewey, I trust you won't be quite as distracted for Friday's performance?"

I can hear Liam's laughter behind me as I apologize to Mr. Hannigan.

When I turn around, Abigail is nowhere to be seen. Shit, have I missed my chance?

"Are your pants on fire?" Liam asks.

I hold up a finger and check out the hall. My eyes dart around until I find her. I only see the back of her head, but that hair is unmistakable. She looks down at something and then turns, gazing left, then right. Perfect.

"I have to go," I tell Liam before I take off in her direction.

"Dude!" he calls after me.

I run up behind her. "Abigail." I touch her elbow. "You look lost."

She looks at my hand on her arm, and I can't tell if she's happy or mad about it. Maybe she's just surprised.

"Abby," she says, smiling sweetly.

Happy then. And I was right—blue eyes. Damn.

She looks relieved that someone is talking to her. It must suck to be the new kid, especially in the middle of junior year after everyone has already found their cliques.

"Okay, Abby." I love the way her name sounds, and I know I'm going to work it into some lyrics. "I'm Crew."

She's amused. "Your name is Crew Rewey?"

I laugh. "My real name is Christopher, but most people call me Crew. Christopher Rewey is a mouthful, and a teacher in elementary school shortened it to Crewey, then it became Crew. My parents don't call me that; they call me Chris." I fidget, knowing I'm rambling and she probably doesn't give a shit. "Sorry, you probably couldn't care less."

"No, it's actually interesting." She extends a hand. "Well, Christopher, it's nice to meet you."

I take her hand in mine, and more lyrics bombard me. I can't wait to get home and put them to music. I don't tell her no one calls me Christopher, because I think I like that she would be the only one.

After a few seconds, we realize we're still holding hands and pull apart at the same time. She blushes, and her tanned skin turns a sexy shade of pink.

"You look lost," I repeat, nodding to the schedule in her hand. "That was the last class of the day, you know."

"I know, but I only got here fifth period. I don't even know where my locker is. I wanted to wait until tomorrow, but my mom insisted I start right away. I missed a week of school during the move."

I look at her schedule and note her locker number. "Why don't you tell me where you're from while I walk you to your locker?"

"Okay," she says, looking more than a little relieved. "I haven't had a chance to meet anyone. You are literally the first person to talk to me other than teachers."

"Sweet." I clear my throat. "I mean, I'm sure plenty of people will talk to you. Come on." I motion down the hall. "Your locker is down there. Looks like you got stuck in the ninth-grade hallway. That sucks, but those are probably the only ones left."

I glance over my shoulder and see Liam leaning up against the wall, watching us. He's waiting for me. He always waits for me; he's my ride home. I pull out my phone and text him that I'll see him at practice.

He shakes his head, snickering, and walks away.

"Do you have to go?" Abby says, seeing me on my phone.

"No. Sorry. You were going to tell me where you used to live."

"San Diego."

That explains her tan. I'm not sure if it explains her super pleasant demeanor. I've never met anyone from California. Not that people on the East Coast aren't nice, but some of them, a lot of them, are entitled narcissists.

I raise my brows. "That's a tough break. Why would your parents want to leave there to come to Connecticut?"

"My dad is an interim minister, so we move a lot."

I've only known her for a few minutes, and I'm already bummed she might not be here long. "That sucks. How long do you think you'll stay?"

"He promised we wouldn't move again until I graduate."

I try not to let her see how relieved I am. "What exactly is an interim minister?"

"He fills in until churches can find a permanent one. That usually takes a while. We were in San Diego for two years. Prior to that, we were in Idaho. Before that, Arkansas."

I point to her locker. "This is yours. I can't imagine moving around that much."

She shrugs. "I can't imagine what it's like to be in one place. It must get kind of boring."

I think of growing up on the same street, with the same friends, doing the same things. "You're right. It's boring. But I think things are about to get more exciting."

She blushes again and fumbles with the lock, then gives up and leans against the wall, watching freshmen students walk by on their way out. "They all look so small. That was us two years ago. Hard to believe, huh? I can't believe I'm going to be stuck with a bunch of fifteen-year-olds for the rest of the year."

"I'd be happy to share my locker with you. It's big enough. I mean, if you want to get out of the ninth-grade hallway."

"Really?" She looks hopeful. "Are you sure? What if my books smell like perfume? Or worse, BO. How do you know I'm not a colossal slob who leaves junk everywhere? Or maybe I'm a criminal, and I'll steal all your stuff." She laughs and my dick gets hard.

Fuck. Now she *has* to share my locker.

"You want to steal my chem homework, go right ahead, but I have to warn you, you'd be doing yourself a disservice. I'm not exactly a straight-A student. Academics aren't really my thing."

"What is your thing, Christopher Rewey?"

Fuck again.

"Music."

"As in the trombone?"

"As in I'm in a rock band."

"You play trombone in a rock band?"

I chuckle. "I sing and sometimes play the piano."

"What's the band's name?"

"Naked Whale."

She looks shocked. "That's unusual."

"That's *original*. Like our music." I look down the hall. "So, Abby Evans, what's it going to be? Sharing a locker with a sub-par student who plays in a rock band, or being stuck with fifteen-year-olds who can't control their erections?"

She breaks into laughter. I join her.

Her laugh is so sexy, my pants get tight again. I hope she doesn't realize I might not be any better than those fifteen-year-olds.

"Lead the way," she says.

I look at her schedule as we go to my locker. "You're in my English class. It's right before lunch. That means you'll have C-lunch, like me. If you want, you can go with me, and I'll introduce you around."

"That would be great. I don't mind new schools much, but if I had to pick one thing I could do without, it's the first few days of awkwardness when I don't know anyone."

"I doubt you'll have any trouble making friends."

She snorts. "You'd be surprised."

A group of girls go by, eyeing Abby with disapproval. "I guess girls can be kind of cliquey. Don't worry. You'll be safe with me."

I hand back her schedule after imprinting it on my mind. I plan on being around her every chance I get.

"Why the name Naked Whale?" she asks.

"You really want to know?"

"I think the reasoning behind a band's name says a lot about the band."

"I think you're right."

Ten minutes. I've known this girl ten minutes, and I think I'm in love. Not that I'd know what that feels like. I've gone out with a lot of girls but none I've felt an instant connection to, like I do Abby.

"So ... the name?"

I'm staring at her and mentally give myself a slap. "Oh, right. Well, when you're onstage, you're vulnerable, ripped open for everyone to see. Sometimes it feels like being naked. At the same time, it's larger than life, you know, like a whale. There you have it. Naked Whale."

"You're the one who came up with the name?"

"I guess. Liam and I started it two years ago. He plays guitar. Brandon plays drums, and Jake plays bass. We tossed around some names and that one was mine."

"I like it. Do you play anywhere?"

"Mostly in Jake's garage. But we have played charity benefits, and we've done a lot of talent shows and school dances. Stuff like that."

"I'd really like to hear you."

"You want to come to our practice? I'm going there now."

She shakes her head. "My dad would freak. I'm sure he's waiting at home to get a play-by-play of my first day."

"Some other time, then. We practice most days." I stop and bang on metal. "Here's my locker ... er, our locker." I pull out a pen and grab her hand to write on it.

"What are you doing?"

"I'm writing down the combination."

"It'll come off the next time I wash my hands. Why don't you write it on a piece of paper?"

I look into her eyes. "I wanted to touch your hand again."

Aaaaand there's the blush.

"Let me try it," she says, looking at the numbers on her hand and then opening the lock. She gets it on the first try.

She examines the contents of my locker. "Wow, you really don't like school, do you? Where's all your stuff?"

I take my backpack off. "In here." I take out the books for my first two classes and put them in the locker, knowing if I leave them here, I'll get to see her in the morning. "Do you want to leave anything?"

"I don't have anything yet. I'll get my books tomorrow before school."

"Great. I'll see you then. You know, I won't mind if you put chick crap in there."

"Chick crap?"

"You know, lipstick and stuff."

She laughs and raises a snarky brow. "What about tampons? Can I leave those in there, too?"

"Uh ..."

"I'm kidding, Christopher. I keep those in my backpack."

"Oh, okay."

I don't know why mentioning tampons to a guy she just met makes me like her even more, but it does. Maybe she isn't afraid of anything.

"I'd better get going," she says. "I still have a lot of unpacking to do at home."

"I'll walk you out. Is your dad picking you up?"

"I have a car. They let me park in a visitor spot today, but I'll get my assigned spot tomorrow. Where do you park?"

I look at the floor. We may live in one of the most affluent parts of the country, but that doesn't mean my family is rich. It's just me and my mom. We live in a small house on the outskirts of town, not even technically in the city of Stamford, but we're zoned for the high school, since it's the closest. "I don't have a car. Liam gives me a ride." We leave the school and stroll to the lot.

"Did he wait for you?" She looks around. "Where is he?"

"He bounced already."

Her face falls. "I'm sorry. That's my fault."

"It's no biggie. I can walk. It's only forty or fifty blocks."

She zips up her coat. "You will not walk. I'll drive you." She motions to a small Nissan. "This is me. If I tell you to duck, duck. I'm not allowed to drive around with boys my father doesn't know."

"Got it. How big is your dad, anyway?"

She giggles. "Not very. His bark is worse than his bite, but he holds my future in his hands. Best not to get on his bad side."

I mime writing on a notepad. "Right. Don't piss off Mr. Evans."

"Dr. Evans. He has his PhD in ministry."

"Shit, Abby. I'm glad you told me that. That way, when I meet him, I won't look stupid."

"When you meet him?"

"If I'm going to take his daughter on a date, I'll have to meet him, won't I?"

I climb into her car, but I don't fail to hear a giddy "Yes!" as she goes to her side. I wasn't meant to hear it, so I probably shouldn't let on that I did. Something about her. I just can't figure out what it is. But I swear to God it's going to make me a better musician.

I turn to her. "I've written two songs in my head since I met you. Not to scare you away, but I think you've become my muse. And just so you know, once that happens, there is nothing that will keep a musician from it. Plan on me being around a lot." I take her hand in mine and squeeze.

She smiles and squeezes back. "I think I like the sound of that, Christopher Rewey."

I'm not positive, but I think I just asked her to be my girlfriend.

Even better, I'm pretty sure she said yes.

Chapter Seven

Bria

As I go onstage for the last time, I try not to think of the papers that were handed to me earlier today. Just as Liam warned me, and as I had feared, my contract was not renewed for the European tour. Some small part of me hoped they would still want me to join them because of my talent, but I've been reminded more than once how replaceable I am. I guess that meant onstage as well as in Adam's bed.

I'm not nervous like I usually am for a performance. I'm not even pissed. I'm just … sad. I hope this doesn't turn out to be my one and only shot.

I remember who's in the audience tonight: my brother, Brett, his fiancée, Emma, and her daughter, Evie. I put on the best show I can for them. And maybe a little bit for me too—to prove I'm not a worthless piece of shit who can so easily be tossed aside.

Afterward, I look out at the massive audience and walk off the stage with tears in my eyes that make Aimee smile. I keep my head down and try not to look at anyone. They need to be here, but I don't. I never go back and join them for the encore. My job is done.

In the dressing room, I fall face first on the small sofa and reach for my earbuds. I turn on my Reckless Alibi playlist. I've listened to nothing else this past week.

Someone bangs on the door. I pop up and wipe my eyes, suspecting the gallon of mascara they made me wear is all over my face. I peek through a crack in the door, then open it. "Oh, gosh. I'm so sorry. Please, come in."

I move aside and let Brett, Emma, and Evie into the tiny room. I'd forgotten I gave them backstage passes.

"Bria, what's wrong?" Emma asks, touching my arm.

"You must be sad about this being your final show, eh, kiddo?" Brett says.

"You were soooooo good," thirteen-year-old Evie says. "I love your dress."

I move to the mirror and grab a tissue to run beneath my eyes. "Let me clean up, and I'll show you around."

Evie stands in the open doorway, hoping to catch a glimpse of the band. Emma comes up behind me. "It's not only that this is your last show, is it?"

I lock eyes with her in the mirror. She knows it goes deeper than that. She turns to the others, fingering the lanyard around her neck. "Brett, why don't you take Evelyn wherever you're supposed to take her with these passes? I'll help Bria gather her things."

"But don't you want to meet the band, Mom?" Evie asks.

She shakes her head. "It's not important to me, but I know it is to you. Go. It's okay."

Emma and Brett have some kind of telepathic conversation and then Brett takes Evie out of the room and the door shuts.

"What's really going on?" she asks.

Feeling claustrophobic, I peel off the too-tight dress and slip into my robe. "I feel so stupid." I sit.

"How can you say that? You were fabulous. I knew you would be, but I had no idea I'd be able to hear you. I thought your voice would blend in with the band. But you had solos. You completely blew me away, as I'm sure you did the other ten thousand people here."

"Thank you. But that's not why I feel stupid." Hot tears travel down my cheeks.

Emma sinks into the couch next to me. "Tell me."

I hesitate.

"Come on," she says, taking my hand. "We're about to be sisters. We haven't had a chance to bond because you've been on tour, but that's going to change. I suspect we're going to be more than sisters. We're going to be good friends."

I look at the floor, embarrassed. "I never even told Brett. I'm not sure why either. At first, I couldn't believe it. Then I thought I might jinx it."

"Are you pregnant?"

My eyes snap to hers. "God, no."

"Then what is it?"

I close my eyes, wanting this to be the last time I mention it to anyone. "I was dating Adam Stuart."

"Adam Stuart," she repeats. "Who's that?"

I laugh. "Lead singer of the band you came to see."

"I came to see you, not them." She gives me a sympathetic look. "You said you *were* dating him. So I guess it's over now."

"Since last week."

"Oh, Bria, I'm so sorry. Did he end it because the tour is over?"

I shake my head. "I'm the one who ended it. I can't believe how stupid and naïve I was to think he'd be faithful to me. I should have known better. I see what goes on, but he was good at hiding it, and so was everyone else. It's almost like part of their job description was to keep me from finding out about his indiscretions." I pull the robe tightly around me. "Am I that gullible?"

"Sweetie, no." She rubs my back. "This was all surreal for you, I'm sure. You got caught up in it. It's understandable that when Adam turned an eye your way, you'd be flattered. I'm sure he was very charming." She's silent for a beat. "Did you ... fall in love with him?"

I wipe my tears for the hundredth time. "Love? No. I think I'm embarrassed more than anything. And I'm upset that I ruined my chance to join them on the next tour."

"I'm so sorry."

"It's okay. I was being silly. They probably never would have kept me on anyway. They've never had the same backup singer two tours in a row."

"Maybe there's a pattern there."

I look at her. "As in you think Adam sleeps with every backup singer?"

She shrugs.

My head droops. "Oh, my God, I bet you're right. I did some research when I was auditioning for them. Every single one of their backup singers was pretty." I think back to the final audition. I was so nervous I didn't realize the unattractive women were dismissed immediately. "I wasn't hired because of my voice, was I? It was a goddamn beauty pageant."

She smiles. "First off, you *are* beautiful which, like it or not, gives you a leg up in life. Secondly, you have an amazing voice. It's why you beat out everyone else to get to the finals. You deserved to be out there, Bria. I promise you will be again someday. Just not with a bunch of philandering Brits."

"I've been offered an audition with another band. Actually, they've all but guaranteed me the gig."

Her eyebrows shoot up. "Really?"

"They aren't successful yet, but I have a feeling they will be. They opened for White Poison a few weeks ago. They live in Connecticut."

"How good are they?"

I pull the earbuds out of my phone and play her a song.

"Wow. They are good," she says. "That song, though. It would be better if a woman sang half of it."

"A lot of their stuff is like that. It's almost as if they were written for two singers, but Crew is the only one who sings them. He doesn't want to hire me."

"Crew?"

"Chris Rewey. They call him Crew. He's the lead singer and one of the founding members of the band. If he doesn't want me, there's no chance I'll be hired."

"But you said they already offered you the job."

"The other three did. They said they would get him to come around. They want me to sing with them, see if we're a good fit."

"It sounds like an exciting opportunity for you. You can get in on the ground floor, become an integral part of the band."

"They have a lot of potential. Then again, if something sounds too good to be true, it usually is." I glance around the dressing room. "Case in point."

"This wasn't one of those times. You went on tour with White Poison. You'll have that on your résumé until the day you die. It's going to be a pivotal point in your life. Everything happens

51

for a reason. Even if this didn't exactly turn out the way you expected. Even if your heart and your pride got damaged." She pulls me in for a hug. "You're going to do great things, I just know it."

I laugh. "I think my big brother has rubbed off on you."

"You might be right."

"Do you think I should audition for Reckless Alibi?"

Her mouth falls open. "Reckless Alibi? Interesting name. Tell me about Chris Rewey."

I give her a sideways look.

"Oh, come on. It's always the holdouts who have the best stories."

I couldn't agree with her more. I know he's got one, but the last thing I should do is get close to another lead singer. His story will have to remain just that—his.

Evie bursts through the door and shoves a T-shirt in my face. "Look! All four of them signed it. Can you believe it? I actually met them. Oh my God, I think there is even some sweat on it." She turns the shirt over and points to a tiny wet spot. "See? Adam Stuart dripped sweat right here. I will never, ever, ever wash this as long as I live." She hugs me. "Thank you so much, Bria. You're the best."

I smile at the feisty girl who's about to become my niece, then get up, throw on some clothes, and quickly pack what little I have. "Come on, I need to go home and sleep for a week."

"Yup," Emma says. "Because you've got big things waiting for you."

"What big things?" Brett asks.

"It's a long story," she says, giving me a wink.

Chapter Eight

Crew

She enters our rehearsal studio, which is Liam's uncle's barn. Our eyes meet. She knows I don't want this. She quickly looks away and greets the others.

"Thanks for coming," Liam says. "You won't regret it."

She gives me a quick glance. "We'll see."

She appraises Garrett's full sleeve of tattoos. She's no stranger to tattooed musicians, but this is the first chance she's had to study us. Her attention moves to Brad, perusing his arms for nonexistent ink, and then to Liam and me. She focuses on my right bicep, where I have my one and only tattoo. I lift my left hand to cover it, as if I'm somehow protecting it from her. She quickly averts her eyes.

"We listened to your album," Garrett says. "Thanks for sending it over. It's phenomenal."

"Tell that to the thirty record labels and agents I sent it to."

"Screw them," he says. "They don't know shit. In this business, it's become less about talent and more about who you know." He nods at Liam. "We're lucky to know someone with connections."

"But you *are* talented," she says.

"And so are you. Maybe more than we are. You got the White Poison gig on your own. We got it because of Liam's uncle. I'm happy to report that in the past few weeks, we've gotten some calls."

"Calls?"

"You know, from agents and managers."

"Don't you already have those?"

Liam shakes his head. "We've been managing ourselves, but based on the influx of interest, it may be time to bring someone else on."

"Two someones," Garrett adds, giving me the side-eye.

Liam shows her our stage. "You may have hit the jackpot, getting in with us on the way up."

"A bit cocky, are we?" she says with a rise of her brow.

I look away. I don't like the way she does that. She has this confidence about her, yet an innocence all the same. How she got tangled up with Adam Stuart is beyond me. Maybe she thought he would better her career. I laugh quietly. Quite the opposite. He dropped her like a hot potato as soon as she got onto him. He's probably on a beach in Fiji right now on top of Amanda or Amy or whatever the hell her name is.

I remain on the couch. "Can we get this over with?"

Bria says, "Listen, if you aren't all okay with this, it will never work."

"Shut up, Crew," Garrett says.

Liam hands her a mic. "This is just for fun. We're not deciding anything today. Let's just jam."

The guys take their places.

Bria sees that I don't move from my seat on the couch. "Uh … aren't you going to sing?" she asks.

"I'm going to sit this one out. They want to hear you, not me."

She nervously shuffles from foot to foot.

"You do know the songs, right?" I ask sharply.

"Of course. I learned all of them."

"Why don't we start with something easy," Liam says. "How about 'Black Rose'*?*"

They play, and she belts out the first few words, her voice shaky and not at all how I remember.

"Sorry," she says. "Mind if we start again? I'm a little nervous."

"Bria, you sang with White Poison," Brad says. "You can sing with anyone."

She closes her eyes and nods as Garrett counts off the beat with his drumsticks.

She starts again, this time with a clear and steady voice, much like the one we heard on her album. My heart races and my pulse pounds, sending me back seven years to a place I don't want to remember. I jump up and go to our makeshift bar for a beer. When I return to the couch, she doesn't look at me. She doesn't look at me through the entire song. Or the one after that. I try to ignore her amazing voice.

"You guys mind if we try that one again, and I sit at the keyboard?" she asks.

The guys look at each other and shrug. "Fine by us," Liam says without consulting me.

I get that I'm against this whole thing, but they could at least have the decency to let me in on the goddamn decisions.

I chug the rest of my beer, then go outside to take a piss. When I'm done, I hear her playing the keyboard. I lean against the side of the barn, freezing, and listen to the song. I swear to God, if she'd had any other voice; a soprano maybe—anything but that throaty, sultry, all-too-familiar voice—I'd jump up and down. Regardless, she's taking what we've done and making it better. A whole lot better. But I'm not going to tell them that.

I don't want this.

I go back inside when the song is over.

"Holy shit, Crew, you have to hear this. Let's play it again," Liam says.

I hold up my hand. "No need, I heard it."

"Then you know it's fucking off-the-charts good."

I admit nothing.

"Stop your whining, and get up here and sing already," Garrett says. "We need to hear it with both of you."

All four of them stare at me.

"Fine. One song." I turn to her. "Do you know which parts are yours?"

"It's pretty evident," she says. "I'm kind of surprised you've never had a female singer before."

The guys all look at me.

"We've gotten along just fine without one."

Garrett counts us off. Bria stays at the keyboard. I consider telling her to move—the song was not written with keyboard—but she already played it once, and obviously the guys have no issue with it.

She sings. I watch her, then turn away when it's my part. When we hit the chorus, I don't expect her to join in, but she does. Damn if she doesn't hit just the right pitch to mix perfectly with me. Liam's smile is a mile wide.

When it's Bria's turn again, I try not to look at her, but every time I turn away, my heart pounds and I have to remind myself it's Bria, not *her*.

I don't like this. I don't like it one damn bit.

The song ends, and the guys are salivating—even Brad, who rarely shows emotion. It's clear I'm the only voice of dissension.

Everyone goes to the bar for a drink.

"You have to sing with us this weekend," Garrett says, handing Bria a cold beer.

Liam nods. "I second that. It will be a trial. You know, to see how it goes at a real gig."

Everyone stares at me. Liam begs me with his eyes. Bria looks hopeful. I know her dreams got squashed when she found out Adam cheated on her, but what did she expect? Still, she's biting her lip and looking at me like this is her last chance or something.

"Fine. One gig."

Liam and Brad high-five. Garrett pumps his fist. Bria's smile widens, showing off her perfect teeth.

"Let's get started then," Liam says, handing her our playlist for this weekend. "We have four days to practice. Are mornings good for you?"

"Don't you have regular jobs?" she asks.

"Crew and I work at my uncle's car dealership. Brad does freelance IT work. And Garrett ..." He turns to Garrett and scratches his head. "We still haven't figured out what the hell Garrett does, other than sit around and wait to collect his trust fund."

"Fuck you." Garrett pulls a drumstick from his back pocket and throws it at him. "I practice, you douchebag. Ten hours a day, unlike you amateurs. Why do you think we're so goddamn good?"

"Yeah, 'cause clearly the rest of us suck," Brad says, picking up his bass and playing it as if it's the first time.

Bria laughs at the antics.

I cringe. I don't like her laugh.

"Do you have a day job?" Liam asks her.

"Not at the moment."

"What about the drive? It's more than an hour from the city."

She shrugs. "You do what you have to do."

"Looks like we're in luck then," he says. "We'll put in a few more hours tonight, then meet again from nine to noon the rest of the week. Sound good?"

She looks at me. I'm not sure if she's waiting for my approval or for me to walk out and slam the barn door. I don't move.

"What are we waiting for?" she asks, picking up the mic.

My head falls back and I look at the rafters. *Fuck*.

Chapter Nine

Bria

Sweat trickles down my back and is absorbed by the waistband of my skirt. I twirl around, my flowy skirt getting some altitude but not enough to show off my ass like that other band I sang for. At least these guys let me pick my own clothes.

I feel high. Higher than when I sang with White Poison—and about a million times less nervous—even though I'm out in front this time.

There is a good crowd in the bar, maybe a hundred people. I don't miss that most of them at one time or another have stopped talking to pay attention to us.

I didn't know what to expect from Crew, but in my wildest dreams, it wasn't this. After the first song, we fell into an unbelievable synchrony. It's like we've been singing together all our lives. Every so often one of us will go rogue and sing an octave too high or low, and it's amazing that when it happens, the other one doesn't miss a beat. Our voices go together like peanut butter and jelly. Or maybe Jack and Coke if you ask one of the guys.

Crew locks eyes with me during the chorus. It's kind of a sappy song, and the audience probably expects us to do it, but still. He's different: animated, passionate.

The next song is almost like a fight between us. I was told they rarely sang this one because it most definitely required a second singer. He leans into me during his part, and I lean toward him during mine. We sang this in rehearsal, but we never did what we're doing now—not even close. At the end, when we "make up," he runs and slides over on his knees, begging me with his lyrics. I forgive him with mine, and he climbs up my body so we sing the final chorus together into the same microphone.

The crowd goes wild, begging for more when we walk offstage. Liam, Brad, and Garrett look ready to run back out for an encore. Crew hesitates.

"Come on, brother," Liam says. "They fucking love us. When have we ever played an encore? Let's give 'em what they want."

Crew looks indecisive. "'Revolving Door'," he says.

I don't sing on that one. It's all Crew. I pretend I'm cool with it. "Fine by me."

Everyone, including me, goes back onstage. Instead of getting a tambourine and perching on a stool, I sit at the keyboard. Crew doesn't see me, since he's busy with the mic. Garrett counts us off. When Liam and Brad start to play, I join in. Crew spins toward me and blows out a long breath. We hadn't practiced this song, and he wasn't aware I'd learned it. But not only did I learn it, I adapted it for the keyboard.

I shoot him a snarky grin. *Thought you were gonna do this one without me?*

Liam smiles at me. I'm not sure why he likes that I challenge Crew, but he seems to get off on it.

I'm a little weirded out, though. The whole time we were singing, Crew and I had a connection. I've never felt this with anyone I've worked with before. But the minute we stopped, he turned into a different person. It's like he remembered he's no longer the sole lead singer of Reckless Alibi. Not that I've been offered a job yet, but with how well things are going tonight, I can't imagine any other outcome.

The encore ends, and we leave the stage. The owner of the bar greets us with a tray of drinks. "I want you back here every Friday night for a month—maybe longer. Can you do that?"

Liam, the unofficial manager of the group, steps forward. "We might be able to accommodate you, but based on this crowd, I'd be doing our band a disservice if we didn't ask for fifty percent more."

The owner smacks his lips together as he thinks about it. The crowd is triple what it was when we started playing ninety minutes ago. No one has left. "Twenty-five percent more, and I'll give you five percent of the profits during your set."

"Make that from an hour before we play to thirty minutes after, and we've got a deal," Liam says.

"Deal. You kids really got something."

"Thanks," Liam says. "We'll see you next week."

The owner walks away.

"That was amazing, man," Brad says. "Looks like we don't need a manager. You handled that great."

"This is a bar," Liam says. "It's going to be a whole lot different when we play bigger venues and go on the road." He turns to me. "Shit. I didn't even think to ask—are you good with this? His offer was for the band he heard tonight. That includes you."

Crew is brooding, and I feel bad. What's going on with him?

"We might as well make it official," Garrett says, lifting one of the drinks off the tray. "What do you say? Did Reckless Alibi just become a party of five?"

"We're not even going to talk about this?" Crew asks.

"What's there to talk about?" Liam says. "You two were phenomenal. With both of you, we'll pull in male and female fans. You should have seen yourselves. Mark my words, we're about to take the world by storm."

Crew backs against the wall and slumps.

"Give us a minute," Liam says.

The three of us find a table as the two of them talk.

"What's with him?" I ask. "I mean other than not being the only one in the spotlight anymore?"

"You were pretty hot up there," Brad says. "And the two of you together were on fire. Maybe that makes him uncomfortable."

"Why?"

He shrugs. "Maybe he thinks you'll want to date him, like you did Adam Stuart."

"That's crap," I say. "He had a stick up his butt long before now. And who says I want to date him? I mean, I learned my lesson with Adam. But what would it matter if I did? I'm sure plenty of women do. That's not a reason to hate me."

"He doesn't hate you," Garrett says. "He also doesn't date women."

"Oh." I look over to see Liam and Crew having an intense conversation. "Is he gay?"

Garrett and Brad almost fall out of their chairs laughing.

Liam and Crew join us. "What's so funny?" Crew asks.

"Bria was asking if you're gay," Brad says.

Liam is doubled over, guffawing. Crew and I are the only ones not laughing.

"I'm not gay," he says sternly. "What the hell made you think I was?"

"They said you don't date women."

"He doesn't date them," Garrett says. "He fucks them."

Crew hits him on the back of his head. "I'm standing right here, douchebag."

I twist my lips. "So you're no better than Adam Stuart."

"That's bullshit," he says. "I don't string them along. They all know the score. And quit looking at me like I'm some kind of man-whore. It's not like I take a girl home every night. Just because I get more action than these cocksuckers doesn't mean I'm a player." He tosses back his drink. "I'm not like him."

"Sorry," I say. "I shouldn't have said that, but you're standoffish with me." I motion to the stage. "Except when we're up there."

"Everyone has to play their part."

I narrow my eyes. "Well you do it very well."

Liam nudges Crew. "Go on. Tell her."

"You do it," he says.

"She won't believe it if it comes from me."

Crew absentmindedly rubs his tattoo. He does that a lot. I've never asked him about the knife piercing flowers. Like his notebook, I get the feeling it's super personal.

He sticks his hands in his pockets. "I guess ... welcome to Reckless Alibi."

I bite my bottom lip to suppress my girly squeal. "Really? You mean it?"

"Yeah," he says dryly, then mumbles something about déjà vu. "Listen, I'm going home. I'll catch an Uber."

"You don't want to stay and celebrate?" Brad asks.

"Headache."

"Let him go," Liam says. "The rest of us can stay."

Before he leaves, he turns back to the stage and gazes at where we were singing moments ago. Then he catches me staring. He runs a hand through his hair and walks out the door.

"Don't mind him," Liam says. "He'll come around. He knows this is what's best for us. Give him time to warm up to you."

"Does he have a problem with women singers?" I ask. "Or just with me specifically?"

Liam stares at the front door. "He … has his issues. He'll work through them. This is a good thing." He picks up a shot glass and hands it to me. "To Bria. Welcome to RA!"

I clink my glass against theirs, almost as excited about my future as I am curious about Crew. Issues? What issues? And what do they have to do with me?

Chapter Ten

Crew

Seven years ago

Abby rolls off me and snuggles into my side. "When's your mom going to be home?"

I glance at the clock as I remove the condom. "Not for another hour."

"Good."

"It's okay, you know. She's well aware you come over when she's not here."

"That doesn't mean I want her catching us in bed."

"We've been dating almost six months. I'm pretty sure she knows we're sleeping together."

She puts her head on my chest. "Why can't my parents be more like your mom? You know I had to swear to my dad that I would stay a virgin until I got married?"

I tense under her. "Shit, Abbs. He's gonna kill me."

She grabs my hand under the covers and holds it over my heart. "He won't find out. But if he did, he wouldn't kill you. He does like you in his own reserved way. But I'd be grounded until I was twenty-one for sure."

"Where did you tell him you were going today?"

"Work. No ... Janine's."

I hate that she has to lie to her parents.

"Hey, speaking of work, I forgot to tell you Rob got fired yesterday."

"The creep who was always staring at you?"

"Yup."

"Thank God. I was wondering when I was going to have to kick his ass."

She stares at me, her head propped on my chest. "You'd really have done that?"

"Hell yes, I would have. You're all mine, and any guy who looks at you the way you said he did, deserves a black eye and a swift kick in the nut sack."

She smiles. "My protector." She inches her way up to press her lips against mine.

I love the taste of her. My dick springs back to life, but like Abby, I'm not too keen on Mom finding us naked in bed, so I don't do anything about it.

I wipe a piece of hair from her forehead after she settles onto the pillow next to me. "God, you're beautiful."

Her cheeks flush. "Christopher."

I kiss her. "It's true. I think God put you on earth just for me." I get out of bed. "Wait here." I run across the room and grab my notebook and a pencil, then jump back in bed.

She giggles. "Did you get inspired again?"

"You always inspire me, babe."

I sit against the headboard and look at her as words effortlessly flow out of me and onto the paper. She scoots up and sits next to me, looking over my shoulder as I work.

"Is that the way you really feel?" she asks.

I drop the notebook and pull her close. "I love you, Abby Evans." I look her straight in the eye. "I swear I'll never say that to another woman."

"Ever?"

"Ever."

She breaks into a brilliant smile. Then she picks up the notebook and sings the lyrics I wrote, sounding like a goddamn angel. She sings even better than she plays the flute. Every word makes my heart pound. She finds just the right melody to bring the lyrics to life, and I vow to record it exactly like she's singing it.

When she's done, I trap her under me. "Join the band. Do you know how big we'd get with you as our lead singer?"

"You already *have* a lead singer, and he's brilliant."

"Okay, co-lead singer. You can play the tambourine or something. That would be so sexy. With your throaty voice you'd be like a young Stevie Nicks."

"I'm not singing for Naked Whale. My dad would never allow it."

"What if I asked him? I can be very convincing."

"You'd do that?"

"Of course. That's how much I want you."

She smirks. "Are we still talking about singing?"

I lean down to kiss her. "Maybe."

She wiggles out from under me. "Let's get dressed. It's almost time for your mom to get home."

I pull on my boxers. "Are you working tonight?"

"No."

"Why don't you come with me to rehearsal? Sing a few bars. See how it feels."

She looks at the floor. "I don't know. Maybe you shouldn't push your girlfriend on the rest of the band."

"Are you kidding? They love you. Come on. Just one song. Then we'll see what happens."

"Which song?"

I know exactly what I want to hear her sing. I wrote it as a duet, even though I sing it solo. "'Across the Room'."

Her eyes meet mine. "That's the one you wrote the day we met."

"Maybe I sensed even then you'd be a great addition to the band."

She holds up a finger. "One song. That's it. I mean it, Christopher. I'm not promising anything."

I race around the bed and pull her into my arms.

"Don't get too excited," she says. "There's the whole getting my dad on-board thing, and you know how he hates rock bands."

"We'll start singing Christian music, then." I wink.

She laughs loudly. "Naked Whale singing Christian songs? I don't think so."

"You have no idea how far I'd go to get you."

She wraps her hands around my neck. "You already have me."

"And that makes me the luckiest man alive."

We hear the garage door opening, so we go to the living room and turn on the TV. Mom walks in with an armful of groceries. Abby hops off the couch even before I do.

"Hi, Mrs. Rewey. Can I help you with that?"

"I've got it," I say, taking the bags from my mom. "What's for dinner?"

"I was thinking pot roast. Abby, would you like to eat with us?"

"That sounds wonderful. I just need to clear it with my dad."

"I'll text him and let him know I invited you," Mom says, fully aware of Dr. Evans and all his rules. "Seven o'clock work for you?"

"Seven sounds great," I say. "We're going to rehearsal in a few. Abby's going to try singing today."

Mom puts down the milk carton in her hand. "You don't say? I think that's a fine idea. You have such a lovely voice, dear. I'm sure you'll be a great addition to the band."

"See? Now why can't my parents react like that?" Abby says.

Mom laughs and touches her shoulder. "You're a girl. That's the difference. I'm not sure I'd be okay with everything Chris does if he weren't a boy. I know that's sexist, but it's just how it is. Cut them some slack. They only want you happy and safe."

Mom's always been my biggest cheerleader. It's hard for me to imagine parents being any other way. But Abby's parents—her father in particular—don't seem to want to give her any room to become her own person. Hell, it took three months before they would agree to let her come to my house, and then only if my mom was here and they had proof of it with a text from her.

When we go on dates, they insist we go with another couple, as if that would in some way prevent us from having any alone time. I've spent half this year setting up Liam and the guys with random girls from school so Abby is allowed to go out with me.

Abby takes my hand. I love that she knows she can do that in front of my mom. "I *am* happy and safe," she says. "I can't imagine being any happier."

I don't miss Mom's proud smile. "I guess I did something right," she says. "Not that I can take all the credit. His dad must have had something to do with it."

"I'm pretty sure it was all you, Mom."

She hums a tune as she puts the groceries away. A Naked Whale tune. I have the coolest mom.

"Bye, Mrs. Rewey," Abby shouts over her shoulder as we head out the door. "See you at seven."

Abby hands me the keys. She always lets me drive—as long as her father isn't watching.

"Don't forget to stop by Janine's," she says.

"Right."

Abby's dad tracks her phone. Unless Mom has explicitly told him she's home and Abby is invited to be there, Abby's not allowed to come over. So she leaves her phone with Janine or one of her work friends. If her parents text her, the friend will get in touch with me, and Abby tells her what to text back.

I hate all the lying and sneaking around, but I'd hate not being with Abby even more.

Luckily Jake's house, where we practice, is right up the street from another one of Abby's friends. It's made it quite convenient for her to watch our rehearsals without having to stash her phone somewhere.

"Hey, Abby," Liam says when she walks in behind me.

Jake and Brandon greet her too. She's been at more rehearsals than not. She critiques us, tells us what she thinks works and what doesn't. She's got a great ear for music.

After we warm up and play a few old regulars, I motion for Abby to take the mic. She hesitantly picks it up. "Is this okay?" she asks everyone.

They smile. "It's about goddamn time," Liam says. "I'm tired of singing all the girl parts this pansy writes."

Her hands are shaking.

"It's just us," I say. "This is no big deal."

She nods. I motion for Brandon to count it off on the drums.

My part comes first. I always look at her when I sing, but this time is different. She's going to sing back to me. I'm as excited as a kid on Christmas morning.

She closes her eyes at first, which is probably good, because when I hear her voice through the amp for the first time, I almost shed tears. Holy shit. She was made for this. I knew she was fantastic, but with the music behind her, and the way she's projecting—my God, I know her voice shouldn't make me love her more, but it does.

When she opens her eyes and sings the lyrics I wrote because of her, it's like we're the only two people on the planet. The music comes to life in a way I never imagined. I sing better. The guys play better. Everything is perfect.

The song ends, and the garage becomes almost eerily quiet.

After a moment, she breaks the silence. "So?"

Liam comes up behind her, hugging her and picking her up. "I think I love you, Abbs. I mean, why the hell haven't you done that before? I'm pretty sure I speak for all of us when I say you have to do that again. Like all the time. Right, guys?"

Jake and Brandon don't speak. I think they're in shock, but they nod.

"I told you," I say. Then I turn to Liam. "Hands off my girl, dude."

He backs away, holding up his hands in apology. "Are we all in agreement that she becomes a member of the band?"

Abby sits on the chair in the corner, looking sad. "You realize my dad will never allow it."

"But you come to almost every rehearsal," Jake says.

"Yeah, but what about your gigs?" she asks. "If he found out, I'd be grounded for sure."

I sit on the arm of the chair. "I told you I'll talk to him. Even if he says no, we sometimes play in Jersey or New York. It's only an hour away. He wouldn't find out about those. Tell him you're with Janine."

"Come on, Abby," Liam begs. "You have to say yes. We need you."

She stares at the microphone stand. Then she looks around the garage, biting her fingernails like she does when she's thinking hard. Then she looks at me and smiles.

Chapter Eleven

Bria

I love singing for Reckless Alibi. The past few weeks have flown by between all of our rehearsals and the new gigs we got after singing in the bar. And the best part is we're starting to make money.

I put most of my White Poison pay toward my credit cards, so I'm back to living on a shoestring budget. The cost of gas to and from Stamford five or six days a week is killing me.

Hopefully I'll soon be able to start paying Brett back all the money he's loaned me. He did it out of love, but let's face it, he's a firefighter, it's not like he's rolling in dough. I know he had to scrimp and save to be able to help me.

I still wonder if Mom would be disappointed in me. I mean, I quit college after the first year—college that was completely paid for because I was a child of a 9/11 casualty. It just seemed pointless to sit in a classroom day after day when I already knew what I wanted to do with my life. So I hired voice coaches and dance instructors and image consultants to make sure I was giving off the right vibe to be a singer. Not to mention all the money I spent—Brett's money—on hiring a band to cut the album.

It's not like we're making bucket loads of cash. Most of what the band makes we put into equipment and advertising. We all agreed to put aside half of what's left for travel expenses so we don't end up staying in crappy motels if and when we start touring. Effectively, what I end up taking home isn't much more than any waitress job I held while waiting for my big break. Is *this* my big break?

I thought singing for White Poison was.

It wasn't.

Other than being on some YouTube videos taken by concertgoers, my likeness was never shown on signs or promos. My name was never mentioned during interviews given by the band. I never got recognized. That was probably because I didn't look like myself when I was onstage. They put so much makeup on me, I looked like a different person.

It's different with Reckless Alibi. I get to look like me. I get to *be* me. And even though we're still a smalltime band, it's everything I've ever dreamed of.

I pull up to the barn, wondering why Liam wanted us here an hour before our scheduled practice. He was very hush-hush about it.

The usual cars are parked in the makeshift gravel lot next to the barn. Liam's is the flashiest, no doubt because his uncle owns the largest car dealership in three counties. Garrett and Brad drive decent enough vehicles, ones you might expect men in their mid-twenties to drive. It's Crew's car that makes me scratch my head. It's an old Nissan. It might be twenty years old. Considering he works for Liam's uncle, surely he has the opportunity to drive something better.

I see a big white SUV. Its wheels and running boards are gray with slush and street salt. I peek inside on my way by, but don't see anything that clues me in as to who might own it.

I slide open the heavy barn door and go inside. A man stands and claps his hands once. "Good. Now that you're all here, we can get started."

I walk over.

"Bria, I'm Jeremy Halstead."

We shake hands.

"Nice to meet you." I look at the guys. "What's this about?"

Garrett, Brad and Crew look about as clueless as me.

I sit on an empty chair across from the couch. Jeremy walks in a circle around the furniture in the middle of the barn. "I'm a friend of Dirk's."

I'm confused.

"Liam's uncle," he clarifies.

Oh. I nod.

"I've got a background in entertainment and I'd like to become your manager."

Eyebrows shoot up. Pulses quicken. Excitement emanates.

Crew says, "You have a pretty nice ride. I'm not sure we can afford you."

Jeremy waves him off. "How do you think I'm able to afford such luxuries? By finding garage bands like yours and putting them on the map, that's how." He looks at our surroundings and chuckles. "Or in your case, a barn band."

"Still," Crew says. "We're barely able to cover our expenses and pay ourselves."

"I'm not asking for any of what you already have," Jeremy says. "I'll only take a cut of the gigs I get for you."

"How much of a cut?" Garrett asks.

He hands us each a printed contract. "It's all right here. This is a standard contract, but by all means, feel free to have your lawyer look it over."

By the way he says it, I get the feeling he knows we don't have a lawyer.

"We're booked through April," Brad says. "And the calls keep coming in. I think we're doing pretty well on our own."

Jeremy laughs. "Yeah, if you want to play in bars the rest of your life. I'm talking about getting you into bigger venues. Amphitheaters and festivals and eventually tours."

This gets the attention of everyone. "Tours?" Garrett asks.

"Eventually."

Crew thumbs through the contract. "Yeah, but how much of our souls will we have to sell?"

"It's not like that," Jeremy says.

"What will we have to do?" Garrett asks.

"The first thing you have to do is get into a recording studio and re-record your album with Bria. While you're focusing on that, I'll start courting record labels."

I don't fail to notice Crew's disappointment at Jeremy's mention of adding me to the album.

I don't get him. When we're up onstage it's like we're a couple who's madly in love. He sings *to* me, not just with me. He smiles. He's full of an energy that the rest of us seem to feed on.

But the second he puts down the mic, he goes back to being this, well … jackass. He's bipolar for sure.

"What else do we have to agree to?" Garrett asks.

It's not lost on me that Liam is not asking questions. It makes me wonder if he already knows all this or is being forced into this by his uncle, who's practically funded the band until now.

"I may hire someone to come in and work on your image," Jeremy says.

I shake my head. "I'm not wearing tight skirts that show my ass cheeks, and I refuse to paint my face so I don't even look like myself."

Jeremy laughs. "It won't be like that. Just a few tweaks here and there, I promise."

I sink back into the couch wondering if what Crew said is right. Are we about to sell our souls to the devil? Maybe that's what's necessary to get to the next level in this business.

"And?" Crew says. "There must be more."

"New material," Jeremy says. "You have to churn out new songs. I'd like you to have another album cut by June."

"June?" Garrett shouts. "You're crazy. There's a handful we've been working on, but ten? *By June?*"

"I was thinking more like twelve, maybe more." Jeremy nods to me. "Bria has some that will work, don't you, honey?"

I stand up and hand him the contract. "If you call me honey one more time, I'm walking out that door."

He pushes the papers back to me. "Feisty. I like it. Okay, *Bria.* I've listened to your work, and I'm impressed."

"Great," Crew says, sounding more than a little pissed. "I'll just play the goddamn tambourine or something."

"Don't worry, big man," Jeremy says. "That's not what I had in mind." He turns to me. "I'd like to change some of your songs, adapt them for two singers. Do you think you could do that? I think there's a lot of untapped potential there."

I try not to smile and give anything away. What he doesn't know—what nobody knows—is that I've already been doing that. I shrug. "Maybe."

"What do you say?" Liam asks. "Are we doing this?"

Crew puts down the contract. "We need some time to think about it. You know, talk about it as a band?"

Jeremy hands each of us a business card. "As you should, but don't take too long. I have to give SummerStage an answer by Friday."

"SummerStage?" Crew asks, perking up. "An answer to what exactly?"

"With a little help from Liam's uncle, I've secured you a spot in the lineup this summer. As you know, it's the largest outdoor music festival in New York City. The exposure could be even better than opening for White Poison."

Garrett's jaw drops. "SummerStage? Are you shitting me?"

"That's just the beginning." Jeremy crosses to the barn door and turns. "Friday," he says before leaving us staring at each other in stunned silence.

Slowly, a smile creeps up Brad's face. "Holy shit!" He flips through the contract. "Where do I sign?"

Crew stops Brad's hand. "Hold on. What do we even know about Jeremy?"

All eyes focus on Liam. "I only just met him. Dirk introduced me to him yesterday. He may be my uncle's buddy, but I did some research. He's legit."

"How is it we're only now hearing about this?" Crew asks. "If he's legit, why didn't Dirk tell us about him a long time ago?"

"He didn't want to get our hopes up. But after our gig with White Poison and all the attention we've gotten lately, he finally gets that we're the real deal."

"The real deal?" Garrett asks. "As in he didn't think we were good enough before?"

Everyone looks at me. I cringe.

Liam touches my shoulder. "I told you good things would happen if we brought her in."

Crew skirts the back of the couch. "Re-record *all* of our songs? That's a lot of damn work."

"Work that will pay off in the long run," Liam says. "You know it will." He turns to me. "Are you up for it? This puts a lot on you, too. We'll help where we can. But Crew's our lyricist, which means you'll have to spend a lot of time together, reworking your songs."

"Great." Crew looks less than excited as he gets a bottle of water from the mini fridge.

Liam slings his guitar over one shoulder. "Listen, if it was up to me, this would be a done deal. But it has to be unanimous. If you want to go in a different direction, well, that's the way it will have to be."

"But … SummerStage," Garrett says, pouting.

Crew smiles for the first time today. "I have to admit performing there would be pretty sweet."

Garrett hops off the couch and goes for his drumsticks. "Come on, then. We have a lot of work to do. We have until Friday, so we don't have to decide today." He walks around his drums and sits on his stool. He leans forward, close to his mic, then he belts out in an announcer's voice, "SummerStage presents the hottest up-and-coming rock band in the tri-state area—Reckless Alibi!"

Chapter Twelve

Crew

New material by this summer.

I shake my head for the umpteenth time since meeting Jeremy Halstead a few hours ago. I admit, it's what we've been working so hard for all these years, so why, now that it's happening, do I feel so apprehensive about it? Of the four of us, I think I'm the only one questioning any of it.

I blow out a breath and let my head sink back onto the couch—the *five* of us.

I make sure everyone is gone and then pull out my notebook. It's almost always with me so I can jot down lyrics when they come to me. But nobody gets to see it. They all know it's private until I complete a song.

Getting comfy on the couch, I open it to some of the first pages, knowing we could use some of it for the *new material* Jeremy is demanding. I just don't know if I can, though. I flip through the pages knowing some of them I could never sing—not even if a gun were pointed at my head. But there are a few that could work. Mom still has a few of my notebooks—surely there are bits and pieces I could turn into songs. I'll have to make a trip into the city and see if I can find them.

I open the "Abby" photo album on my phone and look at the pictures. Would she be okay with that? Would I?

There are two songs I wrote when we were dating that weren't really about her at all. One was about her dad, specifically about being controlled by someone who wanted to dictate your life. It could be about anyone. I'd have to adapt the song for Bria. The second song is about a turtle. I still remember the day Abby and I helped it get from the sidewalk to a pond. The lyrics I wrote about that damn turtle were stupid, but if I changed them a bit the song could be about finding your way and letting people help you.

Some of the songs I wrote about Abby were shared with Naked Whale. We even put them to music. They were pretty damn good, especially when Abby was singing with me. Liam is the only member of RA who's ever heard them, and he knows better than to bring them up.

But these two … I run my fingers across the lyrics I wrote about Abby's father and hum the tune in my head, remembering it all these years later.

I go to the keyboard. *It's for the band,* I tell myself.

I position my hands over the keys and close my eyes. Then I play. I mess up a few times, but then I find the right melody and sing. I don't need to look at the words. Every lyric I've ever written is burned into my memory.

"Not bad," Bria says from the door when I finish.

Surprised, I step away from the keyboard. "I thought everyone was gone."

"Car won't start," she says.

I go over to the couch and close my notebook. "I think I have jumper cables."

She follows me out. "Is that something you've been working on?"

"I wrote it a long time ago." I close the barn door behind us.

"I've never heard you play it. It's a shame, because it's good. Are you thinking of adding it to our lineup?"

Our lineup. I stop myself before I say something I shouldn't. She's a member of the band now, like it or not.

"Maybe." I open my trunk and get the jumper cables. "It's cold. Go sit in your car while I get it started." I pull over and get her hooked up, then start my car. I roll down the window. "Try it now."

Her car doesn't start. I go through the motions again without success.

Her forehead meets the steering wheel. "What am I going to do now?" She opens her purse and gets out her wallet. I see a few twenties. "How much do you think it will cost to Uber back to the city?"

"It's an hour drive. So a lot. You know they don't take cash, right? Surely you have enough in your account to cover the ride."

She sighs. "I have some overdue bills." She gets out of the car and slams the door. "Could you drop me off at the train station then?"

"I'll do you one better. I'll drive you to the city myself."

She's surprised. "You haven't wanted to spend one minute alone with me, not to mention an hour."

"There's something I need to take care of there. Something I need from my mom's house."

"She lives in the city? But I thought you grew up here in Stamford."

"I did. She moved there a few years ago after she met the guy who's now my stepdad."

She looks at her car and then at me. "Are you sure?"

"Leave your keys in the car. I'll text Liam to ask one of his uncle's mechanics to take a look. I'm sure they'll have it fixed in no time."

"You don't have to work today?"

"It's Tuesday, my day off."

"Right." She looks as though she'd rather get in the car with a serial killer. "Okay, thanks. Give me a sec."

She retrieves a notebook from her vehicle. It looks a lot like mine. "Don't tell me—it's where you write down your lyrics."

"How did you know?"

I get in the car and flash her my notebook. "Got one of my own." I toss it in the backseat.

She gets in and puts on her seatbelt. I look out my side window as I back up. When I look out the front window again she's got my notebook in her hand. I swipe it from her. "No."

I toss it in the back again.

"Jeez, touchy are we?"

"Nobody reads it, Bria. I mean it."

She stares at me for a minute, looking genuinely sorry. She runs her hand over her own notebook. "Crew, I'm sorry. I shouldn't have touched it. I know how personal it can be. I won't do it again."

I start driving.

"Can I show you something?" she asks.

"Sure." I put the car in park.

She opens her notebook to a page and hands it to me. It takes me a minute to realize what I'm reading. She's changed one of her songs, adding lyrics for *me* to sing.

"When did you do this?"

"I've been working on it a while."

Familiar with the song from when I listened to her album, I play it in my head. "Bria, this is great. Jesus, the guys will salivate over this."

She smiles. "You think so?"

"Hell yes. Are there more?"

She nods, then looks at me strangely.

"What?"

"Nothing. It's just … that might be the first compliment you've ever given me."

"No way." I think back. I've complimented her many times. Haven't I? At least I have in my head.

"Yes way."

I'm a real prick. *Way to go, Chris.* "I'm sorry. I don't mean to be a douchebag."

"To some it comes naturally." She elbows me in the ribs, and I roll my eyes.

I put the car in gear. "We have to get going. How about you sing them for me on the way?"

"Okay."

She sings the one she showed me, both her parts and mine. I ask her to sing it a second time and then once more. This time I sing my part, then we join in on the chorus, only I do it differently.

"That's brilliant," she says. "I like it your way much better. Can we try it again from the top?"

We sing it two more times, and I'm smiling ear to ear. I haven't had this much fun singing in a car since—*fuck*. I briefly close my eyes, remembering whose car I'm driving, and guilt washes over me.

"Crew!"

I slam on the brakes; traffic has stopped because of an accident.

"Damn." I crane my neck, looking ahead. "Looks like we might be stuck here a while."

She opens her notebook. "Want to try another to pass the time?"

Ten minutes later, we've mastered another one of her songs. She wrote my parts better than I ever could. She's a better lyricist than I am—hell, she's becoming a better *me* than I am. And suddenly, I question the need for Chris Rewey in Reckless Alibi.

"You look sad," she says.

"Just questioning my existence." I say it like a joke, but I think she sees through my bullshit.

"None of this would work if it was just me or just you. You guys were good before me, and I was good before you, but together it just …"

"Works," I say.

She nods. "Yeah. It does."

I stretch back and retrieve my notebook from the backseat. I open it to a page near the front. "Tell me what you think of this one." I give her a pointed look. "But *only* this one."

"Got it," she says, laughing. She mimes the sign of the cross. "May lightning strike me dead if I turn the page."

I'm beginning to appreciate Bria's strange sense of humor.

She reads the lyrics. No, she studies them. She scrutinizes them. "Why did you name this song 'Viaje de Tortuga?' That's Spanish, right?"

"It is. It means 'turtle's journey.' We wrote it … er, *I* wrote it when I was helping a turtle get to a pond."

She laughs.

"What?"

She looks at me and laughs harder.

"What's so funny about the song? It's not supposed to be funny."

She wipes her eyes. "No. I know it's not. It's just, the coincidence."

"What coincidence?"

She flips through her notebook, then shoves it at me. "Read," she says, covering the top of the page with her thumb. "I wrote this when I was thirteen."

I read her lyrics, but I don't get why that has anything to do with me or my turtle song. Her song is about somebody always in a hurry. It's childlike and nonsensical. "I have no idea what I'm reading. And I'm not sure how to say this, but it's really bad."

She laughs again. "I know. Like I said, I wrote it when I was a kid."

"What's so funny then?"

She finally moves her thumb and shows me the title: 'The Race of the Cottontail.'

I skim the lyrics again, and it makes a little more sense. "You wrote a song about a rabbit?"

She looks at me like she's waiting for me to get it.

"What?" I ask again.

"Don't you get it? It's the tortoise and the hare."

"You've lost me."

"You and me—we're the tortoise and the hare. You know, in the old story."

I shake my head, confused.

"You are fast, overconfident, and distracted," she says, amused.

"What does that make you?"

"Slow but relentless."

I chuckle. "Relentless. I'd agree with that. But the tortoise won the race. Are you saying I'm a loser?"

"It's true the tortoise won, but only because they didn't work together. You and me, we're working together, and that makes us unstoppable, just like when we're up onstage."

She's right. We're amazing when we're together. "What does that have to do with the story of the tortoise and the hare?"

She shrugs. "I don't exactly know, but I'm sure there's something there we could make into a song."

She closes her eyes tightly and bites her lip. She's thinking hard. Then a luminous smile lights up her face and she belts out a lyric.

Holy shit, is she for real? Damn it if she doesn't inspire me. The traffic is still not moving, and as I stare out the window, it comes to me. I recite the next line.

She's quick to come up with the next one, then it's my turn again. It's like we're in each other's heads. It's fucking unbelievable. This feeling—it's exhilarating.

Our gazes lock in a moment of sizzling awareness. Without thinking about it, I lean across the console and kiss her. I kiss her hard. She resists, as if I took her by surprise, but then she lets my tongue into her mouth and kisses me back. Her lips are lazy and teasing. Pulse waves ripple through me, tingling my groin. Every nerve ending I have comes brutally to life. Holy shit times two. This kiss—it's the best goddamn kiss I've ever had in a car.

I remember where I am and pull back. I'm not just in any car. I'm in *Abby's* car. Guilt hits me a second time.

A horn blasts behind me. Traffic is finally moving again.

"Sorry," I say, my eyes locked on the road in front of me. "I shouldn't have done that. I won't do it again. Let's keep this between us, okay?"

She doesn't answer, but I can feel her eyes burning into me. I can't look at her, though, because if I do, I fear Bria might not be the girl looking back at me.

Chapter Thirteen

Bria

This week has been a whirlwind. Crew stayed at his mom's in the city every night so we could work on songs going to and from practice. But after that first day, he insisted on driving back and forth in *my* car. I find it strange, because I swear he has some kind of unnatural attachment to that old Nissan. He loves driving it, but he doesn't seem to want *me* in it. Not after that day. I thought maybe he didn't want to spend money on gas, but he insisted on paying for mine. The man is a puzzle. I'm just trying to figure out if I want to bother solving it.

He hasn't tried to kiss me again. It's as if it never happened. Which is probably for the best all things considered. But when I look at him, all I can think about is that kiss. It was the best one I've ever experienced, but also the worst, because I shouldn't have let it happen. We have a good thing going. I can't let this turn out like before. We need to keep it professional.

That day in the car, I felt we had a breakthrough—right up until he kissed me. Now the tension between us is worse than before but in a different way. Singing or writing lyrics are the only times things feel normal between us.

Tonight we're all on a high. We signed the contract with Jeremy this morning, and we're playing our last show at the same bar where I played my first RA gig.

The audience has tripled in size since our first time here. In fact, they had to hire bouncers to keep the place from going overcapacity. Word definitely got out that the opening act for White Poison was playing. I'm sure the bar owner will try to negotiate additional gigs. I'm also sure that our asking price has probably doubled since signing our new manager.

After a short break, Liam stops us before we go back onstage. "Let's play it."

We all know what he's referring to. We've been rehearsing one of my altered songs. "I'm not sure we're ready."

"Liam's right," Brad says. "We should play it. After today we might not have as much control over our set list."

"This is true," Garrett says, twirling a drumstick.

Crew shrugs. All of them look at me. I'm not sure when I became the deciding vote. Maybe because it's my song, only it's *not* mine anymore. It's *ours*.

I glance at the crowd. "Let's do it."

I'm both excited and nervous. This will be the first time I've ever sung one of my songs in public. What if they hate it? Crew must sense my anxiety, because he whispers in my ear, "I haven't told you this yet—probably because I've always been the songwriter—but this might be the one that puts us on the charts."

I smile, more confident now. Garrett counts off with his drumsticks.

My part is first. I sing to Crew. Not because I'm afraid to look at the audience, but because in some strange way, even though there is tension between us, he gives me strength. When it's his turn, he sings to me. When we sing the chorus, we do it like we did it in the car, because his way is a thousand times better than mine.

The rest of the set is just as good. The audience is on its feet, and the dance floor is packed with sweaty bodies. The energy is palpable, and the connection between Crew and me is indescribable. Sometimes it's like we're making love to each other with our words, our actions, our eyes. It's hard not to be turned on by it, especially after knowing what his lips feel like on mine.

I've had more than one fantasy about Crew since our kiss. Despite his insistence that it won't happen again, I've seen the way he looks at me. He's fighting it, just like I am.

But he doesn't fight it when we're singing together. That's when he feeds on it. He feeds on it like a starving man at a buffet.

When our set is over, people storm the stage. They want a piece of us. They want to touch us, get our autograph, say they know us. It's scary and exhilarating at the same time.

I break away, needing to pee badly from my nervousness. I hurry to the bathroom, hoping I can get there without being accosted. Thankfully nobody is inside, but I hear someone enter the room while I'm in the stall. I wonder if it's a fan who followed me in, or just some random girl who has to pee. I flush and then open the metal door to see it's not a fan. It's not even a girl. It's Crew.

He locks the bathroom door. Then he looks at me. His gaze slides casually down my body before rising to meet mine again. He lunges toward me and pins me to the wall. He kisses me. He kisses me like he sang to me, with passion and fire. It almost feels like we're still singing to each other, because this is what it's like. And even though I know how wrong it is, it makes what's happening between us kind of make sense.

Sensations I've never felt before run through me as his tongue strokes my lips with strong, sensual licks. He cups my face and then runs his hands through my hair. I pull him closer. His erection presses into me, and a ball of need forms in the pit of my stomach. His hands are unruly and untamed as they work their way over my body. I'm drowning in him—his taste, his feel, his scent. Then suddenly, I hear lyrics in my head. I'm afraid that if I don't write them down, they'll be lost.

I don't want to push him away, but the songwriter in me does it anyway. He backs off, breathing heavily. He shakes his head to clear it, like maybe what just happened wasn't really what he wanted. His forehead creases, and he turns to unlock the door.

"Crew," I say, wanting to tell him it was nothing he did, but when inspiration strikes, you need to go with it.

He looks at me, but it's like he's looking *through* me. Before I can explain, he's out the door without uttering a single word.

A girl walks in with a friend. "Oh my God, that was him!" She notices me. "And you're *her*. You guys are so good. Are you dating? Of course you're dating. You were practically humping each other on the stage. Is he good? Stupid question, right? I mean look at him. Are you playing here again? Are any of the other guys in the band single?"

I ignore her ramblings because I have so much going on in my head right now. "Do either of you have a pen?"

One of them checks her purse and hands me a ballpoint. I pump the paper towel dispenser until I have a good length and then I put it on the counter and write. By the time I leave the bathroom, I think I've written Reckless Alibi's newest song.

I walk toward my bandmates. Things have died down, but there's still a crowd around them. Crew's easy smile drops when he spots me. He scratches an eyebrow repeatedly as he eyes me, like he's sorry about what happened. I weave my way through the crowd and shove the paper towel at him. He looks at me wondering why I'm giving him a paper towel. I nod at it. He notices my scribbling and the corner of his mouth turns up. Before he reads it, he locks eyes with me as if he now understands why I pushed him away.

He walks away, reading my deepest innermost thoughts. I wrote about wanting him but not being able to have him. About not letting history repeat itself. About the incredible sensation of his hands on me. He brushes off a few fans that trail after him. He leans against the wall as he reads. I can tell he reads it more than once. He scrubs a hand across his face—the way guys do when they're in a state of confusion.

He looks at me from across the room. He's fighting something. I wonder if it has anything to do with the issues Liam spoke of.

He flags down a passing waitress. She pulls a pen from behind her ear and hands it to him. He lays the paper towel against the wall and writes. He shakes the pen and writes again. After a few minutes of this, he comes back over, gives me the paper towel, and walks out of the bar.

I look at what he wrote. He marked out some of my lyrics and changed others. My mouth hangs open. With his modifications, I think we've just written one of the saddest love songs of our time.

What happened to him that could invoke such loving yet painful words?

I look at the empty doorway and wonder why he feels so much pain, even as I realize that pain may be about to make us a shitload of money.

Chapter Fourteen

Crew

Seven years ago

Abby and I stroll past store after store in the mall until I stop our progress and pin her to the wall with my stare. "What's the matter?"

She looks at the floor.

"You've been acting strange for days. You *love* shopping, but we've yet to go into a single store. What gives? Are you sick?"

"Not exactly."

"What does that mean?" I swallow and take a step back, fear crawling up my spine. "Is there someone else?"

Her eyes snap to mine. "God, no."

Relief.

"Then what is it?"

A single tear falls from her lashes. "I ... oh, Christopher." She grabs her stomach. "I feel sick. I need a bathroom."

I rush her to the nearest restroom and wait outside for ten excruciating minutes, wondering what's going on.

When she finally emerges, her eyes are red and puffy, and she looks exhausted. I think of the past few days—the past week actually—and realize she hasn't been acting strange per se, just tired.

"You *are* sick," I say, leading her to the nearest bench.

She shakes her head. "I'm not."

She gives her belly a rub, and my heart falls.

"Abbs, really?" I grab her hand. "Are you sure?"

She sniffs away more tears. "There's nothing else it could be. I'm late. Really late. Three weeks or more. I lost track of time and didn't think about it until I started feeling … funny."

"But it could be something else. You could be sick. Maybe you have the flu and that's the reason you're late."

She shrugs weakly.

I stand and pull her to her feet. "Come on. We have to be sure." I gesture to a drugstore.

She holds me back. "Are you kidding? We can't go in there. Look around. I see four people from school. And who knows how many people from church could be here. I can't risk someone seeing us buying a test and telling my parents."

"Right. We'll try the next town, and you can stay in the car while I buy one."

She's still trying to hold back tears. "You'd do that?"

I raise her hand to my mouth and kiss it. "I'd do anything for you."

"You're not mad?"

"I'm definitely not mad. Scared maybe. Surprised. But not mad. I'm just as much to blame as you are. More maybe, since I'm the one who buys the condoms."

We leave the mall, reach her car, and get in. "You wore one every time," she says. "How could this be happening?"

"We're not sure it is. Your period has been whacky before."

"It's different this time. It's like I know."

"Or you're scared and imagining the worst-case scenario."

"What would we do?"

"Let's not think about that yet, okay? One thing at a time."

I hold her hand for thirty minutes while I drive. Thirty minutes of silence, both of us surely contemplating what will happen if what she fears is true.

"Stay here," I say after pulling up to a drugstore.

I reach in the backseat and put on a baseball cap I left in her car. Then I raise the collar of my jacket around my neck. I probably look like I'm going to rob the place, but I can't risk anyone recognizing me and going to Abby's father.

I peruse the pregnancy tests and pick the most expensive one, thinking it must be the best. Then I grab a bag of M&M's on the way to the register. I'm not sure why. I don't even like them, and it's stupid to think that because I'm buying candy, the lady behind the counter will fail to see the pregnancy test, but I do it anyway.

Back in the car, I hand the bag to Abby. "What now?" I ask.

"I want to do it now and find out for sure."

"There's a bathroom inside. Go in there, but don't look at the results. The box says to wait three minutes. Come back out. I want to be with you when we find out."

We lock eyes, both hoping this is all a bad dream. She takes the box and gets out of the car.

I turn up the music, wanting to drown out the thoughts in my head. How can this be happening when everything is so perfect? We have so many plans. Abby has become an unofficial member of Naked Whale. Though her father refuses to let her sing with us, she comes to almost every rehearsal and even joined us last month for a gig in Jersey. Some high school hired us to play at their prom. It wasn't exactly Radio City Music Hall, but it's better than a stupid talent show.

We're good, and people are starting to notice. Liam's uncle is kind of a bigwig. He lined up some local county fair performances for this summer. Abby turns eighteen in August. Her parents won't be able to control her then. She says she wants what I want, to be part of a band, cut albums, and go on tour. Everyone else thinks it's a pipe dream. Everyone but Abby and me.

She gets in the car and hands me the test. "I can't look."

I take a deep breath, deeper than any breath I've ever taken, and look at the clock on my phone while the minutes tick away. "It's going to be okay."

She stares out the window.

I look at the white stick. It's not one of those tests where you have to figure out if it's one line or two, crossed lines, or pink or blue. This test tells you flat out. PREGNANT.

I try to think of anything but what our reality could be. I love her. I'll never love anyone but her. I take her hand. "Let's get married."

Her head falls back. "I knew it." Her chin quivers.

"Abby, this isn't the end of the world."

"That's easy for you to say. My dad will kill me. He will literally ground me for the rest of my life. I'll never get to see you again. He'll be so ashamed. He'll say I've disgraced the family. He might even make us move away."

I pull her across the console and into my lap. "Then we won't tell them."

"You mean get an abortion and pretend it never happened?"

"We're not getting rid of our baby, Abbs. I mean we won't tell him until you're eighteen. You can hide it. Wear big shirts and stuff. It's not like you spend a lot of time with your parents anyway.

You're either with me or Janine or the band, and when you're home, you stay in your room."

"What about church? I can't exactly wear oversized frumpy clothes there."

"You'll be eighteen in four months. How big do you think you'll be by then?"

She looks at me in surprise. "Do you really want to do this? Have a baby?"

"It doesn't look like we have a choice, does it?"

"I have no idea about anything, Christopher. I mean, what do we do? Do we go to a doctor? And since I'm a minor, how do I do that? If we keep it, we have to make sure it's okay, don't we?"

I do some quick internet searches on my phone. "What time do you have to be home?"

"Not until dinner. I have all day."

"Good. We're going to the city. We're halfway there anyway. They have tons of free clinics. I don't even think you have to give your real name."

"You mean like where the drug dealers go?"

I raise my brows. "Babe, I doubt drug dealers go to doctors. I'm sure homeless people do, but also people without insurance. Lots of regular people don't have insurance. I'm sure it will be fine. Unless you have a better idea."

"There is no better idea. It's our only choice."

I program the address into my phone. "Call the guys. Tell them we're missing practice today."

Two hours later, I'm staring at a black and white photo of the peanut that is our baby. Eight weeks, that's how pregnant she is. By August, she'll be almost six months along. The doctor said she'll be showing, but with the right clothes, she may be able to hide it. He said to come back once a month to make sure everything is okay.

He sent us on our way with the picture and a bottle of prenatal vitamins.

Back in the car, I take her into my arms.

"Did you really mean what you said?" she asks.

"I've said a lot of things today."

"About getting married."

I wipe her tears and cup her face. "I'd marry you tomorrow if I could."

She nods over and over. "I'd marry you too."

"We'll do it as soon as you turn eighteen, before the baby comes."

"What about school? What about my parents? I'll still be living under their roof. How will it work? What about the band? What about—"

I put my fingers over her mouth. "It's going to be okay. Plenty of girls have babies in high school. You'll take a few weeks off or something. I'll help you with your studies. We'll take the same classes. If we're married, we'll live together. I'm sure my mom will let you move in. Your parents won't be able to say or do anything. As for the band, we've got paid gigs lined up for the summer. We'll save every penny for the baby. I'll get an extra job if I have to. And as for the kid—we'll take him on tour with us. Maybe buy him his own little guitar."

For the first time in days, she smiles. "Him?"

"Just a feeling."

She stares at the sonogram. "It doesn't seem real."

I put my hand on her belly. "This may not have happened like we planned, but we're going to be together forever, Abbs. This just made forever happen a little faster."

I reach into the glovebox and pull out a pen and paper.

She laughs. "You're writing a song? *Now?*"

I scribble some lyrics. "Are you kidding? Of course I'm writing a song. Shh, let me think."

She looks over my shoulder as I write. "You won't be able to sing this until we tell everyone."

"I know, but I have to write it down while I'm inspired."

"I love you."

"I love you too." I touch her belly again. "Both of you."

Chapter Fifteen

Bria

Nearly two months have gone by. Seven weeks to be exact. Seven weeks of insurmountable tension, stolen kisses, and forbidden gropes. Forbidden because we're in the same band, and it could complicate things. I know why I'm fighting it. I don't want this to end badly, like it did with Adam. Is that why Crew is fighting it?

He hasn't come right out and said that he is. Then again, he has. With his lyrics. The songs he's written lately—they're all about wanting something you can't have. I'm just not sure if the songs are about me or someone else. Someone from his past. Someone who lives in the notebook he carries around with him like a Bible.

It doesn't happen after every gig, but sometimes, like right now, when neither of us can control the emotions we had onstage, he pulls me into a back hallway or storage closet, and we make out until we can no longer breathe. We don't talk about it, we don't plan it, we don't apologize for it, it just happens. Afterward, though, it's like it didn't.

He pulls away, clearly done with today's make-out session. We're in a closet this time. He opens the door. "You go first."

I walk into the hallway, trying to look like I just came from the bathroom. He'll wait a minute and then follow. He doesn't want anyone to think we're together. Because we're not. I tell myself this isn't as bad as the Adam situation. Crew and I aren't sleeping together. As far as I can tell, he's not sleeping with *anyone*. I think back over the past few months and try to remember a time when he left a gig with someone. I can't think of one, though the guys once told me it's what he often did.

"Bria Cash!" someone says behind me. For a moment I hope it's him, calling me back.

A man is exiting the restroom.

"You were great up there." He shuffles his feet uneasily.

"Thanks."

"I saw the band play at another bar last year. They're much better now, with you up there."

"I appreciate the vote of confidence."

"Where will you be playing next weekend?" he asks. "I'd like to check out more of you … uh, your band, I mean."

I laugh at his nervousness. "We'll be at The Vogue Friday and Ripple on Saturday."

"Great. I'll be sure to catch one of them. Or maybe both."

"Thanks for the support."

Crew comes out of nowhere and latches on to my elbow. "We have to go."

He drags me back into the bar. I look over my shoulder at the guy in the hallway. "Uh … bye." I turn to Crew. "What just happened?"

"Why did you tell him where we're playing next?" he asks with an aggressive slash of his brows.

Has he lost his marbles? "Why do you think? Because we make money when people come see us."

His lips are pinched together, nostrils flaring. I try to hide my smile. He's jealous.

He drops my elbow after realizing he's still holding on to me. "You shouldn't make a habit of talking to strange men in dark hallways."

I itch to call him on his jealousy, but I don't.

"Let's rejoin the others, okay?"

Garrett, Liam and Brad look at us strangely when we sit down at the table.

"What?" Crew bites out.

"Nothing," Liam says, shaking his head. "Good set today."

"It *was* good," Crew says.

My cheeks pink, and I turn away. What was good, our songs or what happened in the storage room?

I don't miss how Liam scrutinizes Crew and me the rest of the night. Does he know about us? Not that there's anything to know really. If he does think there is something between us, he doesn't look mad about it. Concerned maybe, but not mad.

I'm reading too much into it. Liam's always been concerned about me when it comes to Crew. All the guys have.

I accept my ceremonial drink to end the evening, and we toast to another successful performance.

~ ~ ~

Crew and I enter the barn together. He stays with his mom in the city some days so we can put the finishing touches on the songs we've been working on.

All eyes turn to us, including Jeremy's.

"What's up, guys?" Crew asks.

Jeremy opens his briefcase and removes papers, handing one to Crew and another to me.

I read the top line. "An addendum to our contract? What's this about?"

"This is about the two of you having a sexual relationship," Jeremy says.

Crew steals a glance at me. I'm sure I turn beet red. The guys act mildly embarrassed for us.

"We had to say something," Liam says sheepishly. "It could get complicated. We're just getting started. None of us want anything to screw this up."

Crew hands the paper back to Jeremy. "We don't have a sexual relationship."

Jeremy follows him over to the seating area. "Do you deny it?"

"We're *not* having sex," Crew says. "End of story. You guys can take your addendum and shove it up your asses."

"Come on," Liam says. "I saw you go into the storage closet together Friday. You didn't come out for ten minutes, and then it looked like you were having a lover's quarrel."

"A lover's quarrel?" Crew says. "You're seeing shit, man. We're not sleeping together."

"Maybe not yet," Garrett adds.

I rub my forehead in frustration as the men in the room discuss my love life. *This isn't happening.*

"Listen," Jeremy says, shoving the paper back in Crew's hands. "This is just a precaution to protect the band. Nothing else. It doesn't define your relationship with Bria."

"Like I said," Crew snarls, "we're not in a relationship."

Jeremy motions for everyone to calm down. "That may well be, but these guys seem to think you are, and they want to protect themselves and your brand."

I skim the addendum. It states that if either of us ends up leaving the band, we give up all rights to the music we brought in and recorded as RA. Not only that, we forfeit any and all future royalties earned by that music.

Crew reads it too, then huffs. "Seems to me all of us should be signing this, not just Bria and me. What if Garrett quits tomorrow because he and Liam got into a fight? He's played on all the songs we've recorded. How is that any different than Bria or me quitting?"

Jeremy nods, thinking about it. "Crew's right. I'll have the addendum modified to include all members of the band."

Garrett stands. "How did this turn into *our* problem?"

"Problem?" Crew says. "There is no problem. There is no relationship. So we kissed. So what? No need to alert the goddamn press. It didn't mean anything."

Why my heart falls into my stomach when he says that is beyond me. *Did I want it to mean something?*

"Still," Brad says. "Maybe the two of you should think twice before sneaking into any more closets. Look at the bigger picture. We have the band to think about."

"Says the guy who's been in it about two seconds longer than Bria," Crew spits out.

"Crew," Liam warns. "We don't need to fight about this. We just want you to be responsible. That's all."

Crew tosses the addendum into the trashcan and crosses to the stage. "Are we going to rehearse or what?"

"That's not all," Jeremy says.

"There's more?" Crew runs a hand through his hair. "I can't wait."

"This is the good part. You'll want to hear this."

Crew rejoins us.

Jeremy's smile grows as he reaches back into his briefcase. He throws a thick folder on the table. "We have an offer to sign with a label."

"Are you serious?" Liam asks.

"I am, but before you get too excited, it's not a major record label. It's an independent."

"What's the difference?" I ask.

"Indie labels come in all shapes and sizes. Some even operate like major labels. The smaller, grass-roots labels concentrate on promoting, selling, and publicizing releases. They wear many different hats, with one or two employees bearing the brunt of A and R, arranging airplay, working with distributors, and coordinating publicity."

Liam picks up the folder. "I'm assuming we got an offer from the latter kind."

"We did, but that's not a bad thing," Jeremy says. "It's a move in the right direction. It will allow you to dip your toes in the water before diving in headfirst. Because they are a small label, their offer is negotiable. I've gotten them down to a three-year contract."

"What does that mean exactly?" I ask. "And not to sound stupid or anything, but what is A and R?"

"Artists and Repertoire," Crew says. "They're the ones who locate new talent and work with bands on song selection and recording studios."

I'm not sure if I feel naïve for not knowing that or impressed that he does.

"They'll have the rights to all your recorded material for three years," Jeremy says. "After that you can re-negotiate or move on. There is also a buyout option. Say you climb the charts to number one, and you need more PR than they can handle. You give them a lump sum and part ways."

I smile to myself, happy I'm not completely unaware. I know PR stands for Public Relations.

"How much is the buyout?" Liam asks.

Jeremy turns a few pages and points to the figure.

"A million dollars?" Liam shouts. "We'd be stuck with them for the full three years if we do this."

"It's a good possibility, but three years is nothing in this business. A blip on the radar, during which time you'll figure out how the industry works. I've had an entertainment attorney look it over. It's standard issue. My advice is to take the bird in the hand because you never know what's going to happen."

"They'll get us on the radio?" Garrett asks.

"Most definitely."

The five of us look at each other and smile.

"We'll need time to discuss it," Crew says.

"As you should," Jeremy responds. "Why don't I meet you back here in two days? I'll bring the new addendum, and you can ask me any questions you have." He leaves.

We stare at the folder in Liam's hands. Then we high-five and hug each other. Everyone but Crew and me. We keep our distance, and Liam notices. He looks between us and shakes his head.

"Holy shit," Garrett cries. "We made it!"

"Hold on," Crew says. "This is amazing. It's exactly what we've hoped for. But you heard the man. We'll be at their mercy for three years. They'll control us. They will tell us where to play, what to play"—he glances at me— "maybe even what to wear."

"But we can make demands of our own," I say, "Can't we?"

Brad laughs. "What, like, 'I refuse to wear a skirt more than five inches above the knee?'" he says in a hideous falsetto.

I throw a pillow at him.

"Actually," Crew says, looking at me protectively, "exactly like that." He paces around the back of the couch. "Like Jeremy said, they're a small label and more likely to negotiate. That means we can ask for stuff we wouldn't normally ask a major label."

I smirk at Brad.

Liam puts the folder down. "We have two days. Why don't we all write down the things we think are negotiable and regroup before Jeremy comes back."

We nod.

"Now," Garrett says, smiling, "let's rock the roof off this barn. We're going to be fucking famous!"

Chapter Sixteen

Crew

I've avoided her for three weeks. I've avoided her through eight gigs and twelve days in a studio re-recording our first album with Bria singing.

I sang with her. Even put on a pretty good act onstage. But that's all it was, an act. I even quit riding to and from the city with her.

But the truth is, I'm not sure if I'm avoiding her to validate my proclamation that we're not together, or if it's because I really don't want to be with her.

Bria and I signed the addendum, along with the rest of the band, even though everyone knew it was meant just for us. We also signed something else that day, a three-year contract with Indica Record Label. Jeremy is introducing us to our label rep next week.

This should be the best week of my life. I glance over at Bria. So why isn't it?

I screw up on the keyboard, and Garrett throws a drumstick across the barn floor. Everyone stops playing. "I'm so tired of this shit," he says. "We all are."

I walk over and flick his snare. "Like you've never missed a goddamn beat before. If I called you out on every one, we'd never get anything done around here."

"You're kidding me, right?" Garrett snaps. He turns to Liam and Brad. "Are you hearing this?"

"Crew," Liam says, putting down his guitar.

"What?"

"Garrett's right. The three of us are tired of this."

"Tired of what exactly?" I say, like I don't know what's going to come out of his mouth next.

He motions between Bria and me. "You. Tiptoeing around each other because of the goddamn addendum. For the love of God, will you two just get over yourselves and fuck already?"

Bria's jaw drops. I step forward, wanting to punch him. "What the hell, Liam?"

"I'm only saying what everyone else is thinking. Get over your shit and do something, because the two of you avoiding each other is not working. You sucked at our gigs last weekend. If Jeremy had been there, he'd have torn you each a new asshole." He turns to Bria. "No disrespect."

"Right," she says dryly.

"We did not su—"

"Shut up and let me talk, Crew. This conversation is long overdue. You're damn lucky you two recorded in separate booths at the studio, or that shit would have sucked, too. Whatever is going on with you affects all of us. We have four weeks before we go back to the studio to record our new stuff. Four weeks, and you've still got two more songs to write and three to complete. Not to mention the time it'll take me to put them to music and for us to rehearse them. So yeah, go fuck—then write a song about it. Then fall in love and write a song about that. Then break up and write another fucking song. I don't care as long as you both get over this shit and do your damn jobs."

Bria sits on the couch. "Maybe my joining the band was a mistake."

Garrett hops off his stool. "It wasn't. We're ten times better than before. This is going to work. You need to figure out how that's going to happen."

I pick up the mic. "Stopping in the middle of rehearsal is not going to help."

Liam turns off the amps. "We're finished with rehearsal."

"We're not even halfway through," I say.

"We're done until you finish the songs." He goes to the door with Garrett and Brad. "Do whatever you have to do to make that happen, and don't come back until then." He gives Bria a sharp look. "That goes for you, too."

"What about work?" I ask.

"Leave that to me," Liam says. "Dirk knows the band is what's important."

"Seriously?" Bria says as they leave. "Are you tough-loving us?"

Liam looks guilty. He knows this is my fault. Everyone here knows that.

I narrow my eyes at her. "Tough-loving us?"

"Cutting us off until we do what they want."

I sit on the chair across from Bria and let my head fall back. "Fuck!" I shout into the rafters.

"What do we do?" she asks.

"We write the damn songs."

"You realize that means spending time together. Lots of time. A car ride to the city isn't enough."

"I know." I try to think of a solution that will work. "I guess we could go to my place."

She shakes her head. "We're talking ten- or twelve-hour days, Crew. Liam's right. We have to finish. I'm not about to sleep on your couch. You'll have to come to the city."

"We can't work at my mom's place. My stepdad works from home."

"We'll use my apartment then. You can sleep at your mom's. It'll be just like before except—"

"We'll be at your apartment instead of in your car." I work my neck from side to side, thinking of what will be there. A couch. A bed. Hours and hours of us alone.

"What do you suggest? Writing songs at Starbucks?"

"Fine. Let's take your car."

"Don't you need to go by your apartment for some things?" she asks. "And why can't we ever drive *your* car? Do you know how many miles I've put on mine in the last few months?"

Notebook in hand, I head for the door. "I keep clothes at my mom's, and we take your car because mine's a piece of shit." It's true, but that's not why I don't want her in it.

"Mine's not much better."

"Can we just go? We have a lot of work to do."

"Okay, but we're going halfsies on gas."

"I'll pay for the damn gas."

She jingles her keys. "You'll get no argument from me."

~ ~ ~

We ride in silence to the city. I stare out the window and she drives, glancing at me when she's not looking at the road.

"Giving me the silent treatment isn't helping," she says.

"What do you want me to say? We'll figure it out when we get there."

"Whatever," she says, turning up the radio.

I flip through my notebook, making no progress at all in the seventy minutes it takes to reach our destination.

A card from her visor gets us into a parking garage. None of the other cars are much nicer than hers. It's a bargain garage for sure. Half the security lights either don't work or flicker. I look in the corners to see if they have cameras. They do. We walk down three flights of stairs and pass the security booth. Bria knocks on the window, waking up the old man who's sleeping on the job. She waves, and he salutes her.

We cover eight or nine blocks in silence. "Could you have picked a garage any farther away? How much longer?"

She stops and her stare all but pins me to the wall. "You try living in New York City on what we've been making. I'm lucky to have a car and a place to park it. Most people don't."

"But you were the backup singer for White Poison. Surely you made enough to upgrade your parking accommodations."

She laughs. "Oh, I can't wait to see what you have to say about my apartment. I was only their backup singer for one tour. Three months. I couldn't exactly change my standard of living on that. Plus I have a lot of debt."

Across the street a kid runs out of a store, followed by a yelling man carrying a gun.

"Jesus, Bria."

"That's the city for you."

I expect her to be scared or upset, but she's not affected at all. Some kid not fifty feet away robbed a store, and she's acting like it's no big deal.

Our surroundings say it all. Broken windows line some abandoned storefronts. Homeless people lie in the alleys. I'm certain we've seen more than a few people making drug deals. "How can you live here?"

"Not everyone grows up with a silver spoon up their ass."

Like Bria, most people assume if you're from Stamford, you're wealthy. For the most part, it's true. I'm one of the exceptions.

We turn a corner.

"My place is over there." She points at a vape shop.

We approach a door adjacent to the shop, she unlocks it, and we go up a stairway into a hall with four apartments. There are more stairs leading to higher floors. Maybe I watch too much TV, but this looks like a damn crack house—water stains on the wall, peeling plaster, and what on earth is that smell? She lives *here*?

Bria sees my expression. "Before you say anything, I know it looks bad, but my brother had the building checked out. He's a firefighter in Brooklyn. It's far from being condemned."

I try not to cringe as we come to her door. "Well, I guess there's that."

Part of me wants to go inside, pack up her things, and take her back to Stamford. I may not live in the Taj Mahal, but my apartment is the goddamn Ritz compared to this shithole.

I come to the city often. So do the guys. We've been playing gigs here for years. Have I just ignored the fact that people live like this? Or maybe I've just never been to *this* part of the city.

"Your brother lets you live here?"

"I'm a big girl, Crew. He doesn't *let* me live here. I choose to. You shouldn't judge a book by its cover."

She opens her door and we enter her small apartment. I glance around and am surprised yet again because this place is not anything like the outside of the building or the hall.

"Wow." It takes only a few seconds to see the entire apartment. It's all one room, except for the bathroom. But what she's done with it—I *could* be at the Ritz or an ultra-urban version of it. I run my finger along the handcrafted shelves, which hold an impressive collection of vinyl. I spot one in particular and carefully extract the rare album cover. "Holy crap. How did you …?"

"I go to flea markets. Can you believe I got that one for a dollar? The lady selling it had no idea of its value."

I put it back where I found it. "Was the place like this before you moved in?" I ask, taking in the wall that looks like exposed brick. When I move closer, I can see it's been expertly painted. Her small open kitchen is sleek and modern, and there's not a hint of rust on anything. The furniture is sparse but tasteful, and the lighting is fabulous.

"Nope. I did this with a little help from Brett and his friends."

"Brett?" I ask, a gnawing in my gut.

"My brother. He and a few of his firefighter buddies helped me. And he has a rich friend who was redecorating, so I inherited some amazing furniture and light fixtures. Brett bought me the mini kitchen. You should have seen the place before."

"I can only imagine but"—I peer at the many locks on the door— "is it safe?"

"It's safe enough."

My insides twist.

"Listen," she says, seeing my concern, "I know all my neighbors. Well, except the guy who just moved in on the third floor. None of them are drug dealers. They're regular people like me, waiting for their break."

I go to one of the two large windows and then the other, testing the locks and making sure they're secure. I examine the fire escape, wondering how easy it would be for anyone to climb up from the street.

I glance into the alley and swear I see someone who looks like *him.*

"What's with you?" she asks, eyeing my balled-up fists. "You look like you want to kill someone."

I retreat from the window. "You really have no idea how vulnerable you are, do you?"

"You need to relax, Crew."

I open my mouth to speak, but she shuts me up by gripping my arm, twisting it behind my back, and pushing me up against her wall.

"What the hell, Bria?"

She releases me. "Just showing you I can take care of myself, that's all. Brett made me take some classes." She opens her small fridge and gets out two bottles of Bud Light. "Beer?"

I check the time on my phone. "It's barely noon."

"And you need to chill. How are we going to get any work done with you being all judgy?"

I take a beer and sit on the couch, then open my notebook to the last page. It's a song we were working on three weeks ago. One of hers. It's almost finished. It'll be the easiest one to complete. I'm not sure I have enough creativity flowing through my veins to do anything else. Not after seeing that man in the alley.

She twists off the top of her beer and sinks into the couch next to me. She leans close to see my notebook. I can smell her. My first instinct is to scoot away—protect myself. I gaze at the window again, then at her, knowing I'm not the one who needs protecting.

Chapter Seventeen

Bria

We didn't get much done yesterday, not with all of Crew's questions about my apartment and the neighborhood. Going out for a quick bite didn't help either. He criticized something on every street corner. I get that he's from Connecticut, but his high and mighty act is getting old. He needs to realize not everyone lives a charmed life.

I haven't told him about my family, outside of Brett. I don't need people feeling sorry for me. I want to tell him, though. I almost did yesterday to get him to quit with the third-degree about where I buy my groceries, what restaurants I go to, are the streets well-lit at night, and do I carry mace in my purse.

I've been on my own for a while now. I grew up in a house with a father, but he wasn't really there. He may as well have died along with my mom. He wasn't the one who raised me. Brett was. The minute I graduated from high school, Harry Cash hightailed it out of New York. The day of my graduation, he handed me a card with a few thousand bucks in it and told me he'd sold the apartment, and I had until the end of June to move in with Brett or find my own place.

If Crew had seen where I wanted to live that first summer, he'd have had a coronary. Even Brett put the kibosh on that one. I lived with Brett for a few months, but I couldn't stand Amanda, his wife at the time, so I moved into the dorm. Until I quit school, that is.

My phone rings. It's Crew.

"I'm downstairs," he says before I can say hello. "Can you buzz me up?"

"Be right there."

I run downstairs and let him in. He appraises the door and the walls surrounding it. "There's no way for you to open this from your apartment?"

I snatch the Dunkin' Donuts bag from him. "You must be confusing this with Park Avenue."

He follows me up the stairs. "You shouldn't leave your door open."

"It was only for a minute so I could let you in."

"A lot of things can happen in a minute." He looks disgusted as he hands me my coffee. "You should keep your door locked at all times. Promise me you will."

I stop blowing on the coffee. "What's with the big brother act?"

He blindly reaches into the bag I'm holding, extracts a donut, and rips through it with his teeth. "I'm not your goddamn brother," he says around a mouthful of food.

"I see your mood has improved since yesterday," I jest.

I'm perusing the donuts when he recites some of my lyrics. "'People tell me all about you. Your picture hangs up on my wall. I was forced to grow without you—'"

I race over and close the notebook I left open on the coffee table. I give him a hard stare, and he knows he crossed the line. We don't look at each other's notebooks without an invitation.

"You're the one who left it open," he says. "That makes it fair game." He stands and thoughtfully checks out my apartment, his attention landing on a picture of my mother hanging on the wall next to my bed. "Is that your mom?"

It's the picture I gaze at each day and wonder how things might have turned out if she'd lived. "She died on 9/11."

"Shit, I'm sorry."

I shrug. "I was three. I don't really remember her. Sometimes I think I do, but they are probably just memories I've created based on what Brett's told me. He was eleven."

"Was she a first responder?"

"She was a nurse. Worked at a nearby hospital. They ran over to help."

He leans down and runs a finger across the top of my notebook. "I'll bet you have a lot of songs in here about her. Dozens maybe."

He says that almost like he knows what it's like to lose someone.

He shoves another donut in his mouth. "We'd better get started."

We sit and stare at our notebooks for long drawn-out seconds. Then we laugh.

"Any ideas?" I ask.

"Remember the one we were tossing around last month about that car on fire at the side of the road?"

"I don't know. I kind of thought it sounded too much like 'Man on Fire'."

He nods. "You're right. We have to come up with something more original. Something we can shove up their asses."

He's still mad at the guys for kicking us out. I am too, but I understand why they did it. We were acting like adolescents.

His phone chirps with a text. "Liam just told me to open my email. Says it's something for both of us." He taps on the screen. "He sent me an MP3 file."

He plays it. It's a guitar riff. Not much, twenty seconds or so, but it's good. Crew plays it two more times.

"He wants us to succeed, you know," I tell him.

"I know."

Liam writes the majority of the melodies for our songs. Sometimes he'll come up with one and Crew will put words to it. Other times, Crew will give him lyrics, and Liam will write a melody to fit them. It's a symbiotic relationship my presence has thrown a wrench into.

I've often wondered if either of them regrets bringing me on. If maybe they're intimidated by me. I write lyrics and melodies. I never intended to threaten their jobs. Because of that, I hold back and let them take the lead. But I think I have to put both hats back on and see what happens.

"Can you play it again?" I ask.

I listen with my eyes closed, hearing the timing of where the lyrics should go. I then flip through my notebook to see if I have anything that will fit. Crew does the same.

After a while, he says, "I might have something. It's not a lot, but with some work ..."

"Can I see?"

He hesitantly hands me the notebook. These lyrics, located at the back, are relatively recent.

He looks over my shoulder as I read them silently.

On that stage is where I find you
Each and every night
On that stage is where I find you
Dancing left and dancing right

"Play it again," I ask.

I listen to the riff while singing in my head. I turn to Crew. "It's missing something. The verses should be separate, and we need to add a third line."

He ponders my suggestion. "That could work."

I motion to his phone. "Play it on a loop."

I close my eyes and listen. Then I scribble down some possibilities. When I look at Crew, I see he's doing the same.

Sometimes it feels uncomfortable, writing lyrics that are obviously about each other, but ask anyone in any band, and that's the nature of the beast. We write about what's important to us. What affects us. What has destroyed us.

"I think the first verse should be mine," I say, leaning forward to stop the music. "How about this?"

I take a deep breath and sing, "On that stage is where I find you. Each and every night. Doesn't matter if you're here or far away from me."

"Again," Crew says. On his notepad, he does more scribbling as I sing.

"You got something?"

"How about this for my verse?"

I look at what he wrote:

On that stage is how I see you
Dancing left and dancing right
Looking just as though it's where you're always meant
to be

"Perfect," I say. "Now the chorus."

I look at the words he'd written for the chorus.

On that stage, on that stage, I see you on that stage
I'll always see you like you were that daaaaaaaay
That day I saw you up on that staaaaaaage

I walk over to my keyboard and mess around until I find a melody that goes with the riff. I tweak it, changing the key until I find the best one.

"That's it," Crew says, jumping off the couch. "Let's try it."

We sing the chorus together, doing it a few different ways, both of us making notes. I don't fail to notice that he keeps his back to me as we sing.

He turns and smiles. "It's good."

I go to the couch and play Liam's riff again. "We need a third verse."

We both listen and think.

The riff loops again and he sings, "On that stage is where you slay me. Even when I pick a fight."

Without missing a beat, I add, "Never saying what it really is you want from me."

"Yes," he says, writing down my lyric. "From the top, the whole thing. Acapella."

We sit on the couch, each of us staring at the wall as we sing our new song.

"Again," he says.

This time, as the song unfolds, we look at each other as we sing. And somehow, the song gets better. It gets better even though there's no music. It gets better because we bring more emotion to it. More passion.

At the end, we naturally sing the chorus twice. Then we stop, the apartment dead silent except for the sound of our excited breaths.

His eyes flare with heat and the edges of his mouth turn up in a sexy, roguish grin. We reach for each other simultaneously and our mouths collide. His full, firm lips brush back and forth against mine. Without hesitation, our tongues mingle. He lays me back on the couch, kissing me even harder. He tastes like chocolate and me—cherry. The flavors mix together almost as well as our bodies do.

I can already feel his erection as he presses into me. Every hormone in my body zings to life. I pull him more tightly against me.

He moans into my mouth when I suck on his tongue. His hand works up and under my shirt, and my breasts grow heavy, weighted with need. He grips one, then the other. My bra gets pushed up. He cups my bare skin, then his thumbs lightly graze my rigid nipples.

"Oh, God," I mumble incoherently.

He sits up, straddling me, and removes his shirt. I see his tattoo up close for the first time, but before I can explore, he's ripping off my shirt and bra. Then his lips are on me again. They're all over me: my neck, my collarbone, my breasts. He spends a lot of time on my breasts. I weave my fingers through his hair, begging him silently to go lower. I want to feel his mouth on every part of me.

He slips a finger under the waistband of my jeans, teasing my skin before he unzips my pants. His lips blaze a trail down my abdomen, finally joining his hands as they work to shimmy my pants over my hips.

He abruptly stops kissing me and jerks away.

I look down, thinking maybe he's removing his pants. But he's staring at my stomach. At the scar from having my appendix out. He doesn't look like he wants to sleep with me anymore. He looks like he's going to be sick.

He hops off the couch, picks up his shirt off the floor, and throws it on inside out. "I have to go." He retrieves his phone and notebook and bolts to the door, glancing back at me like he wants to say something more, but he doesn't.

I stare at the door after he leaves. What just happened?

I get dressed and read the last lyric I wrote, thinking how nothing has ever been truer.

Never saying what it really is you want from me.

Chapter Eighteen

Crew

Hours later, after doing a lot of soul-searching, I end up at Mom's. I knock, the door opens, and she's there. "Oh, sweetie, what's wrong?"

I step inside. "Is Gary here?"

"He's at a meeting. He'll be home soon." She runs a soothing hand down my arm. "You okay?"

I nod. It's not very convincing.

"I'll put on a pot of coffee."

While she's in the kitchen, I browse the pictures on the wall. Pictures of me, of the two of us together, of her and Gary's wedding. Even one of Abby and me.

"A man who stares at a wall must have a lot on his mind," she says, coming up behind me. She hands me a cup. "Or maybe nothing."

We go to the kitchen table and sit. I sip coffee, stalling.

She cocks her head thoughtfully. "Does this have something to do with Bria?"

"What makes you say that?"

"Oh, I don't know. Maybe because a month ago, when you'd sleep here a few times a week, I noticed some changes."

"Changes?"

"You were … happy." She smiles. "After all this time, it's not something I expected. I'd hoped, prayed even, then it started to happen. I didn't say anything because I didn't want to jinx it. But a few weeks ago, around the time you told me about your record contract, you stopped coming to the city, and when we spoke on the phone, you seemed sad."

"I'm not sad, Mom."

"Okay. Confused then."

I run a hand through my hair.

"We've always been able to talk, Chris. You know you can tell me anything."

"I ran out on her." I sink into my chair like the weasel I am. "I saw the scar, and it just reminded me of … Well, I saw it and freaked."

"Scar?"

"Bria had her appendix out."

She tries not to smile, but I see it anyway. She knows full well what we must have been doing for me to see a scar like that. "Is that so?" She sips her coffee, eyebrows raised.

"What's wrong with me?"

"Can I ask you a question? Have you been with anyone else since Abby?"

I eye her like she's crazy. I am in my mid-twenties. "Mom, it's been seven years."

"So the answer is yes. Surely other girls you've been with have had scars, Chris."

"I don't know. Maybe. But I didn't notice."

Her eyebrows shoot up again. "But you noticed with Bria. That must mean she's important to you." She laughs and gives me a hug. "My boy, it's time you let yourself be happy."

"It's complicated, Mom. There's more to it."

"More to it than letting go of the past?"

"I have the band to think about." I tell her about the addendum Jeremy made us sign.

She smiles. "So it's even more serious than I thought."

"Nothing is serious."

"So you haven't written any songs about her?"

I glance at the notebook. "I write songs about everything."

"Everything important to you."

I sigh and gaze out the window.

"She'd want this," Mom says. "Abby. She'd want this for you. She loved you, Chris. If the tables were turned, would you want her to live her life drowning in the past?"

I shake my head.

"You know what you need to do?" she says. "Do what you do best. Write a song about it."

I pound a fist on my notebook. "I've written several. This morning at Bria's place, we wrote one about when we sing together."

"That's not what I meant. You need to write a song for Abby. You need to let her go."

I close my eyes. "I've tried a hundred times."

"So maybe the hundred and first time will be the one."

I hear the door open and Gary appears. "Hey there, Chris. Nice to see you coming around again."

"Hi, Gary."

I like my stepdad, maybe even more than I like my biological dad. I'm not sure if Dad got used to seeing me less and less, and out of sight was out of mind, but Gary has always made me feel like I'm one of his kids. He has three with his ex-wife. He's a cool dude.

"When are we going to hear a Reckless Alibi song on the radio?" he asks.

"Soon, I hope. We're meeting with our rep next week."

"Looking forward to it. Stay for dinner?"

I shake my head. "No. I have an apology to make."

Mom stands and kisses me on the cheek. "Now that's the boy I raised."

I pick up my notebook and go to the door. "See you guys later."

On the subway ride back to Bria's, I see a mother with her toddler. She's trying to entertain her son by playing peek-a-boo. "I see you," she says. Then she covers and uncovers her ears. "I hear you."

Inspiration strikes, and I open the notebook and scribble a few words.

Can you see me, can you hear me
From wherever you are now

The toddler giggles and my attention is drawn back to them. I watch closely, getting lost in their game. Before I know it, I'm at Bria's stop.

I stand in front of her building, wondering what I should say to her. It starts to come to me in a song, but I shake it off. This is one time I have to man up and not hide behind my lyrics.

I call her from the street. "Hey, it's me. Can I come up?"

There's a long pause. I've taken her by surprise. "Okay. Be right there."

It takes her much longer to come down than it took this morning. Clearly, she's not in any hurry to see me. God, I'm such a dick.

The door opens. "Hey," she says.

"Hey."

She goes up the stairs and I follow. She left her apartment door open again. "Did we not talk about this six hours ago?" I'm reading her the riot act as we go inside. There's a man on her couch—a big fucking guy—and I shut up mid-sentence.

My spine stiffens and my gut twists. Then I realize she wouldn't have invited me up if she was getting it on with someone else. There's an FDNY emblem on the breast pocket of his T-shirt.

He stands and offers me his hand. "Brett Cash. It's nice to know there's someone else looking out for my sister."

"I, uh, … Chris Rewey. Call me Crew. Nice to meet you." I shake his hand. "I shouldn't have yelled at her."

He laughs. "You have my permission as the overbearing older brother to yell at her anytime her safety is involved."

I don't miss Bria's eye roll.

"I didn't mean to interrupt. I can come back another time."

"No need," he says. "I was just leaving." He goes to the door. "I'm a big fan of your music, by the way, and not just because you hired Bria. It's good. I think you really have something."

"Thanks. That means a lot."

He hugs Bria. "We all should go to dinner sometime."

I lift my chin at him as he closes the door. "I'm really sorry. I didn't mean to run him off."

"He was on his way out anyway."

"Yeah, I can see that by the way he was relaxing on your couch."

133

She doesn't laugh. "Why are you here, Crew? I'm not sure I'm up for working on another song today. Can't we pick it up tomorrow?"

"I came to apologize."

She stares at me, waiting.

"I shouldn't have run out like that." I motion between us. "This scares me for reasons I can't talk about. But I like you, and I shouldn't have left with zero explanation. The thing is, though, I can't tell you for sure it won't happen again. I'm … I'm kind of a fucked-up mess, in case you haven't figured it out by now. I'm not sure if that was a real apology or not. I suck at this. I'm sorry, that's all."

Finally, a smile appears. Damn, I love her smile. I could write a song about it.

"You don't suck at this," she says. "And I'm kind of a fucked-up mess myself."

"Not like I am." I glance at the picture of her mom on the wall. "Sorry. I shouldn't presume to know how you feel." I laugh. "I'm apologizing a lot today. Can I buy you a pizza and we'll call it even? No strings, no expectations. Just two co-workers going to dinner."

"Co-workers?" She looks at the couch. "You had your hands on my boobs, Crew. I think we've moved past co-workers."

"Yeah." I chuckle. "I think we moved past that a long time ago."

She palms her keys. "Let's get that pizza and let this sink in for a while. We'll concentrate on the music. Get the last few songs written. The rest—whatever it is—can wait."

Hearing that, it's like a weight has been lifted. I grin when she picks up her notebook on the way out. We're a lot alike. I think about someone else who was a lot like me. But before guilt consumes me, I recall what Mom said. Abby would want me to be happy. I know she would.

I wonder what Bria would think of some of my earlier music. The songs I sang when I was in Naked Whale. Would I be betraying Abby if I showed some of the stuff to Bria?

I'm not sure I could do it. It's too private. We're nowhere near there yet.

"There's a great place down the block," Bria says. "Their pizza is to die for. Garlic crust, loaded with veggies. Sooooo good."

I look up and down the dilapidated street. "You sure you don't want to go somewhere else?"

She gives me a biting glance. "You mean someplace nicer."

"I was thinking someplace safer."

"You think stores don't get robbed on the Upper West Side?"

"I'm sure they do, but not when I'm walking by them."

"You really don't get out much, do you?"

"I get out," I say defensively.

"Crew, this is my neighborhood. That's not changing anytime soon unless I win the lottery or RA hits the top of the charts."

I let out a big sigh as we pass a few thug teens on the street, looking at Bria like she's a piece of filet mignon. "I don't have to like it."

"You don't, but I do, and that's enough."

We reach the establishment, which is not as bad as I imagined. I hold the door open for her. The proprietor greets her like they're old friends.

"Hey, Tony," she says. "I'll have the usual." She turns to me. "It's fully loaded, you okay with that?"

"Sure, and a Budweiser."

"Bud Light for me, please."

"You kids take a seat. I'll bring it to you."

Bria leads us to a table in back. "I wrote a song about my brother."

"I think they call that incest," I joke.

She play-hits me on the arm. "Shut up. Do you want to see it? I've never sung it in public."

"Definitely. I'd love to see *anything* you've written."

She smiles. "Yeah—same." She opens her notebook and leafs through the pages. It's an early one. The title of it is 'Big Blue Door.' "I wrote this when I was fifteen, so don't be too critical. It's got a pop/country beat." She hums the tune to put it in my head.

I read the lyrics.

If you run in will you come out
It's the thought I think about
Every time you walk out that big blue door
That big blue door

(chorus)
That big blue door is where we live
Where we fight, where we forgive
That big blue door is where I go,
the only place that I call home
Will you come through I wonder each day,
or like her will you go away

I read the rest of it, captivated by her words. "Wow, that's powerful. Has he seen it?"

"He's the only one who has until now."

My eyes snap to hers. "Seriously?"

She crosses her chest. "True."

"I'm honored."

Tony comes over with our beers and a basket of bread. "Writing songs again, eh? I can't wait to tell everyone I served you pizza when you become famous. Hey, maybe you could give me a shout-out to drum up business."

"Sure," Bria says.

He saunters away, whistling.

Bria takes a drink. "I showed you mine, now you show me yours."

I mentally go through a dozen songs in my head, not coming up with a single one I want her to see. I pull my notebook protectively into my lap. "I thought we weren't going to talk about work tonight."

Her face falls. "Okay, but I'm not sure we've ever talked about anything else. How about you tell me about high school? Everyone has good stories about that time in their life."

Shit, that topic's not any better.

"No?" she says at my hesitation. "All right, I'll go. But one of these days you'll open up to me, Christopher Rewey."

My heart stops beating, and I'm sure my face goes ashen. *She called me Christopher.*

"What is it?" she asks. "Your beer not sitting well?"

I take a few long swallows. "It's fine. Tell me some stories."

She talks about her best friend, Hannah, who moved away senior year, leaving her high and dry. About singing in the choir. About the awkward way she lost her virginity. About letting go of the disdain she had for her father.

Letting go.

As she tells me more about her dad, I hear lyrics in my head.

'Cause letting go is a fatal blow

I pull out my notebook. "I have to jot something down. Sorry."

"Don't be sorry. It drives my friends crazy when I do that, but I totally get it. She scoots closer. "Can I see?"

I close the book. "It's not our stuff, it's…" I have no idea how to explain it without giving it away.

Her lips form a thin line and then she sighs. "A fucked-up mess?"

I nod as our pizza is put on the table.

Chapter Nineteen

Bria

It seems strange to leave the city with Crew after being banished to my apartment for a week to finish our songwriting. We did, though. We finished everything, and now we have thirteen songs for the new album. The guys should be happy, and we can get back to rehearsing again. Right after we meet our new IRL rep, Veronica Collins.

"You ready for this?" Crew asks.

"Why wouldn't I be?"

"I've heard record label reps can be intimidating."

"More intimidating than Jeremy? I doubt it. Plus, with a name like Veronica, she's probably old. Who names their kid Veronica?" I pull up to the barn near a sleek red Porsche parked next to Jeremy's SUV.

Crew turns to me. "Old, huh?" He opens the door for me.

He's been very nice to me this past week. Opening doors, pulling out chairs, paying for meals. But one thing he hasn't done is kiss me again. It's my own fault for telling him we should concentrate on the album and let everything else wait.

"Welcome!" someone chirps in a high-pitched and somehow totally condescending voice.

The voice belongs to a woman with stick-straight black hair that falls to the middle of her back. Her designer blouse reveals a hint of cleavage, her tight pencil skirt matches the color of her hair, and she's got legs up to there.

Crew and I share a look. Definitely not old. I'd be surprised if she was thirty.

"You must be Brianna," she says, quickly giving me the once-over. "And you" —she eyes Crew up and down— "your pictures don't do you justice." She picks up his hands, holds out his arms, and shamelessly ogles his body. "This I can work with."

"Please call me Bria. It's nice to meet you, Veronica."

"Ronni," she says to me before her eyes go back to devouring Crew. "Jeremy has told me all about you. I'm eager to get started. Come."

She leads us over to the common seating area and pulls Crew down on the couch next to her, forcing the rest of us to take the chairs. I don't miss Liam's eyes on me. Apparently, I'm not the only one weirded out by Little Miss Red-Porsche's behavior.

Jeremy is perched on a barstool. He nods hello and gives Ronni the floor.

"A few things," she says. "First we're going to need one more song for the album."

"We have thirteen," Garrett says.

"Uh, ahyaaaah," she says melodramatically. "Why do you think we need one more? It's bad luck to put thirteen songs on an album."

"Bad luck?" I say incredulously. "That's ridiculous."

"Yes, Brianna. Bad luck."

"It's *Bria*."

"What's that?" she asks, seemingly uninterested in anything but Crew's bulging arms.

"Everyone calls me Bria."

She sniffs in disapproval. "Not anymore. Bria is too cutesy. From now on you'll be Brianna Cash. It's a strong name. A recognizable one."

I point at Crew. "What about him? He's got a nickname."

"Crew," she says, musing aloud. "Also strong and recognizable. It's fine."

I snort. "Of course it is."

"He'll be billed as Chris Rewey on the album," she says. "But he'll be referred to as Crew for all other intents and purposes." Her sculpted lips curl into a cruel smile. "How long will it take you to write another song, Brianna?"

"I don't know, *Veronica*. A day? A week? It's not like we can just pull one out of a hat."

"It's *Ronni*," she says, in that whiny irritating voice of hers.

I give her a hard stare. "It's *Bria*."

Jeremy joins us from the bar. "More songs mean more money, guys."

Ronni finally stops giving me the look of death and addresses all of us. "Remember, I call the shots, or did you forget what you signed? Listen, boys …" She glances at me in disgust. "Listen, *people*, I'm going to get you on the radio. I'm talking serious airtime, not just the three AM lonely-hearts hour. IRL may be a small indie label, but this isn't our first rodeo. You saw my car, right? You have to trust that I know what's best for you. You do that, and one day you could all be driving cars like that."

Three years. We have to put up with this self-righteous bitch for three years?

"First things first," she says. "We need to upgrade your rehearsal space. This place is unacceptable. And it smells."

"What? No." Crew stands and moves around behind our chairs in a show of solidarity. "That will cost money. Money we don't have yet. This place is free and available to us twenty-four-seven. And believe it or not, the acoustics are great."

She pats the seat next to her, as if calling her dog. Crew glances at me and then sits back down.

"Okay, I'll give you that one. But I'll expect you to remember how accommodating I've been."

"Is that all?" I ask.

It seems to pain her to look away from Crew and at me. "Of course that's not all. Do you think I'd drive all the way out here for a five-minute conversation?" She narrows her eyes. "You'll have to cut your hair. It's too long."

I touch it protectively. "I'm not cutting my hair. There was nothing about that in the contract."

"We'll see about that," she says. "You should also get some highlights." She touches Crew's jaw. "This I like. The five-o'clock stubble is sexy. Keep it."

She goes through the rest of her demands, which are more along the lines of what I expected. An hour later, she shakes hands with all the men, her highly-manicured paws lingering on Crew longer than they should for a friendly handshake.

I put my hand out. She shakes it as if I have cooties.

"We have a lot of work to do, boys … I mean, *people*. We'll meet again at the studio. If you need anything, call." She hands her business card directly to Crew. "I mean it. Anything."

"Bye, boys," she says on her way to the door. With her back turned, she raises a dismissive hand. "Bye, Brianna."

"Veronica," I say dryly.

She pauses but doesn't turn around. I get the idea this is going to be how it is with us.

Liam closes the barn door behind her. "Well, that was interesting."

"She can be a lot to take," Jeremy says. "But IRL is our best shot right now." He tucks her notes into his binder. "I'll see you Friday night. Oh, and I hired someone to set up for you. Beginning next month you'll no longer be hauling your own equipment from the van. He'll also be your driver."

"How much is that going to cost us?" Crew says. He glances at me like he's thinking how hiring extra labor means more out of my pocket that's already empty.

"Let me worry about the budget," he says. "We want to present a certain image, and you setting up your own equipment reeks of mediocrity. You have to spend money to make money."

"When is the making money part supposed to happen?" Brad asks.

"These things take time," Jeremy says. "You need to trust me. More importantly, you need to trust Ronni." He opens the door to leave, and I see the dust cloud trailing behind Ronni's car.

"Dude," Brad says to Crew after Jeremy is gone. "That woman wants in your pants."

Crew shrugs like he couldn't care less.

Brad backtracks. "Sorry, Bria. No disrespect."

"How are things between the two of you?" Liam asks.

"We're good," Crew says. He goes to the stage, turning when nobody follows. "Oh, come on. You saw the material, right? You have to admit it's amazing."

Garrett twirls a drumstick. "It's great, but we need one more."

"Seriously? We did our job. Ronni sprung the fourteenth song on us. We should at least rehearse while we're here."

"Time better spent on the last song," Liam says. "Besides, I've got work to do. I've got to write all the music for the ones you gave us yesterday."

"You're kicking us out again?" I ask.

"You know it's not that," he says, ushering us to the door. "We need this, Bria. We're so close to greatness. Can't you taste it?"

Crew whips out his notebook. "Sweet, I like it." He scribbles down some words, mumbling, "We're so close to greatness, we can taste it."

Liam laughs. "See? You're inspired already. Now go and do what you do."

Crew steps through the door, still jotting notes.

"Bria, hold up a sec," Liam asks, holding me back. "Are you guys really okay?"

"I'm not sure what we are, Liam. But we're good."

"If you ever need to talk."

I glance at Crew, standing next to my car. "You've known him a long time, haven't you?"

"Since we were kids."

"He says he's fucked up."

"I know."

"Do you know why?"

Liam shuffles his feet. "Yeah."

I lean against the wall. "But you're not going to tell me."

"Sorry. Bro code and all."

"Was it bad?"

"Bria," he warns.

"I like him. And I guess I'm asking if he's—"

"Worth it?"

"I was going to say damaged. But yeah, that too."

"I think he's both. He's damaged *and* worth it. If you're asking for my advice, I'd say give him time. He'll come around."

"He won't let me look in his notebook. I've shared some of my stuff with him, but he's guarded about his."

"You know better than anyone that songwriters bleed in their songs. There's a lot of fucking blood on his pages, Bria."

"That's what I thought. Thanks, Liam."

"There she is," a large man says approaching the barn.

"Great," Liam says, obviously less than pleased to see the man.

"Bria Cash, I presume," he says, holding out a hand. "I've been wanting to meet you. Jeremy says you're a real spitfire."

Crew comes over and stands next to me. "This is Dirk, Liam's uncle."

"Oh. Nice to meet you, Mr—"

"Just Dirk. How are things going? I trust these boys are treating you right."

Crew inches closer.

"Things are great," I say. "I'm having the most fun."

"Good." He looks at my car. "Is this your ride?" He hands me his card. "Come by and see me, and we'll see what we can do about getting you an upgrade. Unless you're like our boy, Chris, and insist on driving an old piece of shit."

"Her car runs fine, Dirk," Liam says.

How would he know? He's never been inside it. Why is he being so short with his uncle?

"Okay, then. But the offer stands. Liam, I know your aunt would love it if you brought your friends to dinner once in a while."

"Sure thing," he snarls.

"I'm sure your mom would like it, too."

I think I see Liam cringe.

"Bye, Dirk," he says and retreats into the barn.

Crew and I get in the car. "What's with Liam? Seems as if he doesn't like his uncle much."

"He hates him."

"But Dirk has pretty much funded the band."

"You mean he's controlled it. Kind of like he's controlled Liam."

"Controlled him? What does that mean?"

"Nothing."

Crew scribbles in his notebook, ending our conversation.

I'm beginning to think there are a lot of secrets in this band.

Chapter Twenty

Crew

Seven years ago

The baby squirms beneath my hand.

"She likes it when you sing to her," Abby says.

"I know *he* does."

Abby thinks it's a girl, while I'm convinced it's a boy. We didn't find out. We want to be surprised. The truth is I'd be happy with a daughter, especially if she gets all of Abby's good qualities. Like her beautiful eyes, her sense of style, and her voice. I pray the baby inherits her amazing voice.

I sink back into the couch, and she lies on her back and puts her head in my lap. I continue to run my hand across her protruding belly.

She puts her hand on top of mine. "One more week 'till I'm eighteen."

"I know it's been hard for you. Even more so lately."

She laces our fingers together. "Sometimes I can't believe we made it this long without anyone finding out. I have to stop myself from touching my stomach when she kicks. Do you know how hard that is? Don't even get me started on the clothes. I haven't been able to button my jeans for over two months. Even my yoga pants are getting too tight. It will be a relief when we don't have to hide it anymore."

I trace the outline of her jaw with my finger. "What do you think your parents will say?"

"It doesn't matter. We have our plan, and there is nothing they can do about it after next Thursday."

"Do you know how much I love you?"

Her eyes get misty. "If it's half as much as I love you, I'm a lucky girl."

"Then you're the luckiest girl in the world." I lean down to kiss her forehead. Then I muse aloud, "Lucky Rewey. Hmm."

She giggles. "We are not naming the baby Lucky."

"Well, nothing goes well with Rewey, so we're pretty much screwed."

"Abigail does," she says.

"Abigail Rewey." I smile big. "Damn, that *does* sound good."

"How about Kate?"

"Kate?" I shake my head. "Our baby is going to have rock stars for parents. We need to be more creative than that. I was thinking more along the lines of Slash."

"We're not naming our son Slash."

"Who says Slash can't be a girl's name too? But I'm glad you finally agree it's a boy."

"I'm doing no such thing." She rubs her belly. "It's a girl. A mother knows."

A lump forms in my throat. "Shit, Abbs. You're going to be a mother. I mean, I know that, but sometimes reality just creeps up on me. I'm gonna be a dad."

"You're gonna be the best dad."

We gaze at each other. We do that a lot. That's the reason I know we're meant to be together—we never get tired of looking at each other. Even when we don't talk, it's never awkward or uncomfortable.

The front door opens and Mom comes in. Abby doesn't bother lifting her head off my lap. Mom knows all about us. We had to tell her. We can't afford a place of our own while we're in high school. She didn't even wait for me to ask; she invited Abby to move in as soon as we told her she was pregnant. She's well aware of how strict Abby's parents are. For the past several months, we've been planning—all three of us. I think Mom is even a little excited about having a grandchild.

She hands Abby a bag. "I couldn't resist."

Abby sits up and removes a tiny yellow outfit that reads *My Parents Rock*.

Abby and I laugh. It's the first baby thing we've gotten. Somehow it makes this more real than before.

"It's perfect," Abby says, getting off the couch to hug my mom. "She'll wear it home from the hospital."

"You mean *he* will," I say.

Mom snickers. "It'll work either way because it's yellow."

"Thank you so much, Mrs. Rewey. For everything. I don't know how I can ever repay you."

"I think we're past 'Mrs. Rewey,' Abby. You're moving in next week, and you're having my grandchild. You should call me Shelly."

Abby smiles. "Okay ... Shelly. Wow, that feels strange. I'll have to get used to that."

"We'll all have to get used to a lot of things," Mom says. "Speaking of which, do you guys want to go shopping with me tomorrow for a new bed?"

"A new bed?" I ask.

"Surely you don't expect Abby to sleep in your full-sized one. You both may fit now, but in a few months, she's going to need more space."

I cock my head to the side. "You're going to let her sleep in my room? We thought she'd be in the guest room."

"It sounds strange to think it and even stranger when you say it out loud, but it's not like you'll get her *more* pregnant, Chris. What's done is done. Plus you'll be married soon. Why postpone the inevitable? And the guest room is more suited for a nursery, don't you think?"

"Why can't my parents be more like you, Mrs., er, Shelly."

"They'll come around," Mom says. "Wait until they see their grandbaby."

"I think you give them too much credit," Abby says. "I'm fully prepared for them to cut me out of their lives."

"Nonsense. I can see how much they love you. That won't change because you've done something they don't approve of. Don't get me wrong, it's not that I approve either, but you know what they say about lemons and lemonade." She touches Abby's stomach. "This baby is all kinds of lemonade."

"My dad will say I'm an embarrassment."

"Perhaps, but he'll get over it."

"He'll try to make me give the baby up for adoption."

"That's not really his choice, is it?"

"He won't be happy about me moving in here."

"You'll be eighteen, honey. It's your decision, not his. And you never know. They might surprise you. Maybe they'll want you and the baby to stay there."

I tug Abby closer to me. "No way. She's moving here, and we're getting married."

"Even if they say Abby and the baby can live with them?"

I turn and look directly into Abby's eyes. "Even then. I'm not marrying you to give you a place to live. I'm not even sure I'm marrying you because of the baby. I'm marrying you because that's how things are meant to be. You and I were going to end up together no matter what."

Mom tears up. "I raised a hell of a son," she says.

"Thanks, Mom."

"What do you two have planned for today?" Her smile wanes, and she looks at me guiltily. "I almost forgot. You're playing at the fair tonight."

"You're coming, right?"

"I wouldn't miss it for the world. I'm only sad nobody will get to hear Abby sing."

I smile. "This will be the last concert where she doesn't. After next week, she'll officially be a singer for Naked Whale."

Abby giggles and sits back down awkwardly. "Kind of apropos, considering I'll be as big as one soon."

"Are you going to watch them play?" Mom asks her. "Do you want to go with me?"

"I wouldn't miss it, but I work until seven. I'll take a change of clothes with me and go when I get off. I'm sure I'll see you there, Shelly."

Mom is pleased at Abby's use of her first name. "I'll be right where I always am, in the front row."

I call after her as she leaves the room, "My mom. Naked Whale's biggest fan."

She calls back, "Chris Rewey's biggest fan."

"Your mom is so nice," Abby says.

"Yeah. I kind of hit the jackpot where moms are concerned." I look at the time. "I wish you didn't have to go to work."

"Me too, but we're going to need the money."

"Has that asshole bothered you anymore?"

"Rob? Not since you told him to fuck off last week."

Mom pokes her head out of the kitchen. "Don't curse around the baby."

"Sorry, Shelly!" Abby says.

I breathe a sigh of relief. "He hasn't come to the drive-thru?"

"Nope. Someone said he got a job at a gas station on the other side of town."

"Good. I'm glad I was there when he came in and harassed you. Dude creeps me out. He's way too old to be talking to teenage girls."

"Tell me about it."

I touch a lock of her hair. "Old guy or not, I don't want *anyone* looking at my girl that way."

"Babe, you have nothing to worry about. It's like the song we wrote. Do I need to sing it to you again?"

"You know I want you to, but you'll be late for work." We get off the couch. "I wish you could be up onstage with me tonight."

"I will be soon. Do you think people will care that a pregnant girl is singing in a rock band?"

"I think they won't even notice your baby bump once you start singing."

She stretches up to kiss me. "You're *my* biggest fan."

"Hell yes, I am."

I escort her to her car and give her one last kiss through the open window. "I'll see you and Slash tonight?"

I can hear her laughter as she backs out of the driveway. *Damn, I love her.*

Chapter Twenty-one

Bria

I run downstairs to let Crew in. He hands me a coffee, knowing exactly how I like it, and we walk up to my apartment. When I unlock the door, he smiles.

"Ready to get to it?" he asks.

"I hope so."

Yesterday afternoon was a disaster. Neither of us had anything worth working with. There are some lyrics I didn't show him that might have sufficed, but I'm not willing to put myself out there like that.

"What's today?" he asks. "Wednesday? Let's try to get this done by tomorrow night, so we can rehearse Friday before our gig."

"It is Wednesday." I check the calendar. "In fact, today is exactly four months after we met."

"How can you remember that?"

"It was after my sound check. We went to the diner, remember?"

"Yeah, but how did you know it was a Wednesday?"

"I remember everything about the tour. Every concert, every city. Everything."

Crew's jaw tightens. "I bet you do."

I giggle. He's jealous. "You're not thinking about Adam Stuart, are you?"

"He's been in your bed, Bria. The lead singer of one of the most successful bands of our time has been in your bed. It's kind of hard to ignore that."

It's impossible not to smile. If he's thinking about Adam in my bed, then he's thinking about *us* there, too.

"Technically, he's never been in my bed."

"You know what I mean," he huffs.

"Are you worried you won't measure up?" I joke.

His eyes snap to mine. "Are we talking in bed or onstage?"

"Both, I guess."

He rubs his jaw. "Come on, Miss We-Met-on-a-Wednesday, let's get to work."

I stare at him. Then the calendar.

"What is it?"

"Give me a minute." I reach for my notebook. I scribble, mark words out, and scribble some more. "What do you think about this?"

He reads over my shoulder.

It was a Wednesday when I met you
We got some food and dined
I was with him, the future grim
Was getting time to sink or swim

"That might work." He nods his head over and over as he writes. "Yeah, this could work."

"What is it?" I ask, excited. "Show me."

He angles the page so I can see it.

It was a Tuesday when I saw you
Moments burned into my mind
I couldn't stay, I ran away
The image of you still remained

"Crew, that's great! That verse will be first. We can use all the days. Thursday is next. What should Thursday be? Found you? Kissed you? Loved you? Left you? If we have four verses, it makes sense to use love and then left."

He nods. "Right."

I hum a tune that I think will work, then I sing a lyric. "It was a Thursday when I loved you."

Crew cuts in and sings, "Even though I'm not inclined."

"Perfect," I say. "What's next?"

We gaze at each other, waiting for the words.

"Crap," I say. "It'll come to us."

"No, wait." He flips to the previous page, then back, making some notes. "How about this?"

I read the verse.

"It was a Thursday when I loved you, even though I'm not inclined, so close to greatness, we can taste it, let's embrace it, never waste it."

"You're a genius," I say. "Now the chorus."

He shakes his head. "We're on a roll, let's write the fourth verse."

"It was a Friday when I left you," I say. When he doesn't come up with the next line, I add, "Alone and far behind."

He stares at the wall and recites, "You're in my head, filled with regret, sometimes I wish we'd never met."

I close my eyes, hoping he didn't come up with those words because of me.

"Damn, this is good," he says. "Now the chorus. Something about days." He writes down some notes. "How about this: Not a day goes by without thoughts of you."

I stare at the side of his head. "Without tears of you."

He looks up at me. "Without fears of you."

"I look at you and want the future, but all I get's your past."

"Yes." He closes his eyes tightly, thinking. "Day after day I wonder if we were meant to last."

He writes the whole thing in its entirety. "Shit, Bria, this may be the fastest song we've ever written."

"I think you're forgetting about the one we wrote on the paper towel."

He laughs. "Right. Dang, woman, we're good at this."

We bang out the rest in record time, then spend the next few hours getting a head start on a melody for Liam.

"Should we call and tell everyone?" I ask.

"Nah. Make them sweat it out."

"So we're finished for today?"

"We should celebrate. Dinner?"

"I can't. It's Wednesday."

"I think we've already established that."

"Every Wednesday I have a standing date with Brett if he's not on shift."

"You do?" he says sadly.

"Come with us. I'm sure he can get you in."

"In?"

"We're going to a Nighthawks game. In a suite. Brett has connections. They're playing Kansas City tonight."

"You like baseball?"

"You don't think I'm a jock?" I tease.

He laughs. "Bria, you had to ask what a three-pointer was when we had you sing 'On and Off the Court'."

"That's different. That's basketball. Nobody watches basketball."

He grips his chest like he's having a heart attack. "Oh, you did not just say that." He kisses his fingers and puts them in the air. "LeBron, she's kidding. We love you, man."

I roll my eyes. "Do you want to go or not?"

"Hell yeah, I do."

~ ~ ~

"Having fun?" I say, sneaking up behind Crew after I went to the bathroom.

"Are you kidding?" he asks, staring out at the game in the ninth inning. "This has been the best day. Thanks for this."

"Oh, you thought this was it?"

"There's more?"

"How would you like to go to Sawyer Mills' place afterward?"

He looks down at the field in shock. "Sawyer Mills, as in the Kansas City shortstop that used to play for the Nighthawks?"

"That's the one. He still has a townhouse here." I nod to Denver Andrews, a firefighter Brett works with. "He's Denver's brother-in-law. Caden Kessler and Brady Taylor from the Nighthawks will probably be there, too."

"Shit, Bria. I've died and gone to heaven."

159

He really is happy. Is it the game or me? *Can* I make him happy? I've asked myself that a hundred times. Crew is not exactly the kind of guy who's naturally upbeat. He likes to have fun, and when he's onstage, he's completely in his element, but happy? It's not the adjective I'd use to describe him. Morose maybe. Content at best.

Yet somehow I'm drawn to him. His intensity. His dedication. I've never seen a man get so immersed in a song. Not even Adam Stuart. I'm pretty sure Adam didn't even do it for the music anymore. I can't imagine that ever happening to someone as passionate as Crew.

"What?" he asks, catching me staring.

Heat flushes my cheeks. "I was wondering if you were ever going to kiss me again."

"That's why you've been watching me all night?"

"We finished the songs. We said we'd wait on everything else until then. So here we are. Done. So, what's next?"

His gaze darts around the room. "I'm not going to kiss you, Bria. Brett is standing right there. Besides, it wouldn't be spontaneous now that you brought it up."

My insides tingle. So he *is* going to kiss me.

"Am I interrupting?" Brett says.

"Nope," I say. "There's nothing going on over here."

Crew smiles.

"I'm heading out," Brett says. "You're coming to Sawyer's place, right?"

"We'll be there."

"Emma called to say parent-teacher conferences are finished. I'll swing by to get her and tuck Leo into bed. We'll meet you at Sawyer's."

"Oh, good. I can't wait to see her." I turn to Crew. "In case you're wondering, Leo is my nephew. He's three and completely adorable."

"But you're not biased at all." Brett laughs. "See you soon. Glad you could make it, Crew."

Crew lifts his chin. "Thanks for including me."

"He likes you," I say after Brett leaves.

"How can you tell?"

"Because you're still here. You wouldn't be if he didn't like you. My brother has scared away more than one guy because they looked at me the wrong way."

"Shit, really?" He drops his voice. "Did you tell him how I walked out on you last week?"

"I might have."

He takes a step back. "I'm toast."

"Like I said, he likes you. He thinks you're a lot like his fiancée."

"In what way?"

"She was, um … reluctant."

"How so?"

"She didn't want to date him."

"That's nothing like me. I want to date you, Bria."

My mouth curves indulgently. "You do?"

"Yeah." He looks at the floor. "I'm just not sure how good I'll be at it."

How could he not be good at dating? "When's the last time you had a girlfriend?"

He sighs. "Been a while."

"How long?"

"Long."

"You're kind of cryptic sometimes. Most of the time, actually."

I'm a fucked-up mess, I hear him say in my head.

"Sorry. You ready to go?"

"Sure."

We get caught in a herd of people waiting for the elevator.

"Hey, you're that girl," a man shouts, giving me the once-over.

Is he talking to me?

"You're that girl," he says again, coming closer. "I saw you onstage with White Poison."

It's hard not to smile. After all these months, someone finally recognized me.

"What's your name?" he asks. "Who are you singing with now?"

Crew steps in front of me. "It's not important."

The man tries to catch my eye. "It's you, right? I'd remember those legs anywhere."

"Back off," Crew says.

"Crew, it's fine."

"It's not fine," he growls and turns. "I said back off."

"Who are you, her bodyguard?"

"Yeah," Crew says, his posture stiff and muscles rigid. "That's exactly what I am. Now back the hell up before I *make* you back up."

The man holds up his hands in a gesture of innocence and backs away. "Jeez, it's not like she's famous or anything. I mean, she's only a backup singer."

The elevator opens, and I step in. Crew waits at the doors, making sure my fan doesn't come in behind him. We ride down in silence, him brooding, me watching him brood.

"You mind explaining to me what happened up there?" I say after we exit.

He guides me into an empty hallway and traps me against the wall, the intensity of his dark gaze hinting at a soul full of secrets. He swipes the hair off my face, then his finger caresses my bottom lip with unexpected tenderness. Heat, frustration, and hunger drive through me. He knows how he's affecting me. His lips curve into a dangerous smile right before he kisses me. I let him, because having his lips on mine again is everything I've fantasized about.

I've stopped fighting it. I've stopped trying to rationalize it. The bottom line is—I want him. I want him more than I've ever wanted anyone. So I give in.

I weave my hands through his hair, clutching his neck so he can't pull away. He tugs me closer. His hands snake around my back to hold me tightly. We kiss until we run out of breath, then he presses his forehead to mine.

"I kind of like jealous Crew," I say. "I feel like Jane to your Tarzan."

"Jealous? I'm not jealous." He averts his eyes. "Whatever."

I shimmy into him. "I kind of like spontaneous Crew, too."

"You do, do you?"

He watches my tongue as I lick my lips. He kisses me again. He kisses me until a ballpark employee tells us to get out of the hall.

Holding hands, we run out to the curb.

"I can't believe I'm about to meet Sawyer Mills. He was one of my idols growing up." He tucks in his shirt. "Do I look okay?"

"Are you nervous about meeting baseball players?"

"Hell yes, I am."

"You know what I think? Someday they'll be telling people about the time they met Chris Rewey, the lead singer of that famous band."

He squeezes my hand. "Co-lead singer."

I squeeze back. "Right."

"We were on fire today, weren't we?" he says.

I cock my head. "Are we talking about the song or the kiss?"

He draws me to him and gazes into my eyes. "Both. Definitely both."

Chapter Twenty-two

Crew

It's been two weeks since we wrote that last song. Two weeks since I've had a reason to come to the city every day. Two weeks of making up excuses not to be alone with her.

I like Bria a lot, and I don't want to hurt her, but part of me knows I'll end up hurting her anyway. Girls want a relationship with a future, and I'm not sure I can offer that to anyone. I made a promise.

I hear Mom's voice in my head. *You need to write a song about it. You have to let her go.*

Every time I write more than a few words, the past comes rushing back. I can't think about it. If I do, I won't be able to sing. I won't be able to write. I won't be able to breathe. Mom has my best interests at heart, but she has no idea what writing a song like that would do to me.

Today we played a gig in the city, a Sunday afternoon charity event put on by FDNY that Brett brought to our attention. Jeremy and Ronni thought it was a good idea for exposure and image.

Funny that a lot of their good ideas result in money flying *out* of our pockets instead of *in*.

We're packing up the gear in Liam's uncle's van when Jeremy finds us. "Great set. With a little polishing, you'll be ready to record in a few weeks, eh?"

I know he means well, but every compliment he doles out is a passive-aggressive dig.

"Does he have to come to *every* gig?" Bria whispers as she tosses something in the back.

"Wait until we go on the road. We'll practically be living with him."

Her eyes widen. "You don't think Ronni will go, too, do you?"

It's almost comical how much Bria hates Ronni. I get it though. Ronni rubs her the wrong way, and she's everything Bria's not: businesslike, polished, elegant. I consider it a good thing that Bria's not like that. She's real. I'll take the girl next door over a sophisticated floozy any day.

"I don't think so," I say. "But even if she did, no way would she stay in the kind of hotel we can afford. She'd stay in Porsche hotels. We'll be in—"

"Honda?" she says, laughing.

"I'd love to stay in a Honda hotel. I was going to say Gremlin. Do you remember those cars? My buddy in high school had one. It must've been thirty years old. A real piece of shit."

She cringes. "Do you really think we'll be in flea-bag motels?"

I shut the back door of the van. "It probably won't be that bad, but nothing like what you got used to with White Poison."

"Did I ever tell you about Adam's list of riders? The hotel had to make his bed with thousand-count sheets that had never been used before. Same with the towels—they had to be brand new, and not just once. Every time he used one, it had to be new. He threw used towels in the trash."

Everyone has been listening in. I turn to them. "Please kill me if I ever become like that."

Liam snorts. "If we ever turn into that, we'll have more money than God."

"Don't laugh too hard," Jeremy says. "You'd be surprised what happens to a band when they find fame."

I shake my head. "It's not going to happen to us. Right?"

"No way. Not us," Brad says.

"Are you saying I can't hire a roadie to wipe my ass?" Garrett says. "Damn, I was really looking forward to that."

Bria punches him playfully while the rest of us crack up.

"Okay," he says. "I'll have to settle for a harem bathing me."

"As if you need any of that," Liam says. "You'll be wiping your ass with hundred-dollar bills as soon as you turn twenty-five."

"Fuck off, Campbell." Garrett is pissed. He looks disgusted, like he's unhappy about having a trust fund—a trust fund he never talks about. Right along with the family he never mentions.

"We can't let that shit happen to us," Brad says. "Let's make a pact. In fact, Jeremy, maybe you should write up another addendum that says if any band member becomes a diva, we can kick him out."

"You don't want to do that," he says.

"Why not?"

He's solemn. "Listen, I've seen bands go from zero to sixty, and I've seen them fade into nothing, but they all have one thing in common—fans. When people worship you, it gets in your head. Some people get a god complex. A lot turn to drugs and alcohol. Sometimes bands break up before they have a chance to hit the top because of disagreements between members. You never know what's going to happen, and you don't want a contract dictating who gets to stay and who goes. You're going to have a hard enough time navigating the waters if everything goes right."

"Fine. No addendum," I say. "But I'm telling everyone right now, I will personally kick your ass if you insist on a new fucking towel every time you wash your hands. Now bring it in." We form a circle and stack hands in the middle. "On three: one, two, three."

"Let's get reckless!" we shout.

It's something we started doing for luck before each show, and it's become our way of bonding. It's like a pinky promise. It makes us blood brothers—and sister.

Brad checks his watch. "Can we get going? I have a date with Katie."

Liam elbows him. "That's the third time this week. You getting serious about her?"

"I might be. You guys should try it."

"What, having a girlfriend?" Garrett grabs his junk and motions to some fangirling teens on the other side of the fence. "And give up all that available poontang?"

Liam pushes him to the van. "Easy, Casanova. They're jailbait."

"Casanova?" Garrett says, glancing at me. "But that's Crew's handle. You giving up your title, man?"

Liam's eyes dart to Bria and back. "Of course he is, you tool." Liam punches him in the arm.

"Will you guys quit punching me?" he whines. "I play drums, you know."

"Pussy," Liam says.

"So can we go?" Brad asks.

"Can we drop you off, Bria?"

"Sure. Thanks." She hops in and slides over on the bench seat.

On the way to her place, my phone vibrates with a text.

Bria: Want to come over for dinner?

I look at her and she raises her brows. I text her back.

Me: My car is in Stamford.

Bria: So stay at your mom's tonight, and I'll drive you back tomorrow for rehearsal.

I hesitate. Out of the corner of my eye, I see her smile fall. I feel like a dick, having avoided her for two weeks. And other than the car thing, I can't think of a good reason not to go. The truth is, I *want* to.

Me: Sounds like a plan. I have to make a stop first.

Her smile reappears, then she bites her lip. Dammit if my dick doesn't start to swell in the middle of a bunch of sweaty men.

"Liam, can you drop us at my mom's?"

He looks at me in the rearview mirror. "You stayin' the night?"

"I think so. She just texted me."

I'm not sure why I lie to him or why I text Bria instead of having a conversation everyone can hear.

Fifteen minutes later, we're stepping out on the sidewalk in front of Mom's place. "Later," I say to the guys before I shut the van door. Bria stares at me as we walk into the building.

"What?"

"Taking me to meet the parental units? That's a big step, Christopher Rewey."

I stop. "Why did you call me that? It's the second time you've done it."

She looks surprised. "Isn't that your legal name?"

"It is, but nobody uses it. I'd prefer you didn't."

"Sorry," she says, taken aback.

"It's okay, but if you don't want to call me Crew, use Chris."

"Fine, *Chris*. But it's funny your name is what you objected to in that sentence."

"What are you talking about? You've met my mom. She's been to a few gigs."

"Met her, yes. Sat and talked to her while you take a shower— no."

She's right. This will be the first girl I've brought home since … Maybe I didn't think this through.

I lean against the wall.

She sees my face and turns around. "Why don't I just wait in the lobby? You'll be quick, right?"

Pushing the gnawing in my stomach aside, I take her hand and guide her to the elevator. "You're not waiting downstairs, and for the record, it's not a big deal. We work together. We're having dinner. I have to change clothes. End of story."

She knows I'm full of crap. We more than work together and everyone knows it—including my mother. If I say it out loud, will that make it more real? Will it nullify the past?

I drop her hand and unclasp the pen from my notebook, writing a few words down before we reach Mom's floor.

"Always working," Bria says, still in good humor.

"Chris!" Mom brings me in for a hug as soon as she opens the door.

"Mom, you remember Bria Cash?"

She hugs Bria. "Of course I do. You're a wonderful singer, sweetie."

"Thank you," Bria says, taking everything in. "You have a lovely home."

"That's Gary's doing," she says. "He's my sugar daddy, and I'm his trophy wife."

"I heard that," Gary says, joining us from the kitchen. He kisses Mom's head. "Not that it's not true."

I introduce Bria and Gary and glance briefly at the photos on the wall, hoping Bria doesn't look at them too closely. "Sorry to barge in on you like this, but we just played a gig, and I'm all sweaty. Abby wanted to go out to dinner, so I popped in for a shower and change of clothes."

Everyone is looking at me funny.

"What?"

"You called me Abby," Bria says.

I run a hand through my hair. *Fuck.*

Mom looks at me sympathetically. "Bria, why don't I show you around while Chris cleans up? We have a spectacular balcony." Mom drags her away.

"You okay?" Gary asks.

I shake my head.

"It took me twenty years to get over my first wife. Who has three kids, turns thirty-five, and decides they don't want to be married?"

"She divorced you. Big difference."

"It's the only frame of reference I have. The therapist I used to see told me divorce is a lot like death. Apparently you go through a lot of the same stages of grief."

"No way could it be the same."

"Probably not." He sighs. "Has your mom told you I've called her Helen before? More than once, and usually when I'm snapping at her."

I motion to the photo of Abby and me. "I looked at the picture. I didn't mean to call her that."

"Is she the kind of girl you think you might open up to?"

I shrug. "I don't know anything right now."

"Seems to me she's something special. Maybe you should start thinking about it, before it's too late."

Chapter Twenty-three

Bria

Both of us are quiet on the way to my place. I glance at his notebook. Is Abby the one who lives in those pages?

Crew looks at me like he knows what I'm thinking. He shifts the notebook to his other hand, as if protecting it from me.

At my apartment, I go straight for a bottle of wine. "Here." I hand him a glass. "Make yourself comfortable. I need a shower too."

I notice my notebook on the coffee table where I left it. I decide to leave it where it is. Will he look through it? If he does, will my songs about him scare him away? Would I look through his if I had the chance? I know it would be tempting to do it, but at the same time, so wrong. Then again, he'd never leave it out for anyone to see. I didn't miss the fact that he took it with him to the bathroom at his mom's. His *mom's*. That should be a safe place. Which makes me wonder if the only person he's hiding it from is me.

I turn the radio on for Crew then go to the bathroom. I look in the mirror, wondering what Abby looks like. Does he still talk to her? I swallow. Does he still love her?

I'm almost finished when Crew screams my name from the other side of the door. "What? I'm in the shower."

He opens the door and shoves my robe through the shower curtain. "We're on the radio!"

I pull back the curtain. "You're messing with me."

"Am I?"

I don't bother drying off. I throw on the robe and trot to the living room, water dripping down my legs and trailing across the floor.

I hear myself singing, and it finally sinks in. It's one of the RA songs we re-recorded last month. Ronni did it! It's six-fifteen, Sunday, June eighteenth. *Remember this*, I tell myself. "Shh," I say loudly when Crew looks like he's going to speak again.

We look at each other as we listen to the rest of the song. Our lips move with the words. It's not like we haven't heard ourselves before, we have. All the time. But this is different. He's never been on the radio. I haven't either. This could quite possibly be the best moment of my life. Better even than when I got the job as the backup singer for White Poison.

After the song ends, I scream and jump in his arms. "We were on the radio!"

He kisses me more passionately than he sings to me onstage.

He carries me to the bed and lays me down. My robe falls open. He gazes at me like he's never seen a naked woman. I warm under his perusal, aching for his touch.

He runs a hand across my inner knee to my thigh, then touches me *there*. It's like he's asking for permission. I bite my lip and nod my head. He puts a finger on my clit and I shudder. He works it to the beat of the song on the radio. If I weren't so aroused, I'd laugh.

He slips a finger inside me, then another. I raise my hips, pushing onto them. I'm climbing, climbing. I've never been turned on this quickly and thoroughly. I should be embarrassed but I'm not. I'm lying naked before him, and he's fully dressed. I'm not nervous either. I'm a bomb waiting to explode.

He's working me with his thumb, his fingers still exploring inside me. Thrill after thrill shoots through my body as he possesses me.

"Bria," he says softly.

Him saying my name is all it takes for me to clamp down and shout, "Oh, God!"

My head falls back on the bed and I breathe deeply, feeling the final surges of my orgasm.

When I open my eyes, he's staring at the scar on my stomach. I grab his belt. "Now you."

He hesitates, and I get the strange feeling he's about to get up and run out the door. But he swallows and takes off his pants.

I'm not sure what just happened, but I think whatever it was is good. He sits next to me and pulls off his shirt. He might be the sexiest man I've ever seen. Adam was sexy, there's no denying that, but he was sexy in a *I-know-I'm-sexy* way. Crew is sexy for other reasons. And I could be wrong, but I think he's exposing more than his body to me right now. In some way, I think he's exposing his soul.

I take his cock into my hands, and he inhales sharply. I run my hand up and down the shaft. He's long, thick, solid, and velvety soft. He leans down. "Do you have a condom?"

I point. He opens the nightstand drawer, looking in it and then back at me. I can see it in his eyes; he wants to ask me how often I open this drawer, but he doesn't, because if he asks me about my past, he'd have to tell me about his.

He opens a pack and puts the condom on in record time, then gets on top of me. "Is this okay?"

I nod.

"Say it, Bria," he commands.

Ooooo, I like demanding Crew. "I want this."

His eyes burn into mine as he enters me. Then he fucks me fast and hard. I barely even have time to feel it before he comes. He groans into my shoulder and lies on top of me for a minute. I wonder if I've ever had quicker sex in my life.

He rolls out of bed and vanishes into the bathroom. I listen to him wash up.

A few minutes later, he opens the door and stands naked in the doorway. He grips the doorframe above him and shakes his head. "Were we really on the radio?"

I roll onto my stomach and let out an excited scream. "We really were."

He sits beside me. "I should apologize. It's been a while."

I can't help my smile. "How long?"

"Five months or so."

My lower lip works its way into my mouth as I calculate how long ago we met.

He touches my bare butt. "What about you?"

I shrug nonchalantly. "About five months or so."

"Adam?"

I nod.

"How did I compare?" He puts a finger to my lips. "You know what, don't answer that."

I chuckle. "Well, you were so quick, I don't have enough data to answer the question."

"Not enough data, huh?"

I nod seductively. His cock dances. I reach out and give it a tug. His mouth twitches into a grin. He gets hard in my hands.

"I want a do-over," he says, getting another condom.

I lie on my back, exposing myself to him. He sucks my nipple into his mouth and blows on it, giving me a chill. Then he ever so lightly nips me. I shake involuntarily and feel his smile against my breast.

"You are so responsive."

I arch into him. "I aim to please."

He growls—actually growls like a bear—and climbs on top of me, testing me with his fingers before he pushes himself in. He seats himself fully and then retracts until just the tip remains. He does it again, building me back up. He makes love to me slowly this time. His lips are moving, and I wonder if he's writing a song. The thought has me clawing at his back. He slips a hand between us and pinches my nipple. I groan. His thrusts come more quickly.

He flips me over and yanks me to my knees, slapping against me as he sinks into me over and over from behind. I grab a pillow and lean into it, moaning at the way he feels inside me. He reaches around and rubs my clit with one hand, his other hand grabbing my waist.

"I'm gonna come," he announces, pushing me over the edge for a second time. We both shout.

We collapse, sweaty and satiated, and laugh.

"We should definitely write a song about that. Jesus, Bria."

I giggle. "I thought you were. I swear I saw your lips moving, and since you're always writing …"

"Lyrics by sex," he says, stroking my side. "You're very inspiring."

"I could say the same about you."

"I still can't believe it."

"I know it's a lot to process, being in bed with a famous singer and all, but you're going to have to realize I'm a person, too. But on your way out, my head of security will ask you to sign an NDA."

He hits me with a pillow.

I rise on one elbow. "Do you think it's been on more than once, or do you suppose we heard the very first time?"

"Hard to say, but what are the odds that we happened to be listening the first time it was on?"

"Do you think the guys heard it?"

He retrieves his phone and gets back into bed. "No texts or calls."

"Maybe we should tell them."

He puts down his phone and straddles me. "Hmm, or maybe …" He shimmies against me, getting hard again.

We call them after round three, and Ronni finally texts to let us know we were on the radio. *Thanks for the heads up, Veronica.*

After round four, I revel in the events of the day and realize Crew's asleep. I strain to see the outline of his face. I stare at him for a long time. Long enough for the moon to come up and shine through the window.

"Abby," he mumbles, snuggling against me.

I fall asleep before dawn after staying up most of the night crying, because the man in my arms thinks I'm someone else.

The bed creaks. I cover my eyes to block the light. I hear Crew use the bathroom. He crawls back into bed and wraps his arm around me and kisses the back of my head. His breathing slows; he's going back to sleep.

"Crew?"

"Yeah?" he says sleepily.

I face him knowing I shouldn't ask, but I can't help myself. "Who's Abby?"

Suddenly he's wide awake, but he doesn't speak, or get off the bed, or run away. He just turns away from me and pulls the covers up.

Guilt consumes me. He wasn't baring his soul to me after all. And now ... now he's burying it.

Chapter Twenty-four

Crew

Seven years ago

Where is she?

Between songs, I check the time. Abby's never late. We're almost finished with our set.

Liam shrugs at me. He knows as well as I do our final song was going to be my early birthday present to her. I've been working on it for months. I started writing it the day we found out she was pregnant. No way am I going to sing it if she's not here.

Two more songs go by. Mom's out front, and she's searching for Abby too. *'Where is she?'* she mouths. I shake my head.

I check my phone during the guitar solo. No new texts. I quickly send her one. She doesn't respond.

We're finishing up the next to last song when Liam says, "Yes or no?"

I make a cutthroat sign to let them know we're wrapping it up.

I hardly thank the crowd at all. Usually, I make a big production of who we are and where they can find us, but I only nod and hustle offstage.

I call her. She doesn't answer. I call Janine and a few of her other friends. They all say they thought she was coming here.

Freaking out, I say to my bandmates, "Can you pack up without me? I have to find her."

"Sure thing," Liam says. "I hope everything's okay."

"She was probably held up at work," I say, but I don't believe it. She'd have texted me if that were the case.

Mom appears, and I hurry over to her. "Can I borrow the car? I'll drop you at the house first, then I want to swing by the restaurant. I don't get why she's not answering my texts or calls."

"It's on the way home. I'll go with you, and you can drop me off after. I'm sure there's a perfectly good explanation."

"Thanks."

"You were great tonight," she says as we leave the venue.

"*They* were great. I was worried about Abby, so I sucked."

"You didn't suck, Chris. I see a big future for you in the music industry, with or without Naked Whale. Promise me you'll always be smart about it. Promise me you won't get caught up in the drugs and narcissism." She touches my shoulder. "I don't want you to lose the incredible man you've become."

"I promise."

Twenty minutes later we park at the fast food restaurant. Abby's car is in the lot, and I've never been so relieved. I get out and go over to it, and something crunches under my shoe. It's a cracked cellphone, and I can tell by the case it's hers. Not far away from it is a scrunchy, like the one she wears to work. I pick it up; there's a lot of hair in it. Abby's hair.

"This is hers," I say, holding it up for Mom to see through the open window.

She comes around to my side of the car, and we follow a trail of things on the ground—a crushed bottle of hand sanitizer, a package of tissues, a pen, a tube of Chapstick—and end up at a purse.

My heart is pounding, and my mouth goes dry. "That's hers."

Without thinking, I reach for it, but Mom stops me. "Don't touch anything. Run inside and see if she's there."

"You think something happened to her?" I feel dizzy.

"Maybe she fell on her way to the car and had to be taken to the hospital."

"Oh shit, the baby."

"Hurry. I'll wait here."

I run inside and cut in front of people at the counter.

"Dude," someone says. "Not cool."

I ignore him and ask the employees, "Is Abby Evans here?"

"She's not working right now," a man says.

"When did she leave?"

"Dunno. A while ago."

I slap the counter. "I need to know how long she's been gone."

He shouts to someone in the back. "Chet, when did Abby clock out?"

"Seven."

"Exactly seven?"

"Hold on. Six fifty-five."

"Happy now?" the annoyed cashier says to me.

I glance at my phone. It's quarter to nine. "Are you sure she's not in back?"

"In the plush employee's lounge?" he says sarcastically. "Yes, I'm sure. She said she had to go to her boyfriend's concert. I'm guessing you're the boyfriend. Guess you got stood up, man."

"Can you do me a favor and check in back? Maybe she's sick or something." I turn to a female employee. "Can you check the bathroom? Please. It's important." I follow her and wait outside the restroom.

"There's nobody in there," she says.

I return to the front counter. The man shakes his head. "She's not here. Sorry."

Running back outside, I try to call Abby again. Then I remember her phone is smashed on the ground.

Mom is on her cell.

"Abigail Evans. Abby. She's seventeen. Light brown hair with streaks of blonde. Blue eyes. About five-two. How about Abigail Rewey? R-E-W-E-Y," she spells out. "Yes, I'm her mother." She glances at me, and I see the worry in her eyes. "Okay, thank you." She puts her phone away. "I take it she's not inside."

"They said she left almost two hours ago."

"I called the three closest hospitals. None of them have admitted a girl by her name or description in the last few hours."

I gaze at Abby's things strewn across the ground. "Mom, this is so messed up. I'm scared."

She puts an arm around me. "We need to call her parents and then the police."

A huge lump forms in my throat. "Mom, no. You don't think—"

"Chris, let's not go there yet."

Her scrunchy is still in my hand. I sit on the curb and stare at it as Mom calls Dr. Evans and then the police. As I listen to her, an eerie feeling washes over me. A feeling that my life will never be the same again.

I jump to my feet and get sick in the bushes.

Samantha Christy

Chapter Twenty-five

Bria

The ride to Stamford is uncomfortable. Neither of us brings up him twice calling me Abby.

It's obvious we're dancing around it by talking about what else happened yesterday. Our song was on the radio! It's everything I ever dreamed of. Crew obsessively changes stations, trying to hear it again. We're pulling off the highway when it finally comes on. I'm so excited I have to pull into a fast-food parking lot.

Crew makes a call. "Liam, dude. It's on again!" He tells Liam what station, then puts his phone on speaker. We sit and listen to our song. When it's over, the guys whoop loudly.

"We're fucking famous!" Garrett yells.

I get back on the road again. We stay on the call, listening to them rave about it until Crew and I arrive at the barn. We run inside, and lots of hugging ensues.

The barn door opens, and Dirk comes in. "You kids hear your song on the radio?"

Garrett and Brad run over to him, and they shake hands, talking jubilantly about it. Liam and Crew, hang back, looking anything but excited. Liam really must despise Dirk, and Crew seems to be the only one who knows why.

"Bria," Dirk says, coming over to kiss my cheek. "You sounded lovely, as always."

"Thank you."

"I told you things would happen." He turns to Liam. "Didn't I tell you?"

"Yeah, Dirk. You told me."

He looks pissed. "Maybe you could show some fucking gratitude then."

Crew steps between them. "We appreciate everything you've done for us, Dirk. None of this would be possible without you."

"That's more like it." He shoots a glare at Liam. "Sylvia would like you all to join us for a celebration dinner tonight. I've invited influential people from the city. Show up at six with bells on."

"Tonight?" I look down at my clothes: jeans and an old Aerosmith T-shirt.

"I'm sure you can find a pretty dress to wear, sweetheart. There's a nice mall a few miles down the street."

No one in the band protests, and I wonder if this is an example of what Crew meant by Dirk controlling everything. "I'm sure I can find something."

"That's the spirit," Dirk says and leaves, repeating "Six o'clock" over his shoulder.

"Shit," Garrett says. "The last thing I want to do is celebrate with a bunch of goddamned suits."

"It's a small price to pay for all he's done for us, though, right?" Brad asks.

"Small price, my ass," Liam mumbles, going over to turn on the amps. "Come on, let's get to work."

After practice, I ask Crew to point me in the direction of the mall.

"I'll go with you," he says.

"Thanks, but you don't have to."

"I'm going, Bria. Malls are cesspools of creepy guys."

"I think you're forgetting where I live."

He shakes his head in disgust. "Not likely."

"You really have a problem with my apartment, don't you?"

"It's not your apartment I have the problem with, it's your street."

"Whatever," I say, walking to my car. "Are we going to do this or not?"

At the mall, Crew becomes more playful, even sneaking into the dressing room to 'help' me.

"Crew," I say, peeking through the curtain. "We'll get in trouble."

"For what? Trying on clothes? Now take off your shirt."

I pull it off. He stares at my chest, and I heat up under his perusal.

"Now the pants," he commands.

I do what he says. He turns me so my back is to his front and locks eyes with me in the mirror. He wraps his arms around me and caresses my hips, stomach, and breasts.

"Who's the creepy one now?" I tease.

Instantly his demeanor changes and he pulls away. "I was trying to have fun." He picks a dress off a hanger and hands it to me. "Try this one. I'll wait outside." He shuts the curtain behind him leaving me confused once again.

"What's the deal with Garrett?" I ask in the changing room.

"What do you mean?"

"I've never met his family, and someone said something about a trust fund."

"You won't meet them. He doesn't talk to them."

"Why not?"

"Beats me."

"And the trust fund? I assume that means the family he wants nothing to do with is rich."

"All I know is he stands to get his hands on a shitload of money the day he turns twenty-five."

I peek out. "There are a lot of secrets in this band, aren't there?"

His brows are drawn. "Maybe there are good reasons to keep them that way." There is an edge to his tone that tells me to stop prodding.

I pick my favorite dress of the four I tried on and take it to the counter. Crew hands over his card before I can give her mine.

"You're not buying my clothes," I say.

"I am, and the shoes, too. Every penny you save is a penny you can put toward your new place."

I roll my eyes, but I concede. He can afford the seventy-five dollars a lot more than I can.

On our way out, a young man approaches us. "You sing for Reckless Alibi, don't you? I've seen you at least a dozen times. You guys rock."

"Thanks," we say at the same time.

"Chris Rewey, right?" He looks at me. "And you're …?"

I open my mouth to tell him when Crew captures my elbow. "Leaving," he says curtly. "We're in a hurry."

"Oh, okay. Bye."

We reach the car and get in. "Kind of rude, don't you think?"

"I wasn't rude."

"If that's not you being rude, I hate to think what it looks like. We have to be nice to our fans. We don't want to get a reputation for being arrogant."

"We're not arrogant."

"But *he* doesn't know that. What if he tells all his friends we are, and they stop coming to our gigs? It can snowball easily."

"If they like our music, they'll keep coming. He'll probably tell his friends he met the singers from RA so he can look good."

"We should be more accommodating."

"Accommodating?" he says with disgust. "You want men following you? *Touching* you?"

He's jealous again. Jealous of someone I don't know. "Of course not. Just be nice. Do you think you can manage that?"

He blows out a breath in frustration. "Whatever."

"So what are we doing the rest of the afternoon?" I ask. "Can we hang out at your place?"

"You want to go to my apartment?"

"Sure, why not?"

"Because it's ... dirty."

I chuckle. "You should have seen Brett's first apartment. I think I can handle it."

He scrubs a hand across his jaw. "Okay."

He gives me directions. It takes longer to get there than I thought it would. We pass the *You Are Now Leaving Stamford* sign.

"It's these apartments," he says. "Turn in up here."

I try not to let my jaw drop. This complex must be fifty years old, maybe older. Paint is peeling off the siding. Dirt, not grass, lines the property. Cars as old as Crew's fill the parking spaces.

"You were expecting the Ritz?"

"No, but—"

"I never said I was rich, Bria." He points to a building. "That's mine. Park over there."

"I assumed—"

"You and everyone else."

"But how can you be so against my place when you live here?"

"It's different. You're in the city, and you're a—"

"Girl? It's different because I'm a girl?"

"Yes."

I snort my displeasure.

"Bria, I don't make up the rules. The fact is it *is* different for girls. I'm not being sexist. Guys can protect themselves better than girls. We aren't as vulnerable. We don't get stalked."

"Stalked? That's ridiculous."

"It's not."

"We're not famous yet. Maybe then I could see it."

"You think you have to be famous to get stalked?" He opens his door. "Forget it. Give me a few minutes, okay?"

"You forget I have a brother. I've seen it all."

He shakes his head. "Wait five minutes and then come up."

"Fine. Jeez, go hide your porn."

He runs up the stairs two at a time and enters the first apartment on the right. Considering where he lives, I feel guilty letting him pay for my dress.

After five minutes, I get my things out of the backseat and go up. He left the door cracked for me. When I step inside, I see a mess on his couch. He darts across the room to pick up the dirty clothes and throw them into a closet.

"It's not so bad." A few old guitars hang on his walls. A keyboard and synthesizer are in one corner. There's also an impressive collection of albums that would rival mine.

"It's not as nice as your place," he says.

"But it's a lot bigger."

He picks up one of his guitars, nervously strumming as I check out his separate kitchen and peek into his bedroom. He's playing one of our songs. I stop snooping and watch him play.

"You're as good as Liam, you know."

"Don't tell him that."

He keeps a lot of rock memorabilia on his bookshelves. One shelf is dedicated to photos of friends and family. I recognize his mom and Gary in some of them. He's with friends in others. I pick one up and smile. "Is this you and Liam? How old were you?"

"I think we were ten."

Crew is "singing" into a broomstick, and Liam is playing air guitar. "You wanted to be a singer even then?"

He comes up behind me, wrapping me in his arms. "I was born to sing."

I look at some of the other photos and notice two clean spots where pictures should be. He didn't just want to tidy up. He came up first to hide her from me.

I want so badly to ask him again. But the way he's holding me; he'd stop doing it if I did. And I decide I want him to hold me more than I want to ask about her.

I spin to face him. "You were a cute kid."

He pulls me tightly against him. "What about now? Am I still cute?"

"Cute? No. Incredibly hot? Absolutely."

"You think I'm hot?"

"Oh yeah," I drawl.

"You're not half-bad yourself."

I stand on my toes and peck him on the cheek. He momentarily glances over at the photo shelf and then back at me. Then he kisses me hard, with tongue.

"Wow," I say breathlessly. "What was that for?"

"I've wanted to do that since rehearsal. You were great today. You're great every day, but today there was something more, if that makes any sense."

"It's amazing what a few orgasms can do for a lady."

He laughs. "Why don't I give you a tour of the place?"

"I've seen it."

"Let me clarify. Bria, do you want to see my bed and maybe let me strip you naked and add to your orgasm count?"

My cheeks flush. "Lead the way."

~ ~ ~

We drive to Dirk's house. Correction, his mansion. "Holy crap. You didn't tell me Liam's uncle was a billionaire."

"What did you expect? He owns a huge car dealership and half the city."

I park to one side, embarrassed to be driving my old car. I get out. Among the vehicles in the massive driveway are a shiny red Porsche and a white SUV. "He invited Ronni and Jeremy?"

Crew shrugs.

A big black limousine pulls up to the front walk, and a man and women get out of the back.

"Who's that?" I ask.

"Could be anyone. Dirk has lots of friends in high places."

I look down at my dress. "I feel underdressed, like I should be wearing a tiara or the Hope diamond."

He takes my hand. "You look amazing."

"Thanks. So do you."

Watching Crew get ready for this thing was nothing less than spectacular. Seeing him put on a suit was almost as fun as seeing him remove all his clothing before we have sex. I've never seen him wear anything other than ripped jeans and T-shirts. He's gorgeous.

Crew nods to the end of the driveway. "Here come Brad and Garrett." They park and join us. Crew walks to the door.

"What about Liam?" I ask. "Shouldn't we wait for him?"

"He lives here."

"But he hates his uncle."

Garrett says, "Yeah, but not enough to pay rent on some dive instead of living in the damn White House."

"Says the guy living in a dive instead of on his family's estate," Crew says.

Garrett shoots him a biting glance. "Whatever."

Before we can ring the bell, the door opens, and someone who looks like a waiter greets us. "Welcome. Mayor Campbell and his guests are waiting in the salon." He points us in the right direction.

"Oh, my God," I whisper to Crew. "This house has a *salon*."

"It's a fancy word for another living room," he says, clearly not as fascinated as I am with our surroundings, maybe because he's been here so many times. I don't care how often I come here, I'll be impressed every time.

Dirk sees us and hurries over. "Ah, the guests of honor. Let me introduce you."

Along with Liam, we are paraded around the room and introduced to lawyers, a Wall Street tycoon, the owner of the Knicks, and two politicians.

"All this for us?" I ask.

Liam snorts. "It's not for us. We're Dirk's shiny new toy now that we've gotten airtime. He probably had this dinner planned for months, but he wants you to think otherwise."

"But then why are Jeremy and Ronni here?" I ask.

"Not just them," Liam says. "Ronni's boss too. The head of IRL."

"Really?" Crew says, suddenly interested.

"He probably couldn't turn down an invite from someone as influential as my uncle. Hell, he probably didn't even know we'd be here. But as much as I hate this mingling shit, if the head of the record label likes us, we'll probably get some serious attention. It pains me to say this, but we should try to be on our best behavior."

"You? Behave at a party?" Garrett jokes. "They'd better lock up all the alcohol."

"Shut up," Liam says. "And take your sticks out of your back pocket, dude. You're wearing a damn suit."

Garrett lays a protective hand over his drumsticks. "They go everywhere with me."

Brad laughs. "I'll bet you even take them to bed, don't you?"

"Sometimes. They're inspirational. We should all sleep next to something that inspires us."

Crew and I share a smile.

We meet Niles Armentrout, Ronni's boss. I play nice and don't call her Veronica when she calls me Brianna. He barely gives us the time of day; maybe Liam was right, and he didn't know we'd be here. I'm getting the feeling Dirk is the kind of guy who works every situation to his advantage.

All the bigwigs go off and talk politics. Liam leads us out of the room. "Let's play pool until dinner. They won't even miss us."

He guides us through a maze of hallways to the billiard room.

"Wow, this is incredible," I say. "I didn't know you lived with your uncle."

"Not for long," he says. "As soon as I can afford it, Mom and I are getting out of here."

"Your mom lives here too? I'd love to meet her."

"She doesn't come to these things."

"Shame."

Thirty minutes later, the same man who let us in the front door beckons us to dinner.

"How did he know where we were?" Brad asks. "This place is ginormous."

Liam points to a small plastic dome in the ceiling. "Cameras."

Brad stiffens. "I hope there isn't one in the bathroom. I might have snooped through a closet."

Crew slaps him on the back of the head. "Fucking tool."

On our way to the dining room, we run into a woman stumbling out into the hall. Liam runs over to her. "Mom, let me help you back to your room." Steadying her, he escorts her into a different wing. When he returns, he doesn't say a word about his mother almost doing a drunken face-plant in front of his friends.

Crew pats Liam on the back like he understands. The rest of us pretend nothing happened.

Over the course of the next few hours, Dirk manages to endear us to Niles, the head of IRL. I hope Liam's right. If he decides we're worth it, big things could happen.

When we leave, I ask Crew, "What's in it for Liam's uncle? Why go through all the trouble?"

"He's a businessman. He can profit from this."

"But I read all the contracts. His name isn't mentioned. He won't make money off us."

"That's where you're wrong."

"I am?"

"Yeah, big time." He glances at the mansion. "He didn't get this rich by inheriting money. He knows how to make it. And believe me if we make it big, he'll profit. Maybe he's got secret ties to IRL we don't know about. Maybe he owns a radio station and will profit from advertising. Maybe he owns a clothing store, and we'll end up promoting his product. Whatever it is, you can bet he's thinking about it now. On the other hand, if Dirk Campbell thinks we have something, he's rarely wrong, and though I don't want to be, I'm excited he's so into us right now."

"Why don't you want to be?"

"Dirk isn't always what he seems. He's not someone I want to be in bed with."

I raise my eyebrows.

"It's a figure of speech, Bria."

Crew opens my car door. "Is there *anyone* you want to be in bed with?" I ask in a sultry voice.

His slow smile has all kinds of promise in it. "Now I'm getting hard."

I graze my hand seductively across the front of his pants. "What are we going to do about that?"

"Woman, you're going to kill me." He shuts my door and runs around to get in.

I giggle. "Yeah, but what a way to die."

His smile vanishes and distant Crew is back. "It's been a long day. You probably want to get back to the city."

"Did I say something wrong?" I was secretly hoping we'd sleep together like last night. After all, it's late and I have to be back here tomorrow anyway.

"No. Let's get out of here. I think we both need to get some shuteye."

Maybe he remembered his dream and is afraid of what might come out of his mouth if I stay over.

I drop him at his apartment, only remaining long enough to change back into my other clothes. He walks me to my car, looking guilty. "Bria, I want …"

I wait five whole seconds for him to finish his thought. "It's okay. You're right. We both need sleep. I'll see you tomorrow."

He pinches the bridge of his nose. "Text me when you get home."

I see him in my rearview mirror watching me as I pull out of the parking lot. And on the way home, I write a song in my head about the mercurial man I think I might be in love with.

Chapter Twenty-six

Crew

It's our last day in the recording studio, and we're putting the finishing touches on our second album. Bria's in the booth, re-recording some of her parts. We lock eyes as she sings the lines we wrote together. Damn, she's good. Bringing her onboard is the best thing we've ever done. We killed it this week. Bria and I sound better than ever.

Sometimes I wonder why she puts up with me, though. It's been two weeks since I called her by Abby's name. Neither of us has mentioned it. She's figured out Abby was a big deal to me. I'm pretty sure Bria realizes that when I fuck things up, it's not because I don't like her. But tension is growing between us, and not in a good way.

"We're going to get rich from this," Garret says, coming up behind me.

Garrett always says that, which is strange, considering he has a trust fund waiting for him. But I hope one day it will be true. Money would be nice, but I just want to be on a stage, singing to thousands of people, and I want Bria right up there with me.

"You good with that?" Jake, the sound engineer, asks Ronni.

"Yes. We can break for lunch now."

It doesn't slip past me that Ronni rarely gives Bria a compliment though she raves about the group as a whole. It must be a woman thing. They're both beautiful but in very different ways. Maybe that's intimidating to them.

Ronni takes me to the conference room, where a catered lunch is spread on a table. "There's a charity benefit in the city next Thursday. I'd like you to go with me. It would be good exposure."

"I'll check our schedule and make sure everyone's free."

"I'm not inviting Reckless Alibi. I'm inviting Chris Rewey."

I give her a sideways look. "Why would we need exposure for me and not the band?"

"I'm looking out for you," she says. "You have a big future in the music business."

My bandmates are digging into a pile of sandwiches, and I wonder when Bria will show up. "Ronni, I'm part of Reckless Alibi. We're a package deal. I don't *have* a future without them."

"I think you're wrong, but don't come as a singer then. Come as my date."

Liam overheard Ronni. He stops eating mid-bite.

"Maybe Jeremy didn't tell you, but I'm with Bria."

Her lips curl in disgust. "You and Brianna? No. That's a train wreck waiting to happen. I forbid it."

Everyone in the room is listening to our conversation, and I'm glad Bria isn't here yet. I reach for a plate. "It's not a train wreck. We've signed papers protecting the band if anything were to happen."

She addresses Jeremy. "Is that what the addendum was all about? You should have been up front with me. I'd have advised against any personal relationships among band members."

"I advised them against it too, but do you know what happens when you tell someone they can't do something? Forbidden fruit, Ronni. I took measures to protect the band, that's all. There's nothing more we can do."

She growls and turns to me. "How serious is it?"

"I don't know," I say, taking a sandwich. "We go out sometimes. It's no big deal."

"No big deal, huh?" She scowls.

"That's right."

Bria comes in, and everyone looks at her. "Did I suck or something?"

"You were great," I say. "Wasn't she great, guys?"

Everyone agrees. Everyone but Ronni.

All through lunch, Ronni sits across the room, appraising me, appraising Bria.

"Brianna, you need to cut your hair," Ronni says frigidly.

I protest mildly, "I don't think that's necessary. Guys dig chicks with long hair."

"It's true," Liam says. "We do."

"It's unkempt," Ronni says.

Bria looks offended. "Are you calling me sloppy?"

"Your hair is perfect," I whisper to her. "Don't listen to her."

"I have to agree with Crew and Liam on this," Jeremy says. "We want men and boys to follow us as much as we want women and girls. Bria's beautiful. The young generation would even call her hot." He smiles at Bria. "No disrespect."

"None taken."

Ronni clearly disagrees with him. "But I'm putting my foot down on the highlights. She needs them. Brown hair is boring. She needs to look more edgy."

"What do you say, Brianna?" Jeremy asks. "In the name of compromise, will you consider highlights? I think you'd look spectacular."

She shrugs. "I could try it. It's something I can undo if I don't like it."

"I'll set it up," Ronni says. "I know a stylist in the city. I'll have him reach out to you."

"I'll go with you," I tell her. "It might be fun."

"Be sure to tell him *no* haircut," Bria tells her.

Ronni gets up, leaving her plate for someone else to clean up. "Jake said he wants you both in the booth for the track-eight chorus. After that, we'll work on Liam's riff on track eleven."

Track eight is 'On That Stage.' It's become one of our favorite songs to sing together.

After Ronni leaves, Bria throws her plate in the trash, covers the remaining food, and stashes it in the studio fridge. She'll take it home; she's been doing it all week. It makes me feel bad that she relies on leftovers to feed herself. The money hasn't exactly been flowing in lately. We've been working more on the album than onstage performances. It's been tough on most of us, having to put what little we do make back into the band, but especially on her, as she lives in the city. I wish I could help, but I'm barely scraping by.

Before I return to the booth, I take Jeremy aside. "Is there anything we can do to help Bria with expenses? She drives an hour both ways to rehearsal, five times a week. It hasn't been easy."

"We're operating on a shoestring budget as it is," he says. "Maybe she should move to Stamford, or even better, one of the towns nearby. Rent would be a lot cheaper, and she wouldn't have to use her car as much."

"I don't know if she'd do that. Her brother lives in the city, and they're very close."

"I'll ask Ronni if IRL will front her some money."

"Don't do that. They're relationship is tenuous at best. We don't need to make it worse."

"Agreed."

"I'll think of something," I say.

"I don't doubt that you will." He pats me on the back. "I'll try, too."

When I join Bria in the booth, she's already got her headphones on and Jake has her singing so he can calibrate the synthesizer. I'm glad she doesn't have to cut her hair. I like it the way it is. I pretty much like everything about her.

The music starts. Bria sings, then stops.

I missed my cue. "Sorry. Can we start again?"

She knows why I messed up. For the next half hour, we watch each other as we sing the chorus over and over until Jake is one hundred percent satisfied.

The way she looks at me when we sing. It's like her hunger and need match mine. I'm surprised I don't have a boner.

Hours later Ronni calls it a wrap. Jeremy pulls out several bottles of champagne, and we toast to the completion of our second album.

"Give me a month to get a couple of these tracks on the radio," Ronni says. "We'll need that much time to master and market it."

"I'll drink to that," Liam says. "More songs on the radio. I think I've died and gone to heaven."

"I have something else for you to drink to," she says. "I spent the better part of the afternoon on the phone and I've lined up a performance next Friday at the most exclusive club in New York City. The band that was booked cancelled. I want you to sing your new stuff, so make sure you rehearse plenty. I'll get you a playlist in a few days." She turns to Bria. "And get that hair done."

Jake finally kicks us out at seven. I hang back, knowing Bria doesn't want the others, especially Ronni, seeing her take the leftover food.

She has the bag from the fridge in her hand when Jeremy walks in. Her cheeks flame. "It shouldn't go to waste. You know, with all the starving kids in Africa and all."

Jeremy hands me an unopened bottle of champagne. "Maybe you kids can put this to good use."

"Don't mind if we do," I say.

He hands an envelope to Bria.

"What's this?"

"A little something to help cover your gas. I know you travel a lot to and from the city."

"Where did this come from?" I ask.

"Dirk," he says. "He asked me to give it to her."

I narrow my eyes at him. We only talked about this a while ago. How could Dirk have given him money?

In the envelope is a stack of fifty-dollar bills. I take it from her and give it back to Jeremy. "Please thank him, but she's got it covered." No way do I want her indebted to that slime ball. "We'd better get that food back to your place before it spoils."

"We?" she asks, smiling.

"I thought I'd go back to the city with you. My mom asked me for dinner tomorrow. You can come too."

"Tomorrow? But what are you going to do until then?" The amused gleam in her eyes is breathtaking.

My pants get tight. "I'm sure we'll find something."

We get in her car. "Crew?"

"Yeah?"

"Why didn't you want me taking the money?"

"Because Dirk always has ulterior motives. He never does anything that won't benefit him."

"Maybe he thinks paying for my gas will keep me in the band and *that* could benefit him."

I shake my head. "Like I said, you don't want to be in bed with him."

"Okay, but my credit card is getting a lot of use lately."

"So is mine."

"We're paying our dues, right?"

"Yup."

Halfway back to the city, she asks, "Why do you think Ronni wants me to cut my hair so badly?"

"Honestly? I think she's jealous of you."

"She drives a Porsche. How would she possibly be jealous of *me*?"

"You're the one with all the talent, and you're gorgeous too."

"I believe you're a tad biased. Maybe Brad was right. She wants you and she sees me as competition."

I don't mention what happened earlier. "That's ridiculous."

"You haven't picked up on her subtle advances? Are you really that blind?"

"She doesn't want me," I lie.

"Maybe *I'm* jealous. She has looks, money, and power. Why wouldn't you want a woman like that?"

"I wouldn't. I don't. You have nothing to worry about. We're good."

She squeezes my hand. "Is there a *we*?"

"Yeah, there's a *we*."

She smiles as she watches the road in front of us.

Me—I feel guilty for adding to the secrets I'm keeping from her.

Chapter Twenty-seven

Bria

I hand Crew my phone before we go inside. "Snap a picture of my hair. I want a before and after photo." I strike funny poses as he snaps away.

"Did anyone ever tell you that you should be a model?"

"Actually, yes."

"Really?"

I nod. "Back in high school, I was approached by someone after a choir performance."

"What happened?"

"The guy made Brett uneasy and he scared him away."

"I like your brother."

"It wouldn't have mattered. I've never had any desire to be on the cover of a magazine unless it was a result of my singing."

"*Rolling Stone?*" he asks with a smirk.

"That's the holy grail, isn't it? But I was thinking more like *Spin* or *Billboard*."

"You've got to think bigger than that."

A girl passing by stops. "Are you Chris Rewey?"

Crew smiles and offers his hand. "I am."

"Oh my God, I love your songs. Reckless Alibi is like my favorite band of all time, and now you're on the radio. Can I have your autograph?"

He signs a page in her notebook, and she takes their picture. "This is like the best day of my life. You really are my favorite."

"Thanks. We have a new album coming out soon."

She squeals.

"This is our other lead singer," he says. "Brianna."

I look at him sideways. He's never called me that before.

"Nice to meet you," she says, looking about as impressed with me as the bum on the corner bench.

"We'd better get going," Crew says.

"Right. Thanks again," the girl says before bouncing down the street.

I put my hand over my heart. "O-M-G," I say dramatically. "I can't believe I just met *the* Chris Rewey. Isn't he dreamy?"

"Shut up," he says, yanking me to him.

"And he touched me. I'll never wash my hand again."

"Will you quit it?" He pushes me against the side of the building and kisses me. "You're the only one I want to touch."

"Are you famous or something?" a man asks, taking his phone out. "I saw you autograph something for that girl and then you posed for a picture with her."

"Nope," Crew says sharply. "Not famous. If you'll excuse us."

He hurries me toward the hair salon and I'm left wondering if he's always nicer to the female fans.

As soon as we open the door, a flamboyant man dances toward us. "Ah, my dear Brianna. I've been waiting for you. I'm Carlos."

"Uh, hi. You know who I am?"

"I make it a point to read up on my clients." He circles me. "Ronni's description didn't do you justice. You're simply gorgeous, darling, and once I'm done with you, you'll be nothing less than breathtaking."

"I don't want my hair cut."

"Why would you? It's perfect." He runs his fingers through my hair. "I'll give you a few layers here and some highlights there. I'll sculpt your brows. Oh, my. I must thank Ronni for sending me such a fine specimen."

"This is my friend, Crew." I blush. I've never had to introduce him to anyone before, and I'm not sure how to do it. He did say we're a *we* the other day.

"Friend. Right. The two of you together will burn down the house." He squeals. "Oh, the hotness. I wish I could bottle it."

"Where do you want me?"

He escorts me to a chair in front of a large mirror, then drags another one over for Crew. "Sit, my boy. Your hair is simply delicious. I'm sorry to say there's not a thing I would do to it."

We sit and listen to Carlos gossip about his other clients, most of whom are either famous or rich. An hour later, I'm taken back to the sink to get my hair washed. It's heavenly the way Carlos massages my scalp.

"You're going to look fabulous. Trust me," he says, wrapping my hair in a towel. "Now don't peek until I'm finished, okay?"

He turns the chair so I can't see myself in the mirror. My back straightens when he gets out his shears. "Carlos—" I lean away from the scissors. "I know Ronni wants me to cut my hair, but I'm really against it. I mean it when I say please don't."

He puts down the scissors and leans in, his hands on the arms of my chair. "Sweet Brianna. I don't care if the Pope himself tells me to cut your hair. I won't do it unless you say so. A few layers only. I give you my word."

"Okay. My friends call me Bria."

Carlos smiles and picks up the scissors.

I'm still nervous, especially when I see hair falling on the floor, but Crew's smile assures me it's okay. I watch him the whole time.

After Carlos blow-dries my hair, Crew's smile fades. I try to get a glimpse in the mirror, but Carlos won't let me. "What is it? Is my hair orange or something?"

"It's magnificent," Carlos says. "You'll see soon enough."

Crew is looking at me like he's seen a ghost.

"Crew?"

He pinches the bridge of his nose. "Carlos, is there a bathroom I can use?"

Carlos points to the back of the salon. "I hope your friend is okay. He looked a little green."

"I'm sure he's fine." But I'm not sure. His violent mood swings confuse the hell out of me.

Carlos gets out his curling iron and does things with it. "Perfect," he says. "Do you want to wait for him for the big reveal?"

I shake my head, wondering what's taking him so long.

"Here we go," Carlos says and turns the chair around.

I'm stunned. It's me, only better. Sun-kissed highlights span the length of my hair and wispy long layers give it a casual, beachy look. My brows are sculpted in a way that make my eyes stand out more than they did before.

I turn and hug Carlos. "I love it!"

He hugs me back. "Of course you do. I'm a genius with hair. Tell all your famous friends."

"I don't have any famous friends."

"I suspect you will soon, honey."

Crew returns, and his eyes are glued to my head. Carlos was right. He looks green. I twirl around in a circle. "What do you think? I could easily pass for a California girl, right?"

Crew heads for the door. "I'll wait for you outside."

Carlos shrugs. "It must be the smell of the color that got to him. Some people can't handle it."

"Yeah, must be," I say, not believing it for a second.

I get out my wallet, but Carlos pushes my hand away. "Your visit has been covered, including tip. You're good to go, girl. Promise me you'll come back every month for a touchup."

"I promise."

I exit the salon. Crew is sitting on a bench. I sit next to him. "You don't like it?"

"It's not that."

"Then what is it? You're acting really strange."

He runs a hand across the cover of his notebook. "There's something I want to show you."

"Okay."

He flips through it, stops on a page, and bends the cover back. He hesitates for the longest time before placing it on my lap.

I'm almost afraid to look at it, but when I see the first few words, I can do nothing but smile. I run my finger under the lyrics as I read them.

When your eyes locked with mine,
I went out of my mind
I fell head over heels for you
Though we never had words

and we came from different worlds
Somehow I felt I always knew

(chorus)
New girl, you slay me
The way you disobey me
New girl, you own me
As if you've always known me

I'm grinning so big, my face splits. "This is beautiful."
Crew still looks sick. "Keep reading."
I look back at the page for the second verse.

That California sky,
reflected in your eyes
You put me under your spell
We were only seventeen,
going after our own dreams
We told the world to go to hell

With a kind of shock, I realize the song is not about me. It's about *her*.

I read the rest of it. He was in love with her, that's for sure.

"This is about Abby."

He nods.

"Was she your high school girlfriend?"

He looks down the street in the other direction. "I can't talk about it."

"Then why show me the song?"

"Because you need to know how fucked up I am."

"What happened, Chris?"

He takes his notebook from me and stands. "I'll walk you home."

We are silent, though I want to ask many questions. He moves farther and farther away from me with each step we take.

When we're almost to my place, a familiar man comes out of the alley, asking for money. He touches my arm.

"I don't have any cash," I say, recognizing the homeless man as Jonah, one of the regulars who begs on this street.

Before I realize what's happening, Crew punches him in the face. Blood instantly appears on Jonah's lip. "Crew! Stop it," I yell, yanking him off. Jonah runs away. "What's wrong with you?"

"He was robbing you."

"No he wasn't. He was asking for money. There's a big difference."

"He put his hand on you," he says, staring at the place where Jonah touched my arm.

"Jonah didn't mean anything by it."

"Jonah? You *know* him?"

"He's a nice man. A little slow but harmless."

"Are you kidding me? Nobody's harmless."

"He's hungry, Crew. Sometimes I give him my leftovers."

"You encourage him?"

I'm confused by his behavior. "What's going on here?"

"Nothing. Sorry. I overreacted."

"You think?"

I unlock the outer door, and we go upstairs. Crew doesn't follow me into my apartment. He's staring at my hair again.

Finally, he averts his eyes. "I promised Gary I'd help him do some painting. I have to go."

"You're not staying for dinner? I was going to make spaghetti."

"I really have to go." He backs away, putting more distance between us. "Another night. Lock the door."

"Crew?"

"Sorry," he says and runs down the stairs.

I sit on my couch, remembering the song he shared with me. Is that his way of letting me into his past—or telling me I can't be his future?

Rather than drive myself crazy, I fetch peroxide and bandages, and make a quick turkey sandwich, wrapping it in tin foil. Then I go in search of Jonah.

Chapter Twenty-eight

Crew

Garrett gives me the stink-eye during our break and corners me in the hallway. "What's up with you tonight? Are you sick or something?"

"No."

"Then why do you sound like my goddamn grandma?"

I don't argue with him. I know I don't sound great tonight, but I can't look at her, and that prevents me from singing the way I need to sing.

"You have to get it together," he says. "We're playing at the hottest club in Manhattan on Friday. Whatever the problem is, find a way to fix it."

He walks away. I force myself to look at Bria. Why did Ronni make her do that to her hair? Worse, Bria seems to like it.

I go to the bar and order a shot of whiskey, but I stop after one. No matter how much I want to drink, I won't be any good onstage if I do. I can't perform drunk.

Every song I sing, I do it with my eyes closed, trying to give the crowd the performance they deserve. When I play backup guitar, I look at the strings even though I don't need to. But it's better than looking at her.

When our set is over, the proprietor escorts us to a table and offers us free drinks. I make sure to sit next to Bria so I don't have to look at her across the table. She puts her hand on my thigh. I squeeze it to let her know all is well.

"You really found your stride after the break," she says.

"Is that your way of telling me I sucked during the first set?"

She leans close. "You never suck."

I try not to look at her. I reach for another drink.

A few women approach us. One of them leans down, flashing her cleavage. "Mind if we join you?"

Garrett hops up, offering Big Boobs his chair as he pulls over a few others.

"Hi, ladies," Liam says, making room for them.

I move my chair closer to Bria's.

"You guys were really good up there," the brunette says. "I'm Lisa, and this is Alyssa and Tara."

Lisa seems enamored with Garrett and his tattoos.

Alyssa and Tara are focused on me. "Can I buy you a drink?" Tara says, looking directly at me.

I raise my glass. "I'm good, but thanks for the offer."

"Is there anything else I can do for you?" she asks, running a finger from her chin down to the top of her low-cut shirt.

Her friend elbows her. "I think they're together."

Tara looks between me and Bria. I drape my arm around Bria's shoulders.

"Just my luck," Tara says. She turns her attention to Liam. "What about you? Are you single?"

He gives me a withering look. "Why do I always end up with your sloppy seconds?"

Alyssa and Tara lean into him. "There's nothing sloppy about us," Alyssa says. "Take us in back, and we'll show you."

Liam downs a shot. "Lead the way."

Bria looks shocked. "Is he really going to have sex with them? *Both* of them? *Here?*"

"Stranger things have happened," Brad says.

Brad and I have a long conversation about Liam's sexual antics. I realize I'm ignoring Bria. I hope she doesn't notice. I sneak a look at her, wondering if the more I drink, the less her hair will bother me.

She eyes the many shot glasses in front of me. "If you're just going to sit here and get drunk, I'm leaving."

"It's dark outside. You're not leaving."

"I *am* leaving, Crew. There's really no point in my being here anyway." She wiggles out from under my arm and stands.

"I'll walk you home then."

"No thank you."

"Bria, it's late."

"I'm perfectly capable of finding my way home. I'm not the one who's been drinking."

Brad stands. "I'll make sure she gets home."

"I do *not* need an escort," she insists.

Two girls cross to our table. I roll my eyes, not wanting to deal with more fans, but instead of talking to me or the guys, one of them hugs Bria. I go on full alert, and I'm about to pull them apart when Bria squeals, "You came! I wasn't sure you'd make it."

"We saw your last four or five songs. Brutus at the door wouldn't let us in until some people left."

Bria turns to us. "Did you hear that? We had the place packed!"

"Sweet!" Garrett says, taking a break from sucking face with Lisa.

"These are my friends, Katherine and Lola."

I hold out my hand. "I'm Crew, and that's Brad and Garrett. Liam should be back soon."

"Crew," Lola says. "Right. We know all about you."

They do? Bria's expression gives nothing away, except she's still mad at me.

"I was getting ready to leave," Bria tells them.

"You're not going home, are you?" Katherine says. "We haven't hung out in ages. Come clubbing with us."

"Yes, Bria, go clubbing," I say with a tight jaw. "Oh, wait, we're already *in* a club."

She hooks elbows with them. "We're leaving. See you at rehearsal."

"Guess you don't need to walk her home," I say spitefully, pulling out Brad's chair for him.

Brad looks at me sideways. "You don't want her going out with her friends? Or you don't want her going with them when she's pissed at you?"

I down another shot.

"What's wrong with your girlfriend?" Lisa asks.

"She's not my ..." —I run a hand through my hair— "Forget it."

I take another shot and get up to use the bathroom. Alyssa and Tara storm past me, going the other way.

"Your friend is a pervert," Tara says. "What kind of creep doesn't want a girl to touch his dick?"

Alyssa brushes against me. "I'll bet *you're* not a pervert, and your girlfriend will never know."

I push her away. *"I'd* know."

She huffs her displeasure and they leave, presumably to find their next conquest.

Liam comes through a door in back, sees me, and tries to act all cool. "Got a cigarette?"

"You don't smoke."

He gestures vaguely. "Yeah, but after that. Wow."

"You're such a liar, dude. I just ran into them. They said you were a perv."

He laughs. "Yeah, that about sums it up. Some girls just don't want to go down on each other while you jack off watching."

My jaw drops. "You asked them to … *here?*"

"I saw an opportunity."

"Dude."

"Right. Like I'm any more fucked up than the famous Chris Rewey. Don't act like you aren't, man. You can't even look at her, can you? It's the hair. I noticed it too. You should tell her."

I lean against the wall. "Tell her what? That every time I look at her it hurts like hell because all I can see is my dead girlfriend?"

"She needs to know. You're acting like a douche. It's not fair to her."

"She'll dump me."

"Maybe that's not the worst thing. If you can't get over this, you shouldn't be together."

I continue to the bathroom door. "You don't know what the hell you're talking about."

He clamps down on my arm. "I may be a dozen shades of fucked up, but I know you can't keep doing this. It's eating away at you. I can see how much you like her, and I'm pretty sure she's in love with you."

My eyes snap to his. "She's not."

"You wouldn't know, would you, since you can't look at her and all. But I see how she looks at you. We all do."

I sink against the wall. "Fuck."

"Either tell her and let the chips fall where they may, or end it and let her get on with her life."

"Says the guy who can't get on with *his* life."

"Hey now, we're talking about you, not me. I'm all too aware that I'm a therapist's wet fucking dream." He points to the bathroom. "Go take a whiz. I'll order us a few more shots. Looks like we both need it."

"Better make it more than a few."

When I return to the table, it's covered in shot glasses. "Think it's enough?" I ask Liam.

"It's a start."

A half-hour later, Brad shakes his head at all the empties in front of Liam and me. "You guys better not puke on the way home."

"It's a good thing Jeremy hired us a driver," Garrett says, downing another.

"I could have driven," Brad says. "I promised Katie I'd stay sober tonight and stop by her place after."

I shove a glass at him. "Not when we're done with you. Come on. Misery loves company."

"I'm not miserable. In fact, I've never been happier."

"Well, aren't you the golden child. Perfect fucking Brad, with his perfect fucking girlfriend and his perfect fucking life."

He clinks his glass against mine. "I'll toast to that."

"How come Katie never comes to our gigs?" Liam asks.

"She's not into rock music. Or drinking."

Liam looks at Brad like he's crazy. "And that makes her the perfect girl for you? At least pick someone who's going to support your chosen profession."

"She supports me. She just doesn't like the scene, that's all."

Liam snorts. "It'll never last."

"You're wrong," Brad says defensively. "This is the real deal."

Liam turns to us. "You guys want to take bets on this?"

"On whether Brad's relationship crumbles or not?" I ask. "Count me out."

"Hey, want to get high on the way home?" Garrett asks when Lisa leaves to find her friends.

"Hell yeah," Liam says. "Wait—no. Is this another one of your practical jokes?"

Garrett pulls a joint out of his pocket. "This is some real shit. A buddy of mine who came to the show gave it to me."

I may be drunk, but I know that isn't something Liam should get into again. He smoked pot all the time in high school. It took me years to convince him to stop. I lived every day in fear that it would lead to something else. "Put that shit away."

Liam thinks I can't hear him when he whispers to Garrett, "Count me in."

"Don't do it, man," I say.

"Don't you have enough of your own problems?" he says, handing me another shot. "Quit worrying about mine."

An hour later, we stumble out to the van. Bruce, our driver, already packed up our gear. He grins when he sees us. "You can sleep it off on the way back."

I tap on his shoulder from the seat behind him. "I'm not going back. Can you drop me at Bria's?"

"Do you think that's a good idea?" Liam slurs. He thinks about it. "Actually, yeah, drop him at Bria's." He leans close. "Drunk people are more honest. Just lay it all out there."

"That's not why I'm going."

"Midnight bootie call," Garrett shouts.

I high-five him.

"She seemed pretty upset with you, Crew," Brad says. "Maybe we should stick around until you're sure she'll let you in."

"She'll let him in," Liam says. "She luuuuuuvs him."

"Shut up," I say, punching him in the arm.

"You all see that shit? If I can't play tomorrow, you'll know why."

"If you can't play tomorrow, it's because you got shit-faced."

"All's good," he says and passes out.

I'm glad. It means he won't get high with Garrett.

Bruce drops me at Bria's. I walk around to the alley and look up at her dark windows. Maybe this wasn't such a good idea after all. I tug on the door in case it's not locked, but it is. I get out my phone and call her.

"Crew?" she answers sleepily. "Is everything okay?"

"I'm downstairs."

"You're *here?*"

"Yeah. Can you let me in?"

"Are you drunk?"

"Very. You?"

"No." She sighs. "I'll be right there."

She comes to the door wearing a short robe. I look around, making sure nobody else is watching.

"You shouldn't walk around your building like that," I say, pushing her up the stairs.

"You shouldn't come to my place at two in the morning."

She turns on the light when we go inside. I immediately turn it off. "I feel a headache coming on," I lie.

"Did you come here to have sex?"

"No."

"Liar."

I lead her to the couch and drop my notebook on the table. "No, really. We can just sit here."

"You want to sit?"

"Sure, why not? So what did you do with your friends?"

"We had a drink at another bar, then came back here to talk. It was fun. I haven't seen them since last fall. I was so consumed with White Poison and then RA that I've let a lot of my friendships slide."

I can see her gazing at me in the moonlight. It's not bright enough to see the color of her hair, for which I'm grateful. I touch it, rubbing a lock between my fingers. "You really like the new hair?"

"I do. Kat and Lola said they loved it. Don't you?"

Her phone vibrates, saving me from having to answer.

"Who's texting you at two in the morning?"

"It's probably Brett. He's always checking up on me. He texted me earlier, wondering why I left the bar right after our gig when we usually stay after. I was catching up with Kat and Lola and forgot to get back to him. He's on shift tonight."

"You told him you left early?"

"No. He saw on that app that tracks my phone."

"Your brother tracks your phone?"

She laughs. "He does. I guess it makes him feel better when he knows where I am."

I pick up my phone and tap around on it until I find what I'm searching for. Hers vibrates. She reads the message, alerting her to my request. "You want to track my phone, too?"

"It might make *me* feel better." I can just make out the smile on her face.

"That's getting dangerously close to girlfriend territory, isn't it, Chris?"

"Just accept the damn invitation."

"Fine, but it goes both ways. I get to see where you are, too." She puts down her phone.

I hand it right back to her. "Text him back."

"I'll do it later."

"Do it now."

"What's the big deal?"

"The big deal is that he's worried about you, and it's two in the morning." I take the phone from her and type a text as if I'm her.

"You're worse than he is," she says, scowling.

It may be dark in here, but I'm not totally blind. Her robe falls open, and she's wearing sleep shorts that barely cover her ass. I touch her thigh. "I think we've done enough sitting."

"So this *is* a bootie call?"

"Is that such a bad thing?"

She shrugs, sinking deeper into the couch. I scoop her into my arms. Moonlight falls across her face, and all I see is Abby. I carry her to the bed and draw the curtains, making it darker. I join her under the covers and will myself to think only of Bria. When I touch her, I close my eyes and picture the brunette she used to be.

Chapter Twenty-nine

Bria

Crew takes off his clothes before stripping me of what little I'm wearing. I can taste the alcohol when he kisses me. He's drunker than I've ever seen him. It's not so dark that I can't see his eyes are closed. This makes me sad, because he's always looked at me when we're in bed.

He crawls down my body, putting his mouth on either breast, then my stomach. He hesitates when he reaches my scar, as always. Sometimes I wonder if it bothers him. Does he somehow see me as damaged?

He feathers kisses along my inner thighs, puts a finger inside me, and groans when he finds me wet and ready. When his tongue circles my clit, I inhale sharply. My insides coil, and I'm surprised at what I'm allowing. I'm angry at him. I almost pull away, feeling like maybe I shouldn't be doing this with him when he's been acting so indifferent lately.

Indifferent. Yes, that's it. I couldn't put my finger on it until now. Maybe he's trying to figure out how to dump me. "Crew."

He doubles his efforts, thinking I'm saying his name because I'm about to come. For the second time in my life, I fake an orgasm. I buck my hips and squeeze his fingers with my walls, hoping he doesn't see through me.

Sadness washes over me when I remember the last time I faked it. Am I going down the same road all over again?

He moves up beside me and passes out. I'm relieved. I'm not sure what I would have done if he'd wanted to make love.

I get up and collect my sleeping clothes on my way to the bathroom. I close the door and stand at the sink. "Why did you let him touch you?" I ask the girl in the mirror. "He doesn't even seem to want you anymore."

Tears flow as I sit on the toilet and feel sorry for myself. I can't believe I let this happen again. I shouldn't have gotten involved. "You're so stupid," I say.

"What'd you say?" I hear from the other side of the door. I quickly dress and splash cold water on my face before opening the door.

I leave the light in the bathroom on. Crew is sitting on my couch with a beer. He's wearing only boxers.

"Didn't have enough yet?" I ask bitterly.

"You're mad at me," he slurs.

"You think?"

"I'm sorry," he says, rubbing the front of his boxers. "It doesn't work so well after a dozen shots. I'll make it up to you later."

"I'm not mad because you couldn't get it up. Relieved is more like it. Just go to bed."

The front door handle rattles. Someone is trying to get in. Crew may be drunk, but he flies off the couch and opens the door to Brody, my upstairs neighbor. He stumbles inside, looking unkempt with his straggly beard and wrinkled clothes.

"What the fuck do you think you're doing?" Crew yells.

Brody looks at Crew, taking in his half-nakedness, then at me. "What are you doing in my apartment?"

"This isn't your apartment, Brody. Yours is one floor up."

He looks around at my stuff. "Well shit, I did it again."

"You know this asshole?" Crew says.

"No need to call me names, buddy. Honest mistake."

"You're honestly wasted."

I snort and say, "Said the pot to the kettle."

He flashes me an annoyed look, then shoves Brody into the hall, closes the door, and engages all four locks. "How many times has he mistaken your place for his?"

"Once or twice."

He grabs his beer and drinks. "Shit." He stumbles over the coffee table, knocking everything off it, including a glass of water. I run to get a towel.

"Let me," he says, taking it from me.

"Fine. I'm going back to bed. Turn off the light when you're finished."

I crawl into bed and hug the pillow tightly against me. He's quiet, and I wonder if he conked out on the couch. But a few minutes later, he turns off the bathroom light, comes to bed, and spoons me. "I'm sorry."

"What are you sorry for?"

"For whatever I did. The water. The sex. Everything."

"Okay. Go to sleep."

He breathes evenly in my ear. When I think he's drifted off, he surprises me by saying, "I think you should move in with me."

I stop breathing. "Where did *that* come from?"

"Don't you want to?" he slurs.

I turn and face him, barely able to see his eyes. "Crew, do you love me?"

He stiffens. "That's kind of a loaded question, don't you think?"

"Maybe, but it's an easy one. Either you love me or you don't."

He rolls onto his back. "I told you, Bria, I'm fucked up. I'm not even sure I'm capable of that."

"Capable of love? Or capable of commitment? Because moving in together seems like one hell of a commitment." I get up and pace. "What's going on here? One minute you can't look at me and the next you're asking me to cohabit. Yeah, that's all kinds of fucked up, if you ask me. What's come over you lately? I thought earlier you might want out of this relationship, or whatever it is we have, and now you throw *this* at me?" I go to my fridge and get a bottle of water. "I just faked an orgasm. Do you want to know why? Because I didn't know if you liked me anymore, and I'm so confused that instead of pushing you away, I faked it. Who does that? Not to mention you're so drunk you answered the door in your skivvies." Realization dawns, and I lean against the kitchen counter. "We shouldn't be having this conversation, considering the state you're in. You won't remember it in the morning. Just go to sleep."

He doesn't respond.

"Crew?"

I go closer and hear him snoring.

I sit beside him, half hoping he'll wake up so we can clear the air. I poke him but he doesn't move. "Just great."

I cross to the sink and stub my toe on the coffee table because Crew put it back the wrong way. Sitting on the couch, I rub my toe.

My phone pings with a text. It's Brett, thanking me for replying. It lights up the coffee table, and that's when I see Crew's notebook, and it's open. Did he leave it that way on purpose or did it happen when the table fell over?

I close my eyes and bite my lip. *Don't do it.*

Really, though, is it my fault he left it like that, open for anyone to read? If I look but don't touch it, am I breaking the rules?

I hesitantly pick up my phone and turn on the flashlight, looking back at Crew to make sure he's still sleeping. Then I scoot to the edge of the couch and look. As soon as I see the title at the top of the page, 'Right to Die,' I know I'm going to read it. I take a deep breath.

I'm alone with my bottle
Searching for a friend
Looking for my heart
Coming up empty again

(chorus)
I have no right to die, or I'd have gone long ago
I'm living as a dead man—no hope, no soul
Never knew it'd hurt this hard.
Limb by limb being pulled apart

My heart jumps when I hear a sound. I turn the flashlight off and glance at the bed. After my eyes adjust to the darkness, I see he's turned over. I turn the light back on.

Give me blue, brown, or clear
Don't care if it's plastic or glass
I'll drink until it's empty
Drive until I'm out of gas

The pain becomes too much
It's blinding and complete
I know what I have to do
I have to die so we can meet

There's one more verse, but I can't read it through my tears. I close the notebook, knowing I've violated his privacy by reading his most intimate thoughts. He wants to die? I open it again. The song is near the beginning, so it's old. Does he still feel this way? He has to die to be with her?

I sink back into the couch, two thoughts clouding my head: one—Abby's dead? How awful for Crew, that must have been horrible; and two—Abby's dead. How do I compete with a ghost?

Chapter Thirty

Crew

Seven years ago

I am horrorstruck as police cordon off Abby's car and the surrounding area. An officer says to Mom and me, "We'd like you to come to the station to give a statement."

"Right away." Mom starts to her car, then pauses. "Chris, you coming?"

I hear her, but I can't move. My feet are cemented to the ground as a cop places a numbered piece of plastic next to Abby's phone and then takes fifty pictures of it. I've seen this a million times on TV. They think this is evidence, but of what? My stomach flips again, but there's nothing left to bring up.

I feel Mom's hand on my shoulder. "Chris?"

I look at her and then back at Abby's car. I don't want to leave. I feel if I go, I'll never see Abby again.

"Folks, we need you to clear the area," a cop says.

Mom tugs on my arm. "They need us at the police station."

As we walk away, I see the police talking to some of the employees I spoke with inside the restaurant. One of them points to me.

Mom drives us to the police station across town. My phone blows up with texts. After glancing at a few of them, I realize word has spread. I can't look at it anymore. I shut it off and put it in the cup holder.

At the station, we're escorted down a hall. We pass a room with a glass door. Abby's parents are inside. They look up and see me, their terrified expressions matching mine.

Mom is introduced to Officer Hanley, who will take her statement at a desk in a room with other desks. I am taken into a private room by Detective Abrahms. We sit at a table across from one another. Behind him is what is probably a two-way mirror, and I wonder if anyone is watching me.

"What's going on?" I ask.

He puts a pad of paper and a pen on the table. "Your full name?"

"Chris Rewey. Uh, Christopher."

"Mind if I have a look at your driver's license?"

I take it out of my wallet and hand it to him. "Sir, can you please tell me what's happening?"

"Your relationship to Ms. Evans?"

"Boyfriend."

He makes notes and hands me back the license.

There is a notch in the table. A notch where one might hook handcuffs to keep someone restrained. "Am I in some kind of trouble?"

"That's what I'm here to determine."

I narrow my eyes. "Don't you have to read me my rights or something if you're going to question me?"

"Do I need to read you your rights?" he asks, features hard.

"No. Of course not."

"I'll start by getting your statement then. You are welcome to have a lawyer present when I take it."

"Why would I need a lawyer? I told everything to one of the officers at the restaurant."

He flips through the pad. "You said you were looking for Miss Evans because she didn't show up at a concert?"

"That's right."

"Is there anyone who can corroborate your attendance at the event in the hours leading up to Miss Evans's disappearance?"

"Only about three hundred people. I'm the lead singer for one of the bands that performed. I was there all afternoon leading up to the concert. Listen, if you think I had anything to do with whatever happened to her, I don't. I'm her boyfriend. I love her."

He raises his eyebrows at me.

I draw back. "And the boyfriend is always the chief suspect, huh?"

"You catch on quickly, son."

He gets a call on his phone, stands up, and paces while listening, staring at me the entire time. Putting his phone down, he gazes at me with sympathy.

"What? Will someone please tell me what's going on?"

"I just got word that you aren't a person of interest in this case."

"What does that mean?"

"It means you don't need a lawyer, and we're not going to detain you."

I stand. "Then I can leave."

"Yes, but I'd appreciate it if you stayed. If you're as close to Miss Evans as you say you are, you may have information pertinent to the case."

"There's a case?"

"We've confirmed she's missing. It's my job to determine if it's voluntary or not."

"As in she threw all the shit from her purse on the ground, left her car, and took off?"

He shrugs. "It happens more often than you think."

"That's not what happened."

"How can you be sure?"

I contemplate not telling him, but I'm scared shitless and protecting our secret is the least of my worries. "Because she's pregnant."

"How far along?"

"Almost six months, but no one knows except the two of us and my mother."

He makes more notes on the pad. "Who's the father?"

"Who do you think? I am."

He gives me a hard stare. "Are you sure about that?"

"Yes. She's never been with anyone else."

"You're certain there isn't another man?"

My jaw clenches. "I'm positive."

"What about a male family member? Are you aware of any history of abuse?"

"Abuse? No. That's crazy."

"So there's no possibility she was sexually assaulted, which led to a pregnancy she's trying to cover up? No possibility someone could have hurt her?"

"Why would anyone want to hurt—" Bile rises in my throat, and I swallow convulsively. "Oh, shit."

"What is it?"

"There's a man Abby used to work with. He's older than we are. He liked her to the point of being stalkerish. He got fired but still came to the restaurant to talk to her. I was there when he came in last week. I confronted him and told him to fuck off. He was pissed, but he left." The blood leaves my face. "You think he could have taken her?"

"His name?"

"Rob. I don't know his last name. He's in his thirties, I think. He works at a gas station now. Her manager can tell you his full name." I groan. "This is all my fault, isn't it?"

"How could it be your fault, son?"

"Because I told him to fuck off. I told him if he ever came near her again, I would hunt him down and" —I scrub my hand across my face— "...kill him."

He lets out a sigh.

"Am I in trouble now?"

"No. Wait here a minute."

He leaves the room. While he's gone, I sit again, and the tears I suppressed when he was here finally fall. *What did I do to her?* I look at the clock. More than four hours have passed since she went missing. Part of me hopes the detective is right about people wanting to disappear. Maybe her dad found out she was pregnant and threatened to make her give up the baby, so she ran away. It almost makes sense. She'd only have to hide for a week. But would she really go so far as to fake an abduction? No, she'd have told me, and she'd have skipped work if there was trouble at home.

Detective Abrahms returns and sits. "We've issued a BOLO for Robert Vargas. He'll be brought in for questioning." He gets out his notepad. "I want you to tell me everything about Abby Evans, from the moment you met her."

Chapter Thirty-one

Bria

I knock on the door, worried that I'm crossing a line, but I don't know what else to do.

The door opens, and Mrs. Rewey pales, like she's seen a ghost. She blinks a lot and doesn't speak.

"What's going on?" I ask. "You're looking at me the same way Crew does lately." I sink against the doorframe. "He's going to break up with me, isn't he? I knew it. I'm sorry to have bothered you."

Before I can escape, she hauls me into her apartment. "There's something you need to see."

She takes a picture off the wall and hands it to me. It's a photo of Crew when he was younger and thinner, standing next to a girl. A girl whose hair looks exactly like mine. They're singing into the same microphone. He's gazing at her the same way he looks at me when we sing. Or the way he did until recently.

"This is Abby?" I say.

"He hasn't told you about her?"

"I'm confused. He started to act strange after I got my hair done. It's not like he was altogether normal before that, but this last week has been horrible. I have to know, just who is she?"

"Come. Sit."

We settle in the living room. I take the picture with me. I can't stop staring at it. Abby is gazing straight at the camera while Crew is looking only at her. It's clear he's in love with her. "What happened, Mrs. Rewey?"

"Please call me Shelly. Can I get you a drink? Water maybe?"

"Yes, thank you."

While she's in the kitchen, I go to the mirror on the wall and look at myself next to the picture. Aside from our hair, which is the same color and length, we don't look alike. She has blue eyes, mine are green. I have more freckles and a thinner nose. I'm taller than she is.

Shelly comes back, catching me at the mirror. "It's mostly the hair."

"And we're both singers."

"There is that."

"Tell me what happened. I know he was in love with her. I've seen some of his songs."

Her eyes light up. "He showed you?"

Guilt consumes me. "He showed me one. I thought it was about me at first. Then the other night, he left his notebook open, and I ... I shouldn't have, but I couldn't help myself."

Shelly touches my arm. "You were curious. It's human nature. Don't beat yourself up about it."

"But the song was so private. I think it was about him wanting to die."

She inhales sharply. "It was a tough time for him, after Abby died."

My eyes snap to hers. "She died?"

She looks guilty. "I thought you knew."

"I suspected, but I wasn't sure. How did it happen?"

"Bria, I don't mean to be rude, but Chris needs to tell you in his own way. It would be better for both of you."

"I guess you're right, but it's hard."

"He likes you very much, I can tell. He showed you one of his songs about her. That's a step in the right direction."

"I thought he showed it to me to let me know he could never feel that way about me."

"I doubt that. Chris might feel more than the average person. Maybe that's why he writes good songs. I suspect you're the same way, which is why this is so hard for you. I can see how much you care for him. Not many young women would have the courage to show up and ask questions. It tells me you're willing to fight for him. And perhaps that's exactly what he needs."

"Maybe now it will be a little easier. How long do you think he needs to get over her?"

"Grief doesn't have a timetable. To some, seven years is a lifetime. To others, it can seem like yesterday."

"She died seven years ago?"

She nods.

"They were high school sweethearts?"

"Yes."

"And you were close to her?"

"She was like a daughter to me."

That makes me sad.

Shelly sees the tears pooling in my eyes. She puts her arm around me. "But that doesn't mean there's not room for more. In my heart and Chris's."

"My mom died."

"I know. Chris told me."

"He talks about me?"

"Yes. I'm very sorry about your mom. What a horrible day that must have been."

"I was so young, I don't even remember her."

She touches the picture. "That's why photos are important. They help us remember the faces of those we've loved. It doesn't mean we can't love others just because we keep them around."

I think about the empty spots on Chris's bookshelf, where he obviously keeps photos of her.

"Do you think he's still suicidal?"

"He's sad, stuck in an emotional rut. He's also holding on to a lot of guilt, but he's not suicidal. Music has helped him when nothing else could. I think you're helping him, too."

"Me? I think I'm making things worse."

"You are forcing him to come to terms with the past and making him think about a future. You're doing everything right. Don't change a thing."

I look at the young girl in the picture. "Can I ask you one more question? Did she call him Christopher?"

She nods, then she takes the picture from me, walks across the room, and hangs it. She stares at a blank spot on the wall. "There is an empty spot right here that needs another photo." She glances at me. "I bet it won't be too long before I'm hanging a picture of you."

I drop my eyes.

She sits next to me. "You love my son, don't you?"

"Is it that obvious?"

She laughs. "No, but you wouldn't be here if you didn't. Give him time, Bria. I promise he's worth waiting for. Why don't you stay for lunch? I'll make sandwiches. You need energy for tonight's performance. Chris tells me it's a big one."

I stand, ready to accept her invitation, and catch a glimpse of myself in the mirror. "Thanks for the offer but I'll have to take a raincheck."

"My door's always open," she says. "I mean that. Sometimes a little motherly advice is just what the doctor ordered."

I smile. "Motherly advice. I'd like that. Thank you."

As soon as I'm out the door, I make a call. "Carlos, I have an emergency. Can you work me in right now?"

Chapter Thirty-two

Crew

Ronni wanted us all to meet at IRL before our big night. The guys and I arrived a little while ago. We're waiting on Bria.

"Sit," Ronni says after squirting something in her hands.

I eye her suspiciously.

"Just do it, Crew."

I sit in front of her and she rubs goo through my hair. She plays with it for a few minutes, circling me until she gets it just right. Her boobs almost touch my face as she leans over.

"There," she says.

I go to the mirror. My hair is spiky and haphazard. I try to touch it, but she bats away my hand. "Leave it. The girls will love it. It looks like you rolled out of bed, and they want to fantasize it was *their* bed. Some of the guys will like it too."

I turn to Garrett. "What do you say? Does this make you want to fuck me?"

He throws a drumstick at my head. I duck and it flies by, narrowly missing Ronni. She jumps into my arms to avoid it. We fall back onto a chair and I catch her on my lap. She looks down at me, laughs, and shimmies. "Maybe I should thank him for that."

The door opens, and Bria walks in. Her eyes open wide when she sees Ronni on top of me. I quickly stand and put her on her feet. I feel guilty even though I didn't do anything. She keeps watching me, but instead of being mad, she smiles.

I can't take my eyes off her, and it takes me a few seconds to figure out why.

"Brianna, what the hell have you done?" Ronni spits.

Garrett walks around Bria. "Wow."

She's gone back to her old hair color—I guess she didn't like the new highlights after all—and she's cut it, even though she was so against it. It falls just below her chin and is uneven, with longer layers in front and short in back.

I push past Garrett. "Dang, I've changed my mind about long hair being sexier. I kind of like Bria 3.0."

She laughs. "I'm glad you approve."

"Approve? I love it."

"This is not what we agreed on," Ronni says, looking displeased. "It's so boring."

"I didn't like it the other way," Bria says. "So I thought I'd compromise and go back to brown but cut it like you wanted."

Ronni is pissed. I'm not sure why, because Bria looks fantastic.

"The car's here," Jeremy says. "We hardly have time to do anything about it now. Besides, I think Brianna is stunning."

"You mean hot," Liam says.

Bria smiles.

"What car?" Garrett asks. "I thought Bruce was waiting out back with the van."

"You're not going in the van," Ronni says. "Come on."

A stretch limo is parked outside. The driver is holding the rear door open.

I say, "We can't afford this. Some of us are barely making rent."

"It's all about image," Ronni says. "If you arrive in a passenger van with all your equipment, people think you're a street band, working for pennies."

"Ronni, we *are* a street band working for pennies."

"Listen. If you show up in a limo, people will assume you're important. Pretty soon, if enough people think you're important, you'll *be* important."

"It won't matter how important we are if we're living on the streets."

She motions for me to get in, then climbs in after me, sitting next to me and leaving no room for Bria. Bria sits next to Liam, who continues to tell her how hot she is, probably because he's the only one who knew she resembled Abby. She looks nothing like Abby now. Relief washes over me.

"You'll play two sets," Jeremy tells us. "Ronni would like you to mingle with the club patrons after."

"What exactly does that mean?" Brad asks.

Ronni says, "Be chatty. Sign autographs. Pose for pictures. Dance with people. Make them want more of Reckless Alibi."

Bria cocks her head. "You mean flirt."

"If that's what it takes, yes," Ronni says. "There will be a lot of money in that club. Important people. Influential people. You want them on your side."

Ronni and Jeremy give us more instructions along the way. When we arrive, there is already a crowd at the door. The driver waits until he can pull up directly in front of the building. Ronni instructs him to stay inside the car for five minutes. "We need to build excitement. People will wonder who's in the limousine, and the longer we wait to exit, the more hype there will be. I'll text the manager and have him send out two bouncers, so it looks like you need security."

When she's convinced enough time has passed, she tells the driver to open the door. Ronni moves so she's boxing Bria in. She puts an arm across Bria, preventing her from getting up. "Boys first. Crew, you go."

I start to protest but Bria stops me. "It's fine. Go."

I flash Ronni an irritated look.

"Remember," she says. "You're stars. Act like it."

I exit the car. People swarm closer to get a look at us. Phones come out to snap pictures, but I doubt they even know who we are.

The bouncers are overdramatic when they "hold" people back. I'm beginning to think this entire night has been orchestrated.

Ronni comes out of the limo before Bria. I step back, ready to go in and get her, but Jeremy hustles me forward. "Stars," he says. "Come on. Brianna is a big girl."

Bria is the last to leave the car. It's ridiculous. I vow to talk with Ronni about this. We shouldn't have to put up with this shit. Bria is as much a part of RA as I am.

Ronni stops, letting Bria by, and shouts to the crowd. "Reckless Alibi will be available after the show for pictures and autographs. Thank you all for coming."

We're led through the bar to a back room that is our staging area. Food and a few bottles of liquor are on a table against one wall. Large buckets of ice are filled with cold beers and bottles of champagne. Liam goes right for the drinks.

"Might want to limit yourself to one or two until after the show," Ronni tells him.

"You trying to say something?" Liam asks.

Ronni ignores him, but it's obvious she's caught wind of his drinking habits. I might need to run interference where that is concerned. While I'm not excited about the amount of alcohol he consumes, I know why he does what he does, and it's none of her business. Liam and I have had each other's back since we were six. That won't change now.

Jeremy pops his head in. "Bruce has everything set up, and the sound check is complete. You're good to go."

I pour shots for the five of us, and we gather in a circle. "Ronni, can you give us a minute?"

She hesitates then spins on her stilettos and walks out the door.

"We need to put on our best performance. None of us are happy about how Ronni goes about things, but she's right. People have to think we're something more than we are. Let's go show them. On three."

"Let's get reckless!" we shout, clink our glasses together, and down our shots.

I let the others leave while discreetly holding Bria back. "Earlier, when you saw Ronni in my lap? Garrett threw a drumstick. She fell on me while dodging it."

"I didn't ask," she says.

"I know, but I just wanted you to know." I cage her to the wall and rub a lock of her hair between my fingers. "You're beautiful."

She smiles, eyes sparkling and cheeks glowing.

I lean close and whisper, "You're sexy, too." She pushes against me, and my dick twitches. I step back. "I'm not about to go out there in front of five hundred people with a boner."

She grabs my hand. "Come on, Chris Rewey, let's go rock this place."

For the next two hours, we rock the shit out of it. Bria and I put on a show like no other, and when I look at her, I see *her*.

Everyone in the club is on their feet, crowding the stage. The five of us are all smiles. Bria and I feed off each other, getting better as the show goes on. This is more exciting than opening for White Poison. The crowd there might have been fifty times bigger, but we weren't headlining. It's just us here. Reckless Alibi. We're making a name for ourselves, and it's the best feeling in the world.

When we leave the stage, people chant for us to come back. Rarely do we play encores in clubs or bars, but they're begging for more.

Jeremy finds us. "Can you hear that? Want me to tell the sound guys you're going back for another?"

"Ronni didn't include an encore song on the play list," Liam says.

Bria and I look at each other. "'On That Stage'," we say in sync.

"Hell yeah," Garrett says.

We run back out. The crowd goes crazy.

I cross to the mic. They get quiet. "Here's one I think you'll like. It's a personal favorite."

Ronni's at the end of the bar, talking to the manager. She doesn't look happy. She hates it when we play this one. Although Bria and I write all new material together, this song is clearly about us, and no matter how many times I've told Ronni we're together, she can't seem to accept it.

Garrett counts us off. Bria and I gaze at each other when Liam and Brad start to play. The first verse is hers. She sings it to me like she always does. Mine is next. I walk around behind her, and she dances while I sing. She shoves me in the chest during the third verse. I love it when she touches me onstage, and she knows it.

The song ends to thunderous applause. Bria runs over and jumps in my arms. I put down our mics and kiss her.

"We nailed it," I say.

We run offstage. Ronni is waiting, and she's pissed. "Do *not* kiss her onstage."

"Oh, relax," I say. "We were a little excited. The crowd was great, don't you think?"

Ronni steps closer, flames of anger simmering in her eyes. "Don't do it again. Ever."

"Don't you get it?" Bria says. "She thinks you'll be more desirable if the ladies think you're single."

I give Ronni the stink eye. "I'm not single."

"I don't see a ring on that finger," Ronni says. She cuts between Bria and me. "Until you're so famous that your image doesn't matter, you'll leave the decisions to me. Now come with me. There are people you need to meet." She looks over my shoulder. "Jeremy, please make sure the rest of them mingle."

"Just me?" I ask as she escorts me to the VIP section on the upper floor.

"The others will meet them too, but I think one at a time is best. That way, they'll get to know each one of you."

"Who is *they?*"

"Entrepreneurs, restaurant owners, radio execs—there's even a film producer here. I made the rounds during your show. They're all eager to meet you. I expect you to be on your best behavior."

I hate it when she treats us like children. "I'll try not to sneeze in their Cristal."

"Stop it," she says, irritated. Then she starts laughing like I said the funniest thing ever. It takes me a moment to realize the fake laugher is meant to draw attention to us.

For the next twenty minutes, Ronni introduces me to a dozen people with whom I have nothing in common. She doesn't leave my side the entire time, her arm laced tightly around my elbow.

I lean in and say, "For someone who doesn't want me to look spoken for, you sure are keeping me close."

She throws her head back and laughs again, putting on a show.

Somebody shoot me. She's even more fake than I gave her credit for.

A man takes her aside, and I finally get a chance to duck away. I stand on the balcony, watching the people below, scanning the crowd for Bria and the guys. She's near the bar, surrounded by three men. I look for Jeremy or one of the others, but nobody is with her. One of the men hands her a drink. She takes a sip.

I hurry downstairs and across the floor until I reach her. I take her drink and put it on the bar. "Come with me." The back hallway is quiet and dimly lit.

She smiles wryly. "Here?"

"Bria, what are you doing?" I ask sternly.

She's confused by my question. She looks out at the crowd and back at me. "I'm mingling, like Ronni told us."

"You took a drink from a stranger."

"I was standing at the bar."

"But your back was to it. He got the drink from the bartender and handed it to you. He could have slipped something into it."

She looks concerned. "Did he?"

"No, but he could have."

She slumps against the wall. "Crew, four band members and Jeremy are looking out for me. Nobody is going to drug me."

"There are five hundred people in this club. How long do you think it would take for the five of us to notice you're gone? Ten minutes? Five? By that time, you're in the back of someone's car."

She touches my cheek. "You're going a little overboard. I can take care of myself."

"I'm going back out there with you."

"Ronni's not going to like that very much."

"Screw Ronni. Maybe I'll stick my tongue down your throat on the dance floor."

She looks at me seductively. "You want to stick your tongue down my throat?"

I brush her hair behind her ear. "I want to stick my tongue in a lot of places."

She exhales slowly. "How long do we have to stay here?"

"There you are," Ronni says, coming around the corner. "You ran off. We're not finished."

I motion to Bria. "I think it's her turn. You did say you wanted us all to meet them, right?"

Ronni's expression sours. "You work the floor down here. Brianna, follow me and try to look sophisticated."

Bria follows her, but mimes someone tightening a noose around her neck behind Ronni's back.

I smile. Because, holy shit, I really like this girl.

Chapter Thirty-three

Bria

The limo pulls up in front of my place. Ronni's eyes are glued to the window. "You *live* here?" She looks up and down the street. "God, it's hideous."

Crew says sarcastically, "Yet you keep spending our money on frivolous things, like limos."

"Well, it's obviously needed," Ronni says. "We sure as hell don't want people thinking you live in squalor."

I'm tired of her condescension, but I decided long ago not to let it get to me. "Bye, guys. Great set tonight."

Crew gets out after me. Before he closes the door, I hear Ronni say, "That hair."

"Don't listen to her," Crew says. "Your hair is incredible. She's just jealous."

"Yeah, right," I say, stumbling.

He catches me. "Whoa. You okay?"

I smile. "I am now."

"You're drunk."

"Maybe a little, and so are you. How could we not be, with all the drinks pushed our way?"

He laughs. "A lot of *expensive* drinks."

I unlock the door. "I haven't had champagne like that since I was on the road with White Poison."

"Maybe you should get used to it."

"Do you think people really get used to drinking bottles of two-hundred-dollar champagne?"

"Did Adam?"

"Oh yeah."

"That's not going to be us, Bria."

"I hope not." We go into my tiny apartment, and it's like I'm seeing it for the first time. "It will be strange to go from this to that, don't you think? *If* it happens."

He captures me, tugging me to him. "It'll happen. We were good tonight."

I wiggle against him. "Really good, and you were amazing."

"It's because of you."

I did the right thing going back to Carlos. It's like the old Chris is back. No, he's better. "They treated us like celebrities. It was surreal."

"We may not like Ronni, but I have to hand it to her. She knows how to make things happen."

I run my fingers through his stiff hair. "I guess she does, but I can't say I'm a fan of this."

He snorts. "Me either. Mind if I shower and wash this crap out?"

I shrug seductively. "Not if you don't mind if I come with you."

We drop everything and quickly shed our clothes. My shower is tiny, and the curtain sticks to us every time we move. He puts his head under the water and lets me wash his hair. I've never washed a man's hair. It's so intimate. When I finish, he opens his eyes and looks at me. I swear he's looking at me harder than he ever has before, like earlier when we were singing. He radiates strength, determination, and heat. And I wonder who he's seeing—her or me?

He shoves me against the wall, exploring me with his mouth and tongue. He's hard as he grinds into me. I break our kiss, laughing when I look at his erection and it jerks with needy expectation. "I'm happy to see you didn't drink *that* much tonight."

He frames my face with his hands. "Nothing is going to keep me from being with you right now."

I palm his cock, and he inhales sharply. I stroke up and down his length, the water making him slippery. He braces himself against the wall behind me.

He cups my breast and toys with my nipple. He runs a hand down my slick body and puts his fingers between my legs. He groans as he pushes them inside me. I want him to go farther, deeper.

I spin around so I face the wall, desperately wanting him to make love to me. He pins me against the tile, kisses my neck and upper back, one hand fondling a breast and the other on my clit. I lean over as far as I can, reaching behind me to guide him inside.

He hesitates, his hands still on me. "Are you sure?"

"I'm on the pill."

He enters me. "Jesus, Bria … this feels … oh, God, I'm not going to last long." He circles my clit with a finger. He whispers in my ear, his hot breath and sexy words taking me higher. "Uhhhhhhh," he cries, as he makes his last thrusts. His explosive groans vibrate through me.

Him coming inside me with nothing between us—it's so freeing. So trusting. I lose myself in his orgasm and come.

He pulls out of me, lathers his hands, and washes between my legs. He lingers over my skin until the water turns tepid. I turn off the shower. He wraps me in a towel and helps me out of the tub. "Sit," he says, putting down the toilet lid.

He dries himself, then, still naked, runs the towel over my hair. He carefully combs through it and stares at me for a long moment before wrapping a towel around his waist and leaving the bathroom without a word.

What just happened?

I put on my robe and follow him out. He gets his notebook and sits on my couch, writes a few words, chews on his pen, then writes a few more. I laugh silently, happy to have provided him inspiration.

I go back in the bathroom, dry my hair, and slip into bed, letting him work. Sometime later he joins me, his movements waking me.

"Was it good?" I ask.

He shimmies against me. "It's always good."

I giggle sleepily. "I meant the song you wrote."

"Yeah, it's good."

I turn, just able to make out his face in the moonlight. "Do you remember Wednesday night?"

"Vaguely."

"You asked me to move in with you. Do you remember that?"

He stiffens. "I … I thought it was a dream."

"I know why you asked me."

He skims a hand along my thigh. "So we could do this all the time?"

"You asked me because you want to protect me, right? Like you did at the club tonight. Like you always do."

"Whatever. I was drunk."

"I know, but I get the feeling you meant it. Don't worry, I'm not trying to trap you. We're not moving in together. I know why you asked, but I'm not her."

He inches back. "What are you talking about?"

"I know about Abby. Well, not *all* about her. But I know she died."

He sits up and swings his legs off the bed. "You read my stuff?" he says angrily.

I don't answer. He turns on the light and looks at me. I don't want to admit I read that song. "I went to see your mom. She looked at me the way you did this week—like she'd seen a ghost. She showed me the picture of Abby."

He jumps out of bed. "She *what?*"

I sit up and wrap myself in the covers. "I didn't know what to do. The way you've been acting lately, I thought you were going to break up with me. As soon as I saw the picture, though, I knew it was my fault, not yours. I'd made myself look like her. I'm so sorry. I can't imagine how it must have felt. And she was a singer, like me."

"Jesus," he says, pacing around the room. "What the hell did she tell you?"

"Nothing. She showed me the picture and told me Abby died a long time ago. I asked her to tell me more, but she wouldn't. She said you needed to tell me in your own time."

He puts on his underwear. I think he's going to get dressed and leave. Instead, he looks back at me. He runs his hands through his hair, clearly frustrated. Then he sits on the edge of the bed. "It's not your fault you colored your hair. You had no idea. And I liked it, I did, but ..."

I scoot over and wrap my arms around him. "It's okay. I get it."

He tenses, then relaxes. He turns off the light and lies next to me. I lay my head on his chest. "I'm not going anywhere, and I'll wait for you to tell me." I glance at him. "As long as you don't act like a douche anymore."

He kisses my head. "Deal. I'll try to dial down the fucked-up."

"We're all fucked up, you know. You don't own the rights."

"I know."

I give him a squeeze. "You didn't really want me to move in with you, did you?"

"I don't know. It's no secret I don't like you living here by yourself, and it would save us a ton on rent, but—"

"But those aren't the right reasons."

"No."

He rubs my back, and I start to drift off, his heartbeat strong and steady under my ear.

"Bria?"

"Mm?"

"Did you fake an orgasm the other night or was that a dream, too?"

I chuckle. "That really happened. You were drunk and ..."

"And what?"

"You wouldn't look at me."

He flips me over so I'm under him, and he turns the light back on. "I'm looking at you now, and I swear you'll never fake another one again."

He slips a hand beneath my panties and keeps his promise.

Chapter Thirty-four

Crew

We stick around after rehearsal. Ronni hired a photographer to do a shoot. No matter how much she complains about the barn, even she had to admit it has a great rustic feel.

As we wait for Ronni and the photographer to arrive, Bria tries to help Liam with a melody for a new song. He's been in a slump lately. She sits at the keyboard, trying different variations as he strums his guitar.

I watch her. I've been doing a lot of that lately. She's so easy to look at. Our eyes meet, and she smiles.

Something has changed between us since last Friday. And it's not just her hair. Ever since she found out about Abby, she's been acting differently. More accepting. She asks fewer questions. She gives me more space.

I pick up my notebook and attempt to work on the song Mom suggested I write. I've made some progress this week. I even feel like it might be finished someday. But a part of me doesn't want to finish it. It would somehow make things so final.

Dirk comes into the barn with an armful of food. "Thought you kids might be hungry. I hear you have a long day."

Garrett and Brad race over to him. The rest of us hang back.

"You're not hungry?" Dirk asks Liam.

Liam ignores him.

"Or just not grateful," Dirk says. He crosses to his nephew. "It'd do you good to remember who supported you when no one else would."

"Can we not do this here?" Liam says.

"Why not here? You never talk to me at home. At *my* home."

Liam sees us watching. "Jesus, Dirk." He gets up and leaves. Dirk follows, slamming the door so hard it pops back open. We pretend to eat as we listen to their argument.

"What the hell is your problem, Liam?" Dirk shouts.

"What do you think it is? I'm sick of you thinking RA owes you. That I owe you. That everybody in the goddamn world owes something to Dirk Campbell."

"You'd do best to remember your place," Dirk says. "The way I see it, you *do* owe me. Or have you forgotten about White Poison, SummerStage, and all the other shit I've done for your band? Not to mention what I do for your goddamn mother."

"Don't talk about my mother. And let's face it, *dear uncle*, you're the one who owes me. I could ruin you, and you know it."

"That's bullshit," Dirk says. "You couldn't, and you won't. Who would take care of Colleen? You really think your alcoholic mother would survive on the street?"

There is a loud *thump* against the wall.

"Don't fucking call her that," Liam yells.

"Get your hands off me," Dirk says. "That is unless you like them there."

Oh shit. I start toward the door, thinking Liam is about to go ballistic, and hear a car pull up.

"Go to hell, Dirk," Liam says. "Either kick us out of the barn or stay the hell away from us."

I slip out the door. Dirk is straightening his tie.

Ronni gets out of her car and looks at the three of us. "Did I miss something?"

Dirk goes over and kisses Ronni's cheek. "Liam was just thanking me for bringing lunch, weren't you, son?"

Liam's hands ball into fists. He hates it when Dirk calls him that. He returns to the barn, and I follow. He pulls me aside. "I need to get out of Dirk's house. I can't write any fucking music lately. And Mom—she's not good. I have to get her out of there too."

"Everything okay?" Bria asks.

"Yes," I say.

Liam snorts. "Sure, if my uncle being a prick is okay. You guys think you live in shitholes, but you have no idea how much I'd give to be in a place like one of yours."

"Why don't you?" Bria asks. "Maybe you and Crew could get a place together."

Liam shakes his head. "I have to think about Mom."

Bria doesn't press the issue. I haven't told her much about Liam's family situation and nothing about his past.

Liam shuffles away, still brooding.

"Trying to pawn me off on someone else so you don't have to move in with me?" I joke.

She wrinkles her nose and shrugs.

"Come on," I say. "Let's eat."

A few minutes later, Ronni comes inside with someone in tow. "This is Kai Hansen. He's going to do the shoot." She looks at Bria from head to toe. "Please tell me you brought different clothes. Those look like they came from the same place you got your apartment."

"Give it a rest, Ronni," I say. "We all brought several changes of clothes."

"Good, because there's no way she would fit into anything of mine. Everything I own is a size four. She'd look like a stuffed sausage."

Bria is tense, like she's holding back. Ronni has a stick up her ass, for sure. I wonder if she's always been able to get her way with clients. Something tells me she always gets what she wants, and that pisses me off and also scares me a little, because Ronni seems to hate Bria.

Kai unpacks his gear, bringing in several screens and lights. He motions to us. "You look strong, mates. I saw bales of hay outside. Let's pile a few of the smaller ones behind the drums."

I'm surprised by his British accent. Does it remind Bria of Adam? But she doesn't seem affected, and that makes me happy.

I drop off a bale and ask Ronni, "What's this going to cost us? I've seen his equipment. He can't be cheap. We have no money, but you keep making us do expensive shit."

"This one's on IRL. Niles likes you, so make it good. We're sticking our necks out for you."

"He likes us, huh?"

She runs a finger down my chest. "What's not to like?"

"Ronni," I warn, glancing at Bria to see if she's watching.

"You're no fun at all, are you?" She leans close. "One day you'll give in to me, Christopher Rewey."

I push her away. "Nobody calls me that, least of all you."

"We've already established I can call you whatever I please. Now don't you have some more hay to move?"

After we've moved everything around per Kai's directions, we get changed for the shoot. Ronni tries to take charge, positioning Bria behind me, like she always does. Kai calls Bria to the front, and Ronni protests.

"You're paying me to take the best photos. You need to trust me," Kai says to her. "You'll see I'm right." He turns to Bria. "Sweetheart, you're the eye candy. I want you out front with Crew."

I expect her to tell him off for calling her sweetheart, but she doesn't. Maybe she's so happy he's going against Ronni's wishes that she's letting it slide.

Ronni sits on the couch, pouting.

I try not to laugh when Kai poses Bria and me in sexy positions on the hay bales. He hasn't the slightest idea we're a couple. No way would Ronni have told him. Her head must be about ready to explode.

Kai tucks Bria's hair behind her ear. "Has anyone ever told you that you should try modeling?"

Bria blushes. "I never had any interest. Music is my passion."

"Shame," he says. "You'd do very well."

I scoot closer to her. "She's doing very well with *us*."

"I've heard your stuff. It's quite brilliant." He fixes her hair again. "I think I like it better this way, when it frames your face. Beautiful. Stay like that, luv."

He returns to his camera. Garrett snickers behind me.

"Shut up," I snarl through my teeth.

"Let's take five," Kai says a while later. "I want to check my images, and then we'll change the background and take some on your stage."

Jeremy comes in and goes straight to Liam. "What's going on with you and Dirk?"

Liam shrugs. "Same shit, different day."

"Maybe it's time to work your shit out."

"Not likely."

"You do realize it's not wise to bite the hand that feeds you."

Liam gives him a harsh stare. "That's why we hired you, isn't it? To help us make money so nobody else has to *feed* us. When do you think that might start happening? Because from where I sit, the only one making any money here is you."

"It takes money to make money," Jeremy says.

"Where have I heard that before?"

"Dirk is a wise man. Got him where he is today. You could learn a lot from him."

Liam laughs bitterly. "Learn from him? He's a fucking bottom-dweller. He only does things that benefit himself, or haven't you learned that by now?"

"Ah, the life of a politician."

"They're all fucking corrupt," Liam says.

"Maybe, but they're also people who are good to have as friends."

"Says you."

"Okay," Kai says. "We're ready."

We go over to the stage. "I didn't realize things were so bad between Liam and Dirk," Bria says.

I shake my head. "You have no idea."

"Did something happen recently?"

"Something happened a long time ago."

I don't elaborate, and she doesn't ask any more questions.

"So, Kai seems like a real asshole," I say.

"I think he's nice."

I bite the inside of my cheek.

Kai spends an hour taking pictures of us fake-playing and singing. "Okay, mates, now perform a song so I can get live-action pictures. Something with energy. No sappy love shite."

"How about 'Can't Stop Me'?" Ronni suggests, picking one of the songs where Bria's not singing lead.

Bria whispers to me, "She's in rare form today. She hates me more than usual."

I turn to Ronni. "We should pick one where Bria sings as much as I do. That's the point here, isn't it?"

"I'd have to agree with Crew," Kai says. "What's that one I heard on the radio this morning? Something about the days of the week."

"You heard that on the radio?" I ask, surprised.

"On my way here," he says. "I only knew it was yours because the DJ announced it. What are the odds of that?"

The guys and I share fist bumps, and I hug Bria.

"Please," Ronni says. "It's not like you haven't been on the radio before."

"Why didn't you tell us the new songs were on?" Bria asks. "This is huge news!"

Ronni looks at Bria like she's an inconvenience. "Listen, you'd better learn to act like professionals and not a bunch of toddlers every time you hear your songs on the radio."

Liam strolls over to Ronni. "No, *you* listen. You may have been doing this long enough so you don't give a shit, but for us— hearing our songs on the radio is like winning the fucking lottery, and I'll be damned if you're going to ruin that for us. Because you know what? It's a big fucking deal. So let us have a minute to process it."

Kai walks over to Ronni and puts an arm around her shoulders. "Ah, to catch them on the way up, eh, luv?"

She straightens her skirt. "You have no idea how much work they are."

"Okay, mates, we should get this show on the road. At five-hundred-bucks an hour, you probably don't want me hanging around longer than I have to."

"Five hundred bucks an hour?" Bria says, her forehead wrinkling in despair.

"Don't worry," I say. "IRL is picking up the tab."

"Great," Liam says. "Another person who thinks they've got us by the balls."

Ronni steps forward. "Or *thank you* will do."

Liam picks up his guitar. "Whatever. Let's get this over with."

A half-hour later, after Kai is sure he's gotten what he needs, he calls it a wrap. Bria turns on the radio and cleans up the lunch debris. The guys and I help Kai haul his gear out of the barn.

"Thanks, mates. I just have to pop back inside for one more camera." He opens the trunk. "Put these bags in the back."

"Dude," Garrett says to Brad. "You just can't smash his bags in there. The equipment is delicate, like my drums." He repacks everything with care.

I'm laughing when I return to the barn, but suddenly things aren't so funny. Kai has Bria cornered near the bathroom, and she looks uncomfortable. I run over and remove his arm from the wall.

"Sorry, mates," he says, looking at me. "Was I stepping on someone's toes?"

"Yeah," I say, working myself between them. "You were."

"So you and him?" he asks Bria.

"That's right," I say, puffing up my chest and taking a step toward him.

"I wasn't asking you, mate."

"Who the fuck do you think you are?"

"Crew, stop it," Bria says. "I was about to tell Kai that we're together."

"Down, boy," Kai says. "Honest mistake."

My hands ball into fists. "You should leave."

Kai reaches into his pocket, pulls out a business card, and tries to hand it to Bria. "If you ever change your mind about modeling."

I intercept the card and tear it up. "She won't."

"Crew," Bria warns.

I glare at Kai. "The door's over there."

He takes his camera from the table and leaves.

Bria's hands are on her hips. "What was that all about?"

"He was coming on to you."

"Yes, he was. Spoiler alert—guys come on to me, Crew. Just like girls come on to you." She points to the door. "Case in point drives the red Porsche. I can handle myself, so drop the jealous act. It's not very becoming."

"Jealous? I'm not jealous."

She narrows her eyes. "You're kidding, right?"

"I'm not jealous, Bria. I'm not that insecure."

"Yet you practically pummel every guy who gets within ten feet of me. This is really going to become a pr—"

"Guys!" Liam yells. "Listen!"

One of our new songs is on the radio. Garrett runs over and turns it up. We're completely silent, watching each other come out of our skin as we listen to 'Not a Day' blast through the speakers.

"Screw Ronni," Liam says. "This will *never* get old."

"Shh, listen," Brad says.

The DJ on the radio says, "It's twofer Tuesday, so here's another one by Reckless Alibi. If you haven't heard of this up-and-coming band, you'd better get out of your Barcaloungers and get with the program. You heard it here first, people. These guys will have a gold record."

Our collective jaws hang open. Everyone gets on social media to post about the songs.

"Did you hear that?" I say to Bria, gathering her in my arms. "He thinks we're going gold. We're going to be famous."

She swallows and looks up at me. The problem is, I can't tell if she's happy or sad. "Yeah," she says. "I'm afraid you might be right."

Chapter Thirty-five

Bria

Crew is suspicious of every man who comes up to me and even some of the women. He assesses everyone who passes our dinner table like they will ask me out or take me away from him. He claims he's not the jealous type, but his actions speak loudly.

The past few weeks have been so good between us that I haven't said anything further about his behavior. In the beginning, it was even a little endearing that he was jealous. Now it's annoying. I think Brett and Emma have caught on too, as the more he drinks, the more that side of him emerges.

Emma says, "Have you always lived in Stamford, Crew?"

"Uh-huh." He shovels bread into his mouth to avoid talking about his past.

"You must be so excited," she says. "I've heard your songs on the radio at least a dozen times."

"It's all a bit surreal," I say.

"Even though you've already sung with a famous band?" Emma asks.

"That was different. I wasn't really part of White Poison. Reckless Alibi is *my* band."

Crew grabs my hand under the table and smiles. It's taken me a long time to be able to say that. I felt like an outsider for months, but lately it's becoming hard to remember a time when I wasn't with RA.

"Who came up with the band name?" Brett asks.

"It was a collaborative effort between Liam and me," Crew says. "We used to sing in another band. But it broke up a long time ago. When we got older and wrote new material, my mom told us we were reckless rock stars. *His* mom always teased him and said he'd better have a good alibi because he was so often out half the night. We wrote a song called 'Reckless Alibi,' and we liked the title so much we decided to use it for the band instead."

"I think it's a great name," Emma says.

"At least they didn't have to change it when I came on, like if they'd been called the Backstreet Boys or something."

"What happened to the song?" Brett asks.

"Changed the name. It's now called 'Can't Stop the Train'."

"Emma Lockhart!" a woman shrieks.

Emma stands. "Mallory!" They hug. "It's so nice to see you again." Emma flashes her engagement ring. "It's soon to be Mrs. Cash."

"Congratulations!"

A man joins her, and my jaw drops. I nudge Crew and whisper, "Is that who I think it is?"

"Mallory and Chad Stone, this is my fiancé, Brett, his sister, Bria, and her boyfriend, Crew."

Boyfriend. I like the way that sounds. I peek at Crew who doesn't seem to mind that Emma just put a label on our relationship.

The men shake hands. I stare at Mallory's husband like an idiot. "You're ... you're ... Lt. Jake Cross."

He shakes my hand. "Friends call me Chad."

Brett motions to two empty seats at our table. "Care to join us? We haven't ordered yet."

They glance at each other. "Sure," Mallory says. "It would be great to catch up."

Our waitress comes over, looking at Chad like she's no longer bummed about working tonight. She recognizes the famous actor who's starred in over twenty films, including the blockbuster *Defcon* trilogy. She takes their drink orders and hurries to fill them.

"I'm sorry," I say, "you said your name is Chad? I feel kind of silly. I thought it was *Thad*."

"That's my stage name. My agent made me change it when I first got in the business. My real name was too similar to that of another actor."

I laugh. "Agents can be annoying like that."

"You have one?"

"Well, a manager and a record label. Crew and I are in a band. They make me go by Brianna. It's my real name, but I've gone by Bria my whole life."

"Did they come up with the name Crew as well? That's pretty original."

Crew tells him how he got the name.

Mallory says, "Being in a band sounds like fun. You must be kind of a big deal if you have a manager and a record label. What's the name of your band?"

"Reckless Alibi," Crew says. "We're small potatoes right now, but with Bria singing with us, we hope that's all going to change."

"You're new to the band?"

Crew puts a proud arm around my shoulders. "She used to be a backup singer for White Poison, but we snatched her away. They have no idea what talent they let slip through their fingers."

I squeeze his leg in thanks.

"White Poison?" Chad says. "I know Adam Stuart."

I stiffen. "You do?"

"Not well, but we've crossed paths a few times. He's one narcissistic Brit." He hears what he just said and scrambles. "Uh, sorry if you're friends with him."

"No, not friends."

"He's a real prick," Crew says succinctly.

I change the subject. "How do you and Emma know each other, Mallory?"

"We're both teachers. We met through some charity work six or seven years ago."

I'm caught off guard, surprised the wife of an A-list actor would work.

"She's not currently teaching in a school," Emma says. "But she's very involved in making curriculums for kids who travel with their parents."

Chad holds Mallory's hand. "I wanted her and the kids on location with me."

"How old are they?" I ask.

Mallory shows me a picture on her phone. "Kiera is nine, and Kyle is three."

"They're beautiful."

"Thank you."

"My future stepson, Leo, is three," Emma says. "We should get them together. And you wouldn't believe how much Evelyn has grown since you've seen her."

Throughout dinner Emma and Mallory catch up and talk about their kids. Crew and Chad bond over music and films. I'm still in awe that I'm sitting next to a man who has an Oscar on a shelf in his house.

"Sorry, Bria," Emma says when dessert comes. "We didn't mean to ignore you. Mallory and I haven't seen each other in ages."

"I'm enjoying listening to you reminisce."

"Tell me about your band," Mallory says. "How long have you been singing with them?"

"Most of this year. To be honest, it's kind of scary."

"How do you mean?"

"We're doing a lot of shows. Nowhere big, mostly bars and clubs. But our songs are on the radio now, and we're playing at SummerStage next month. People are starting to recognize us. I'm a little nervous about losing who we are and where we came from."

Mallory nods and glances at Chad. "That's all too easy to do."

"Case in point—Adam Stuart," he says.

"That's not going to happen to us," Crew says, and I nod agreement.

Chad refills wine glasses. "It's easy to go down the wrong road when everything is being handed to you on a silver platter. I imagine it's even worse in the music business. There is a lot of truth to the saying 'sex, drugs, and rock and roll.' I saw it happen to Adam and a lot of actors. If you're smart and stay grounded, you can navigate the waters. Don't let it mess up what's important to you, and I'm not talking about the music. That's part of who you are, but your relationships are what define you."

"You say that like you have personal experience," Crew says.

"I do."

Mallory smiles at him. "Let's just say we missed out on a lot of years, but we're good now. You can have fame, and everything that goes along with it, and still lead a relatively normal life."

The wait staff is snapping photos of Chad from the kitchen doorway.

"First rule is don't let that bother you," Chad says. "If you pretend they aren't there, you'll enjoy your evening a whole lot more. Be nice to the fans. Sign autographs and pose for pictures, but make your personal time your own. *Never* let your ego get too big for your head."

"You okay?" Mallory asks, looking at my anxious hands.

"Honestly? I still can't believe I'm sitting here with *Thad Stone.*"

"Well, get over it. He has his moments, but deep down, he's just like the rest of us. He snores. He leaves his socks on the floor. The bathroom stinks after he's used it."

"Seriously?" Chad says to her.

I chuckle. "Nope. I don't believe it. Thad Stone's poop can't possibly stink."

"Don't get caught up in all the bullshit," he says. "At the end of the day, it's just a job."

The waiter brings three separate bills, but Chad takes them all. "Just because I said all that shit doesn't mean you can't be extravagant once in a while. If you've got it, share it."

"Thank you so much," I say. "I can't tell you what a pleasure it's been meeting you both."

Someone comes to the table. "Mr. Stone, there's a crowd out front. When you're ready I will escort you out the back door if you like."

"We'd appreciate that," Chad says.

They get up, and Mallory hugs Emma, then leans over and hugs me. "I just bought your albums with my phone. I can't wait to say I knew you when."

After they leave, I say, "Did that really happen?"

"It did." Brett turns to Emma. "You've been holding back. I didn't know you knew such influential people."

"Oh, like you aren't friends with half the New York Nighthawks?"

Crew shakes his head. "Your collective list of friends reads like the who's who of New York."

"And it looks like we're about to add a few rock stars to that list," Emma says. "I have a feeling fame and fortune are right around the corner for you."

We almost make it out the front door and then Crew tells me he left his phone at the table.

"You guys go on," I tell Brett and Emma. "I'll see you soon."

"Okay, kiddo." Brett gives me a kiss.

"Aren't I getting a little old for you to be calling me that?"

"You'll always be my baby sister."

The restaurant foyer is crowded and stuffy, so I step outside, surprised to see so many people still hanging around. I guess they didn't get the memo that Thad Stone snuck out the back.

"Are you Brianna?" someone shouts. A girl is recording me with her phone. "You're the lead singer for Reckless Alibi, right?"

"One of them, yes."

I'm reeling. Maybe Ronni was right. This girl referred to me by one name, like Cher or Beyoncé. My smile is about to split my face in two.

She squeals and then suddenly, all the people in earshot take a sudden interest in me.

"Can I get a picture with you?" she asks.

"Sure." I lean in, and she snaps a few.

"Thank you."

"Are you famous or something?" a man asks.

"Me? No."

"Yes she is," the girl says. "Look." She must pull up our album or a band picture on her phone.

"Shit, you *are* famous," he says. "Let me get a picture with you, too."

"I want one!" a few others say.

Out of nowhere, Crew appears and drags me away. He pulls me down the street like a child who's being punished until we lose sight of the crowd.

"Crew, what are you doing?"

"Those people were there for Thad Stone, not you."

"But they knew about us. A girl called me Brianna. Just Brianna. Isn't that amazing? We should go back. They wanted pictures."

"You're not going back there."

"Why not?"

"Because you're not. They were manhandling you."

I look at him sideways. "They were not. They were getting close for pictures."

"Hey, how about that picture?" the guy from the restaurant calls behind us.

Crew, moving fast, pins the man to the building. "Are you following her?"

"No," he says fearfully. "I, uh, she's famous, right? I wanted to show my friends."

"Get the hell out of here," Crew says, locking him against the wall for a few more seconds. He finally lets him go and he runs away.

Needing distance from Crew, I hurry down the street. When someone else approaches me, Crew yells, "You want some of that, too? Go—get the hell away from her."

"Crew, stop it!" When he grasps my arm. I jerk away. "I'm so tired of you acting this way. I've had to bite my tongue more than once this past week, because things have been going so well between us, but you have to get over this. We're in a band. We're on the radio. We play in public places. We get recognized. It's only going to get worse. You can't threaten everyone who says hello to me."

"But—"

"But nothing. You should go find that guy and apologize."

"Apologize, my ass. He *followed* you."

"He wanted a picture, not a date."

"Bria—"

"Go home, Crew."

"I'm not leaving you here on the street."

"I'm a big girl, and I'm tired of you treating me like a toddler."

He tries to hold my hand.

I pull away. "You can't act like that and then pretend nothing happened. You have serious issues, Chris. I know what happened with Abby must have affected you in ways you may not be aware of, but you're taking it too far."

"How about we leave Abby out of this?"

"Maybe we've left her out of this far too long."

He bites his lip, then grips his head like he's having a migraine. "You promised, Bria."

"And you promised you wouldn't be a douche anymore. News flash, Chris, you're being an asshole!"

I'm yelling, and people are watching.

"Can we not do this here?" he says.

"We're not doing this *anywhere*. I'm leaving, and don't follow me." I hail a cab. When Crew tries to get in behind me, I yank the door closed. "Drive," I tell the cabbie.

I turn around to see him standing on the curb, stunned. My phone pings.

> **Crew: I'm sorry, Abby. Please text me when you get home.**

Tears run from my eyes as I read his text. I immediately get another one.

> **Crew: Shit, Bria. I'm so so so sorry.**

> **Me: I'm sorry too, Christopher.**

I turn off my phone.

Chapter Thirty-six

Crew

Seven years ago

It's been a week, seven long days, since Abby went missing. I sit on the couch, staring at the present I made for her. It's a framed picture of her eighteen-week ultrasound, along with the lyrics of the song I wrote for her birthday, the one I started writing the day we found out she was pregnant.

Every so often I look at the front door, half expecting her to appear at any minute. She's eighteen today, the day we've been waiting for, when she can make her own decisions without her parents' approval. I play with the wedding rings I bought for us last month—another birthday surprise—and think about all the plans we made.

I put down the picture and place the rings on top of it. In the kitchen I force myself to make lunch. Mom walks in. "I'm glad to see you eating again."

I squirt mayonnaise on some bread and pile lunchmeat on top. I take a bite and taste nothing. I haven't been able to taste anything in a week. I haven't been able to *do* anything except drive around and look for her. After dropping Mom off at work, I use her car to go to all the places Abby and I used to frequent: the park, the abandoned paper mill, the mall. I've even driven into the city and sat at the free clinic for hours, hoping she'll show up.

"Maybe you could invite your friends over," Mom says. "Or we could go shopping. You'll need new clothes for senior year."

"You think I give a shit about school?"

She doesn't know what to say to me. Nobody does.

I sit at the kitchen table and put my head in my hands. "I'm sorry. I don't mean to be a dick. It's just that today is …" I can't bring myself to say it.

"Her birthday. I know, honey."

"I keep thinking maybe she'll come home today. Maybe this was all some big misunderstanding with her father."

She looks at me sympathetically, knowing as well as I do that's not what happened.

Last week, after Detective Abrahms finished with me, I went straight to the room where I'd seen Dr. and Mrs. Evans and told them about the baby. It was obvious they had no clue. They broke down, not even mad at me. Their only concern was with the whereabouts of their daughter—and after I'd revealed the information about Rob—her safety.

Her mother came to my house and asked to see the ultrasound pictures. It was devastating. She kept telling us she now had two people to mourn. Mom ended up asking her to leave.

I've tried a thousand times to picture a life without Abby in it, but I can't. I've only known her for nine months, but I might as well have met her the day I was born, because she is so much a part of me, I feel incomplete without her.

I go to my room and look at the keyboard, wishing I had the urge to play something, anything. But it's like my will to live disappeared right along with Abby. I throw myself down onto the bed, hoping for the millionth time that this will turn out to be a bad dream.

I must've fallen asleep, and when my eyes open, it's dark outside. I check my phone, something I do obsessively in case Abby tries to contact me. It's almost nine o'clock. I sit on the edge of the bed and run my hands through my hair. I watch my tears drop to the hardwood floor. She'd have come by now.

There's a knock on the front door. I jump up and hit my knee on the bedpost in my haste to run out of my room. I barely notice the pain. All I care about is getting to her. I beat Mom to the door and rip it open, heart in my throat.

It's not Abby, though. It's Detective Abrahms.

"Hi, Chris," he says. The grave look on his face tells me he's not bringing good news. "Mind if I come in?" I back up with an uneven step and an indescribable emptiness in the pit of my stomach. He motions to the couch. "Sit down, son."

Chapter Thirty-seven

Bria

Despite what happened between Crew and me a few days ago, I'm excited as I go to the production studio. Today we're shooting Reckless Alibi's very first music video.

On the subway, I browse the many apology texts Crew sent me. I'm still mad at him for ruining a perfectly good night. Surely he must understand we have to interact with our fans. *Our fans.* I look up from my phone as it dawns on me. Abby was a singer, like me. What if something happened to her because of a fan? The possibility almost makes me feel guilty for yelling at him.

At the studio the first person I see is Crew. He's loitering by the door as if he's been waiting for me. Guilt is written all over his face, and my anger melts away. I walk directly to him, and he grabs onto me like a drowning man.

"I'm so sorry," he says into my hair. "I promise I'll do better."

I get lost in the feel of his arms around me. For two days I've wondered if I'd be in them again. But now that I'm here, I know it's where I want to be. I just have to give him more time. "I'm sorry, too. I shouldn't have shut you out like that."

"I was a dick. You had every right. Can I get a do-over tonight? I want to make it up to you. Let me take you to dinner."

I smile and nod.

"Can we please get started," Ronni says, interrupting our private moment. "Time is money. Brianna, you go with Elsie. She'll do your hair, makeup, and wardrobe. Crew, you and the guys will be with those two over there. I'll supervise."

Of course she will.

I kiss Crew's cheek. He smiles before heading off with Ronni.

"Brianna," Elsie says. "It's lovely to meet you."

"You can call me Bria."

"Actually I can't." She nods to Ronni. "She told us we have to call you Brianna."

I feel a sudden urge to smack Ronni, and I'm not a violent person. I smile coldly. "Do what you need to do, but I prefer Bria."

She takes me into a dressing room and seats me in a large chair in front of a mirror. There's all kinds of makeup on the counter in front of me. "You're going to make me look like a slut, aren't you?"

"You're making a sexy video. I love your music, by the way."

"Thanks."

I let her do her job. I can't make small talk because my face moves when I speak. When she's finished, and I gaze into the mirror, I'm astounded. My eyes are smoky-black, and my lashes are an inch long. I consider asking her to teach me how to get that effect.

"I'm not done yet," Elsie says, pulling out bins filled with hairstyling equipment.

"Can I talk now?"

"Sure. In fact, tell me about that hot singing partner of yours."

"What do you want to know?"

"Is he taken? Can you slip him my number?"

"Yes and no."

"Hmm, that's a shame. So a one-night stand is out of the question? A lot of guys are taken but still play on the side."

"Not Crew."

"Are you sure? I can be discreet."

I tighten my lips. "I'm sure."

Her hand goes to her mouth. "Are the two of you …?"

"Yes."

"Shit, I'm sorry. What about the others? Can you give *them* my number?"

My cosmetically enhanced eyebrows rise. "All of them?"

She doesn't even have the decency to look embarrassed. "Improves my chances."

"I'm not in the habit of matchmaking, but I'll pass along your number. Might want to stay away from Brad, though. He has a serious girlfriend."

"Which one is he?"

"Bass guitar."

"Noted."

After another twenty minutes, she takes me over to the wardrobe hanger. "I'm supposed to wear *this*?"

"That's what I'm told. Why? What's wrong?"

I give the outfit a once-over. It's pretty but demure. I figured Ronni would have me in a short, tight skirt with cleavage spilling over the top. This is something I could almost wear to church. "Nothing. I thought it would be sexier." I look at the other two identical outfits. "Why are there so many? Are they different sizes?"

"They're all your size. These are extras in case you tear one or sweat too much."

"I guess I have a lot to learn about making music videos."

Elsie escorts me down a hall and onto the set. It looks nothing like I imagined. It's like I've entered another world. Hot lights hang from the ceiling and down the walls. Cameras and operators are everywhere. There is an expensive-looking convertible on one side, an empty stage on another, what looks like a bedroom against a wall, and there's band equipment that's not ours. Behind everything are massive green screens.

A man comes over. "I'm David Holland, the director. The rest of your band is over here." We must pass fifteen or twenty people along the way. "That's my production staff. If you need anything, ask one of them."

We enter a large conference room. Crew and the others stand around. Crew is always gorgeous, but, oh my God, they've got him in tight jeans and a leather jacket, and the shirt under it is ripped so I can see his abs.

He starts over to me, and Ronni rushes between us. "No touching. I don't want you to have to go back to hair and makeup."

We stare at each other from a few feet away.

"You look hot," he whispers.

"You, too."

Crew gives me a sly smile. "I can't wait to get you alone tonight."

"Are you finished?" Ronni says bitingly. "David wants to go over a few things."

We take seats around the table, except for David, who paces as he talks. "I understand you've never made a music video before, so a few things. First, every minute of your song will take two to four hours of shooting. This will be a long day. The more you cooperate, the earlier we'll get out of here. Second, ideally we'll have several good takes for every scene, so don't be surprised if I ask you to do it again even if you think it's perfect. Third, it's easier to play your instruments than to pretend. To make picture editing simpler, the amps are unplugged, the mics aren't on, the drums have been padded with pillows, and the cymbals are stacked. I don't care what you sound like as long as you stay in sync with the music being piped in. Lastly, think of this more like making a movie than a music video. Your job is to evoke emotion from the viewer. To entice them to follow you and buy your stuff. But don't overact; it has to be believable."

The door opens and four gorgeous women stride in. They're wearing what I thought I'd be given—short skirts and slutty tops.

"Ah, the eye candy is here," Ronni says.

I lean over to Crew. "I thought it was going to be the five of us."

He appears to be as clueless as I am.

"What's this about?" I ask. "Are they supposed to be backup singers?"

Ronni belts out a harsh laugh. "This song is about fast cars and fast women. It's sexy. So we needed a lot of sexy."

I sink back in my chair. "Great."

Crew takes my hand under the table.

David's assistant arrives and hands him a bunch of large poster boards. He puts them on easels around the room. "These are storyboards. Ronni and I have worked for weeks to perfect them. There's one for each scene. Study them so you'll know what we expect from you. I have to speak to the extras."

"Extras?" I look at the four slutty girls. "I thought that's what they were."

Ronni laughs. "They aren't extras. They play a big part in the video. David is going out to brief the hundred or so people who will stand in front of the stage and pretend to be your diehard fans."

I cross to one of the storyboards. There is a sketch of four women surrounding a man in his car. Another one has them in bed with him.

I look at Ronni. "Seriously? This song is about *one* woman."

"That all depends on your perspective. Too late to change it now. We've put a hundred hours into pre-production. Do what David asks and maybe we'll be out of here by midnight."

Crew nudges me. "So much for those dinner plans."

I cross my arms. "Like you'd want to go to dinner with me after having those four draped over you all day."

He tries to hide his amusement. "Who's acting jealous *now?*"

I lean into him. "Try not to forget who's yours at the end of the day."

His blue eyes dance with happiness. "Are you saying you want to be mine, Bria Cash?"

"If you want me."

He shuffles his feet. "Let's get this over with, then."

Garrett eyes the storyboards. "Some guys have all the luck."

I punch him in the arm and walk away.

Two hours later, we're finally shooting. We do the stage scene first, with the five of us playing and singing like we're performing at a concert. All one hundred extras swarm the stage, with the four sluts front and center.

Everyone acts like they're at a concert, but they are completely quiet. A hundred people are dancing and mashing, but no sound comes from them other than the shuffling of their feet.

David has us go through the song seven times. Then the slutty girls crawl up onstage, one at a time, and surround Crew. They push me out of the way, and I'm supposed to act all pouty and mad. They glide around him in circles, taking turns touching his neck and chest, and two of them slide their hands under his shirt.

And then they do it three more times.

I don't have to act pouty and mad. I *am* pouty and mad.

Between takes, I don't miss the huge smile on Ronni's face when she looks at me. She loves what this is doing to me, and there's plenty more to come.

"You're doing great," Crew says between takes.

"As if you'd have time to notice with eight hands groping you."

He gives me a sympathetic look. "It'll be over soon."

I look at the clock. "Like in ten hours."

"Places!" David calls. "Crew, I need you in the R8."

I see the excitement on Crew's face. He gets to sit in an Audi R8, something he will never do again unless we make it big.

It's harder to watch this scene, because I'm barely in it. All I do is walk past the car and sing a few lines.

Liam pulls me aside. "You don't have to watch, you know."

"Yeah, right. Kind of like trying not to look at an accident on the highway."

"He's acting, Bria. They're all acting."

"I'll bet some of them wish they weren't."

Elsie says, "You need powder. We don't want any shine."

She works on me for a few minutes, and I'm happy to have an excuse not to watch. Then I find a quiet spot and close my eyes. I know what's coming next. I'm going to be tortured by having to watch Crew in bed with four women. I'm supposed to saunter around the bed, singing as he makes love to them. I'm willing to bet Ronni was the one who scripted it that way.

During a break, David catches me glued to the storyboard. "I hear you and Crew have a thing." He nods to the set. "This is entertainment. It doesn't mean anything."

"I know, but I wish we could have stayed true to the song. It's about one woman's battle within herself, not her battle with four sluts who want her man."

He laughs. "After hearing it over a hundred times today, I can see that." He stares at me. "I like you. You're feisty. No disrespect to them, but you're prettier than any of those girls. I hope you know that. I'll take the girl next door any day." He taps his lips, deep in thought. "I have an idea, but it involves us going rogue."

I avert my eyes from the storyboard and give him my full attention.

"I'd like to try an alternate ending to the video. Something along the lines of good girl wins over bad girls. Maybe you throw them out of bed or kick them off the stage and the two of you drive off in the car."

I smile. "Ronni would kill you."

"I'm the director. I have creative control. Maybe we can distract her, and by the time she figures out what's going on, we'll be half finished. Might be worth a shot. I'm a huge music fan and a big believer that each song has deep meaning. If that's what it means to you, I think we should give it a try. We show our videos to a test group before release. We'll let them decide which ending they like."

"Can I do anything?"

He gestures to Liam, Garrett, and Brad. "Maybe they could have some kind of emergency after the scripted ending scene."

That's the one where Crew abandons me onstage and leaves with the four girls.

"I'm on it," I say, happily going over to conspire with the guys.

An hour later, I'm less upset seeing Crew in bed with four girls. Ronni has a smug smile on her face. I swear she wants him and is so jealous she'll do anything to make me jealous, too.

It's still hard to watch my boyfriend in bed, naked, with so many other women. They aren't really nude. They have shorts on, and sheets cover their breasts. David has to cut when one of them reveals her boobs. She giggles, and I get ticked. But Crew looks away while she rights herself, and that offers me a tiny bit of relief.

"Again," David says. "Crew, you're in bed with four beautiful women. You're not sure you should be, and maybe you're having an internal struggle, but come on, you need to look a little excited about it. Don't worry, they won't bite."

Crew looks at me apologetically.

I nod at him.

They start shooting and I sing my lines as he gropes the girls. Then I have to stand there and watch them during the guitar riff that seems to last forever. It's all I can do not to stomp my foot and run off the set, but I'm not about to give Ronni that satisfaction.

Between takes, Ronni goes to the bed. "Crew, you have to kiss them."

"No."

"That's ridiculous. We all know it's pretend, but you have to make it believable. You're not going to be in bed with four women and not kiss any of them."

David says, "She's right."

"I'm not going to kiss someone in front of my girlfriend."

"Oh, for Christ's sake," Ronni says. "You've already touched their asses. Can we be adults and get on with it?"

Crew cocks his brow at my silence. I love that he's asking permission. "Just do it."

He sighs and pinches the bridge of his nose. "All right, but I'm not using tongue."

David laughs. "Nobody said you had to. Queue the music."

I almost start crying when he kisses one woman, then another. Is he turned on by this? Is he getting hard? I fight tears, and then realize some of the cameras are on me and my reaction is exactly what's needed. The scene ends, and I'm not sure I can take doing this another three or four times.

"That's a wrap on that one," David says.

I'm surprised.

So is Ronni. "You said we needed several good takes of each scene."

"I had four cameras rolling on that one. I'm confident we got what we need."

"But—"

"Ronni, you hired me because I'm one of the best. Trust me. It's going to be great."

She stalks off, getting on her phone like she always does, and we film the scene where Crew leaves me. It's short and we get through it quickly.

"Are we good?" Ronni says.

David makes some notes on a pad. "Just about. I want to get a few more shots of them on the bed."

Ronni smiles, thinking that will piss me off. "Take all the time you need. I'm going to step outside and make a few calls."

David winks at me.

Garrett and Liam come over. "We'll make sure she doesn't come back in for a while."

"What will you say?" I ask.

Liam shrugs. "I'll tell her some bullshit about needing more money or something. She'll go off on me for an hour if I let her."

I laugh. "I don't doubt it."

"Are we doing this or what?" David says. "We don't have all day."

"What's going on?" Crew asks.

"Bria and I have decided to film an additional scene. Your girlfriend is going to kick some ass, and you're going to carry her to the car and drive off into the sunset."

His smile is the highlight of my day. "Ronni's going to flip out."

I snicker. "I know."

A half-hour later, we're finished. Garrett and Liam managed to keep Ronni busy the entire time.

Crew is delighted. "She'll never know what hit her."

"I'm not sure any of this matters," I say. "David said the screening will be the deciding factor, and I'm sure they'll want the other ending."

"Are you kidding? Everyone wants the nice girl to win over the 'hoes'. We'll get the ending we want." He leans down and whispers, "And now we're going back to your place, so I can get the ending *I* want."

"Crew, can I speak with you?" Ronni says from across the room.

I thumb to the door. "I'll wait for you outside."

I go through the large steel door onto the production lot. There are a few stragglers still hanging around. Extras, I think, though their part was over hours ago. One of them approaches me.

"Brianna, hi, I'm Xavier. I was one of the extras. They wouldn't let us mingle with you earlier, but I'm a big fan of your music. I was wondering if I could get a picture with you."

"Sure."

He takes some selfies with me. "Thanks." He hesitates. "I was wondering if you would like to go for a cup of coffee or something."

"It's nice of you to ask, but I have a boyfriend."

"Okay, well, nice meeting you, and thanks again for the pictures."

He pulls me into a hug. I try to push him away, but he's strong. I get ready to kick him in the nuts. "Xavier, you need to let me go."

"Oh yeah, sorry."

Before I know what's happening, Xavier is on the ground, and Crew is punching him.

"Crew! Get off him!" I shout.

Garrett and Liam run over and yank Crew off Xavier.

"What the hell is going on?" Liam asks.

"He was groping her." Crew lunges, but they stop him.

"I was *hugging* her," Xavier says defensively.

"It didn't look like she was very goddamn happy about it," Crew complains.

"I was handling it," I say.

"Go on," Garrett tells Xavier. "Get out of here."

"And stay the fuck away from her," Crew calls after him.

I look at Crew, aghast.

"What? Did you want him touching you?"

"Of course not, but you can't punch everyone who does. I can handle myself."

"It didn't look like you were handling *anything*."

"You have got to stop doing this!" I shout.

"Doing what? Being your boyfriend? Because clearly that's what I was doing."

"You fighting every man who talks to me is not being my boyfriend. You promised to do better. You said that less than ten hours ago, yet here you are, doing it again. I've had enough." I turn to Liam. "Take him home."

"But we're going out," Crew says.

"No, we're not. I don't want to be around you right now. I'm not sure I can be around you at all if you don't stop treating me like a goddamn possession."

"I'm not doing that."

"You are! Go home. We have a few days off. Take some time and decide if this is really what you want."

"It is what I want," he says. "You're what I want."

I hail a cab. "Then prove it."

Chapter Thirty-eight

Crew

Liam takes me aside. "What just happened?"

"He was all over her."

"That's not how she told it." He gives me a hard look. "What's going on?"

"She doesn't understand how many psychos are out there."

Liam's face softens. "So this isn't about Bria at all. It's about Abby."

When I don't respond, he touches my shoulder. "You've got to reel it in, brother, or you're the one people will be calling psycho."

I shrug his hand off. "I'm not a fucking psycho. I'm nothing like him."

"Then do what Bria asked you to do. Prove it."

"I'm supposed to sit back and let people grope her?"

"What's going to happen if we really make a name for ourselves? She's going to be sought out by lots of people. She may even get stalked by crazies. It happens all the time to celebrities. Are you going to kill all of them?"

299

I lunge at him. "Shut the hell up, Liam."

He dodges me and raises his hands in surrender. "I shouldn't have said that, but someone has to say something to snap you out of it. You're going to lose her, man. Worse than that, RA might lose her."

"Are you coming?" Brad calls from the van.

"I'm going to my mom's," I say.

"Good idea," Liam says. "Take a few days and figure this shit out."

Ronni comes out after they drive away. "Trouble in paradise?"

I snort and turn away.

"You know that little stunt you pulled inside? It's not going to work. My opinion is the only one that matters."

"You'll completely ignore the results if our new scene tests better than yours?"

"Your way is a fairy tale, and people are sick of them."

"You're wrong. People want a happily ever after."

"But that's not always what life gives us, is it?"

"You're goddamn right about that."

"Looks like you could use a drink. I know a good bar around the corner."

I can't believe I contemplate going, because a drink sounds good right now. But I'm already in the doghouse. I don't need to make things worse, and drinking with Ronni would make things a whole lot worse.

"Thanks, but I'm going to my mom's. See you."

"My door's always open."

I'm sure it is, I think, *among other things.*

~ ~ ~

"Chris, you've been moping around here all day," Mom says. "Is everything okay?"

"We've been going full speed for weeks, and we have gigs this weekend. I'm resting up."

"How about coming to dinner with Gary and me?"

"Thanks, but I'm going to get takeout and work on a few new songs."

She sits next to me and takes my hand in hers. "Did you ever write the one we talked about?"

"You mean the one *you* talked about." I shrug. "Some of it. It's not the easiest song to write, you know."

"That's what makes it necessary."

Gary comes in. "Ready, honey?"

Mom kisses my cheek. "Don't wait up. We might catch a show after dinner."

After they leave, I belatedly notice a vase of flowers and a card. It's their anniversary. Damn, I forgot.

Mom and Gary are a lot alike. They were both left by their spouses, both devastated by the person they loved. But they moved on and found each other. I try to rationalize that happy endings are possible. If they can do it, why not me?

Because it's different. Because Abby didn't stop loving me, she died.

I get a beer, sit at the table, and stare at my phone, hoping Bria will call. She's walked away from me twice. I open the app that tracks her phone and try not to think of how obsessively I've done it over the past twenty-four hours. She's been at home mostly, but she's not there now.

She's moving. Must be in a cab. I follow her progress for hours, refreshing my screen every so often to keep up with her. She's barhopping.

I leave my fourth beer half-full and walk out the door. Thirty minutes later, a cab is dropping me off in front of an English pub in downtown Manhattan. It's crowded for a Thursday. Groups of people go in and out of the front door. I follow one of them in.

The place is dark. Most of the tables are full. Lots of men are watching the baseball game on TV. I stand to one side and scan until I see her. She's with the two friends I met at our gig last month. She's smiling and laughing. I find a place at the bar where I can see them without them seeing me.

"What'll you have?" the bartender asks.

"Jack and Coke."

I feel like a total douchebag that I'm even here. She's enjoying a night out with friends, and I should leave.

"Is this seat taken?" a woman asks.

"No, go ahead," I say, not looking at her.

"Are you here alone?" she asks.

I nod.

"Want to buy me a drink?"

I turn. She's a cute redhead. "Does that mean *you're* here alone?"

She smiles. "I am."

I glance at my phone. "It's ten o'clock. This is the city. You shouldn't be alone."

"I don't have to be." She touches my thigh.

I move my leg away. "You shouldn't come to bars by yourself. There's safety in numbers, you know. You should bring a friend."

A waitress is bringing Bria a drink. She points to someone at the bar. He raises his glass. Shit. He sent her a drink. She politely shakes her head and puts the drink back on the tray.

Attagirl.

The redhead says something. "What?"

"I said, I don't have any friends. I'm new to the city. I'm looking for someone to show me around."

"I don't live here, so I'm not your guy."

"We could explore together."

"I don't think that's a good idea."

"You're not interested in buying me a drink or … anything?" She runs a finger down to her cleavage.

"Still not your guy."

"*I'll* buy you a drink," the man on her other side says.

She smirks at me over her shoulder. "Your loss."

The guy who sent Bria a drink is standing at her back. He leans down and says something to her. She smiles and shakes her head. He says something else. She shakes her head again. He puts a hand on her shoulder.

"Fuck this shit." I toss money on the bar and stride over to her table.

Bria sees me approaching and is dumbfounded.

"Want to get your hand off her?" I say to the man.

"Didn't know she was with anyone." He removes his hand. "My bad," he says and leaves.

"What are you doing here?" Bria asks.

"I'm having a drink."

"A half-hour from your mom's? Are you here alone?" She narrows her eyes. "Are you *following* me?"

I take out my phone and wave it at her. "You were all over town. I was making sure you're okay." I glare at the jerk. "Obviously you weren't."

"You track her phone?" Katherine asks sharply.

Bria picks up her phone and taps around on it. "Not anymore."

"What are you doing?"

"You can't show up when I'm out with friends."

Lola huffs. "Are you stalking her?"

"I'm not stalking her. I'm her goddamn boyfriend."

"And you think that means you can't be stalking her?" Lola says accusingly.

"You should go," Bria says.

"I think I should stay."

The man who sent the drink is back. "Is there a problem?"

Bria shakes her head. "No problem."

"Yes there is," Katherine says.

The man puts a hand on Bria. "Maybe you should leave. The lady obviously doesn't want you here."

His hand on her makes me see red, and I ball my hands into fists. "I'm her goddamn boyfriend."

He laughs. "Doesn't look like it from where I'm standing." He takes Bria's hand. "Come on. You'll be safe with me."

I tackle him, then punch him. Bria and her friends scream at me to get off him. A bouncer comes over and lifts me off the jerk. He bends my arm against my back and escorts me outside.

I crane my neck around and see Bria is crying.

The bouncer thrusts me out the door, and I fall to the sidewalk. "Get out of here before someone presses charges. We don't allow that shit here."

Bria doesn't come after me. And the jerk is still in there with her.

I sit on a bench for an hour, watching everyone who leaves the bar. Finally, the jerk comes out with his friends. Bria isn't with them. They get in a cab.

I breathe a sigh of relief but wonder how many more like him are still inside.

She hasn't come out at midnight, and I leave. But I don't go home.

~ ~ ~

I shift around on the pavement, my ass getting sore from sitting here for so long. A cab pulls up. I check the time. Bria opens the door and stumbles out.

"Really? It's two in the morning, and you just fell out of a fucking cab."

"What are you doing here?" she slurs.

"How drunk are you?"

She fumbles with her keys. "Not drunk enough to forget that my so-called boyfriend tracked my phone, stalked me, and then punched someone out—again."

"He had his hands on you!"

"Crew, be quiet. Someone will call the police."

"Let's talk upstairs then."

"You're not coming inside."

"Why not?"

"When are you going to learn you can't act like this?"

"Like what?" I say stupidly.

"God, Crew. Seriously? Like a jealous maniac."

"I told you, I'm not jealous."

"Bullshit. How many people have you punched for coming on to me? Hell, for even talking to me."

"That's not because I'm jealous."

"That's what it looks like to me and everyone else."

"I'm ..." I lean against the building and rub my eyes. "I'm only trying to protect you."

"From what? Guys who come on to me in bars? News flash—men are going to come on to me. They come on to girls all the time. It's a fact of life. Or do you mean protect me from the fans? Fans we need or our band will cease to exist? Either way, it's gone too far."

Someone scruffy walks up to us. "Are you okay?" he asks Bria.

I step over to him and jut a finger into his chest. "You're him. Are you stalking her?"

"Stop it! He's not stalking me. *You* are. Jonah, I'm okay. I think you should go, though."

He hesitates. "If you're sure."

"She's sure, asshole. Go."

He turns the corner into the alley next to her building. I wonder if he lives there and consider rousting him from a location too close to Bria.

She stomps her foot in impotent anger. "That is exactly what I'm talking about. You can't treat people that way."

"How do you know he wasn't waiting for you to get home and planned to force his way upstairs?"

"You mean like how *you* were waiting for me? You have a problem, and you're scaring me. I'd like you to leave." She unlocks the door and starts inside. I try to follow her. "No! How can you not see that you're becoming the very person you think you're protecting me from?"

"You're *scared* of me?"

Streetlights illuminate her tears. "I'm scared of a lot of things, not the least of which is that I fell in love with you."

I back away, the wind knocked out of me. "Fuck."

"See? I tell you I'm in love with you, and you curse."

"I told you I'm a goddamn mess."

She sags, and her eyes become vacant. "You did. That makes me an idiot, doesn't it? I knew we shouldn't do this. I've known all along. I tried to resist, but then ... and you're so obsessed with protecting me you didn't notice. Sometimes I think you have blinders on, because any fool can see how I feel. But you make me feel like I'm not here." She closes her eyes. "Or maybe you wish I were someone else."

"Bria, no."

"Don't come back." Tears flow down her cheeks. "I'm done, Crew. Find yourself a different girlfriend. And" —her chin quivers— "I think it's best you find another singer."

"Bria—"

The loud slam of the door makes me flinch.

I sit on the bench at the corner and look up. Lights turn on and then off in her window. She's drunk. She couldn't have meant what she said.

I take out my phone and text her.

Me: I know you didn't mean that. I'm sorry I made you mad. We'll talk tomorrow.

Why isn't my text being delivered?
I send another.

Me: Bria, please answer me.

I call her. It rings once and goes to voicemail. My chin falls to my chest. This happened to Garrett.

My throat closes and a tight pressure makes my chest hurt. Bria hasn't turned her phone off. She's blocked my number.

Chapter Thirty-nine

Bria

I lie in bed, hiding my head under the covers as if that will somehow protect me from my problems. It's ten. I should be at rehearsal. I've been resisting the temptation to unblock Crew's number for hours. He's probably texted me a dozen times, but I can't do it. If I take him back, I'll be accepting his behavior.

What I said to him last night is true. I love him. I think I've loved him for months. But he can't love me back. How can he when he's already in love with someone else? Someone I can never compete with? I know his behavior has everything to do with her, but I can't allow him to treat me that way.

It's the other thing I said to him that kept me awake most of the night. Am I really quitting the band?

My phone pings with a text.

> **Liam: Crew said you're sick. He's busy so he asked me to text you. I hope it's nothing serious. What about tonight?**

He didn't tell them I blocked him? Is he expecting me to change my mind and forget everything that's happened? I read Liam's text again. What *about* tonight? What about *tomorrow* night? We have two gigs this weekend.

Me: I think you'll have to count me out for the whole weekend unless you want me throwing up on the fans. I'm sorry. I know this puts you in a bind.

Liam: That sucks. We'll handle it. Get better soon.

Me: Thanks.

I put my phone away and hide again.

~ ~ ~

For five days I've been wallowing in misery, pretending to be ill. Brett threatened to come get me after his shift if I didn't call him back.

My phone rings. It's Ronni. "Hello?"

"I assume you're here?"

"Where's here?"

"Your apartment. I'm downstairs. Will you please buzz me up before I get hacked into tiny pieces and shoved in the sewer?"

"I'll be right down."

I look around my place. There are food cartons and soda cans scattered about, but I leave them. I catch a glimpse of myself in the mirror. At least I showered last night, so I don't look completely hideous. I throw on a pair of yoga pants and a fresh T-shirt and go down.

"We need to talk," Ronni says, barreling past me. "Which flea-infested domicile is yours?"

"Second floor on the right."

We go upstairs, and she looks at my open door and then at me. "You leave your door open? Are you *trying* to get raped and pillaged?"

I try not to think of Crew and all the times he chastised me for the same thing. We go inside.

"Hmm," she says. "It's smaller than my shoe closet but not as bad as I pictured."

"You thought cockroaches would be skittering across the floor? Sorry to disappoint you."

"You don't seem sick. Jesus, Brianna, you're pregnant, aren't you?"

I can't help it. I laugh. "God, no."

"Then why the hell did you force Jeremy to cancel two performances?"

I sit on the couch and look at the wall.

She huffs out a sharp breath. "It's Crew, isn't it? You're having some kind of lovers' quarrel?"

"It's not that simple."

She pulls out a chair from the small dining table, brushes off the seat, and walks it over to the couch, putting it down across from me. "Listen, if it were up to me, Reckless Alibi would be an all-male band. But in the past several months, IRL has invested a lot of time and money into the band, and your absence has put us in an awkward position. If you were to leave, we'd have to find another singer. Not that it would be hard to replace you. There are a thousand girls who could do what you do, but we'd have to rebrand everything with her likeness." She purses her lips. "When will people listen to me when I say inter-band relationships never work?"

"They can work. It *was* working, but it's … complicated."

"Have you ever been in a relationship that wasn't?"

"Why are you here?"

She opens her bag and hands me a folder.

"What's this?"

"Dissolution papers to separate you from the band. As agreed upon in the addendum you signed, if it's your choice to leave, you walk away with nothing."

I think of all the songs I wrote that wouldn't be mine anymore. "I don't know."

She stands. "You'd better figure it out. I'm not cancelling any more performances. Crew will sing alone until I find your replacement. You have one week to decide. If you don't sign the papers or show up for rehearsal by next Monday, IRL will sue you for damages. We spent fifty thousand dollars shooting a music video, Brianna. Not to mention all the social media campaigns, press, album covers … need I go on?"

I swallow hard. "If I sign, I don't have to pay that?"

"Between you and me, no judge will require you to reimburse us for *everything* we spent on you, but it doesn't look like you can afford even a fraction of it. Make your decision by Monday."

I nod and put the folder on the table.

Ronni goes to the door. "I know about you and Adam Stuart. I did my research on you. Seems like it's your MO to date the lead singer of a band and then wallow in the drama that ensues."

"There was no drama with White Poison."

She chuckles. "Apparently, you haven't seen the video."

"What?"

"Don't you know by now that everything you do is out there? Especially when you're famous or hanging around with those who are." She leaves, slamming the door behind her.

I race to my laptop and google my name, but all it shows are pictures of me with Reckless Alibi. I try Adam's name and White Poison. It takes me twenty minutes, but I finally find it. Somebody recorded me telling off Adam. I notice something in the background and play it a few more times. Crew is standing behind me, looking like he wants to kill Adam. He was protective before we knew each other. When he didn't even like me.

My head falls back against the couch. I'm so confused.

I pick up my phone and send Brett a text.

Me: Can I stay at your place for a few days?

~ ~ ~

I sit at Brett's table, listening to the radio while he makes coffee. One of our songs comes on. I close my eyes and listen. I remember exactly how we sing it onstage. How we look at each other. How we touch each other. The thought of Crew singing it with another woman guts me.

"Seems like I hear you guys every day now." Brett puts a cup in front of me. "Hey, why are you crying? What's going on?"

"I don't know what to do."

He appraises me over the rim of his coffee cup. He puts the cup down. "Bria, are you pregnant?"

"Why does everyone keep asking me that? No, I'm not pregnant."

"Then what is it?"

"It's Crew. I broke up with him, and I may have left the band."

"You quit?"

"Sort of. I have a week to decide."

"Tell me everything."

As I lay it all out for him, telling him about Crew's overprotective behavior, his tracking me, and Abby's dying, I wait for Brett to go ballistic. Maybe I need someone to tell me to cut Crew out of my life and assure me that quitting the band is the right thing to do.

"Wow, you've been dealing with a lot."

"Why are you being so calm about this? Aren't you pissed off?"

"You said yourself he's not hurting you. He's protecting you." His spine stiffens. "You're telling me the truth, right? He's not hurting you, is he?"

"No. Absolutely not. He's really good to me. But he's physically hurt other people, and he tracked my phone. Followed me when I was out with friends. Isn't that way out of bounds?"

"Sounds like some of them might have had it coming. People deal with grief in different ways, Bria. He lost someone. And based on what you told me, Abby was very important to him. Having someone you love die is a game changer, and a lot of the time, the changes are not good."

"I get that he loved her and she died, but it's been seven years."

"Do you know how long it took me to go up in a tall building after Mom died? A lot more than seven years. It's called PTSD, and it presents in a lot of different ways. He lost one woman he loved. He doesn't want to lose another."

"He doesn't love me."

"Are you sure?"

"He loves Abby."

"That doesn't mean he can't love you. I still love Mom."

"That's different."

"I'm not sure it is. The heart has an infinite capacity for love. He'll always love her in some way. Maybe, like you, he doesn't think he can love you both."

"But his behavior … it's not right."

"It's not. He probably needs professional help. You said he's never turned his anger toward you, yet you seem scared of him."

"I am. Well, not *of* him, more like I'm scared *for* him. And for us and the band and any poor guy who hits on me." My head falls into my hands. "Why did I let us get involved? I should have known better. First Adam and now this. When will I learn?"

"Don't beat yourself up. Do you know how many people find love at work? When you're with the same people day after day, it's inevitable. Even more so when you write emotional songs about each other."

"What if we can't be together, Brett? How can I continue to sing with him? I can't imagine doing it. Then again I can't imagine *not* doing it. Ronni already told me she's all too happy to hire someone else."

"So you sing with Crew or another woman does it. Which is the lesser of two evils?"

I pound my forehead on the table. "Honestly, I'm not sure."

"Option one will at least give you a paycheck."

"I know, but is that a reason to stay?"

"You need to figure out if there's another reason."

"How do I make that decision by Monday? What do I do?"

He puts a supportive hand on my shoulder. "Nobody can tell you that." Emma and the kids come in. He looks at them lovingly and then leans close to me. "Emma was scared, too. Like him, she didn't want to lose someone else important to her. Because of PTSD, she pushed me away. I'm happy as hell I gave her a second chance, and a third and a fourth. It was all worth it, kiddo."

Leo runs into his arms. Brett high-fives Evie and then kisses Emma. They're the perfect family.

Brett takes my hand. "Grief is different for everyone, and healing can be a slow, arduous process. Then one day, one moment even, when you aren't expecting it, everything changes."

I wonder if that moment will ever happen for Crew. More importantly, I wonder if I'm willing to stick around to see if it does.

Chapter Forty

Crew

I stand outside the barn, like I have every day this week, hoping she'll show up. I keep making excuses for why she's not here. But it's been a week of zero contact, and it's Friday. We have two shows this weekend. Liam calls out to me, and I kick the side of the barn.

I go back inside. I'm not even sure why we're rehearsing without Bria, but Jeremy insisted on it. He's here today too, which is unusual.

Liam turns on the amps, and I adjust the volume on the mic. When the door opens, I eagerly turn around, but it's Ronni, and she's not alone.

She strolls across the floor, a young woman in tow. "This is Tiffani. She'll be rehearsing with you today."

I stare down Ronni. "What the fuck?"

"Someone want to explain what's going on here?" Garrett says.

"He hasn't told you?" Ronni asks.

Brad steps forward. "Told us what?"

All eyes are on me. I sit on my stool and rub my face. "Bria isn't sick, and I'm not sure she's coming back."

They immediately stop what they're doing and swarm me.

"Tell us," Liam says.

"We kind of got in a fight."

Liam shakes his head over and over. "You mean you were being an overprotective ass, and she called you on it."

I feel all kinds of stupid.

"Shit." Liam goes to the couch and sits down. "So she's done?"

"No. I'm giving her time."

Ronni steps forward. "Well, time is running out, boys. She has until Monday, at which time she'll be officially severed from the band."

"Monday? That's not enough time."

Jeremy joins the conversation. "Whatever your issues, you'd better resolve them quickly or things will change."

I look at the new girl, not even remembering her name. "If we have until Monday, there's no need to audition anyone now, right?"

"We have to move forward," Ronni says. "Tiffani is not auditioning. She knows your material. She's agreed to my terms. She'll be replacing Brianna."

I stand up so fast, I knock the stool over. "No fucking way."

"Whoa now," Garrett says. "It's our band. Don't we get to say who's part of it?"

Ronni gives Tiffani a push toward the mic. "I think you'll find her extremely capable, and I'm not about to cancel two more performances."

"We're not Reckless Alibi without Bria," Liam says.

"Look around you," Jeremy says. "She's not here. She hasn't been here for a week. We have to be proactive about this. You can't wait around for her. If she isn't professional enough to put her personal feelings aside for the band, you shouldn't want her singing with you."

I get in Jeremy's face. "It's not her fault. It's mine."

"Either way, the show must go on."

Ronni says, "Time is money. Let's get started. Stick to the regular stuff. Nothing new." She hands us each a playlist. "Here's what you'll play this weekend. Tiffani has learned all of these songs."

I peruse the list. "No."

Ronni comes closer. "What did you say?"

I glance at the new girl. "I said I won't sing these with her."

"Oh, but you will, or have you forgotten the part where every one of you is replaceable?"

"What if we refuse to play?" Garrett asks.

Ronni belts out a mutinous laugh. "Then you'd be in breach of contract, and IRL will sue you for a million dollars."

"A million dollars?" Brad asks, turning ashen.

"That's what it takes to buy your way out of the contract. Unless you have that kind of money, I suggest you get your asses over there and meet your obligations."

I turn to Jeremy. "Is that true?"

"I'm afraid so."

Brad herds us in a huddle. "Listen, it's one rehearsal. Let's just get through it and then we can figure out how to get Bria back. We have all afternoon to come up with something."

"What else can we do?" Garrett says.

I let out an exasperated breath. "I fucking hate this."

"Then do something to fix it," Liam says. "But right now, we don't have a choice."

We take our places. I hesitate. Tiffani strolls over to me. "I know this isn't what you wanted, but give me a chance. Maybe Brianna will come back, but if not, I'm here."

I rub the tense muscles in my neck. "Her name is Bria."

"Sorry. Maybe Bria will come back." She's not snobby about it, like Ronni. She's actually kind of nice.

I mentally kick myself for putting us in this situation and hold out a hand. "Crew."

She shakes. "Tiffani."

"You really know all the stuff?"

"Ronni called me a few days ago. I've worked for IRL for two years as a house singer. She thought I'd be a good fit. Trust me, I won't let you down."

"Let's go down the playlist," Garrett says. As he counts us off, I hope I can get through the next few hours.

When she starts singing, my hand balls up so tightly that my fingernails draw blood. She's good, but she's not Bria.

The music stops. I missed my cue.

"Again, from the top," Liam says sympathetically.

I take my mic as far away from Tiffani as I can, but the music is all around me. Her *voice* is all around me. She hits every note, every inflection, and I curse myself as I betray Bria and sing.

Two hours later, after Ronni and Jeremy babysit us through the entire rehearsal, Ronni pulls me aside. "I trust you'll put yourself into it during the show."

"I'm doing what you said, Ronni. What more do you want?"

"I want a performance. Nobody wants to see you sit on a stool and sing to the goddamn wall. Take some shots, smoke some weed. I don't care what you have to do to make it happen as long as you make it happen."

"I suppose you'll be there to make sure I don't mess up? You do realize we have a manager."

"I'm well aware of Jeremy's capabilities. He's the one who gets you where you need to be. He makes sure Garrett's drums are set up properly, the sound check gets completed, and there's a place to park the van. But make no mistake, *I* run the show."

I laugh bitterly. "I really thought it was because you were jealous over Bria, but now I know you act like this because you're a stone-cold bitch."

"If that's what it takes to get things done." She turns to Tiffani. "Great job, Tiff. You fit right in, like I knew you would. We can talk details during the ride home."

They leave, along with Jeremy. The barn is eerily quiet as the guys stare at me.

"I know," I say. "I screwed up. I've tried all week to contact her, but she won't take my calls. She blocked me. I even followed someone into her building yesterday, but she didn't answer her door. I sat outside for hours. I think she's gone."

"Can you give us a minute?" Liam asks Brad and Garrett.

They go outside.

"You have to fix this," Liam says.

"I know, but she won't see me."

"You misunderstand me. She's not the one who needs fixing. *You* are."

"What are you talking about?"

"Don't give me that shit. You're so fucked up, you can't see straight. And through all that fucked-up-ness you can't see what's right in front of you. Everyone knows you love Bria. Everyone but you and Bria, that is. But until you work your shit out, Abby will always be in your way. I'm not saying you have to forget her, but you need to let her go."

I pinch the bridge of my nose. "I'm not sure I know how."

"You'd better figure it out fast. You have to get control of this anger that's eating you up inside. You have to figure out how to be with her and not think that what happened to Abby will happen to her, because it won't. The world is fucked up, and there are psychos out there, but you need to reel it in before she's gone forever." He jabs a finger into my chest. "Do whatever the hell you have to do to make this right, and do it now."

He leaves me alone in the barn.

I pick up my notebook and turn to the song I've tried a hundred times to complete. I stare at it for a long time, but there are no lyrics in my head. I can't finish it. I slam it shut and fling it off the table. How in the hell am I supposed to fix this if I can't finish the song?

Finally, I get off the couch. I lean down to pick up the notebook but stop when I see the page it opened to. I've never shown this song to anyone. It's dark, sinister. It's about all the rage that was inside me after Abby died. I read the lyrics and realize Liam's right. Seven years later, and I can't let go of it.

I sit back down and stare at the words.

Realization smacks me in the face. Maybe it's not just *her* I can't let go of.

I sink into the couch, knowing what I have to do, but I'd never get in to see him without an act of Congress. I can only think of one person who might help. I pick up my phone, feeling like a traitor.

Dirk answers on the second ring. "What can I do for you, Chris?"

Several hours later, after being vetted, patted down, and run through a metal detector, I sit in a room wearing a large badge on my chest that reads: BRIDGEPORT CORRECTIONAL CENTER – VISITOR

Dr. Evans walks in, and his eyes immediately tear up. He comes over to me, head bobbing up and down, lips pressed together in a thin line. He sits opposite me at the table.

"I was wondering when you were going to show up," Abby's father says. "It only took you seven years."

"Sorry, Dr. Evans."

"I think we're way past that, Chris. Call me Jim."

I can't help but stare at him. I don't remember him having such deep lines around his eyes and on his forehead. And his hair, cut short, is graying around the ears and temples. The man is still in his forties, but he looks closer to sixty. I guess that's what prison does to a person.

When I can't speak—mostly because I can't get anything past the colossal lump in my throat—I reach out to shake his hand, but the guard clears his throat and motions to the NO PHYSICAL CONTACT sign on the wall.

"It's nice to see you, son," Jim says. "You're looking well."

"You, too."

"Bullshit."

I'm shocked. Never had he uttered a single curse word when I knew him. I guess that's also what prison does to a person.

"I've heard your music, you know," he says proudly. "Reckless Alibi songs are on the radio all the time. Well done."

"How did you know that's my band?"

"Shelly visits me from time to time. She was here last month."

"My mom comes to see you?"

"Not often. A few times a year maybe. At first I didn't like it. It reminded me of you, and you reminded me of Abigail."

My chest tightens at his use of her name. "Why would she come here?"

He shrugs. "She feels bad, I suppose. I lost my child and then my wife left me. She still has you. Over the years I found myself looking forward to her visits. Eventually I liked hearing about you."

I'm still amazed Mom comes to visit him.

"So what brings you to this fine establishment?" he jokes. "I know it's not the food."

I remain silent.

"You can sit there and say nothing, son, but our thirty minutes is going to be over before you know it."

I think of all the things I was going to say to him, but nothing sounds right. Seconds tick away on the large clock secured to the cement wall. I look at it for one full circumnavigation of the second hand.

I go completely off-script and say something from the heart. "I hated you."

He nods. "I hated myself for a long time. Still do most days."

"No, this was before. I hated you for being so strict. For making Abby feel like she couldn't come to you. For making us hide our relationship."

"I know you did. She was my only child. My one chance to show the world what a great father I was. But in trying to do that, I lost her."

"You had nothing to do with what happened."

"That's not what I meant. I lost her love, her adoration. I lost it because I felt I had to control everything. Maybe that's why she was so drawn to you. You represented everything I didn't. Fun, freedom, unconditional love. I'm sure she hated me like you did."

"She didn't hate you. She loved you."

"She loved *you*."

I close my eyes. "I know, but you were her father. No matter what restrictions you put on her, she still loved you. She told me she did."

His eyes mist. "I appreciate you telling me that, but that's not why you're here after all these years, is it?"

"I'm not entirely sure why I came. I just knew I had to."

"Your mom tells me you have a special lady."

Guilt courses through me.

"Abigail would have wanted that for you. After she died, I watched videos of her singing in your band. The way you two looked at each other—that's true love. Anyone who loves you like that wants you to be happy. If this new lady makes you happy, then you can rest easy knowing Abigail is happy for you."

Tears threaten my eyes. "But I made her a promise."

"I made lots of promises, too." He fingers the cross at the end of a long chain around his neck. "One of which was 'Thou shalt not kill'."

I cringe. I could so easily have been one of the inmates in this very institution.

"There's something I never told you, Dr.—I mean Jim. Something I've never told *anyone*."

"I'm not a priest, Chris. You shouldn't be confessing anything to me."

"Maybe not, but I have to tell you this because I think about it all the time. In some twisted way, I sometimes think life would be easier if I were here and you weren't."

"What are you talking about?"

My heart beats wildly knowing that for the first time, I'm about to say what I've never said before. "The last morning of the trial, I went to Liam's uncle's house. I knew that monster wasn't going to get what he deserved, and Dirk would have what I needed. The district attorney told us from the beginning that Connecticut wouldn't uphold a death penalty. But I knew I could make it happen if the judge and jury couldn't. That day at the courthouse, after they sentenced him, I waited outside in the bushes with Dirk's Smith and Wesson."

He goes white in the face. "Lord Jesus!"

"I was going to kill him, but *you* did it instead." I choke on my words. "When I heard the gun go off and he hit the ground, I thought it was me who'd shot him. I didn't remember pulling the trigger, but he was bleeding on the ground. From where I was hiding, I could see the blood spurting from his mouth. I panicked and ran, throwing the gun into a pond, but I couldn't stay away. I had to make sure he was dead. When I returned, you were on your knees, surrounded by police, and the area was being cordoned off. I was part of the crowd watching you get arrested and him get put into a body bag. I felt so guilty that you had gotten blamed for something I did, but then I got home and watched the news. Someone had recorded the whole thing. You appeared with your gun, said something about Abby, and then shot him from twenty feet away before giving yourself up."

Jim reaches for my hand, but the guard warns him about touching, and he pulls back. "I don't know what to say."

I picture myself in his tan state-issued jumpsuit. "It should be me in here."

"No. No way."

"How can you say that? It was *my* fault he took her."

"He was stalking her, Chris. If he hadn't taken her then, it would have been another time."

"I should have protected her."

"You don't think I've told myself that a million times? I'm her father. If I couldn't protect her, no one could. It was *my* job, not yours. You and I both know she was an independent soul. She'd have hated it if you'd become so controlling it overshadowed your relationship. You have to stop blaming yourself. No one does, least of all Abigail."

I wince every time he says her name. "But it should have been me who killed him."

"You don't know this yet because you haven't raised a child, but one day you'll understand, and then you'll know why I did it." He laughs sadly. "I wasn't even sure myself until this very minute. I was a pastor. It went against everything I believed in. I knew it was a sin, even though *he* was the sinner, but I was compelled. Driven. Almost like I was on auto-pilot." He cocks his head and smiles. "But now I know why. I couldn't save her, but I did save *you*."

My throat thickens. I can't speak.

"You're young. You have your whole life ahead of you. Look at what you've accomplished so far. You've made a name for yourself, and your mother is so proud of you. She beams with joy every time she speaks of you. And now you have a new lady. The future is full of possibilities. You have to stop feeling guilty about her, about me. You've just given me the best gift I've ever received. You've given me peace."

"Time's up," the guard says.

"Chris, I assume you're having some kind of internal struggle. This new lady of yours … your mother tells me she's lovely and she loves you. Is she worthy of your love, like my Abigail was?"

I swallow hard and nod.

"Good." A guard comes to take him away. "Trust in that," Jim says over his shoulder. "Don't waste second chances." He points up. "*He* might decide not to give you a third. Goodbye, son."

I sit at the table long after the door shuts behind him. Then I wonder if I have enough time to do something before tonight's gig. When I leave, I text Liam and tell him I'll meet everyone in the city at eight.

Then I do what I should have done a long time ago.

Chapter Forty-one

Bria

I hear a knock. I open the front door and find Crew standing on Brett's doorstep. He's leaning against the porch rail with his hands shoved in his pockets. My heart flips over at the first sight of him in a week, but I take a step back, putting distance between us. My heart doesn't know what my head does.

"Why are you here?"

"Why do you think, Bria?"

"Because you want me in the band."

The look in his eyes weighs heavy upon me. "I do—we all do—but that's not why I'm here."

"Save your breath. I have to figure things out myself." I try to shut the door.

He lunges forward and stops it with his shoe. "Please let me talk to you. I'm ready to tell you everything."

A long, arduous sigh works itself out of me. "I appreciate that, but I'm not sure what that will accomplish. I understand you lost someone important to you. Maybe that explains why you are the way you are, but it doesn't excuse it."

"I know that, but there's a lot you don't know. I'm not making excuses for what I did or asking you to forgive me. But maybe talking about it is the first step to, I don't know, maybe fixing it."

Despite how much I want to lock him out, an equally strong force urges me to give him a chance. He wants to tell me everything. How can I turn him away when I know how hard this must be for him?

I step back and let him in. "Brett's at work, and everyone else is across the street at Emma's mom's house."

He motions vaguely. "Uh, where should we …?"

I go into the kitchen. "You want coffee?"

"Okay."

The townhouse is eerily quiet as I make it. I can feel him watching me. A sick feeling twists my stomach, knowing I'm about to find out what happened to Abby. Do I even want to know? If she died in a car accident, there wouldn't be all this cloak and dagger stuff, would there?

I pour us each a cup and sit across from him at the table.

He stares at the empty chair between us. "I don't know where to begin."

"How about at the beginning? Where did you meet?"

I sip my coffee as he tells me about band class and instantly being a couple. He touches his notebook when he tells me how he wrote songs for her, and she sang them, how she wanted to be a part of his band, but her parents wouldn't allow it. By the time we finish our second cups, I feel like I know her, and I'm genuinely sad to hear what's to come. Because I know there's a lot. I can hear it in his hesitant voice. See it in the tension around his eyes. Sense it in the way he rubs his tattoo. What he tells me will wreck him in ways I can't begin to imagine.

After a long silence, he says, "There was this guy she worked with at the fast food place."

Dread forms a knot in my gut knowing this guy is the reason she's no longer here.

"He ..." —his eyes close, and he takes a shaky breath— "liked her. He requested they be put on the same shifts. He kept asking her out." He rubs his jaw. "He was a lot older than we were."

His phone rings, but he silences it and turns it over. "He got fired but he still came around. He'd order food and stay at the counter, trying to talk to her. Or he'd go to the drive-thru and hold up other cars. One day I was there when he came in." He squeezes his eyes shut and rubs his temples. "I told him to fuck off. Said I'd kill him if he bothered her again."

My mouth goes dry. I think I know where this is going and suddenly everything Crew has done makes sense.

"A week later she didn't show up at the fair where we were performing." His eyes get glassy. "She never missed a gig."

"Crew," I say. "You don—"

"I have to tell you." His coffee cup has long been drained. He picks at a napkin, shredding it into pieces as his story unfolds. "I found her car. Her stuff was scattered on the ground. She was ..." —his words drag on slowly as if he's afraid of them— "gone."

My eyes close, tears cascading down my cheeks. He looks utterly destroyed yet there's still so much he hasn't told me.

"A week went by without any word and no clues as to where she was, other than my telling the police about *him*. Then it was a Thursday. Her birthday." He bites his bottom lip so hard he breaks the skin. Blood beads. "They found her body on her fucking birthday."

I cry right along with him. I want so desperately to reach out to him, but I know he's not ready for that. "I'm s-so s-sorry, Chris."

Skin bunches around his eyes. "I haven't told you the worst part." He swallows hard. "He hadn't touched her. The police speculated he was surprised by her condition. The only marks on her were from trying to escape the room he had her in."

"Her condition?"

"She was ..." He goes completely ashen. "She was—" His chair falls over as he bolts out of it. "Bathroom!"

I point to the door and he runs in and slams it behind him. For five minutes, between agonizing sobs, he retches into the toilet.

When he returns, pale and sweaty, I hand him a bottle of water. He nods his thanks and drinks.

"You don't have to do this."

"Yes I do." He finishes the water and sits again. He gazes at his notebook for endless moments. He leafs through the pages and stops. Tears stream as he pushes the notebook across the table.

"Are you sure?" I ask.

He nods.

Moisture clouds my vision as I read the song title: 'Gone Too Soon.'

My throat tightens knowing this is a song about Abby's death.

You were gone before I met you,
taken dark into the night
Would have fought like hell to keep you,
would have given my own life
It's hell on earth without you,
but I know we'll meet one day

You're gone too soon
Now you're far away

I swallow a painful lump and read the second verse.

I visit you in the tiny grave,
it's all that I have left
Every time you fall upon my dreams
is one more precious gift
Her face I place upon you
every night and every day
You're gone too soon
Now you're far away

I shake in realization. *Gone before I met you. Tiny grave.* This song isn't about Abby. I glance at his tattoo—the knife piercing two roses. Not one, *two.*

My heart sinks as I look up at him. "Abby was pregnant?"

He lets out an agonizing howl. It's the most painful sound I've ever heard. I fall to my knees next to him, and he wraps me in his arms, his sobs shaking both of us. I stay there so long that my knees hurt and my feet go numb, but my pain is nothing compared to what he's going through. What he *went* through.

Sometime later—I don't know how much time has passed—he lets go of me, and I sit in the chair next to him. "You don't have to say anymore." I take his hand in mine.

"You have to hear all of it, or maybe I need to say it."

"All right. I'm listening."

He breathes in and out three times. Deep slow breaths. I know because I'm counting. "Like I said, the police think her condition freaked him out. Or maybe it confused him. After everything came out, they said he was delusional. He wanted her for himself. He fantasized that they were a couple. He was probably going to …" He pulls his hand from mine and rips at the napkin again. "He was probably going to rape her, but they think when he saw her belly, the sicko somehow thought the baby was his. He left her there. Locked her in his basement and went to work. After his shift he … God, Bria, he went shopping for baby stuff."

Bile rises in my throat.

"He was gone all night and most of the morning. He worked the overnight shift at a gas station. He waited outside the baby store for it to open. By the time he returned home …" He hesitates, and I lean over and wipe his cheeks. "By the time he got home, they were dead."

I'm both devastated and surprised. "He didn't do it?"

"He fucking did it, all right. By taking her—them—he caused it to happen. The medical examiner said she was so traumatized she went into early labor. She was dehydrated because he didn't bother to give her a goddamn glass of water. Between that, the emotional trauma that psycho put her through, and the physical exertion of her trying to escape, she had contractions. With no medical help to stop them, she" —he looks away— "she delivered the baby."

"Oh, God," I cry, my hands trembling almost as hard as his.

His lips twitch painfully. "My daughter was too little to survive."

I have no idea what to say as he relives his nightmare. All I can do is be here. Offer him my hand. Share in his tears. Absorb some of his pain.

"She died giving birth?" I ask hesitantly.

He shakes his head. "I wish she had." His words are so thick and gravelly, I have to strain to hear them. "She watched our tiny baby come out of her, then she watched her die." He slams a fist on the table. "Fuck!"

I grab his hand. "It's okay. Let it out."

His eyes are red and swollen, his cheeks pale, and his breathing fast. For the first time today, he looks directly at me. "She watched her die and then she tied a sheet to a rafter and looped it around her neck."

My hand covers the sob that begs to come out. I want to break down, but I can't allow it. None of this is about me.

"He didn't even call the goddamn police when he found them. He cut her down and laid them both on the bed he'd put down there. He kept them there for a fucking week, like they were his family. It wasn't until a neighbor smelled—" He looks like he's going to vomit again.

"Chris." I stand. "Come with me." I lead him to the couch and get him a shot of whiskey. Then another.

He tells me about wanting to kill the guy. About Dr. Evans killing him instead and then about seeing him today for the first time since it all happened. He tells me he planned to name the baby Nicole, which was Abby's middle name, despite how he teased her about wanting to call her Slash. Then, from sheer exhaustion mixed with alcohol, he falls asleep, his head in my lap. I cry as I brush back the hair of this broken man.

An hour later, he wakes, pops up, and looks at the time. "Shit, I have to go. The gig."

I get off the couch with him. "You're going to the show?" I look back at the kitchen table where he spilled his guts to me. "After *this*?"

He fetches his phone and notebook. "Ronni's got us by the balls, Bria. I have to." He holds out a hand. "Come with me."

I step back. "I'm grateful you opened up to me, but it's a lot to process, and I'm not sure it changes the reasons why I left."

"But now you know why I am the way I am."

"But knowing why you act that way and putting up with it because of your loss are two different things. You need help, Chris. Help I can't give you."

"I'll get it, I promise. Anything. Just sing with me."

I shake my head sadly. "I can't."

"Even if …" He looks pained. "Even if I say I might love you?"

My heart twinges. My eyes get glassy. "*Especially* if you say that. I can't be with someone who *might* love me. I know you love her even though she's gone, and I'm okay with that, but you need time. You just ripped off a big damn Band-Aid, and your wounds are raw. You need time to deal with that before you can move forward with me."

"But you only have until Monday, and I don't want to sing with Tiffani."

My eyebrows touch the ceiling and my spine stiffens. "Tiffani?"

"Ronni pulled another dick move and hired someone to replace you if you don't come back. She practiced with us this morning."

I sit on a chair so heavily, it hurts my butt. "She didn't even wait for the body to get cold, did—oh God, Crew, I'm sorry."

"Please don't walk on eggshells around me. That's not why I told you."

"Why exactly did you?"

"Because it was time, and I wanted you to know. I can't explain it, but everything about today was, I don't know … cathartic."

I smile. "I'm glad, and I'm happy you went to see Dr. Evans, but I'm still not going tonight."

"You're not going *tonight*, or you're not going *ever*?"

I try to picture Crew singing with someone else. A wave of nausea comes over me. But jealousy is not a reason to give in. "I can't answer that right now. I have a lot of thinking to do."

He comes close and takes my hand. "There's a reason I never told anyone until now. I know you don't trust me after what I've done, but I swear to you I'm going to change. Give me a chance to prove it to you."

I gesture to the door. "You should go. You'll be late."

He opens it. "I really hope you'll give me a chance, Bria. Give *us* a chance. This is the honest truth. Even if you can't take me back, there's nobody else I want onstage with me. You're the only woman I want to sing with. Our songs belong to *us,* no one else. I'm willing to have you there any way I can get you."

His words resonate in my head long after he's gone.

I love him. He *might* love me. That also means he might *not*. Am I willing to risk it all again? What happens if nothing gets better? What happens if we end up right back where we were? Wouldn't it be easier to make the break now?

But my truth is the same as his. He's the only man I want to sing with, and maybe that can be enough.

Chapter Forty-two

Crew

Seven years ago

A week after Abby's eighteenth birthday, they finally let us put them in the ground. A week of seconds dragging on like hours. Of every torturous minute being a reminder of how alone I am. Of each day feeling like an eternity without them.

I didn't hear a word at the service. All I could do was stare blindly at the caskets, one of them so tiny it's hard to believe they make them that small. Abby's parents asked if I wanted the baby to be buried with Abby, but she was already a person to me. She deserves to have her own place in the world, as she did in my heart. I picked the words for her tombstone.

'Baby Girl Rewey – gone too soon – loved forever'

I was asked if I wanted to speak at the service, but I couldn't. Anything I wanted to say was written in a song that is about to be lowered into the ground, along with her body. I didn't need to stand up and tell everyone what a great person she was or how much I loved her. Everyone knows it. The words belong solely to Abby, and the song dies with her. No one will ever see it. Nobody will ever sing it.

Music is the only thing that's kept me going. I eat when I'm forced to. I sleep when exhaustion claims me. But music is the constant in my life, though I'll never be able to sing again.

But I can write. I want to kill Rob Vargas—I wrote a song about it. I contemplate killing myself—I wrote a song about that too. I can't sing—yup, another song. My notebook fills with lyrics pouring from my heart and soul.

After putting a single rose on each casket, I sit in the front row of chairs at the gravesite. Mom holds my hand while the minister says something about ashes and dust and returning to where we came from. Someone behind me puts a hand on my shoulder. I think it's Liam. He's all too familiar with burying a loved one. The circumstances were different, but he might be one of the only people who understands the hell I'm going through.

On the other side of the caskets are Abby's parents. They look as devastated as I feel. I'm sure they think it's worse for them, losing their only child. They think I'm young and can go on to love someone else. Have another baby even. Replace what I've lost, unlike them. They think that at eighteen, maybe we didn't know what love really is. But they'd be wrong. I loved her. I *love* her. I promised her I'd never say those words to another person.

It starts to rain. Not hard, just a drizzle. I'm glad, because the sun shouldn't shine when two young innocent people are put in the earth. As they lower the caskets into the ground, a song is played. It's Abby's favorite. Liam recorded it a few months ago during rehearsal. We're singing. *She's* singing. Although it guts me to hear her, I know I'll always have this piece of her.

When the caskets go down far enough, and I can no longer see them, I stand up and move closer to keep that connection for as long as possible. When they reach the bottom and get covered, that's it. It's all over.

The song ends.

Hot tears stream down my face as I watch my world slip away. Only two words bounce around in my head.

What now?

Chapter Forty-three

Bria

The last twenty-four hours have been torture. Not only has Crew's horrible story been haunting me, but someone recorded Reckless Alibi last night, and I can't stop watching some girl named Tiffani sing with the man I love.

"You're not going to let someone else live your life, are you?" Brett says.

He's looking over my shoulder. I wonder how long he's been standing there.

I put down my phone. "She's good."

"Not as good as you."

"She's pretty, too."

Brett stands me up and puts his hands on my shoulders. "If you need me to stand here and fluff your ego by saying you're everything she's not, I will. Because I'm the big brother, and that's what we do. But that's not going to solve your problem. You love being a part of Reckless Alibi, so go be a part of it. Get back with Crew, don't get back with him—either way, you know it's where you belong."

I sit. "It's complicated. If I go back, he'll think it's for him."

"Make sure he knows it's because you love the band."

I press my lips together and sigh. "I love *him*."

He smiles sadly. "I know you do, but one thing's for sure: you guys are not going to figure this out if he's onstage with someone else."

I look at the time. "I might be too late."

"For what?"

"We're playing in Jersey tonight."

"What time do you have to be there?"

"Nine. I'd have to go home for clothes. I'll never make it."

"Get something out of Emma's closet. I'll pull the car around."

"You're going to drive me? What about Leo and Evie? Emma's out with friends, so you have to be here."

"I'll text Bonnie across the street. Evie can watch Leo until she gets here."

My heart beats wildly. "Are you sure?"

"I haven't been to a show in a while. It'll be fun."

I bounce out of my chair, suddenly excited about going. I kiss him on the cheek and run upstairs.

~ ~ ~

Brett pulls up to the venue. "Wow, big place. You get out here, and I'll find a place to park."

"Thanks."

"Anytime. Good luck."

I hop out and go through the front door. Wow is right. This place is bigger than the nice club we played in the city. The first floor has a large bar in back, a big dance floor in front of the stage, and what must be a hundred high-top tables in-between. I crane my neck to see the second floor, where there's another bar, more tables, and private VIP viewing areas along both sides.

There's a lot of people here. Bodies mash together, dancing to the piped-in music. I weave my way through them. As I near the stage, I see Bruce setting up our equipment. There are two microphone stands.

I tense. The replacement singer is here. The whole drive over, I was worried about getting here in time. I completely forgot how awkward it would be if I barged in moments before the band took the stage. A sick feeling washes over me. What if they like her? What if they like her more than me?

I'm frozen, contemplating my choices.

"Brianna?" someone calls. It's Jeremy. He looks confused. "Does anyone know you're here?"

I shake my head.

He tries not to laugh. I don't know what's so funny.

He escorts me past a security guard, down a short hallway, and into a room. "Look what the cat dragged in."

Six pairs of eyes turn towards us. The first person I see is Crew. A smile lights up his face when he sees me. Liam, Garrett, and Brad share fist bumps.

I expect Tiffani to pout and be mad. She does just the opposite—strides over and holds out her hand. "Bria, I'm Tiffani. It's an honor to meet you. I'm a huge fan."

Bria? Okay, I don't want to, but I like her already.

Ronni stomps her heel loudly, commanding attention. "I don't know what you're doing here, Brianna, but everyone is ready. The playlist has been set. We're going on as planned—without you."

"Fuck that, *Veronica*," Crew says. He smiles at me. "Are you here to sing?"

345

"If you want me to."

"Hell yes, we want you to."

"But Tiffani's already here," Ronni says, temper flaring. "She's been rehearsing, and she sang last night."

Tiffani says, "It's okay, Ronni. Reckless Alibi is Bria's band. She has every right to be here."

Wow. This is not how I expected this to go.

"You gave her until Monday," Liam says. "It's Saturday. So there you have it. She's back." He turns to Tiffani. "Tiff, we've enjoyed having you. You're a fantastic singer. Thanks for helping us out of a bind."

"Anytime," she says. "I really enjoyed it." She pulls me aside as Ronni and Jeremy have words. "I meant it when I said I'm a big fan. I know most girls would kill for this opportunity, but Reckless Alibi wouldn't be the same without you. Plus, I really like being a house singer for IRL. I love filling in where I'm needed. I'm not tied down to anyone and that's the way I like it."

I hug the woman who might have stolen my job but didn't. "Thanks, Tiffani. I'm so glad it was you who filled in."

She thumbs at the door. "If you don't mind, I'm going to get myself a front-row seat."

Ronni stomps over. "Are you back for good or are you going to quit *every* time you get your period?"

My mouth hangs open.

"Ignore her," Crew says, tugging on my elbow until we find an empty corner.

I look around to make sure nobody is listening. "I don't want you to think ... I'm not back beca—"

"You're back for the band, not me." Disappointment momentarily flashes in his eyes. "Listen, I'm just glad you're back." He touches my hand and a pang of want surges through me.

"Me too."

"You ready for this?" Garrett asks.

I nod. "I'm more than ready. I'm sorry I left you in the lurch."

"You're back now, that's all that matters." He squeezes my shoulders. "We missed you, girl."

"I missed you, too. A lot."

Ronni stalks to the door in a huff. "No point in my staying now."

God, she is such a bitch.

"I'll be out of town for about a week," she says. "Niles has me scouting a new group in DC." She shoots me a look. "Hopefully the band will still be intact when I get back. We've got SummerStage coming up."

Jeremy puts a fatherly hand on my shoulder as he responds to her. "Everything will be fine, Ronni. Things are back to normal. We're all good."

She turns up her nose and leaves.

I used to believe Jeremy was the bad one. He's an angel to work with compared to the catty Veronica. I wonder what they said to each other a few minutes ago. Because, suddenly Jeremy is on our side, not hers.

Jeremy checks his watch. "See you out there. Have a good show." He points to me. "That means you, too, Bria."

He called me Bria! I cock my head at him, and he winks.

"Bring it in!" Garrett shouts.

As we gather in a circle, there is a twinge in my stomach. *Did they do this with Tiffani?*

Crew sees my hesitation and elbows me in the ribs. "We wouldn't do this with anyone but you."

I smile big. He counts us down, and we all yell, "Let's get Reckless!"

For the next few hours, I float on air. How did I ever think I could live without this? The energy between Crew and me is as good as ever. Maybe we can do this and not be a couple, if it comes to that.

His eyes burn into mine when he sings.

Please don't let it come to that.

After the show, we go out front for a drink. I'm nervous. I know what happens after we play. People come up to us. To me. Men mostly. And Crew usually runs them off.

I stiffen, waiting for it to happen, but before anyone can get to us, Brett finds me and gives me a hug. "You were fantastic." He looks at the others. "All of you. Man, you've really got something."

A few men who looked like they were going to approach back away. I laugh, wondering if they saw Brett and thought twice about it. My brother can be intimidating. His arms are as big as my thighs. He towers over me by almost a foot. Crew watches the men retreat. He looks deep in thought. I'm grateful that Brett's here. Maybe he should come to every show.

"I ordered drinks for everyone," Brett says.

Jeremy finds us and says he's taking off after Bruce gets our equipment loaded. The rest of us sit around a table, Brett and Crew flanking me.

"I'm glad you're all here," Crew says. "I need to talk to you about something." Brett tries to get up, but Crew stops him. "This includes you. Sit."

"What's this all about?"

You could knock me over with a feather when, right here in the nightclub as we drink whiskey shooters and beer, Crew tells my brother and all the band members what happened to Abby. He doesn't give them the details, saying only that she was kidnapped and died as a result, and that's why he acts the way he does.

348

Garrett and Brad don't know what to say, but it's obvious none of this is news to Liam. Makes sense. They grew up together. Brett isn't surprised either. I told him everything this morning when he got off shift. I think it's one of the reasons he pushed me to come tonight. Brett has seen a lot of messed up stuff over the years because of his job, and he has a soft spot for survivors.

"Shit, Crew," Garrett says. "That's messed up. I'm sorry, brother."

Brad nods. "Same. I mean … *damn*."

"I didn't share this with you so you'd feel sorry for me. I want you to help me get out of my head when things happen."

"What kind of things?" Brad asks.

"Like when strangers come up and talk to Bria, you can keep me from losing my shit. My therapist said I need to rely on those closest to me to help."

I put my hand on his, but then quickly take it away, remembering we aren't a couple. "You're seeing a therapist? Since when?"

"Since today. I found one who took emergency weekend appointments."

I look at him through narrow eyes. "You're serious about this?"

"Whatever it takes," he says evenly.

"How can we help?" Garrett asks.

Crew snorts. "I haven't exactly gotten that far. I've only had one appointment. But I was thinking you could warn me when I get too protective of her."

Brett clears his throat. "As the big brother, I'm not opposed to you being a little protective."

Crew laughs. He's *laughing* about this. I have to believe that's a step in the right direction. "Yeah, but I need to know when I cross the line between being a little protective and batshit crazy."

"How do we do that?" Brad asks.

Garrett slaps the table. "We should have a safeword."

Everyone looks at him like he's lost it.

"You know, a safeword," he says. "Like when you want to do a chick in the ass, but she doesn't want to, so she yells 'pineapple' or some shit like that."

The five of us simultaneously break into laughter. Oh, how I love being back with them.

"Or," Crew says, when the merriment abates, "you could just tell me I'm crossing a line."

"Fuck that," Liam says. "I'm going with 'pineapple'."

I'm having so much fun that I don't want to leave, but Brett just got off a twenty-four-hour shift. He needs his sleep. When we get up to go, Crew corners me. "I'm glad you're back."

I smile. "I'm glad too." I kiss him on the cheek, because that's what friends do. Don't they?

"Text me so I know you got home?" he asks sheepishly.

I contemplate telling him that's what a boyfriend asks his girlfriend, and I'm not his girlfriend anymore. At least I don't think I am. It's all very shades-of-gray at this point. But he's taken many important steps in the last day, and it's the least I can do for his peace of mind.

"I can do that."

Chapter Forty-four

Crew

After rehearsal, Bria shows us lyrics she's been working on.

"Damn, these are good," Garrett says. "Maybe you two should break up more often."

Liam hits him on the back of the head.

"Too soon?"

Liam swipes the notebook from Garrett and studies her songs. "Garrett's right. These lyrics are good. I wish I could get out of this slump I'm in and write some goddamn music for them."

"It'll happen," Bria says. "You're waiting for your inspiration."

She looks at me like *I'm* her inspiration. God, I hope so.

"I've never needed inspiration in the past," he says. "Shit always just comes to me. It's kind of a gift."

"But apparently not the kind that keeps on giving," Brad says.

Liam broods. "Shut up."

We turn off the amps and clean up our mess. Nobody turned on the radio, and I realize how quiet it is. "You guys hear that?"

They stiffen and listen. "Hear what?" Liam asks.

"The sweet sound of silence. Of Ronni not breathing down our necks, and Jeremy not being her little bitch."

"I don't know," Bria says. "I think Jeremy is coming around."

I raise an eyebrow.

"He called me Bria. He hasn't done that since we signed with IRL. I think he and Ronni had it out Saturday night. Maybe he's getting as tired of her crap as we are."

"If only," Garrett says. "It'd be nice to have him on our side."

The barn door opens, and Dirk walks in. Liam beelines over to him. "I thought I told you to leave us alone."

Dirk laughs smugly. "As this is my property, it's within my rights to tell you to go fuck yourself. But I won't because I'm not as rude as you are."

"What do you want?" Liam asks.

"It's your mother. She's piss drunk. Must be a record, as it's barely noon. The housekeeper got her into bed after she vomited in the hallway, but you'll probably want to monitor her. Make sure she doesn't choke in her sleep or something."

Liam abruptly checks his phone. "Oh, shit, today is—" He turns. "I gotta bolt."

As he runs out the door, Dirk yells after him. "You're welcome!" He lowers his voice. "Little shit doesn't appreciate a goddamn thing I do for him."

After he leaves, I rack my brain. Oh, Jesus. I feel like a douche of a friend. With everything else on my mind, I totally forgot what this day means to Liam. Then again, he did too. I quickly get out my phone and text him.

Me: I'll bring the whiskey. See you around nine?

Liam: Thanks, bro.

Every year on this day, Liam and I get shitfaced. It's a tradition neither of us particularly enjoy, but it's his way of dealing. I have my own ways. I glance at Bria. Ways I hope to change.

Starting now.

I follow her outside, catching her before she leaves. "Are you free this afternoon? There's someplace I want to take you."

Her face falls. She thinks I'm asking her out.

"It's not what you think. I have another appointment with the psychiatrist. On Saturday she said it might be helpful if you came to a session."

"Why?"

"Because you're the reason I'm there." She cringes, and I backtrack. "You're the reason I wanted to get better. I'm doing this for *you*."

Her expression softens. "I hope you're also doing it for yourself, Crew."

"Will you come? Please?"

She leans against her car and thinks about it, then she nods.

"Great. Give me a sec to get my things."

Bria follows me into the heart of Stamford in her car. She said it would make it easier to leave from there. The truth is she didn't want to sit in the car with me. She's back with the band, she's singing with me, but she's making every effort to stay away from me when the music stops. My gut tells me she's giving me space. I hope I'm right, because if she's pulling away, I would be losing one of the best things that's ever happened to me.

We sit in the reception area in silence, both of us fiddling on our phones. I hope this wasn't a bad idea.

We get called back.

"Dr. Hardy, this is Bria."

"Very nice to meet you," Dr. Hardy says. "Please, have a seat on the couch."

I sit on one end. I expect Bria to sit on the other, but she settles on the middle cushion. Not close enough for us to be touching, but close enough to send a message. To whom, I'm not sure.

"What brings you here today, Bria?" she asks.

"Crew asked me to come."

Dr. Hardy jots something in her folder.

Bria asks, "What are you writing? That I called him Crew? You think I should call him Chris, don't you? I do sometimes."

"No, Bria, that's not what I was writing. Crew is his nickname. It's perfectly acceptable for you to call him that. Back to my question: I know you're here because Chris asked you, but why did you come?"

Bria shrugs. "If he thinks I can help in some way, that's good, right?"

"What do you think he needs help with?"

Bria looks at me like she doesn't know what she can say. "It's okay," I tell her. "Dr. Hardy knows everything."

"He needs help getting over losing Abby and the baby. Maybe that will help make him less overprotective. My brother, Brett, said he's probably got PTSD."

"Chris, how do you feel about Bria discussing this with her brother?"

"I'm okay with it. I told Brett and the rest of the band Saturday night."

"What did you tell them?"

"About Abby and the baby. No details, just generalizations."

Dr. Hardy makes notes. "That's good progress. Talking about it with those close to you is a big part of recovery." She looks at Bria. "I'm not sure Chris has PTSD, however."

"He doesn't?"

"He tells me he seldom has nightmares about them anymore. As with any trauma, it's normal to experience intrusive memories, flashbacks and bad dreams after the event, but that decreases over time. What seems to be happening with Chris is that, like most people, he experienced a combination of rage and grief, along with feeling powerless. Those emotions are difficult to overcome, particularly for men."

"And that's not PTSD?"

"I don't believe so. Chris is dealing with behavioral patterns that are rooted in the trauma he experienced. He told me about the overprotective behavior that led to your leaving him and the band. This behavior is born of his belief that the world is a dangerous place, and no one can be trusted. His confrontational response suggests an increase of aggression toward others, which is another trauma-based behavioral feature."

Bria turns to me. "Does that mean you don't trust *me?*"

"Of course I trust you."

"He does but he doesn't," Dr. Hardy says. "For the most part, he doesn't trust other men, but on some level he doesn't trust you to take care of yourself either."

Bria sighs, nodding. "That makes a lot of sense."

"Chris can't control everything and that leads to a lack of trust in himself."

"So what can we do?" Bria asks. "What can I do?"

"A lot of things. We will work on increasing his feelings of safety and security by establishing structures and routines to make his days seem more secure and predictable. This can make him feel more in control. He can also spend time doing activities he likes and excels at, improving self-confidence."

Bria smiles. "He already does that. The structure thing I'm not so sure of. We're in a band. Our schedule changes weekly, sometimes daily. The biggest trigger, I'd guess you'd call it, is when men recognize me and want to chat. How can we control that without quitting the band?"

Dr. Hardy nods thoughtfully. "That certainly makes things more difficult but not impossible. Chris, you say you're close with your bandmates. That's good. Spending time with people you trust is important. We'll work on reviewing your traumatic event and exploring the disoriented thinking that resulted from it. You may have unresolved feelings of guilt over their deaths. You may even still be angry at Abby for leaving."

"Angry at Abby?" Bria says. "Why would he be angry with her? It wasn't her fault."

"It's perfectly natural to be angry at people who have died and left us. On a deep, unconscious level, we may even blame them for vanishing from our lives."

Bria looks sad.

"What is it?" Dr. Hardy asks.

"Sometimes I still get mad at my mom," she says. "She died when I was little. I don't even remember her, but I'm embarrassed to say I often get angry at her for making me grow up without a mother."

Dr. Hardy offers a sympathetic smile. "It's normal to feel angry. Don't beat yourself up about how you feel. It's part of the process."

"So he needs to forgive Abby for leaving him?"

"Perhaps. Chris, would you like to share what you've been doing as part of that process?"

Dr. Hardy asked me to bring my notebook to appointments, since my feelings are bottled up inside it. "I've been writing one song for a long time, and I finally finished it yesterday."

Dr. Hardy looks pleased. "That's wonderful. You must feel relieved to have finished it after all this time."

"I wanted to finish it before …" I look at the calendar on the wall.

She says, "Would you like to tell Bria what tomorrow is?"

"It's Abby's birthday." I swallow. "She would have been twenty-five."

Bria's eyes fill with tears. "That's also the day they found them."

I nod.

"I know the song is intensely private," the doctor says, "and we'll respect your decision if you choose not to, but it might help to share the song with Bria. It could help her understand your grief, your helplessness."

I stare at the notebook.

"You don't have to," Bria says to me. "I know how uncomfortable that can be."

Seconds of silence—maybe minutes—pass. "You can read it." I flip through the pages until I find it, the memory of finishing the song still raw. I hand it to her. The lyrics are burned into my mind. I close my eyes and see them in my head.

Can you see me, can you hear me
From wherever you are now
If I tell you where my heart is
Is it like a broken vow

Though a piece of me stays with you
As I leave you in the ground
I'll cherish you for always
My love for you profound.

Promises were made, now I turn a different way
Letting go is a fatal blow, but I'll get through it somehow
I'm letting go
It's time to grow
I'm letting go right now

So goodbye I say forever
As I put you in the past
You'll be gone but not forgotten
As I walk away at last

The chorus runs through my mind one last time. It's hard not to choke up as I remember everything Abby and my daughter meant to me. Hard? Hell, it's mind-shattering, but after seven long years without them, it *is* time to move on at last. Abby would understand.

Bria clears her throat, and I can tell she's trying to control her emotions. "Crew, it's beautiful. Thank you for showing it to me."

She hands me the notebook, and I try to give it to Dr. Hardy. She refuses. "The song is not for me. It's for the three of you."

"Bria, will you go with me when I give it to her tomorrow?"

"Yes." Her voice is tremulous.

The moment between us hangs suspended, and I fight taking her hand in mine. This isn't the time or place, but the promise of better yet to come is there. For the first time in what feels like forever, I look forward to what's next.

Dr. Hardy smiles. "I'm seeing real progress today, Chris. There are a few things I'd like you to think about before our next session. You're in a band. That's not going to change. I googled Reckless Alibi and am impressed by what I've seen, but your chosen profession promotes lots of fan attention, both wanted and unwanted. Until you learn how to control less-desirable feelings, you need to rely on external safety measures."

"What does that mean?" I ask.

"Start by researching how other celebrities maintain privacy and security. Your band should have an experienced agent who can advise you and implement those procedures. Having experts to turn to, and making security a project that includes all the band members, not just the two of you, will help you feel safer and less alone with your fears. Although you may be more afraid than the others, it's a realistic concern for all of you as the attention to your band increases."

I think about how those men reacted the other night when Brett joined Bria. They backed off, and I was so relieved. I would have been okay with them talking to her as long as he was there. She needs a bodyguard. My face falls. "We can't afford that, Dr. Hardy. We're just getting started."

"That would be an issue, but it's something to think about. In the meantime I have another option for you to consider, and this involves you both. Consider taking martial arts classes."

"I know some self-defense already," Bria says. "My brother made me take classes."

"Knowing self-defense is not the same," she says. "In addition to being able to protect yourself, which would help put Chris at ease, there is a component of discipline and focusing of attention learned in martial arts that could help him manage his feelings and make him feel more powerful and in control."

"Like learn Tae Kwon Do or something?"

For the first time since sitting on the couch, I smile. I love this idea. "What do you say, Bria? Do you want to go all Bruce Lee with me?"

She laughs. "I think that might be fun."

I already feel better and wonder why in the hell it took me so long to do this in the first place.

I gaze at Bria and remember why I'm here. A lock of her hair falls over one eye, and I have the urge to brush it away. Lyrics dance through my head, and I know as soon as I leave, I'll be writing another song.

Chapter Forty-five

Bria

Crew laughs when I struggle to walk up the five steps to the stage. "A bit sore, are we?"

"Sore is an understatement. My legs are on *fire*."

He takes the steps two at a time, and I resist the urge to punch him in the arm. How can he not be in pain after what we went through this week? I think back on the two martial arts classes we attended and how incredibly awkward and uncoordinated I was. Crew, on the other hand, seems to be picking it up like a bad habit.

"Don't worry," he says. "Once the music starts, you'll forget all about that."

He's right. When we're out here singing, everything else seems so inconsequential.

I peek at the audience before we take our places. "Looks like standing room only, and they're already crowding the stage."

Liam takes a look. "Hell yeah! We're going to outgrow places like this in no time."

Why does tonight feel different than last week? It almost seems like they are here for *us* and not the liquor. I look around the corner and see some girls edging each other out to get closer to the stage.

"Go," Jeremy says, giving us our cue.

We run onstage with lots of energy, and the crowd cheers. They are louder than normal. It's not like we don't get applause, but it usually comes after we start singing, not before.

Crew goes up to the mic. "Hey, Bridgeport, we're Reckless Alibi."

"Thanks for having us," I say into mine.

"You're hot!" a man screams.

Crew stiffens, then gives me a crooked smile and says, "Thanks, dude," eliciting laughter from the crowd.

I think about how far he's come this week. He visited Abby's grave and sang the song he wrote for her. Most of it anyway. He couldn't get through the whole thing. Afterward he ripped the page out and tucked it in the dirt by her grave marker. He left two roses, one for each of them, and looked sad but also relieved. We parted ways then; he said he had to go home and finish another song he'd started. Part of me wonders if the one song wasn't enough to say goodbye. Maybe a hundred songs won't be.

I sing and soon forget about goodbye songs, tiny graves, and uncertain futures. Crew always looks happiest when he sings. It's obvious he's in his element. He was born to be onstage, but tonight there is something different about him. During one of our raunchier songs, he does a jumping front kick, a move we learned in martial arts class, and I have to look away to avoid laughing.

When we sing 'On That Stage,' before the break, it's almost like we're back in my apartment the day we wrote the lyrics. The day I knew I had deep feelings for him. The day he ran away but then came back. There is so much emotion between us, it's palpable.

"Stick around," Crew says to the crowd. "We'll be back in fifteen."

The crowd cheers as we leave the stage. "Jesus," Garrett says. "We're really lighting this place up."

We all revel in the applause and then I do what I normally do on break, head to the bathroom. I still get nervous up there, and it makes me have to pee. Before I can get to the restroom, hands are on me, forcing me through a different door. I'm about to karate-chop the person when I catch a glimpse of my captor.

Crew pushes me against the wall and kisses me. His lips are intoxicating, his touch electric. I get lost in his kiss, the way his mouth feels on mine—oh, how I've missed it. Sensation and emotion wrap me in a thick blanket, his masculine groan warming me through and through. I've been kissed by at least a dozen men and could still recognize his kiss out of all of them. My head spins, my stomach dances, my heart flutters.

Which is why it's so hard to push him away.

His eyes burn with desire. "I want you so badly."

I lean my forehead against his chest. "I know. Me, too, but not like this. Singing is foreplay, Chris, but it's not our real feelings."

He thrusts his erection against me. "This sure as shit is a real feeling."

I don't answer, but I don't pull away either. God, I've missed his touch.

He strokes my arm. "You mean to tell me when we sing, you don't have real feelings? Come on, Bria. Those songs are about *us*. They're filled with our feelings."

I work up the willpower to step back and break contact, but it's like a part of me is missing. "You're right. Those are real feelings, but it's too soon. You're just beginning to get your life back after seven years. Don't you want to figure out who Chris Rewey is before you let me have a part of you?"

His hands run through his hair. He nods. He leans down and puts his forehead against mine. "You'll wait for me to get there, won't you?"

Tears prickle the backs of my eyes. "Of course I will." *Because I love you*, I want to say, but I don't. He'll say it back, but he won't really mean it. And that scares me more than anything.

I open the door. "I really have to pee. Meet you back out there?"

I expect him to be waiting outside the bathroom door when I come out, but he's waiting for me at the end of the hallway. That's progress. When we get backstage, Liam runs over. "Where the hell have you been? Look at this."

He holds up his phone. A music video plays. *Our* music video.

"You want to know why the crowd is so happy to see us?" Garrett says. "Look at the number of views."

My jaw drops when I see seven figures.

Crew laughs. "Score another one for Ronni, who forgot to tell us the video had been released." He turns to Jeremy. "You knew about this?"

He shakes his head. "I'm as surprised as you are." He tries to look excited for us, but I can tell he's pissed. He's our manager. He should be in the loop on these things. Hell, we all should.

"Shh," I say. "I can't hear it." My eyes are locked on Liam's phone, waiting to see the last scene.

Crew squeezes my elbow. "A hundred bucks says it's the one we want."

When I see myself push away all the girls and Crew pick me up and put me in the car, I almost cry. I never thought Ronni would let that ending fly, but now I understand why she didn't tell us about the release.

Garrett says, "Holy shit, we have over a million followers on Insta. When the hell did that happen?"

We look at each other in disbelief.

"You're on your way up," Jeremy says. "But right now you have a set to finish. Get out there and give these people what they came for."

I walk up the stairs to the stage—this time feeling no pain. *They came for us.* Not because of the two-for-one drinks. Not because it's Saturday night. For *us.*

Garrett counts us off. Liam and Brad start playing. Crew and I look at each other and smile. And then we sing.

People swarm our table after the set. They ask for autographs, pictures, handshakes. Crew is stoic. He's engaging with people, but I can tell he's trying hard not to lose his shit. A man touches my arm, and he flinches. Another pulls me in for a hug, and Garrett has to hold Crew back. A third gets handsy when I take a photo with him, and Crew stands, his barstool falling over on his way to me.

"Oh shit," Brad says when he realizes what's about to happen. He shouts at the top of his lungs, "Tangerine! Uh, plantain. No, watermelon. Shit, I can't remember the goddamn word."

Instead of things escalating and Crew going off on Mr. Handsy, we break into laughter.

Liam slaps the back of Brad's head. "It's pineapple, you tool."

Mr. Handsy moves on, and Crew takes a breath. *Sorry,* he mouths. I flash him a smile. He's trying.

"Hey, how about we take this party somewhere more private?" I say.

Liam, Garrett, and Brad are enjoying the attention; they don't want to leave. But Liam gets what I'm doing. "Good idea," he says. The others fall in line.

At the van, Bruce is putting away our gear, and Jeremy is helping.

"Anyone know of a good bar around here?" Liam asks.

Bruce says, "I grew up close by. What are you in the mood for?"

"Don't much care as long as they serve whiskey," Liam says.

"I know just the place."

We pile in. When Jeremy looks ready to find his car, I call, "You want to join us? It's your celebration too."

"You want *me* to come?"

I smile. "I do."

He looks at the guys. They shrug at each other. Then Crew says, "Why not? The more the merrier."

Two hours and a bottle of whiskey later, we're the only patrons left in this quaint neighborhood bar. I'm impressed Jeremy's still with us, given he's at least ten years older than we are.

"Reckless Alibi is on the map now," he says proudly. "It's only going to escalate from here. With SummerStage coming up, I can promise you things will happen quickly. Get ready for the ride. Most of you have worked your whole life for this."

Unlike the rest of the band, Crew isn't thinking of fame and fortune. He's thinking of the overzealous fans and potential threats. "Jeremy, I need to talk to you about something."

"Shoot."

"We need security at all shows and major appearances. You saw the crowd tonight. This is the tip of the iceberg."

"But we can't afford it," I say.

"We don't have to. I went through our contract with a fine-tooth comb. Security is IRL's responsibility. They have to provide it when the band feels threatened. You saw those guys put their hands on Bria tonight. It's time to do this."

Jeremy's expression sours. "Ronni won't go for it. They've already invested a lot of money in you."

"Looks like they're about to start cashing in on that," Crew says. "Ronni doesn't have much of a choice. They'll be in breach of contract if they don't provide security. You know how she's always threatening *us* with that shit? Now it's our turn. If they don't want to do it, they don't have to. They can release us, and we'll find someone who will. And I think it's safe to say that we won't have any trouble finding a new label."

Jeremy frowns. "You guys feel threatened?"

Garrett, Liam, and Brad stand behind Crew and me. "We do."

Jeremy stands and straightens his shirt. "Looks like I have to call a meeting with IRL. Leave it to me."

He leaves the five of us to close the place down. "He's definitely growing on me," I say.

The waitress comes over with one last tray of shots. "Two million views," Liam says, handing them out. "On three? One, two, three."

"Let's get reckless!"

Chapter Forty-six

Crew

SummerStage is New York's largest outdoor music festival. It runs all summer long, with concerts in many of the city parks in all five boroughs. Performing acts range from local artists to nationally known bands. Events happen almost every day, and today Reckless Alibi is headlining on the Central Park main stage.

I shake my head in disbelief, thinking again how influential Dirk must be to have gotten us this gig. Not that we're getting paid. Artists perform for free, but that doesn't matter. The exposure is what counts. Unlike when we opened for White Poison, *we're* the main act. Bands are opening for *us*.

The past few weeks are a blur. Everything happened so quickly after the release of our music video. The best clubs in the tristate area are demanding we play for them. Ronni and Jeremy are weeding through offers. Video views have climbed to numbers I never imagined. IRL begrudgingly agreed to security—one man at shows and appearances.

I seldom get nervous before a performance, but it's different this time. The new song I've been working on isn't something we planned. It isn't in the lineup. We're going rogue by playing it, and it's going to blindside Bria.

Girls love that grand gesture shit, don't they? My bandmates agreed to it though they know it will piss off Ronni. Hell, they probably agreed to it *because* it will piss her off.

We didn't have time to score the whole thing, but with some minor changes, we were able to alter one of the existing songs for my new lyrics. We practiced it only a few times after Bria left rehearsal.

"Bruce, don't forget to pick up Bria," I say from the backseat.

"I'm on it."

"You okay?" Liam asks. "You look a little pale."

"I'm good."

"Is this about the song? If you don't think you can do it, give us a sign, and we'll play the original. She'll never be the wiser."

I'm relieved to have an out if I need it.

"What do you think about Thor?" he asks.

Thomas Horton is our new security guy. We nicknamed him Thor. He started last weekend when we played the club in Brooklyn. Big guy. I'm grateful for that. Liam pulled him aside and told him to stick close to Bria. I'm grateful for that too. I finally felt like I could breathe, knowing nobody could get to her. She signed autographs and posed for pictures, but no one tried anything with a brick wall standing next to her.

After the show, she let me walk her home. I still worry about her. She can't have a bodyguard twenty-four-seven. It's one of the issues I'm working through with Dr. Hardy.

Bruce pulls to the curb. I text Bria we're here. I get out and wait for her at the door. When she opens it, she looks green.

"Are you sick?"

"I just threw up, but I'm pretty sure it's nerves."

"Nerves? You sang with White Poison in front of ten thousand people. This is nothing compared to that."

"Except when I was with them, people weren't there to see me. Nobody cared who the girl standing twenty feet behind the lead singer was."

"Would it make you feel any better to know I'm nervous, too?"

"Chris Rewey, nervous? I don't buy it."

I take her hand and lead her to the van. I smile when she doesn't wiggle away. "We're all nervous on some level. This could be our make-or-break concert. They've heard us on the radio. They've seen our music video. They're coming to see if we're the real deal."

She hesitates before getting in the van. "You're *not* helping."

"Sorry. Maybe it will rain and nobody will show up." I wink as she gets inside.

Liam checks his phone. "The weather will be perfect. We couldn't have picked a better day. We might sweat our asses off, though. It's supposed to be hot."

Garrett tells jokes on the way to ease the tension. Brad says he's thinking of proposing to Katie.

Bria says, "You should do it with a song onstage. It would be epic. Crew and I can write one for you."

Brad laughs. "I'm not proposing to my girl in front of thousands of people."

"Girls like romantic stuff like that," she says.

When Bruce pulls into our designated spot, Jeremy, Ronni, and Thor are waiting. We're hours early. Bruce has to set up our equipment and do a sound check. Then the opening acts do theirs. After the gates open, we'll wait another few hours for them to finish their sets. We won't go on until eight o'clock tonight, four hours from now. Because *we're* the headliners today.

"What are we going to do for four hours?" Garrett asks.

"There's a tent over here," Jeremy says. "You can relax and hang out. Eat, drink, sleep if you want. There are couches."

"Sleep. Right," Brad says sarcastically.

"Is there a toilet?" Bria asks. "In case I have to throw up again."

Ronni shoots her a biting stare. "Good lord, Brianna. Try to act like a professional, won't you?"

Bria laughs disingenuously. "You mean professional like Adele, who has readily admitted to vomiting before a lot of performances?"

"Ozzy has extreme stage fright," I add. "Ozzy fucking Osbourne. Even after all these years."

"And let's not forget the legendary Eddie Van Halen," Liam says. "His stage fright led to alcohol abuse."

Ronni rolls her eyes and walks away from us and into the tent.

"Actually," Jeremy says, cracking a smile, "Ronni and I have something to discuss with you."

I study him. "You're smiling. You never smile. What's up?"

"I'll let Ronni tell you, but it may help keep your mind off your anxiety, Bria."

I love that he calls her Bria now, much to Ronni's displeasure.

Jeremy holds the tarp door of the tent aside, and we go in. Ronni is pouring champagne into seven flutes.

She hands one to each of us. "I have great news. Reckless Alibi is going on tour."

Did I hear her correctly? Is this a joke or should we be jumping up and down?

"It's true," Jeremy says.

"Are you shitting me?" Garrett asks.

Jeremy's smile grows even bigger as he holds up his glass.

Bria jumps into my arms, spilling her champagne, then Liam, Garrett, and Brad join us in a group hug. We yell and high-five and dance around. How many years have I been waiting for this moment?

"Don't get too excited," Ronni says. "You haven't heard the details."

Of course it's not as good as it seems. This is Ronni we're talking about. "What's the catch?" I ask.

"The tour will be limited to one state—Florida. We're still hammering things out. Smaller venues, like the clubs you play here. A few larger outdoor amphitheaters for the spring-breakers."

"We're going to Florida during spring break?" Garrett asks.

Jeremy looks almost as excited as the five of us. "For most of March into April. Millions of teens and young adults will vacation there. After they see you, they'll be buying your albums and telling friends back home. It has the potential to be a major stepping-stone."

"By the time you get back, you could be on the brink of celebrity," Ronni says. "We have seven months to prepare. More music videos have to be made and released, and at least one more album. Two would be better."

Liam is in a slump, and we know it. His jubilance abates. "Two more albums? In seven months? No fucking way. We'll be lucky to put out one. I haven't been feeling it lately."

Ronni reproaches him. "I suggest you figure out a way to write the damn music for their lyrics, Liam. It's nonnegotiable."

"He will," I say, stepping forward. "We'll get out an album by then."

"I said *or two*," Ronni clarifies.

"One," I say. "That's all we'll agree to or no deal."

"The deal's already done, Crew, or have you forgotten I make the decisions around here?"

"One album, Ronni."

She drinks her champagne and pours another. "Goddamn musicians. I hate all of you."

Liam pulls me aside. "Thanks for having my back."

"Always, brother. You know that." I grip his shoulder. "It'll happen. You'll be inspired when you least expect it."

He follows my eyes as I stare at Bria.

"I don't want a girlfriend," he says. "You, more than anyone, should know that."

"I didn't say you had to be inspired by a girl. Maybe it'll be a song. A car. Hell, maybe a tree in Central Park will do it." I get an idea and go over to Bria. "Want to take a walk with me? Might help calm your nerves."

She finishes her drink and sets down the glass. "I'd like that."

We stroll away from the stage and all the hustle and bustle. I want to take her hand, but I'm afraid it might spur a conversation I don't want to have. Talk about *us* can wait until after she hears what I'm going to say to her in front of a thousand people. *Damn*—now I feel sick again.

"You're awfully quiet today," she says. "Pretty unlike you."

"I guess I'm still trying to process everything. We're going on tour? That's mind-blowing, Bria. I've barely been out of the tristate area."

"It'll be fun. Do you think anyone down there knows who we are?"

"I'll bet Ronni will make sure of it before we go. She'll contact radio stations, set up interviews, and arrange press conferences and whatever else she thinks we need."

A man jogs toward us. He does a double take and circles back. My heartrate skyrockets.

"You're the singers for Reckless Alibi," he says, jogging in place.

I stiffen. "That's right."

He stops jogging and looks at Bria like he wants to fuck her. "Brianna and ... sorry, can't remember your name."

I'll bet you can't. Anger, fear, and pure hatred crawl up my spine. *It's not him,* I say over and over in my head. I take a breath and try to remember what Dr. Hardy told me to do in situations like this. I hold out my hand. "I'm Crew. What's your name?"

"Greg." He shakes my hand and then Bria's.

"You like our music?" I ask. "Do you have a favorite song?"

"Ah, man, I like all of them, but 'Sins on Sunday' is my favorite. My wife loves 'Not a Day.' She sings it all the time. She's not as good as you guys, but I gotta love her for trying."

His wife. He tells us about seeing us for the first time at a club last month, and I realize he's not looking at Bria like he wants to fuck her. He's looking at her—at me—with awe.

"Hey, she'd kill me if I didn't get a picture with you. Do you mind?"

"We'd be happy to," Bria says. She turns to me. "Right?"

"Sure."

Greg stands between us and snaps a selfie. "Claire is gonna freak."

"Are you coming to the show later?" Bria asks.

Normally her saying something like that would have my skin crawling. Now, not so much.

"Wouldn't miss it," he says. "Especially now. Thanks for the picture and for taking time to talk to me. Not many people like you will do that."

"We hope you enjoy the show." I blow out a breath after he leaves. "That could have gone a lot worse."

"Most fans are like that," she says. "*If* you give them a chance." She glares at me.

"Yeah, yeah, I get it. Hey, at least you didn't have to use the safeword."

"Crew, I'll *never* use the safeword."

I give her a heated stare. "Never?"

She blushes. I haven't seen her do that in a month. My dick thickens.

She clears her throat. Yup, she's thinking about it too. "Do you think we'll need Thor in Florida?"

"I'll insist on it," I say.

"You like having him around, don't you?"

"Yes."

"I've seen some big changes in you, Chris, and not just today."

"I don't want to brag or anything, but Dr. Hardy called me one of her favorite patients."

She chuckles. "You do realize she probably says that to all her patients."

"No way."

We walk for hours, speculating what it might be like on tour. My phone buzzes with a text. "Looks like Queen Bitch wants us back."

Bria pales. "Oh, God. Do you think she'll go with us to Florida?"

"I doubt it. We're just one of her clients. But I'm sure Jeremy will come."

"That's fine. I like Jeremy."

"He's not so bad, compared to *Veronica.*"

My melodramatic pronunciation of her name amuses her. Then her smile disappears. "Does she still come on to you?"

"Nope. She knows I only have eyes for one woman."

There's that blush again.

"Crew …" She looks at me like she's at war with herself.

"I know. You need time. Let's go. We should get back before we get put in a timeout."

~ ~ ~

As the headliner, the stage has long been set up for us. We only have to stand here and wait for the opening bands to clear out, listen to the boisterous crowd, and hope lightning is about to strike.

We've done our pre-show ritual and said everything we needed to say to hold each other up or calm each other down.

We're ready.

"You're on," Jeremy says.

Bria closes her eyes and inhales deeply.

I touch her hand. "Remember, we're in this together. If you feel like you're going to puke, look at me, okay?"

I run out and grab my mic. This feeling of exhilaration is why I do this. Who needs drugs when the high I get from performing is better than anything I've ever felt?

Garrett counts us off. Bria's at the keyboard. We begin with our most popular song, bringing screams from the crowd. Screams! We're all thinking the same thing: *Hell yeah!*

Even after a short break, because come on, we all know Bria has to pee, the crowd can't get enough. Event security has to keep a few women from climbing the barriers in front of the stage.

We're so hyped up, we could play all night. It makes me wish we had more songs, but there's still one left. The one we saved for the encore. We manipulated Ronni into making it our last song, and she's going to be pissed when she sees why. I don't care. Look at this crowd. Even Ronni has to admit it's going better than any of us dreamed.

We run offstage and open bottles of water. The crowd is screaming for more. We catch our breath and wait the requisite amount of time, then run back out. More screaming. Liam is waiting for the signal. I nod, and he smiles.

Mic in hand, I cross to the front of the stage. The people quiet, waiting for me to talk. "There's a girl here tonight I want to sing a song to, if that's okay with you."

They yell their approval while a few girls shout, "Sing to *me*, Crew!"

"She doesn't think I know who I am." I move a stool and perch Bria on it. "But I do, and it's all because of her." I take her mic and hand it off to Garrett. I lean close to her. "You're sitting this one out."

She looks scared. "What are you doing?"

"Something I should have done a long time ago."

I turn to the audience. "I call this song 'The One.' You might recognize the tune, but it's been redone for this occasion." I nod to Garrett and pray this doesn't blow up in my goddamn face.

I pick up my guitar. The original didn't require I play, but I need something to do with my hands, or maybe hide behind if it doesn't go well.

I tune everyone out and look only at her.

"Wanting you's a need I've never known
I'm a car spinning way out of control

You're the one so complicated, never thought that I'd have waited
You're the one ... we've just begun."

She doesn't look away, not even when tears start to fall.

"Needing you's a hurt I can't explain
I'm exploding with some stuff I can't contain.
You're the one so unsurpassed, never thought we'd make it last
You're the one ... we've just begun."

I get to the chorus. Her chin quivers, and she nervously bites her lip. I'm abruptly aware the audience has gone quiet.

"You want to know who I am
There's no doubt that I'm your man
'Cause wanting you, needing you, loving you is all I do
The one ... you're the one ... my only one ..."

During Liam's guitar riff, I wipe my sweaty hands on my jeans. Bria's lips are pressed together and her cheeks glisten with tears. One more verse. I hope I can get through it without my voice cracking.

"Loving you's a dream I thought was gone
Second chances prove that life can carry on
You're the one so unexpected, never thought I'd be affected
You're the one... we've just begun."

I sing the chorus two more times. The music stops, but I don't stop looking at her, and thank God, she doesn't stop looking at me.

Liam takes the mic from me. "Thanks for coming, New York City. We're Reckless Alibi."

I think the crowd cheers and stomps, but I don't hear them. I have tunnel vision, and she's the only one I see.

I never got this far in my plan. For a second I think she might run off the stage, embarrassed. But she doesn't seem to care what's around us any more than I do. She comes toward me, never breaking eye contact, and time almost stops. Things go in slow motion. I see every tear work its way down her cheek, each blink of her eyes, every nuance of her face. When she reaches me, I wrap her in my arms and kiss her. Her salty wet lips press against mine. I am reborn.

I hear the crowd as they explode into applause. Our lips part, and we gaze at each other, smiling. "Did that really happen?" she asks.

"It really did. Are you taking me back?"

Her thumb runs across the stubble on my jaw. "Yeah, I really am."

"What do you say we blow this pop stand and go somewhere with a few thousand less people."

"I thought you'd never ask."

"Oh, I'm asking, now and every day, Bria Cash."

The lump in my throat is the size of fucking New York. But I don't care. I don't need to speak anymore. Everything else I have to tell her won't require words.

Chapter Forty-seven

Bria

Crew and I slip out the back, not hanging around after the show. We run to the street and hail a cab, laughing when we hear Ronni's irritated shouts behind us. Crew gives the cabbie my address.

"Do you think she'll ever forgive us?" I say.

"Probably not, but I don't care." He takes my hand in his. "There's only one thing I care about."

I can't stop beaming. The other song he wanted to write was for *me*. "When did you have time to do that?"

"We stayed after rehearsal a few days last week. I wanted to come up with a whole new melody, but there wasn't time. Besides, with Liam off his game ..."

"He'll work his way back. Maybe the news about the tour will be his motivation."

"Maybe," he says, giving me a heated stare. "Motivation can be a powerful thing."

We can't keep our hands off each other in the cab. He grabs my thigh. I put a hand on his chest. He caresses my neck. I touch his cheek. He skims a finger along my jaw. It's all we can do not to grope each other indecently.

We run up the stairs to my place, the pain in my muscles taking a backseat to the want in my core. We throw our things down. He pins me to the wall, eyes hot with desire. "Do you know how long I've wanted to do this?"

"Then do—"

His lips crash into mine. His tongue flits out, inviting mine to join it. Our kiss is like a song, building with each verse, leveling off with the chorus and then ending with the most powerful words.

His lips move up my jawbone. "I've missed this," he whispers. He nibbles my earlobe. "I've missed every part of you." He sucks my neck. "I'm never letting you go again."

He holds my face and ducks to peruse me with his tongue. He tastes every sweaty, salty inch of my neck, working his way down to my cleavage. I'm squirming with want. Heat pools at my center. I claw at his back, needing him closer.

He removes my shirt, staring at my breasts as if he's never seen them. He cups them through my bra, teasing my nipples and making them stiffen under the lacy fabric. "Take it off," I say, my voice husky.

"Gladly."

His lips lightly brush my nipple. I arch into him. He toys and licks and sucks until I don't think I can take another second, then he switches to the other one. He goes back and forth between my nipples, tension coiling in my belly. "Crew—"

Suddenly, I'm in his arms, and he's carrying me across the room. He lays me on the bed and takes off every stitch of his clothing. His penis is stiff and thick, and it dances as if it knows what's coming next. I start to remove my pants, but he stops me.

"Huh-uh. I want to do it."

He peels off my jeans, leaving my panties on, and touches me over them, rubbing my clit and causing the most pleasurable friction. He lowers his head and puts his mouth on the silky fabric, growling low in his throat when he smells my arousal. I feel the heat of his tongue.

It's driving me insane, having something between us. "Take them off," I beg.

He laughs. It's a sexy grumble that further fuels my desire.

He tries to rip them off but can't. I try to control my amusement.

"They make it look so easy in the movies," he says, finally giving up and pulling them down my legs.

"It's the thought that counts."

He slides a finger inside me. "If I have something to say about it, you won't be thinking *anything* in about ten seconds."

My stomach flutters as he moves closer to my center. When he puts his tongue *there*, I shudder. He flicks my clit back and forth, then does circles around it. Then, *oh, Lord*, he hums against it. When he adds a second finger, I arch into him, needing release. I picture him onstage, singing to me. His words were honest and raw. He put himself out there for me, in front of everyone. It's my turn to give everything to him. "Yes!" I scream through my orgasm. "Oh, God."

He doesn't relent until every contraction of my climax has passed. I fall back, satiated but needing so much more.

He lies down next to me. I run my hands across his chest, chronicling every ripple of his abs into my memory. I want to remember every moment of this night. Every word, every touch, every sigh. I kiss his chest, spending extra time on his nipples. I kiss his neck, his shoulders, his arms. When I kiss his tattoo, he doesn't flinch like he used to. This brings a lump to my throat.

I work my hand down his body and wrap my fingers around his pulsating shaft.

He stops me. "I need to tell you something."

For a moment I'm afraid he might leave. Has he changed his mind about me? Did touching his tattoo bring painful memories back?

He gets up on one elbow and brushes a stray hair off my face. "I promised Abby I'd never love anyone else. "

I swallow hard as tears coat my lashes.

"I need you to know before I make love to you that I broke that promise."

"You did?"

"I broke it a long time ago. I just didn't know it. I had to finally let her go in order to let you in." He gazes at me with reverence, adoration, and respect, and I fall in love with him all over again. "I love you, Bria." His voice cracks. "This is the real thing. It's a more complete kind of love. More mature. The kind you know is going to make you laugh and cry and maybe even rip your heart out at times. The feelings I have for you are so intense, it sometimes scares the shit out of me."

I sit up. "I know what you mean because I feel exactly the same way. I love you too, Chris."

"You can call me Christopher if you want."

I take in a deep, savoring breath. Then I shake my head. "Christopher was hers. It'll always be hers. The rest of you is mine for as long as I can have you."

He smiles. "I like the sound of that. We're talking forever here, right?"

"You bet your ass we are." I kiss him. "We're in this together. If you feel like you're going to puke, look at me, okay?"

He laughs at the words I stole from him. "God, woman." He flips me on my back and plants seductive kisses all over me.

I moan, and he responds like it's the best sound he's ever heard.

"Sing it again," I say.

As he makes love to me, he serenades me with the song that is now burned into my soul. Every thrust is like a new verse, each chorus a promise of things to come. I grip his back, pulling him to me, driving him deeper, wanting him harder. Our thunderous climaxes make him pause, then he lies next to me, eyes locked with mine as he finishes the song. I can't remember another time in my life when I've been so fulfilled or deliriously happy.

I have no idea what the future will bring, but if it's anything like the music we make together, we're in for one hell of a ride.

He straddles me, pins my arms to the bed, and grins devilishly. "Do you know what I want to do more than anything in the world right now?"

I smile. I smile big. Because I *do* know.

We jump up, find our notebooks, and flip them open.

And then we write.

THE END

My dear readers,

Most of you have come to expect an epilogue at the end of my books. However, Bria and Crew's relationship is just beginning. You'll see much more of them in the next few books, so to have an epilogue at this point would be premature. I hope you understand. If you're eager to see more of them and the rest of Reckless Alibi, pick up the next two books in the series, Reckless Invitation and Reckless Reunion.

Thank you all so very much,

Samantha

Acknowledgments

I don't know why it took me so long to write about rock stars. Because I love doing it! And I can't wait for you to see what's in store for Bria, Crew, and the gang in the next two books.

With everything going on in the world at the time of this release (Covid-19), I'm especially grateful to be a writer where I get to work from home doing what I love.

As always, there are many people to thank.

To my special editor who has been with me since the beginning, Ann Peters, thank you for your continued support. Also, a great big shout out to my copy editor, LS, at Murphy Rae Solutions.

To my beta readers, Joelle Yates, Shauna Salley, Laura Conley, Jeannie Hinkle, Julie Collier, and Tammy Dixon—you ladies all have unique ways of finding things that have slipped past everyone else.

My deepest appreciation to Susan Phelan of the Denver-based band, Ryan Chrys and The Rough Cuts. We played in the same jazz band in junior high. I always knew you would make music your life. You've been incredibly forthcoming at helping me gain insight into 'band life.'

Dr. Patti Croft—thank you for telling me what Crew needed to do to begin healing.

And finally, to my Facebook reader group, Samantha's Sweethearts, your daily encouragement is the reason I keep writing.

Rock on!

About the author

Samantha Christy's passion for writing started long before her first novel was published. Graduating from the University of Nebraska with a degree in Criminal Justice, she held the title of Computer Systems Analyst for The Supreme Court of Wisconsin and several major universities around the United States. Raised mainly in Indianapolis, she holds the Midwest and its homegrown values dear to her heart and upon the birth of her third child devoted herself to raising her family full time. While it took time to get from there to here, writing has remained her utmost passion and being a stay-at-home mom facilitated her ability to follow that dream. When she is not writing, she keeps busy cruising to every Caribbean island where ships sail. Samantha Christy currently resides in St. Augustine, Florida with her husband and four children.

You can reach Samantha Christy at any of these wonderful places:

Website: www.samanthachristy.com

Facebook: https://www.facebook.com/SamanthaChristyAuthor

Instagram: @authorsamanthachristy

E-mail: samanthachristy@comcast.net